A Rock the Boat Book

First published in the United Kingdom, Republic of Ireland and Australia
by Rock the Boat, an imprint of Oneworld Publications Ltd, 2025

Published by arrangement with Roaring Brook Press, a division of
Holtzbrinck Publishing Holdings Limited Partnership. All rights reserved.

Copyright © Vanessa Le, 2025
Cover art © Shutterstock/Matrioshka
Cover border © Charis Loke, 2025
Map © Charis Loke, 2025

The moral right of Vanessa Le to be identified as the
Author of this work has been asserted by her in accordance
with the Copyright, Designs and Patents Act 1988

All rights reserved
Copyright under Berne Convention
A CIP record for this title is available from the British Library

ISBN 978-0-86154-957-3
eISBN 978-0-86154-958-0

Book design by Meg Sayre
Printed and bound in Great Britain by Clays Ltd, Elcograf S.p.A.

This book is a work of fiction. Names, characters, businesses, organizations, places
and events are either the product of the author's imagination or are used fictitiously.
Any resemblance to actual persons, living or dead, events or locales is entirely
coincidental.

No part of this publication may be reproduced, stored in a retrieval system, or
transmitted, in any form or by any means, electronic, mechanical, photocopying,
recording of otherwise, without the prior permission of the publishers.

The authorised representative in the EEA is eucomply OÜ,
Pärnu mnt 139b-14, 11317 Tallinn, Estonia
(email: hello@eucompliancepartner.com / phone: +33757690241)

Oneworld Publications
10 Bloomsbury Street
London WC1B 3SR
England

Stay up to date with the latest books,
special offers, and exclusive content from
Rock the Boat with our newsletter

Sign up on our website
rocktheboatbooks.com

Praise for *The Last Bloodcarver*

'You'll gasp, you'll scream, you'll cry, and you'll be begging for the next book.'

Chloe Gong, author of *These Violent Delights*

'Has it all – a wonderfully unique magic system, heartfelt themes of legacy and diaspora, and obsession-worthy characters. I need more Nhika and Kochin now!'

Joan He, author of *The Ones We're Meant to Find*

'The perfect blend of sci-fi, fantasy, and romance, with a world that feels lived in and characters that come alive on the page. A unique and beautifully written novel – Le is a talent to watch!'

Axie Oh, author of *The Girl Who Fell Beneath the Sea*

'*The Last Bloodcarver* is fantasy for the vicious, bloody and unrepentant, but fear not: in Nhika's journey, Le has crafted a story that is, in its heart, about her tender homecoming.'

Em X. Liu, author of *The Death I Gave Him*

'Le skillfully brings to life a gritty world filled with a beautifully crafted cast and an intricate magic system I've never seen before. A smart, lush, and utterly compelling read.'

Marie Lu, author of the Legend series

'Absolutely captivating... Le crafts a richly imagined fantasy world, filled with complex, nuanced characters and a magic system that feels brand new. This is one to be savoured.'

Grace D. Li, author of *Portrait of a Thief*

TO MY BÀ NGOẠI, IN LOVING MEMORY

PROLOGUE

AT FIRST, THERE WAS NOTHING BUT THROBBING, painful darkness. It seeped into every sensation, suffocating and blinding—not the absence of light, but an unfamiliarity with light altogether.

Then light came, a pinpoint of brightness pricking a dark canvas, feeble before it was dazzling. It shepherded in a maelstrom of color: gold expanding like lungs bringing in new air; red perfusing emptiness as blood trickled into skin; blue and silver swirling through it all with the languor of a tired exhale. Beneath it, a lonely percussion ferried in the sound of music:

Lub-dub. Lub-dub. Lub-dub.

The orchestra picked up in earnest, the pull of an erhu growing taut as muscle fibers tensed and the airy notes of a bamboo flute drew and released breath. Heat entered after, painting the suggestion of a body—the core first, wherein nestled a fist-size muscle seized with new life. The heat expanded outward, tracing the length of limbs, flooding new skin, dissipating through gaping orifices. It dragged innervation in its wake like a sunrise, first as needlelike pricks of pain, then as the buzzing calm of warmth. Electricity was last to follow, crackling through old conduits anew, following the familiar patterns of well-traversed footpaths.

The body came together in parts, then all at once.

Muscle tightened against bone, skin flushed with life, and organs lurched with renewed autonomy.

Colors merged like a symphony, electricity settled into the body, and Suonyasan Nhika drew her first breath.

ONE
NOW

NHIKA GASPED AWAKE. A PAIN-CHOKED SOB caught in her throat before she swallowed it and alarms raged across her body. One in her stomach, the line of a scalpel. Another in her shoulder, the hole of a bullet. Her skin felt borrowed, scalp aflame, nails wishing to dig themselves into her chest and drag out her heart.

Yes—that's where the pain was the strongest. Her heart, aching and squeezing and tearing itself in two. She clamped a palm over it, feeling an unsettling absence at her sternum. It took her a moment longer to realize that her bone ring, which she'd always worn on a string around her neck, was missing.

Nhika closed her eyes. A face came to mind, dark brown eyes looking tortured and lips trembling with tears. A name pulled at her lips, the man she'd given her bone ring, her heartsoothing, her . . . life? Yet, she was here.

Nhika stilled. Where was she, exactly? Her surroundings were just beginning to settle in. From how sickly she felt to how foreign this bed was, she might've assumed this was a hospital, but the exorbitance of the room suggested otherwise. Her postered bed sat against one wall, red drapes offering privacy and frame carved with lacquered reliefs, while equally ornate furniture pieces filled the rest of the spacious room: a writing desk, a bench, a wardrobe for clothes she didn't have. The door to the bathroom was cracked, and through it she saw the rim of a porcelain tub. There was even a full-length mirror in the corner, and her image blinked dazedly back at her: golden-brown skin blanched of blood, deep bags beneath her eyes, hair tousled.

Memories of a home came to her in parts: well furnished and elegant, endless hallways of endless rooms, a dining room table always full. A manor. Yet, she'd explored those rooms, and she didn't recognize this one. Outside the window, she found neither the gardens nor the driveway nor the acres of land that she remembered from the manor. Instead, it was just forest.

Everything felt foreign—this view, no shining city that she could see; this room, bathed in moonlight and scented in jasmine; her *body*, with her skin clean and stomach full and heart anguished. They came with the dissonance of comfort and anxiety.

A reassuring reality rooted her to sanity: Her name was Nhika, and she was a heartsooth. All these maladies across her body, she could soothe.

The art came back to her with reluctance, as though she were writing with a nondominant hand. Her influence was shaky, jittery, with a wandering focus onerous underneath her direction. Nhika let out a slow breath, re-grounding herself. Her heartbeat, steady in her chest. Her arms, growing in feeling. Her skin, starting to feel like hers again. With her body resumed under her control, she soothed the little fires, the pinpricks in her fingers and the narrowness of her throat and the flip in her stomach. That pain in her heart, though, was untouchable, no matter how she hushed and smothered it. She felt the tightness of something foreign on her abdomen, and when she lifted her shirt, she found a line of scar tissue where there should've been a cut. Another incongruent feeling hailed from her chest and she pulled down the collar of her shirt to reveal a star of raised skin.

The memory came with pain. A bullet shattering her shoulder, a scalpel traced against her stomach, a hospital turned into a graveyard. And . . . a surgical suite, a boy tied down on the table, Nhika bent over in a—

The door opened.

A girl pushed herself in with her hip, holding a tray with a washbasin and towelettes. Nhika remembered the girl—but not like this. Not in loose slacks, her black hair braided and coiled. There should've been dresses, pinned hair, makeup. She remembered those eyes, touched with blush: looking at her from over a fan, through tears, with anger. But not with doting.

At the sight of her, the girl froze, brows raised and lips parted. Then the tray toppled, and water spilled, and now those eyes were wide, fragile, disbelieving.

"Mimi," Nhika said, her lips forming the name by themselves. A second later, her mind caught up—yes, she knew those eyes anywhere. This was Congmi Mai Minlan, and this place must've been the Congmi manor, but Nhika didn't feel like herself. "What's going on?"

Mimi didn't answer. She only stepped forward once, twice, like her legs were made of cogwork. She closed the rest of their distance like a failing automaton, falling to her knees at Nhika's bedside and clinging to Nhika's hand, as though in prayer.

Then Mimi bawled.

It was a raw sort of wail, grief and pain laid bare. Nhika knew its tune well, had known it thrice with each of her family members. But she had never known anyone to cry over *her*, so she was too stunned to do anything but stare and let the girl weep against her legs.

"I'm sorry," Mimi said, though Nhika wasn't sure what for. "I'm sorry, I'm sorry, I'm so, *so* sorry."

She kept repeating it as though she sought repentance and Nhika were some goddess who might be able to grant it. At last, the stupor lifted and Nhika placed a hand atop Mimi's head, quelling her.

Mimi looked up. Her cheeks were wet with tears. The look was familiar; last Nhika remembered, she'd been bleeding out of her stomach and Mimi had been begging her to seek treatment. But she hadn't, because at the end of that dark hospital hallway, there was a . . . someone had been . . .

Nhika squeezed the bridge of her nose, and the memory disappeared. "I gave you quite the scare, didn't I?" she asked.

"*Scare?* You . . ." Mimi paused, swallowed her words, and shook her head.

She what? Last she remembered, she was . . . dying. That's right—dying for something she believed in. *Someone* she believed in. His name came now, tasting like blood on her lips: sweet before it was bitter. "Kochin."

"You remember, then?" Mimi asked.

"He . . . healed me?"

That was the only way she could've awoken. Nhika didn't

know how, both of them bleeding out on that bed with limited energy between them, but he must've discovered something.

Mimi put on a thin smile. "Right."

"Where is he now?"

At that, something dark passed over Mimi's eyes. "You should probably take a moment to rest, Nhika," she said, clunkily changing the subject. "It's too much excitement. I'll explain it all later, okay?"

Nhika stared at her, dread prickling her throat. "Is something wrong?"

Mimi held her gaze for a moment too long. "No. Everything's fine." She stood abruptly, swiping tears from her eyes and collecting her discarded tray. "I'll go grab you a meal and let the others know you're awake. Make yourself at home."

The offer of a meal was almost enough to make her forgive Mimi's evasiveness, but the suspicion lingered, even as Mimi retreated from the room and closed the door behind her. She had little idea of where she was, how she'd come to be here when the last thing she remembered was the operating suite, but she collected what she *did* know:

Her name was Nhika.

She was a heartsooth.

And she had to find Kochin.

⟫ TWO ⟪

SIX MONTHS AGO

SITTING AT THE BOW, KOCHIN GUIDED THE houseboat forward. Gas gurgled in the fuel tank—he was scraping bottom—but he would be home soon. In this part of Theumas, away from the urban landscape of Central, he could almost forget the life he'd had before. Forget that he ever left. Here there was nothing but limestone cliffs crumbling down into beaches and the little villages along the coast. In the distance, he saw the small delta that marked the border of Western Theumas; home wasn't too far now.

Three years. It'd been three years since he'd been home. The allowances had come home in his place, and the closest he'd come to stepping into that white house had been with *her*, but Kochin didn't delude himself. He was returning as the prodigal son, seeking favors in abundance.

As he approached the delta, he found it dotted with other boats, fishing trawlers and wooden skiffs and a couple houseboats like his own, sitting on silt-thick waters. He nosed through them, his eyes on the swaths of hyacinths that dotted the water with purple. Navigating this area was a tricky game of avoiding the foliage, which caught and tangled against the hull. It was a challenge anew each time—he never came home enough to master it.

He'd thought that changed with Nhika.

He could almost imagine her here, just as she was before: sitting at the bow of his houseboat, bare feet skimming the water as they cut through the brown current of the river. An ache twice-wrapped its fingers around his heart, brought on by the remembrance of a night in a hospital long ago. Kochin squared his jaw against the memory.

After her death, he almost hadn't wanted to come home—he still considered turning his boat back to Central. It felt as though a countdown had started that moment in the operating room, a race to save her before she was truly lost. There were things left to do in Central, people to talk to, but he wanted to come home for just a week. It was a promise fulfilled—*See, Nhika, I'm finally going home.*

The river widened as he traveled farther upstream, riparian vegetation giving way to wetlands and docks jutting into the water. Here the land flattened in a valley, and he could see the low outline of Chengton, patched with terraced rice paddies and farmlands. The farm settlement sat atop the horizon, the buildings so squat and distant compared to what he'd grown accustomed to in Central. But his father had grown up in the city and his mother had spent her childhood running from war; both of them preferred the quiet edges of Theumas. Looking back, Kochin wasn't sure why he'd ever left.

He docked the houseboat where the water stilled and took the dinghy downriver toward town. Each stroke pushed him across tranquil waters, nearer and nearer to Chengton. As he approached the docks, Kochin felt his heart tightening in his chest, as though the organ were calcifying to bone. By the time the dinghy lapped up to the docks, bumping into a variety of skiffs as it jostled its way in, there was only a rigid stone where muscle belonged.

With a grunt of effort, he tied down the dinghy, yanked the knot tight, and stood to face the rural expanse of his childhood home.

The main street welcomed him back as an old friend, immune to the same passage of time that had torn down and rebuilt Theuman streets so many times over. There were still the decrepit wooden storefronts, held together by rusted nails and peeling paint. Still the rooftops that were half-tiled, half-thatched. Still the path, cobbled in some areas and dirt in others. Despite being rural, the place held that characteristic Theuman charm: numbered streets; roofs of dark, glazed tile; and automatons squatting at every other corner. While automatons here were outdated, people still made good use of them, repurposing wheeled service automatons as tillers and broken metal casing as animal troughs.

The hills broke the flat monotony of the countryside. On the first bluff, the one closest to the water, sat a house with enough stories and white paint to be spotted through the tree canopy, with its waving fishing flags and patchy roof. Kochin swallowed the rising lump in his throat.

Home.

Eyes followed him as he passed, and Kochin wondered what set him apart. Was it the silk dress shirt he still wore, unmuddied by the primary occupations of Chengton, agriculture and fishing? Was it the upright, focused stride of an urbanite, a spine more accustomed to dinner parties than back-bending labor? Or was it something else entirely, something unseen but persistent? A pain scraped at his heart, that he'd been gone only three years, yet had changed so much that even boys he'd grown up alongside eyed him as a stranger.

Kochin veered off the main road and their stares tugged away.

His path carved a zigzag up the side of the hill. Here, between the trees, the path overlooked the expanse of the river, and when he passed the right pockets, he could see how the water extended up into the horizon in one direction, down into the ocean in the other. He smiled at the breeze that brought the scent of the river, then remembered his grief.

The last time he'd been here was with Nhika.

Kochin paused near the top of the hill, where he'd stopped then, too. Last time, he'd handed her an envelope, bade her continue forward where he could not. Now, he glanced down at the path, his heart seeing a barrier where his eyes saw nothing but a change in the dirt.

This was the gift she'd given him, wasn't it? The gift to return home?

With a breath to steel himself, Kochin pressed forward.

There sat the narrow white house at the top of the hill, flags snatching the wind as they waved on a long, wooden pole. Since he'd left home, there were six new flags; Vinsen's collection was growing.

Otherwise, he remembered this house in its exactness, as if it hadn't changed at all while he'd been gone. Besides the flags, the only other variable was the garden, overgrown with rosebushes and hydrangeas and cosmos, and from the prevalence of yellows and pinks he knew his mother had planted them all. As Kochin approached the door, a streak of brown rounded the side of the building before a dog leaped against his chest, toppling him.

"Bonbo!" Kochin laughed, diverting the mutt's snout before his sloppy tongue could wipe his face. "You remember me?" Three years had not been kind to Bonbo; his eyes had sunken, nose paled, but he still retained that frenetic puppy energy. Kochin wondered if that came from his mother's meals or soothing.

"Bonbo! Get back here!" A voice trailed the dog from the side of the house before his mother arrived, dressed in an outfit all cut from the same monochrome fabric and balancing a wicker basket on her hip. "I'm so sorry ab—"

She froze. Kochin's smile fell away to hesitation as she stared at him, eyes stunned in a half-widened state and lips forming an unspoken word. Bonbo knew no such ceremony, and circled Kochin as he stood and fell into a bow. "Ma."

"Kochin." The word came out breathless. The basket fell from her hip, scattering clipped herbs across the lawn.

His smile was at once apologetic and relieved. "I know I should've come earlier, but—"

In a second, she'd reached his side and swept him up in an embrace, squeezing air from every lobule of his lungs before setting him back down again, too heavily. She gave him only a moment to regain his footing and breath before examining every inch of him, squeezing his biceps and tapping the underside of his chin. "So skinny. What have you been eating?"

It came out so naturally, like three years were forgotten in an instant. He laughed, a meager thing, taking her hounding as forgiveness. "I've been working."

"Working too much," she determined, narrowed eyes scrutinizing his face. Did she notice the new bags underneath his eyes? The sallowness of his cheeks? He had not slept well in a long, long time. If she saw his tiredness, she only shook her head. "Where have you been, Kochin?"

He pressed his lips thin, eyes deflecting toward the ground. "It's a long story, Ma."

"Well, we'll all want to hear it." A firm hand clamped around his arm as she took him inside, Bonbo following at their heels. Kochin threw a glance over his shoulder. For a moment, he could see Nhika, her back toward them as she admired the sprawling view beyond the hill. The wind caught her hair, the sun warmed her golden-brown skin, and she started to turn; he thought he might even catch a glimpse of the smile in her eyes.

Before he could, his mother shut the door behind him.

The smells of the house were the same as he remembered: fish cooking somewhere, the pungent odor nearly concealed by the fragrance of herbs and flowers. Garden clippings added color to the weathered walls, every counter covered in a variety of glass vases and pots. At the end of the hallway was the open kitchen, filled with waning sunlight.

"Vinsen, Bentri, Holy!" his mother called, the cut of her voice enough to rattle a wood louse out of the walls. "Everybody in the kitchen, now!"

The house rumbled to life—feet pounding down the stairs,

doors opening and slamming, chairs scooting across hardwood. He heard the chatter of his brothers in the kitchen and hitched a breath at Bentri's laughter—his younger brother's voice had dropped in his absence.

His mother dragged him down the hallway. Kochin's throat tightened with a combination of anxiety and anticipation, until at last she pushed him into the entryway.

All eyes turned to him. Kochin swallowed. "Vinsen. Bentri. Ba." He dipped his head in greeting when none of them spoke, too afraid to meet their eyes and the expectations that came with them.

Bentri came like Bonbo had, sixteen years of boyhood crashing into Kochin's chest in a tight hug. The boy had grown taller but not any thicker, though he surprised Kochin with hidden strength as he lifted him off the ground. Then there was his father, who gave him a quiet, stoic smile though his lip trembled with disbelief. He stood from his chair with the gait of an older gentleman as he made his way to Kochin, joining in the embrace. Meanwhile, from the table, Vinsen nodded curtly, jaw set.

When his family pulled away from him, Kochin realized he'd been tensing underneath their warmth, and he let his shoulders relax again. It'd been a long time since he'd known an embrace so tight, so complete. With his presence, his family was made whole again—wasn't this what he'd wanted for so long? Yet, being here felt like a betrayal, felt unearned.

"Kochin, I can't believe you're back," Bentri said. For how tall he'd grown, he was still the same kid, all freckles and knobby joints, wild sable hair and toothy grin. His eyes were wide with elation, which was quick to sour to worry. "How long are you staying?"

"I'm sure Kochin is much too busy to stay for long," said Vinsen, Kochin's elder brother. "Quick, someone pull a chair before he's out the door again."

"Vinsen," his mother scolded. But, as though she saw the merit behind his words, she drew a chair for Kochin at the table and gestured for him to sit. "Kochin, it's been so long. You must have so much to tell us."

Santo, Congmi, Nhika. Three years unwound themselves on his tongue, waiting to spill. Instead, Kochin took a seat at the table and said, "Not really. I suppose work got the better of me, and when I finally managed to catch my breath, three years had passed."

"It's okay," his father said, at which Vinsen scoffed. "At least we knew you were alive."

"I'm glad to see you're all well," Kochin said, back straight and overly formal. After spending so much time in Dr. Santo's society, he'd almost forgotten how else to act. As a crutch, he returned to the language of favors, one he'd learned to speak in Central: "I left my job in Theumas. I was wondering if I could stay at home while I reorient myself. I'll cook, clean, and garden—I just need a place to stay."

"No need to ask, Kochin," his father said, taking a seat across from him. "Your bedroom is still here."

"I'll clear it out," Bentri said, then added sheepishly, "I was using it as a study."

Kochin raised an eyebrow. "Were you, now?" He'd never

known Bentri to be a studier; that had always been his niche, following in his father's footsteps.

His mother stooped behind Bentri, ruffling his tangled hair. "He's trying hard to get into a top university. Just like his brother."

"I'm taking the placement exam early—like you did," Bentri said, his tone cautiously eager, as though awaiting Kochin's approval.

Kochin smiled humorlessly. He supposed his path looked grand on paper—small-town genius who'd attended and graduated from his university early to land a job with a research director—but Kochin wouldn't wish his life on anyone, much less his own brother. So, instead, without much of an expression, he said, "I'm proud of you, Bentri."

"Kochin, the letter you sent weeks ago—after reading it, I didn't expect you'd come back so soon," his mother said.

Kochin's heart fell. That was the letter he'd sent home with Nhika.

"My plans changed."

"What about your friend, the other heartsooth?"

A sudden anguish gripped his heart, too painful to breathe through. It felt almost wrong for his mother to mention Nhika so offhandedly, but how could she know the extent of Kochin's grief? He let none of it show as he said, "She's . . . not with me anymore."

Something fell behind his mother's eyes, and he wondered if she still knew him well enough to see the sorrow beneath his cordial smile, or if the mask he'd perfected in Central worked even on his family. For a moment, no one spoke, until Kochin said, "I left my things in my boat. I'll be back again after I grab them."

Before they could protest, Kochin stood, and his family gave him his space. He strode toward the door, pausing at the threshold of the kitchen to say, "Thank you for having me."

As he closed the door, his eyes wandered to the garden, where a group of chickens sniped at his mother's vegetables. Midstep, he paused, counting their calories in his head before nodding with satisfaction.

Kochin took the smallest of the bunch with him.

His dinghy lapped up to the side of the houseboat. With a final grunt of effort, Kochin rowed it parallel and docked himself. Chicken under one arm, he stepped up onto the stern, ducked past the solarium, and dipped into the body of the houseboat.

Where the main cabin had once been a comfortable living space, room enough for two to find respite together, he'd now pushed aside all the furniture to clear the area for something new: one of Dr. Santo's inventions, a casket to keep a body fresh.

Nhika.

With a slow exhale, Kochin traipsed up to the casket, released the pressure of the lid, and opened it. There she lay atop cushioned satin, looking like she was merely sleeping, a breathing tube between her lips and catheters in her arms. He'd long since healed her body's wounds, melting away the hole in her shoulder and sealing the cut in her abdomen. His frequent heartsoothing kept the machinations of decomposition at bay, but it wasn't enough.

Lungs expanding, organs whole, and yet she was still gone. Skin warm, blood oxygenated, and she still didn't wake. And it was all because Kochin's body could take and take and take, but it could never give. It was against the laws of biology, after all—organs were meant to hoard, not relinquish—and though the heartsooth in him could defy such laws in others, his own anatomy remained stubborn and unforgiving. His heartsoothing had never been enough.

He set his jaw as the chicken fretted under his arm. Then, with one hand buried in its breast and the other placed on Nhika's laced fingers, he began the transfer. A flurry of energy entered his core, an influx of heat in his chest, and Kochin exhaled the taste of it on his breath, felt the buzz of it in his clenched teeth. Before his eyes, he saw Nhika's organs laid bare, skin turned to glass to reveal the layers of her anatomy underneath. Each swarmed with color, not tissue but interconnected systems, and he felt a wave of malaise, the nausea that reminded him he was soothing a corpse. He pressed through the discordance, funneling the heat from the chicken toward her glass anatomy.

Kochin had soothed many bodies before, most of them without their knowledge. The workings of their biology returned to him, the feeling of how a body *should* be. Blood was not so sour, so he bled oxygen back into her muscles. Membranes were not so porous, so he tightened up the loosening lumen with a clenched fist. The skin was not so cold, so he breathed warmth across her core. Drawing stores from the fowl in his arms, he mirrored life atop her body, returning color to her cheeks and energy to her tissue. With a pinch of electricity, he started a beat in her heart to bring circulation to the languid blood.

And yet . . . It wasn't enough. As soon as he drew away his soothing, her heart ceased to beat. Her eyes did not open. Her lips remained still.

With a defeated sigh, Kochin pulled back. Her anatomy settled back into reality, opaqueness seeping over skin and organs dimming beneath her rib cage. Kochin watched her face, waiting for any indication of life, but there was none.

Of course not.

He discarded the chicken, now shriveled and limp, and pulled a chair up to the casket's side. With one hand, he caught the lever and added revolutions to the machine, powering the battery. In his other hand, he turned a ring of bone and onyx around his finger, his skin moving over familiar grooves.

"I'm sorry, Nhika," he said, as he often did. Sorry that he could not give the same way she could. Sorry she had left him to carry her gift of heartsoothing, but it wasn't much of a gift at all.

Sorry for a great many things that had already been whispered around this houseboat—when she awoke, he hoped she would hear and accept them all. Bringing her back would be his act of repentance.

And he *would* bring her back. She wasn't yet gone, not with all the potential his heartsoothing had. He'd suffered under Dr. Santo's thumb for three long years for a reason, and now he saw why: to bring back the girl he loved. "Just give me a little more time."

"And a lot more chickens, hmm?" she asked, appearing beside him.

He let out a breath of humor. "Yes. Something different from fish and mice."

"I appreciate the variety," she said, and when his eyes next passed over her, she was gone, leaving him alone in the houseboat once more.

Kochin leaned back, a sigh on his lips, and settled in the silence. There, beside an uncovered casket, rocked by uneven waves, Kochin cranked the lone lever on and on and on.

⇒⇒⇒ THREE ⇐⇐⇐
SIX MONTHS AGO

KOCHIN WASN'T SURE IF HE WAS STAYING LONG enough to make it worth unpacking. His childhood room, the faded-paint walls and squeaking mattress—it reminded him of home in a way he hadn't felt in many years, but settling down as if nothing had happened in that operating room felt disrespectful to the girl who'd gotten him here. Standing before his trunk and open drawer, he felt something pull him toward Theumas: a shadow of the feeling that had drawn him there in the first place, not the promise of grandeur but the invisible chains of his blood debt to the city.

Deciding against unpacking, he donned an old shirt covered in grease stains and took to the garden in the back, returning to chores he had abandoned for the past three years. If he were to stay here, he wanted to make himself useful.

Since he'd left, his mother had let it all overgrow. The camellias had bloomed beyond their chicken wire, the begonias crept out of the shade, and the crab apples were in dire need of pruning.

It was a little like heartsoothing. Every patient he'd soothed was a different garden, a separate variety of flowers and trees and shrubs, but there were still rules to the flora. Some flowers wanted water like an organ wanted oxygen, while others shied from the sunlight with the astringency of cells to sourness. The soil bound them all like blood. Though he didn't know of a heartsooth who could soothe a plant, he saw the parallel to human anatomy on them: the bloom of cockscomb like a skull split open, the deep tracheae of calla lilies, the pelvic cradle of snapdragons. Before his mother had taught him to soothe, she'd taught him to garden.

His father stood by the hydrangea beds. Where his mother was a gardener, his father was a botanist—but those were just two sides of the same coin, art and science. When Kochin approached him, his father nodded toward the flowers, all pink except a bloom of blues and purples at the center.

"Your mother will be sad," his father said, and Kochin tensed, wondering if he'd been found out—his past sin and the one he had yet to commit. He prepared a dozen denials until his father added, "I've found the pipe leak, but I'll have to dig up her flowers."

One glance at the hydrangeas revealed his father's deduction: They only bloomed blue in acidic soil, so this must've been where the pipes leaked. "They'll grow back," he said.

His father gave him a curious look, like the callous response surprised him. "These are the bushes you and your mother planted together when you were young, remember?"

Kochin did. That was back when his mother had first wanted to make something out of the unruly garden. "The pipe won't fix itself," he reasoned. Then, at his father's crestfallen expression, he added, "I can always replant them with her later."

"You'd have to wait for it to get a little cooler. You're staying home long enough for that?"

Kochin clenched his jaw. "I'll plant them the next time I come home."

His father studied him. "It's hard to leave Central, isn't it?"

"Yes." But not for the reason his father believed.

"Thought you might never come home again."

"So, why did you let me leave?"

"Let you? Kochin, there was no stopping you." He clapped Kochin across the shoulder. "Now, help me dig up this pipe."

They spent the better part of the day digging. It was a shame to pull up his mother's hydrangeas. Kochin remembered planting them—all the splinters in his palms, the sun on his back. And when they overgrew their plot, his mother had spent hours pruning them back into shapely beauty, only for Kochin and his father to cut them all back now.

Destroying was easy. Cultivating was far harder—and as they cut through roots with their spades, Kochin wondered how life might arise from nothing.

They found the cracked pipe, and after his father finished replacing it, he turned to Kochin. "Go test it for me."

Kochin left for the pump at the front of the house. When he worked the handle, an unpromising whistle hissed from the dirt, and he frowned.

"That pump doesn't work anymore." When Kochin turned, he found Vinsen coming up the path with his fishing haul. "It hasn't for years."

"I didn't realize," Kochin said, replacing the handle.

"Yes. A lot has changed around here." Vinsen leaned against the sun-bleached fence, arms crossed. "But the city must move faster, huh? For you to blink and have three years pass?" His voice held a grudge that Kochin couldn't fully read. Though he and Vinsen were close in age, only two years apart, they had taken to different things—Vinsen to fishing and animal handling, Kochin to bookwork. Three years away had only deepened the wedge; it hadn't started it. But Vinsen had never been hostile with him, and now Kochin tried to decipher the context behind his words.

"I'm sorry if I haven't been around to help the family out," Kochin said, words tentative. Was that what had Vinsen upset? "I hoped the money that I sent would atone for my absence."

Vinsen scoffed, a humorless smile on his lips as he shook his head. "You speak awfully stiffly now, don't you, Kochin?"

Kochin wasn't sure how to respond to that. Vinsen wanted him to apologize for something, but the reasoning eluded him. So instead, to cover all his bases, he said, "I'm sorry."

"Don't apologize to me," Vinsen said, sticking his hands into his pockets.

Kochin gave him a questioning look. "To Ma, then?"

"That's a start. Ba, too, while you're at it. And Bentri especially."

Kochin swallowed. His thoughts returned to all the letters he'd penned and abandoned, to forged deportation warrants hidden in a doctor's office. If only Vinsen knew how much he'd ached to come home—and how much fear had stayed his hand.

Now, he'd finally made it, only to lose something else in the process.

But Kochin held his tongue. "It seems like you all managed fine without me."

Vinsen gave him a contemptuous look. "Are you serious, Kochin?" His voice adopted an aggravated edge, but his expression remained calm. "Bentri lost his hero, and Ba and Ma lost their favorite son. As soon as you were rid of us, you never looked back. They weren't doing fine."

Kochin opened his mouth with the instinct to protest, then closed it again. Favorite son? His mother's love and father's pride were endless—too much for one son alone. "They didn't play favorites."

"Mm-hmm," Vinsen said. "You're the only one who could keep up with Ba's intellectual ramblings and the only one gifted at heartsoothing. But sure, they didn't play favorites."

Kochin didn't respond, his jaw set with thought. Vinsen had never been one for competition, so Kochin knew he didn't speak from envy. But that meant he spoke only from the truth, which hurt even more. Those years in Theumas, those letters home crumpled and wasted—that had all been for his family's sake. His family had worked too hard to find peace, for him to bring Theuman terror back upon them, incurred by his own naivete. Kochin wanted to say that, to fight back, to explain himself, but there was nothing to absolve him to Vinsen. The only thing he had to show for those three long years was Nhika, with all her boldness and charm, the sole true diamond he'd found among fool's gold.

She was the one thing that could justify his long absence, and she was gone.

When he didn't answer, Vinsen jerked his chin toward the backyard. "We installed a new handle behind the house. Try that one instead," he said. Before Kochin could thank him, he headed into the house, leaving Kochin beside a broken pump and a ravaged garden.

One week. He'd give himself one week to make amends with his family, but Nhika couldn't wait any longer than that.

Dinner, first. Now, instead of hiding in the gardens, he made himself a permanent fixture in the kitchen, chopping tubers for his mother as she prepared seafood chowder. When the family gathered to eat, he joined in the conversation, regaling them with stories from Theumas—of the aristocrats he'd met, the dinners he'd attended, the technology he'd seen. Bentri's eyes widened at the thought of colored motion pictures, so lifelike that the theater auditorium melted away in the darkness. Even Vinsen raised a brow at talks of the nautical vessels that could dip into the abyssal darkness of the sea, of the marine life they'd discovered down there.

After dinner, he helped Bentri move his study out of Kochin's room and into the cupboard under the stairs, which traded space for privacy. There, the two of them tied bandanas over their noses and got to dusting, sweeping away cobwebs and spiders to make a comfortable little space. With a rug, desk, and chairs, the place spruced up into a tidy office, fit for Bentri's purposes.

At this point in the spring, Bentri's university entrance exams were fast approaching. Kochin helped him bring down all his textbooks, those on differential calculus and microme biology and Theuman history. Kochin didn't envy the kid, but they spent the night reviewing topics while Kochin highlighted the test-taking strategies that had helped him ace his exam.

"Now that you're home, maybe you could take it for me," Bentri joked as he settled in his desk chair, limbs flopping with mental burnout.

"I'd have to soothe myself down to skin and bones to convince anyone."

"Doesn't seem to me like you have anything better to do."

The thought of Nhika and her casket flashed in Kochin's mind. "And you have all the time in the world to study."

"It's just so much. I feel like I forget something old as soon as I learn something new." His eyes fell to the desk, where a chemistry textbook lay open to distillation methods. "But I'm glad you came back. Vinsen keeps trying to convince me to stay in Chengton. Says the city will eat me right up like . . ." He held the rest of his words, but Kochin understood them: *like it did to you.*

And maybe it would. Kochin had shown up as a wide-eyed whelp on Theumas's doorstep, hoping for an easy life of milk and honey. Hoping he could bring change to the big city— because didn't Theumas pride itself on innovation? But it had only taken one man to see the naivete of a heartsooth in him, one man to turn him into a bloodcarver.

"Maybe Vinsen has a bit of a point," Kochin began, but Bentri raised his brow in doubt.

"Are you afraid I might become more successful than you, Kochin?" Bentri teased.

"Awfully bold for a boy who can't recite his gas laws."

Bentri's expression soured at that. "Like I said, it's as sand in a sieve."

"You've overworked yourself. Take a little break. A couple weeks to see if this is what you really want. You don't have to take those placement exams early—give yourself another year to enjoy Chengton." That was something Kochin had wished he'd been told, something that might've made him think twice. But, back then, goaded by his father's expectations and his mother's pride, Kochin had only aimed for the pearlescence of Theumas's top universities.

Then again, Bentri had one thing over Kochin: He hadn't taken to heartsoothing the way Kochin had. It hadn't shaped his worldview. He would not enter Theumas with the naive belief that he could sell magic to a city of scientists.

Bentri only snorted. "You know how much Ma and Ba brag about you to the Suli family? I want them to brag about me, too. I *need* to ace this exam."

Bentri had that same spark of confidence in his eyes that Kochin held. Before Kochin had left, Bentri had never been so academically rigorous. Kochin still remembered the nights he had to drag his brother inside from his romps on the street with the neighborhood kids. He'd sit Bentri down before a book, force a pencil into his hands, and watch as Bentri finished his multiplication tables. Now, it was as though he'd come home to a separate kid altogether.

And, in a way, he had. His chest tightened with a distant ache for years lost.

"Well," he said, patting Bentri on the shoulder. "I suppose you have a lot of studying to do, then."

With an encouraging smile, he turned, but Bentri caught him by his sleeve before he could go. When he met his brother's eyes, they were those of a child again—wide, woeful, the same eyes that had bade him farewell the first time he'd gone.

"Kochin, I know you're staying for a while, but do you really have to go back?" he asked, voice small. "There are jobs in Chengton, aren't there?"

"I . . ." The rest of Kochin's words drove hooks into his throat, refusing to come out. An ache braided itself around his heart like corded wire—because those years in Theumas had been spent dreaming of nights like these, ones spent beside his family with no fear between them. Hadn't this always been what he'd wanted?

Now, a hole had corroded that dream, edges burned in the shape of a girl, a heartsooth like him. So, all Kochin said was, "I can't."

"Why?"

Because this had been his dream before she'd entered his life by storm and flying papers. Before he'd found her at a funeral, wrapped in silk and suspicion. Before she'd woven her breath and heartbeat into every fiber of his body as a parting gift, a lasting haunt.

Kochin felt the levity of the evening darken and looked away to avoid Bentri's disappointment. "I can't stop here."

No, he'd only stop when he brought her back.

FOUR
NOW

AFTER HER SHOWER AND MEAL, NHIKA FOUND A change of clothing sitting on her bed, though it wasn't the dresses and silk pants she'd worn in this company before. Instead, it looked more like what she'd worn when she was on her own, a loose tunic thrown over a thin bodice, trousers, and a sash to belt it all together. After she'd donned the pile of clothing, she realized Mimi hadn't bothered to leave her gloves. Despite how simple the attire, it was an aristocrat who looked back from her mirror, and she appeared more familiar than she should've. The well-rested eyes, uncracked lips, brushed hair . . . There was a welcomeness to Suon Ko Nhika, like soothing out the last bit of discomfort after a wound.

When she was done, Mimi awaited at her bedroom door. At the sight of her, Mimi smiled hesitantly, as though afraid of being too optimistic. "You look much better."

"I can work wonders with a meal." She'd just eaten, but she already felt hungry again, having spent all her calories on fixing the little flares across her body, the things that didn't feel quite right—a tight muscle here, a patch of numbness there. There was still a foreignness in her own skin, but she wasn't sure if it was anatomical or if it was due to the recovery from a near-fatal wound.

"Would you like another?" Mimi asked, as though reading her mind. "Hendon just prepared lunch. Everyone is excited to see you."

Nhika's heart leaped at the thought of lunch, and more so at the thought of seeing the Congmi household again—Trin, Andao, Hendon. Grimly, Nhika realized she hadn't expected to wake up from her last stunt.

"Mimi, what happened at the medical center?"

Mimi turned her cheek, looking evasive. "Well, what do you remember?"

"We bested Santo. You went to call the constabulary, and I went to find Kochin. And when I found him, he . . ." The words choked back down her throat, but she pressed through. "He was dying. And in that moment, I just remember feeling like . . . like I would give my life to save him."

"I know," Mimi said softly. "I know you would."

"I thought I did," Nhika admitted with a sheepish laugh, suddenly self-conscious about her own melodrama. "I just don't understand how I'm here, because there weren't enough calories to save us both. So . . . what happened?"

Mimi gave her an uncertain look, and something dreadful curled around Nhika's stomach. Her mind went to the worst—that they *hadn't* both been saved, that her being here meant something she would not be able to bear. But Mimi only said, "You know I don't understand heartsoothing enough to explain it. Can we talk about it at lunch?"

"I—"

"Follow me."

Mimi whirled and fled down the hall, leaving Nhika no choice but to follow.

As Mimi took her through the house, it dawned on her that she didn't recognize these hallways at all. They looked like they belonged in the Congmi manor, all furnished with stately wallpaper and dark wood. They meandered through the parlors, full of lacquered furniture and bright ceramics, and she didn't recognize a single room. She knew the Congmis had multiple homes in Theumas. She just wasn't sure why they'd moved her to this one.

"Nhika?" Mimi said, calling her back. She'd stopped before an entryway that must've been the dining room, judging by the aroma of ginger from somewhere within. When Nhika turned the corner, she found Andao and Hendon already seated.

It was a homely, square chamber dominated by wood-paneled windows, but the view was just as beautiful: the curve of a cliff, gray stone buffeted by foaming water, and fields peppered with flowers. Where the Congmi manor was grand, this was idyllic like a cottage, and she wondered if the seeming isolation was any part of the reason she'd awoken here rather than the manor.

When she looked back to Hendon and Andao, she found them staring at her like she was an automaton that had gained sentience. Something had changed about both of them, very subtly. Though Andao wore the same style of suit, she could've sworn he had grown taller, or perhaps it was just the over-straight way he held his back now, shoulders squared. It was . . . confident. A good look on him. Hendon, too, seemed so much healthier than when she'd first healed him, weeks ago.

The fat had returned to his cheeks, the life to his eyes, but when he reached for his napkin, his hand still trembled. Two more place settings sat on the table, Mimi's and Nhika's. Wordlessly, Nhika took her seat.

"Nhika," Andao breathed, drawing her attention back to the table. "I . . . I can't believe that you're *up*, sitting at the table." He said it with a sense of cautiousness that made her feel like a skittish animal, one he was afraid of overwhelming.

"Me neither," Nhika murmured beneath her breath. Those swallowed questions returned, but one bubbled to the surface first: "Did you take everything to the constabulary? Did Dr. Santo go to jail?"

"Life imprisonment at the Central Theumas Penitentiary," Andao replied as if by rote. He waved to the dishes on the table. "Please, eat."

Only because she needed the calories, and not because she had an appetite, Nhika spooned herself portions of each dish. It was then she realized the meal had started, and yet . . . "Won't Trin be joining us?"

A dour mood fell across the table, like she'd unstoppered something noxious. But Andao's tone was measured as he said, "He's in Central for the time being."

His wording prompted her to look out the window, and she realized something was missing from that view. If they were in Central Theumas and the mansion faced the water, she would expect to see the dockyards—or even the hint of maritime commerce. But there was nothing but white-faced bluffs, fields, and endless horizon of blue, which begged the question—.

"Where are we?" she asked, pushing her chair back with a harsh screech.

"I should've mentioned earlier," Mimi said remorsefully. "We're in Western Theumas."

Western Theumas. Nhika had been here before. Kochin's hometown was somewhere out here, too, in the rural parts of the city-state. But to have moved her all the way out here, then . . . "How long have I been out?"

Mimi swallowed. "Months?"

The word drove through her like a bullet. *"Months?"* Nhika shook her head. "No, no, that can't be." Everything was bearing down at once, like the firmament was dropping out of the sky, because she'd just awoken in a house she didn't recognize, missing months of time, with two of the most important people in her life absent without explanation—and all those questions only multiplied, each one fighting its way up her throat until she felt she might be sick.

Andao leaned over the table. "Nhika, I know it's a lot, but—"

"Tell me."

"What?"

Her eyes lifted to meet his. "Tell me exactly what happened at the medical center."

Swallowing, Andao pushed silverware around his place setting, like he was making room for his words or avoiding them altogether. "I wasn't there, but as I understand it, you and Mr. Ven encountered Santo at the medical center. And . . . he shot you both."

The wound in her shoulder flared with an ache. It was a little unfair, she thought, that she could heal any wound yet still fear the pain of that night.

"Yes, I remember," Nhika responded, a little bitterly. "He took me to a coffin. He'd been keeping his son's body in some machine to preserve it—had all these plans to bring it back to life. It's why he'd been trapping Kochin, but a heartsooth can't bring a dead body back to life."

They were staring at her like she'd just come back from the Butchers' Row again—not quite sure what she was, treating her with padded gloves.

"What?" she asked.

Mimi shook her head. "Nothing."

"So, you freed me from the coffin. Trin shot Santo through the leg. I went into that operating room." Nhika closed her eyes. She remembered that moment with a surgeon's precision, ribs lined with a scalpel and chest cleaved in two. She could even retrace every moment that drew her toward her decision: the grief, the hopelessness, and her . . . bone ring. On that table, she'd truly accepted her ring; giving it to him had been a bid for remembrance. But Kochin understood such customs—since she lived, he should've known to give it back.

Unless he hadn't had the chance. Nhika looked up, met Mimi's eye. "Did Kochin make it off that operating table?"

"Yes," Mimi answered immediately, and Nhika felt her heart loosen.

"So, I healed him."

"Yes."

"And he saved me?"

". . . Yes."

"How is that possible? Heartsoothing requires energy, an exchange, and there was only enough to save one of us."

Mimi shook her head. "I can't explain the heartsoothing to you—you know I can't. But Kochin left you to heal with us. He planned to return when you were better."

"But he's been gone for *months*."

"And it's taken you months to recover."

Mimi wasn't wrong—but there was something not quite right, either. Nhika's stomach soured when she realized the discrepancy: The Congmis would never let him back into their lives. He'd assured them he'd leave Central Theumas forever.

"Was Kochin . . . sentenced?" Nhika asked. Perhaps she'd misjudged the Congmis. Perhaps, in her absence, they'd decided to enact justice for their father, after all.

"No," Mimi said, almost too quickly. "We wouldn't do that."

Nhika turned to Andao. "Is that the truth?"

He met her gaze without wavering. "Yes," he said, and he was either telling the truth or, some time in the missing months, he'd gotten far too adept at lying.

"Stay, Nhika," Mimi said. "I know this sounds like we're keeping you from him—and believe me, I wish I could—but he left you with us. So, shouldn't you stay here until he returns?"

Mimi's eyes bored into her. Nhika remembered Mimi in her fierceness, her anger, her adamancy. This was something different—something vulnerable, desperate, honest. All that youthful entitlement gone, replaced by a genuine concern.

"Okay," Nhika relented, and something fidgety fingered its

way underneath her skin. She'd never stayed in any place for so long, and she wondered how long she could bear it, staying without even knowing if Kochin was alive. "I'll stay. For now."

Mimi's brow melted with relief. "Thank you," she said, but Nhika didn't know what remained unspoken.

Nhika would stay until she learned just why the Congmis were lying to her.

⇒⇒⇒ FIVE ⇐⇐⇐
NOW

AT SOME ANGLES, THE CONGMIS' VILLA LOOKED like a fortress. At others, it looked like a prison.

It sat on a cliff, with only a weathered stone wall separating the garden from a steep, fatal fall into gnashing white waters. Everywhere else was just forest—other than the thin, lonely road that cut from the villa like a shave line. But if it was a prison, it was an understaffed one; there was an uncharacteristic absence of servants, with Hendon filling the gaps. Nhika might've been able to convince herself it was due to the remoteness, but Trin—whom she'd always considered a head warden—was also gone.

She found herself missing him, the steadfastness of his presence, a ready receptacle for all her taunts and jeers. But, without him, there was no one to watch her every move, and she had free rein to explore the house. She familiarized herself with its libraries, none so expansive as the one in their Central manor, and all the furnished parlors. The only place she couldn't investigate was the carriage house, which had been buckled with lock and key, its windows boarded and curtained. Nhika might've found that strange, but this family didn't need many auto carriages. There was an atmosphere of desolation, with guest rooms standing empty and no random home visits from physicians and their annoying aides.

Hendon, steward turned cook, spent most of his time in their kitchen. When lunch ended, he started making dinner. She might've pitied the poor man but quickly found there was nothing better to do in Western Theumas—and the job was preferable to Mimi's and Andao's, who both spent the day in their offices, on the telephone. It was strange, finding Mimi so busy. She never remembered Mimi to be involved in the family business, but that's all she did now, making phone calls and balancing ledgers.

Right now, neither Mimi nor Andao were in their normal spots. When she sought them out, she spied Mimi on the patio, sitting on a tarp laden with automaton parts, wrenches, oil bottles, and blueprints. The girl sat at the center, surrounded by stray metal plating and strewn automaton parts, dressed in a greasy tunic and loose pants with her hair pinned back. Nhika almost hadn't recognized her.

Quietly, she crept up behind Mimi until she could read the blueprint. MEDI-GLOVE 2.0 read bolded text at the top of an automaton rendering. As the name suggested, the sketch detailed an automaton meant to be worn on the forearm, its compartments armored and filled with medical supplies. At the bottom, the diagram had been signed by Andao.

"What's this for?" Nhika asked, and watched Mimi jump out of her skin.

Mimi collected herself, pushing parts around the tarp. It looked like she wanted to conceal the blueprint, but Nhika had already seen it.

"This?" Mimi said, holding up an incomplete glove. "Just

a prototype for one of Andao's new models. He said it was inspired by you—medicine in the palm of your hand."

"No offense, but it's a bit cumbersome for surgery, isn't it?"

"It's not for surgery. It's for the field," Mimi said. More hid behind her tone, but Nhika couldn't parse it before Mimi slipped the glove on. Angling her wrist back popped open a syringe compartment at the forearm, and she slid open a metal plate along her fingers to reveal suture needles, ready with thread. "Like it?"

It was interesting, a healing device in the shape of a glove. To her, those two things felt exclusive, because she'd never be able to heal through metal, no matter how delicate the plating.

"Andao's been studying his anatomy," she said. There were many corollaries to the human hand, springs in the place of muscle and the tendonous rays on the back of the hand re-created with wire.

"Someone's had to, now that we don't have a trusted physician we can consult."

"If this isn't a partnership, what made Andao dabble in medical technology?"

"Well, technically, it *is* a partnership. Just not with doctors. With—" The rest of the sentence turned into a yelp as Mimi dropped her half-assembled device. She'd pressed the wrong button, and a blade had popped out of its compartment. Nhika hadn't witnessed the cut, but a line of red bloomed against white silk.

"Mother, are you okay?" Nhika asked, drawing forward as Mimi tugged off her glove.

"Fine, fine," Mimi said, but there was water in her eyes.

"I thought you said this wasn't for surgery. Why's it got a scalpel?"

"Well, sometimes . . . sometimes healers need to defend themselves, don't they?" Mimi asked, meeting Nhika's eye. She was still nursing her hand, the bleed growing. It was a shallow cut, but long—a terrible mess dripping onto white silk.

By instinct, Nhika placed cool fingers against Mimi's bare skin until she remembered decorum and snapped herself away.

"I'm sorry," she stammered. "I . . . I mean, I can heal it, if you want."

Mimi gave her a curious look, and Nhika realized that she'd healed Hendon, and she soothed Trin, but never had she used the gift with Mimi. But Mimi said, "Will it hurt?"

"Yes. Unbearably."

"Okay, no need to make fun." Mimi prostrated her palm. "Well then, go ahead."

Nhika almost thought she'd misheard—because she hadn't expected such an easy agreement. The Congmis had always hidden it behind respectful smiles and polite words, but she knew they distrusted heartsoothing. Yet Mimi was looking at her with anticipation—no, *expectation*—and she wondered if her near-death incident had proven something to them.

Nhika cupped Mimi's hand in her palms and let her influence sink in. There came a flinch, like Mimi's natural instinct was to resist it, but the girl didn't move—hardly even breathed. There was reservation, but Mimi was being accepting. Nhika wondered if this was grace, if Mimi knew what it meant to Nhika to soothe another.

The cut itself was small, one that would heal in its own time, but the palm was rife with throbbing nerves. Nhika dampened those first, then stitched up the skin with collagen until the cut pulled tight and the bleeding stopped. Just a simple mend, over in less than a minute.

Mimi's eyebrows lifted in awe as she pulled her hand away and turned her palm, as though looking for the shine of a scar or a new palm line. "I see," she said, as though musing to herself. "I always figured it would feel like an invasion. But it's more like . . . when I would skin my knee and Father would kiss it better."

"Your father's kisses accelerated healing?"

Mimi let out a tired breath. "I can't say I've missed your sarcasm."

With a glance at the glove, the knife still extended, Nhika said, "Don't you Congmis usually hire someone to do this part for you?"

"We're spread a little thin at the moment."

"I've noticed. What happened to the help? Budget cuts or something?"

"Privacy comes at the cost of some luxuries," Mimi answered. "But at least politics and reporters can't follow us out here."

"You could at least ask Andao to help you."

"He's in Central today," Mimi responded. Her expression darkened, and she wrung the glove in her lap. "Visiting Trin."

There it was again, that imperceptible sadness that had clung to the corners of the mansion since Nhika had awoken. The way they said Trin's name sounded like a prayer. It turned Nhika's stomach.

"What happened to Trin, Mimi?" Nhika asked—because she knew something must've. There were only a few things she could imagine that would keep Trin from Andao's side.

Mimi's expression wilted, like she realized she could no longer lie. In a soft tone, she said, "He's in the hospital."

Her throat tightened. "Why?"

"Surgery," Mimi said. "We . . . None of us know how it happened. Just that, one day, he came home and he was . . . he was bleeding from the inside out."

Nhika's blood ran cold. "Well? Is he okay?"

At that, tears welled to Mimi's eyes. "We have to believe so."

A knock came at the patio door, interrupting their conversation. Hendon stood at the entrance to the manor, hands clasped behind his back. At his side was a familiar man: broad shouldered, hawkish brow, black robe thrown over his shoulders. It was Mr. Nem, who Nhika remembered constantly hounding Andao with war talks. Some things didn't change, she supposed.

"Commissioner Nem," Mimi said, swiping tears out of her eyes and hiding the bloodied gloves as she stood. She looked occupied with how unbecoming her engineer's outfit was, while Nhika was still stuck on Nem's title: *Commissioner*.

But of course. Last she remembered, the election was fast approaching, and Mr. Nem had been the natural choice. Yet, it still jarred her—the thought that Theumas hadn't even lurched in her absence when her world had nearly ended that night in the operating suite.

When Nhika looked up, she found Nem's singular attention on her.

"Ms. Suon," he said, lips pulling into a smile. She remembered only sharing a single dinner with him—but Nhika supposed that was the way with commissioners, remembering people's names.

"Commissioner," she greeted, following Mimi's decorum.

"I wasn't aware you'd rejoined the Congmi household."

Nhika glanced at Mimi, feeling suddenly naked without a prepared backstory. Mimi spoke up. "Just for the time being," she said. "She was ill and is now looking to get back on her feet."

"Is that so?" Nem asked, his words still directed at Nhika. His eyes roved her like she was one of Andao's designs, a lump of cogwork to appraise. "Well, it certainly seems like you've made a full recovery."

"That I have," Nhika said.

"I would expect nothing less of the Congmis' hospitality."

"Generous, aren't they?"

"I'm holding a dinner party at the end of the week. I've invited the siblings, but that invitation extends to you, too."

"Commissioner," Mimi interjected. "I'd be happy to meet you on my brother's behalf. Please, follow me."

Nem complied, but his stare lingered on Nhika as he turned toward the house. Just before he entered, he paused to tell her, "I do hope we see more of each other, Ms. Suon."

Nhika didn't know how to respond to that, but Nem disappeared into the house before she had to. Mimi and Hendon trailed after him, leaving her alone on the patio. Nhika found herself back in the past, piecing together Kochin's identity from discrepancies alone. This time, it was Nem.

They'd only met once, yet he remembered her. He was a

commissioner, yet so far from Central. And he'd invited *her*, a Yarongese nobody, to a dinner. The last time anyone had shown that much undue interest in her, she'd nearly died on his operating table. Where she'd grown up, evil was apparent. Evil spat at her in the streets and caught her ankles in catchpoles. Here, evil had to blend in, and she hadn't been so great at noticing it the first time. She'd be smarter the second.

Her eyes fell to the abandoned Medi-Glove on the tarp, and thoughts of Trin returned. She wondered why the siblings built gloves like these when they had her heartsoothing. And when she awoke, the *first* thing they should've asked her was to heal Trin. So why hadn't they?

She'd promised Mimi she'd stay, but it couldn't be helped. Nhika was a healer, so she'd heal.

Growing surer by the step, Nhika returned to the house and scrounged up enough chem for a round-trip train ticket to Central. Then, slipping out between the raised voices of Mimi and Nem, she was off on that lonely road through the trees.

Toward Central. Toward Trin. And toward that haunting building that had once tried claiming her and Kochin both.

⟫⟫ SIX ⟪⟪

SIX MONTHS AGO

BY THE SECOND DAY OF THE WEEK, KOCHIN'S father and Vinsen returned to work and Bentri to school, leaving Kochin at home with his mother. He spent the morning in the garden before the heat could hit, then started making a home of his room again.

All he truly needed of the room was the bed. It was a child's bed; the last time he was here, he'd been Bentri's age. Still, there was more room here than on the houseboat, and he felt he owed his family his presence. Yet, his thoughts were not in Chengton.

They were in Theumas.

In particular, they were in the private study of a delicensed doctor, whose walls were hung with photographs of vivisections and whose shelves bent under the weight of unethical Daltan texts. He'd perused those texts after Santo's house had been cased by the constabulary, but they had not been able to answer the question Santo had been researching, the question Kochin wondered now: Could a heartsooth bring someone back from the dead?

A knock came at the door, and Kochin didn't have time to respond before it opened. His mother arrived, a plate of sliced mango in her hand, which she placed on his bookshelf.

He smiled gratefully. "Thank you, Ma."

Taking that as an invitation, she strutted into the room, pushing past him to fling open the curtains. "So dark in here, Kochin," she scolded as dust billowed into the air.

"I don't mind it."

"I do. Look how pale you've become. You look more like your father every day," she said, shaking her head. She opened the window to let in a breeze and fan out the dust, then paused to ask, "Did you like your job?"

"It had its pluses and minuses." Kochin didn't mean to be so reticent, but he feared opening up a line of questions he wasn't prepared to answer. Questions about why the home visits had stopped when the money hadn't, why he was returning now. If he talked about those things, where did he stop? Did he stop at Santo, the strings Kochin had tied himself in? Did he stop at Mr. Congmi, an industrial titan felled by a physician's aide? Or, did he stop at Nhika, a girl who died in his stead because he could take but he could not give?

"Must've been a busy job, studying and working all the time," his mother continued, voice goading him to reveal more.

He halted his packing and turned from the door. "I suppose it was. Everyone there is trying to climb the ladder, just like me, and it was easy to forget about anything else. It's my fault, really. I just got caught up in the city."

"You know, if you went by train instead of houseboat, it's a shorter trip home."

"It was hard to find time even then."

"Were you ashamed of us, Kochin?" his mother asked, turning from the window and dropping the pretense of tidying.

"No," he said, shaking his head fervently. "Never that."

"You fell in love, then. Was it Nhika?"

"I—" Kochin didn't have the words to deny it, but it wasn't what she thought. "I didn't forget about family, Ma."

"Then why, after all this time, no telegrams or visits, just money and a single letter . . . Why now?"

That was the question he feared. Desperation gleamed in her eyes and Kochin knew that if he didn't give her an answer, she would assume the worst: that he didn't care for his family. That, after having drained his mother's love and father's pride to escape to the city, he hadn't once thought about coming back. Nothing had been further from the truth.

And he could've told her the truth. Santo had been imprisoned; there was no more danger to Kochin's family. But now, it wasn't fear that stayed his tongue. It was guilt—he was here because another heartsooth had died in his stead. And not just any other heartsooth, but Nhika. If he put it into words, voiced it aloud, he feared it might break him.

"Theumas trapped me," he said instead. "I was in a bad situation. But now I'm out."

"Was it debt?" his mother asked. "You should've asked for help, and you didn't have to send us the money. We could—"

"No, Ma," he said, waving off her concerns. "Please, don't worry about me."

His words were only gasoline to a fire.

"I *am* worried about you. It's my job to worry about you—I'm your mother. You came back, Kochin, but you're so quiet and unhappy. You don't smile anymore. You're thin as a twig. You tell me not to worry, but what worries me most is when you don't tell me anything at all. Then I'm just left to wonder," she railed, hands planted on her hips.

If only she knew. Kochin's lips parted, as though he were brave enough to reveal that her assumptions could not come close to the truth. For all his life, he had considered his mother's love unconditional, but he wondered if he'd merely lacked the imagination—how could he have foreseen the crimes he'd commit? Instead of the truth, he said, "I lost something important to me in Theumas, Ma."

"Suonyasan Nhika?" his mother asked.

He nodded.

"Who was she to you, Kochin? She was more than just a friend, wasn't she?"

Again, he nodded.

"She broke up with you? That's why you came home?"

His throat closed—he would take that reality over the truth—but he shook his head. "No, she didn't."

"I don't understand, then. What happened?"

A memory caught him like fingers around his throat: the glow of Nhika's flyaway hairs, illuminated by the surgical light as she bent over him; her lips crushing against his, so sweet only because he'd thought they'd be the last thing he tasted; her body in his arms after, impossibly cold and light as the last trace of her warmth disappeared into his chest. A scar still remained, not fully healed; Nhika had used the last of her energy to place her ring in his fingers instead. Kochin couldn't remember how long he remained on that table, holding her against his body as though that could return her gift of life.

By instinct, he turned her bone ring around his finger. If he thought, real hard, about what had killed her, he found it wasn't the gunshot to her shoulder, nor the cut in her abdomen, nor the bruise against her temple. The events that had led to her death had started far before that night in the operating suite. They'd started the moment he'd taken off his mask.

So, because he should've done the same with Nhika, because the world had punished him for hoping, he simply said, "Things just didn't work out. The city holds bad memories for me now. That's all, Ma."

And as though it were a second skin, that physician's aide mask slipped easily over the grooves of his cheekbones again—wooden finish over his eye bags, theater paint on all his cracks. He could tell he was breaking his mother's heart from the look in her eyes, but he could live with that. Kochin had broken Nhika's heart the same way, and he should've left it broken.

When he had no more words to offer her, his mother backed toward the door. "Okay, Kochin," she said, accepting the answer for now. "I'm just glad you're home."

Kochin didn't respond, not wanting to give her any reason to linger, but it still killed him when she closed the door.

No one could've prepared him for the loneliness—when the one person who'd always known him best no longer understood him at all.

It came down to the brain.

Kochin had soothed enough corpses to know that, on their own, organs might push and pull blood, and the lungs might hold and release breath, but it was the processes of the brain that brought it all together. But Kochin had never been so adept at soothing the brain—had always avoided it, lest his patients feel him. Even with Hendon, during the accident that killed Mr. Congmi, Kochin hadn't been able to heal the collateral damage.

Nhika had done that. She had, somehow, repaired the pathways that allowed Hendon to get out of bed, to walk and talk and laugh again. But to create those electrical pathways out of nothing was like drawing water from air.

Kochin's knife slipped, as he was so lost in thought, and the edge sliced open his finger. He sucked in a breath and drew back, keeping blood off the vegetables he'd been cutting for dinner. Only then did he realize he'd been dicing the tomatoes, when it should've only been the onions—so absentminded lately. His thoughts weren't in the kitchen, as quaint and warm as it was. They were in his houseboat, at Nhika's side, one hand on her arm and his influence mired somewhere in her cranium, trying to create a spark that might keep.

"Here," came a voice: Vinsen, emerging from behind to pass Kochin a napkin.

Kochin accepted it and squeezed it around his finger. "I thought you were on the river today."

"The fish were disagreeable. We'll try again tomorrow morning." Vinsen looked him up and down, then proffered up a hand. "Need a calorie?"

It was a habit from when they were children because Kochin was always taking calories to soothe—second nature, but Kochin had spent so long soothing in secret that the offer stunned him.

"What, don't tell me you don't even soothe anymore after Central," Vinsen said.

"Of course I do," Kochin said. It wasn't something he could ever give up easily—no matter how hard Santo had tried to make him hate it. The doctor had almost succeeded, but Kochin had just needed a reminder—a girl, too smart for her own good, who'd pried apart his mask with bloody fingers. Proof that heart-soothing was beautiful, and it was kind, and it was forgiving.

When Kochin still didn't take the offer, Vinsen stuck his hand back under his armpit. "You were up early this morning. Earlier than me."

Kochin had gone to the houseboat. Santo's machine was enough to keep the decay at bay, but he was still terrified—like he might come back one day to find her unsalvageable. "I was exploring Chengton again. I've been away for too long."

"Yeah," Vinsen agreed easily, and his eyes bored into Kochin. "You know, I found Ma crying, earlier. You have anything to do with that?"

Kochin stepped back, looked away. He'd made her cry when he left; he made her cry when he returned. "I guess I just didn't come home in the way she'd hoped."

Vinsen's expression darkened, like he wanted to say something biting, but he only shook his head. "You're leaving at the end of the week, right?"

Kochin nodded.

Vinsen let out a sardonic laugh, something disappointed hiding behind his dry smile. "Well, I'd say you never really came home at all."

He clapped a hand against Kochin's shoulder—a fraternal gesture, but this one felt cold and distant—as he left, and for all Kochin's heartsoothing, the cut in his finger still bled.

After dinner, he took to the dinghy again—this time, bringing one of the mice that had gotten stuck in his mother's traps. Vinsen's words were still crawling under his skin—but Kochin told himself he'd be home, truly, soon. Just one last task, one final chain to cut free from: his failure to pull his heartsooth out of Theumas alive. Then, and only then, could he find those ideals she'd promised him.

Peace. Freedom. Love. For a night, he had those; in a night, he'd lost them.

When he neared the houseboat, he found something immediately amiss: another skiff tied to the railing. He hurried, rows digging water, and didn't bother to tie the dinghy down before hauling himself on board and shoving his way into the cabin.

Inside, he found Vinsen standing before Nhika's casket.

Kochin left no space for explanations. He just rushed up to Vinsen and shoved him aside, harder than he'd intended. With a cry, Vinsen crashed against the shelves, toppling books in his grapple for balance.

"Did you touch anything?" Kochin demanded, and Vinsen winced at his tone.

"Kochin, I—"

"Did you touch anything?"

Vinsen stared at him, brows lifted and eyes horrified. The way he was looking at Kochin now, it was like they weren't even related—like nothing more than empty space and strewn books connected them.

"Who are you?" Vinsen asked, his voice hollow. "You look like my brother, but you've come back empty. You sound like him, but your words don't mean anything anymore. And now this . . . this . . ."

"Did you—"

"No, I didn't touch a damned thing!" Vinsen snapped, and his anger devolved into an incredulous laugh, like he couldn't decide between horror and disbelief. "So, this is where you've been spending all your time. Mother, Kochin, please don't tell me . . . don't tell me you . . ."

"Don't tell you that I what?"

In a strained voice, Vinsen finished, "That you killed her?"

Kochin's eyes flared. "No." But he might as well have. He turned toward the casket, just to ensure Nhika was still within—untouched, unaltered. "Leave, Vinsen."

"What?"

"Leave. Forget what you saw."

"Not until you explain this to me. Why is there a dead girl in your—"

"She's *not* dead," Kochin interrupted, and the bite of his

words startled Vinsen back toward the shelf. "Not alive. But not dead, either. Somewhere in between, with this machine taking over the function of her organs and my heartsoothing keeping her warm."

"By the Mother, Kochin . . . are you planning on . . ." Vinsen shook his head. "So, all this time you've spent in the city, it's just been to break the natural order, test your limits."

"You don't know what you're talking about." Kochin took a step toward him.

"Well then, enlighten me, Kochin." Vinsen matched the challenge.

"You wouldn't understand."

"Why not?" Vinsen demanded, and Kochin realized how close they'd gotten, eye to eye. "Because I never left Chengton? Because I couldn't possibly be as smart as Ven Kochin, boy genius?"

"You're putting words in my mouth."

"Then tell me I'm wrong. Tell me you haven't spent these past three years gallivanting across Central, seeing the world, while the rest of us were stuck here. Tell me you don't want your name in the stars like all those other Theuman trailblazers. Tell me . . . tell me you're *not* trying to bring a corpse back from the dead."

"And so what if I—"

Vinsen shot out a fist, and knuckles cracked against Kochin's jaw. Kochin stumbled against a chair, cool palm cupping his flaming cheek, and for a moment, all either of them could do was stare at each other in stunned silence.

Then Vinsen said, "When will it be enough for you?"

That wasn't a word Kochin liked, *enough*, so he didn't answer. Following Kochin's silence, Vinsen continued, "You were gone for three years, not a word back until now. Finally found somewhere fast enough for you, not a care whose feathers you plucked to make your wings—and when you do return, it's with a science experiment."

That jogged some sense back into Kochin's skull, though he still reeled from Vinsen's punch. With the back of his hand, he wiped spittle from his lip and mumbled, "She's not a science experiment."

"What?"

"I *said* she's not a science experiment. Her name is Suonyasan Nhika," Kochin enunciated, and drew himself up, scraping together what remained of his dignity. "In Central, I worked for a terrible man. I wanted to come home, but he never let me. He extorted me. Blackmailed me. And I went down a dark, dark path."

Mr. Congmi's murder came to mind now—a raised pistol, something to spook the horses. The gun had been meant to place distance between himself and the unforgivable act, but he'd pulled the trigger all the same.

And after that, his world had gotten so much narrower, and so much colder—like he could no longer take that fox mask off, and all the light he could see came filtered through its taunting jeer. Until Nhika.

He drew up to her casket. Lifted the lid. Dropped his hand into his pocket, where the mouse squirmed—and soothed. Those microscopic cracks across her bone sealed, and he squeezed out the clots in her thickening blood, and everything seemed to let out a long breath.

"I did terrible things in Central, Vinsen," he said, and his throat nearly closed at the words. "But she never judged me. She helped me leave. But it was . . . the last thing she ever did. She gave her life to me. I held her in my arms as she . . . as she . . ."

This time, the words wouldn't come out. Kochin bowed his head over the casket, shut his eyes—but to no avail, because the memory came like a bat to his skull. And each new breath was a growing fracture, until he was sure his head might split into two.

Something solid settled on his shoulder: Vinsen's hand, gentle and reassuring. "You never told anyone?"

Kochin met his brother's eyes. "How could I? Could you imagine Ma seeing what I've become? I already make her cry."

"She would understand. She loves you more than anything."

Kochin shook his head—she couldn't know. Because her heart-soothing was magic and light, while his was . . . wretched. And he still planned on committing the biggest taboo. "You can't tell her, okay, Vinsen? Promise me you won't tell her."

Vinsen drew back, but his eyes were sympathetic. "Okay. But . . . where does this end, Kochin?"

"I'm going to bring her back."

That sympathy morphed—into pity, Kochin realized.

"I *am*," Kochin insisted, and it was the first time he'd spoken the goal aloud. That made it real, like he could no longer turn back. "I have to."

"Kochin . . ."

"I can do it," Kochin snapped—and almost worried Vinsen might punch him again. But he continued, his voice cracking. "My heartsoothing, the thing Ma gave me . . . It couldn't save her. But it can do *this*. I know it can."

It was like all his time in Santo's service had prepared him for this—soothing corpses, inadvertently helping a man who wanted to bring back his son. But Kochin would succeed where Santo hadn't because he was a bloodcarver, and so he'd carve Nhika out of a tombstone. He'd find some semblance of the girl he loved from this lifeless tissue and dull bone.

"It's not . . . It's not that I don't think you can do it."

Kochin met his brother's eyes. "You don't think I should?"

"You remember those stories Ma used to tell us, right? Of heartsooths who had done the same?"

"They're just stories." Kochin remembered the folktales: a shambling army bringing death because they could not have it for themselves, immortal children who called only for the sleep that their mother forbade them. Just as his mother had not raised him to believe in the Mother, Kochin did not believe in horror stories meant to scare children into bed at night. In fact, he *dared* the Mother to take more from him than She already had.

"And if they're not?"

"What choice do I have?" Kochin shook his head. "The Mother can damn me to Hell, but the other option is I just . . . give up, and pretend it's not a possibility. And that blood would never come off my hands, and I'll always be haunted by the things I did in Theumas."

If he buried her, no matter how beautiful the grave, Kochin

→ 59

knew he'd always hear that voice coming up from the dirt—her ghost, haunting him ever since she'd woven her life into his chest. A reminder that he could escape Santo and leave the city but still find himself wrapped in chains.

Vinsen settled back on his heels, arms crossed. "You really didn't come home, did you? You're still there—in the city. Itching to go back."

His words sounded judgmental, but behind Vinsen's biting tone was a somber expression—like he was just beginning to understand the extent of Kochin's desperation. Kochin didn't need him to understand it; he just needed his brother to accept it. To step back from Nhika's casket and let him leave Chengton again. "I'm returning to Central. I'm going to bring her back. And you can't change my mind."

He studied Vinsen's face. His eyes were forlorn, brows drawn with pity, and somewhere behind the frown was disgust—at what Kochin had done, at what he planned to do. He could read Vinsen's thoughts, too: another punch loaded in his white knuckles, like that might rattle Kochin back to his senses. Instead, Vinsen stepped up to Kochin, grabbed him by his collar, and raised him to the balls of his feet. Kochin never had to fear true violence from his brother, and if Vinsen punched him again it was because he deserved it, but he still winced.

But all Vinsen said was, "I don't know who's a bigger fool—you, for trying to do this, or me, for deciding to help you."

Kochin blinked in surprise. "Help . . . me?"

Vinsen set him back down, though his hands still clutched Kochin's shirt. "I just want my brother back," he said, and there was such sadness in his voice—like Kochin wasn't even there, standing before him. Like he was begging a goddess, not his brother. "So, tell me what to do."

There was no bitterness in his tone, only acceptance. Kochin mulled it over before saying, "Keep her safe for me. It'll be hard to bring her back to Central. I'm returning to the city, and when I find my answers, I'll let you know. This machine is all she needs—just don't let it stop running. Can you do that for me?"

Vinsen let out a long sigh. "I *have* been doing that for you. This is nothing new. Just . . . Just promise me one thing."

"What?"

"When this is all over, whether or not you find your answers, you come home, okay?"

Kochin closed his lips, not ready to make a guarantee. He wasn't even sure what it meant for this to be over, because there was only one end to this he foresaw: bringing Nhika back. There was nothing short of that he'd accept, but all he said was, "I promise."

SEVEN
SIX MONTHS AGO

KOCHIN STAYED WITH HIS FAMILY FOR ANOTHER week. In part, it was because he wanted to see the garden restored before he let his mother have her way again. And also, he was beginning to enjoy the nights when everyone returned from their corners of Chengton, with Bentri to his books and Vinsen bearing fresh haul.

But, truly, it was because he appreciated the quiet hours of Chengton. It allowed him to think. It allowed him to plan.

At the end of the week, he was off. While he'd done his best to avoid his family's judgment, they walked him down to the railway station, a single track carving through a barren platform with a flap display schedule that never updated because it never needed to—there was Central Theumas in one direction, the western residential towns in the other, and that was it.

Kochin had little with him, just a handheld trunk. It was mostly filled with his family's gifts, meals wrapped in waxed parchment, a few changes of clothes, and a couple novels he'd promised Bentri he'd read. Few others were gathered on the platform, awaiting the first train of the morning. With nothing to do but wait, Kochin was forced to face his family.

With a breath, he turned. "Ma, Ba, thank you for having me," he said, dipping his head into a bow. "Bentri, Vinsen . . ."

He was disappointing his brothers, he knew, but in different ways. Bentri had never grown out of his boyish expressions, and his despondence was evident in his heavy frown, the droop of his brows. Vinsen, though, held a taciturn look, arms crossed over his chest.

"Come back soon, Kochin," Bentri said, staggering forward as though he intended to hug Kochin. He must've thought better of it, because he swooped into a bow instead.

"I'll write," Kochin offered in lieu of a promise to return, though Vinsen looked unconvinced.

Kochin's mother stepped up to him and cupped his cheek in her palm. The gesture was a quick one, but her heartsoothing pulled at him—full of longing, full of warmth, full of farewell. If he left his mother, with Nhika gone . . . it would be the last time he felt heartsoothing in a long, long time. Real heartsoothing, something more than his own.

"Don't forget about home, okay?"

"I'd never—" he began, but a whistle of the train called their attention to the horizon, where a steam locomotive emerged from the forest. He watched it approach, stepping back from the edge as it rolled up to the platform.

The train exhaled as it came to a stop, and a conductor leaned out the door to announce its final destination: Central Theumas. Kochin grabbed his trunk in preparation to leave but bowed a final time to his family.

"Thank you again," he said, straightening.

His family repeated their farewells, and through them, Kochin met Vinsen's eyes. They shared a moment of quiet camaraderie—and melancholy, like they were both grieving two different things. For Kochin, it was the girl he'd left in Vinsen's care. He promised himself the next time he faced that iron casket, it would be with an answer.

"Don't let the months turn into years, Kochin," Vinsen said, his eyes holding a warning. "And whatever it is you're looking for in Theumas . . . I truly hope you find it."

Kochin felt new remorse bubble up in his heart, and maybe if he set down his trunk, stepped away from the train, he could live here in Chengton, happy and surrounded by family.

But Nhika's face swirled in the wisps of steam, and he tightened his grip around his luggage. No, he wouldn't be able to live with himself if he didn't bring her back, if he didn't at least try.

So instead, he waved a final goodbye to Bentri, who leaned forward on his toes to holler a farewell. To his father, who held up a hand in parting. To his mother, whom he'd made cry again.

And to Vinsen, who knew what it would take for Kochin to return.

The conductor made his second call, and Kochin stepped into the train car. He found a seat in the back, a window facing the platform. When at last the train rolled forward, he could see his family still watching him from the railway station, gathered and close. There was a space there, between his brothers, where he could've fit. But he felt himself pull away from Chengton just as surely as the train pulled out of the station, drawn by the ring around his finger.

"You should've stayed in Chengton," Nhika said, and when

he looked back to the car, she was sitting on the bench across from him. "Family is . . . rare. Precious."

That sounded like something the true Nhika might say. He knew of her family. Knew that she'd lost them much too early, and when she spoke about them, her eyes glowed with a distant softness, a youthfulness returned. Maybe she was right.

"There's always something drawing me back to this city, isn't there?"

"It's a hard place to escape," she rationalized. Nhika flashed her canines in an impish grin. "Well, hard to escape alive, anyway."

Kochin reached Central Theumas's Grand Terminus as the mountains pulled the last of the sunlight from the sky. In its place, the glow of the cityscape bled toward the stars as electronic lights and gas lamps flickered to life. He grabbed his trunk and departed, hopping onto the last trolley to the Pig Borough.

When he'd quit his job, he'd used some of his saved money to clean the shophouse: selling the animals, fumigating the smell. He'd almost considered listing it for sale but was glad he hadn't; now that the houseboat remained in Chengton, he'd have to use this address as a true residence.

When he shimmied the lock open into a cold, barren living room, his heart sank. Silver moonlight cast the silhouettes of his furniture in blue, the floors in gray. Silence threaded through the rooms and settled like dust in the corners. When Kochin fumbled out a hand to dial up the lights, the sparse cobwebs made themselves apparent, wisping along his chandelier and strung across his ceiling.

This had never been a home for him. It had always been a hidden blemish, the place he collected the secrets of his heart-soothing: the animals snuck into the Theumas Medical Center in his pockets, a coat hook for his fox mask and Butchers' Row attire. Then it had become his first wrong move, the initial thread in the tapestry that wove Nhika's death—because he never should have let her go with him.

"It's not so bad," Nhika said, appearing in the corner of the space. "It's just missing . . . plants. And maybe a little light."

It's missing you, he wanted to say. Instead, he tipped off his shoes and dragged his trunk to the bedroom.

It had a bed, but he'd mostly been using the space for storage. The majority was medical equipment that he'd collected over the years, apparatuses from past research experiments or boxes of defective medical kits, unusable at Santo's office. Scattered among them were personal items, relics from a time when he'd intended to make a true home here—wall decorations, clay pots never used, hanging glass terrariums, all abandoned. Discarded medical orders and drafted schedules littered the desk. He pushed all that aside to clear space for a planner, which he opened in the center of the desk.

He'd returned to this city for answers, and as much as it boiled his blood to acknowledge it, there was one person in this city who might be able to supply them. One person who had spent years studying the possibility of resurrection, long before Kochin had ever considered it. He'd spent three years trying to escape this man, but now he'd make an appointment to visit him—hopefully on the other side of prison glass.

Kochin needed to speak with Santo.

Kochin had never been inside the Central Theumas Penitentiary before, though he'd always imagined there was a cell here with his name on it. It was an austere and minimalist place, its waiting room just a row of chairs and lockers for personal items. Two officers stood guard, hands clasped behind their backs and pistols on their belts. Automatic security mechanisms topped every door and window, a series of levers, locks, and shutters prepared to bar all exits in case of lockdown.

He was alone in the waiting room, the only sound the insistent tick of the clock, time pressing forward. Time that Kochin despised wasting.

At last, an official, dressed in a smart navy uniform, entered from the visitation hall. "Mr. Ven Kochin?"

Kochin stood and followed the official out of the waiting room. They passed a hallway adjacent to the visitation room, an open space for convicts and their guests to talk around tables. Santo wasn't among them—instead, the officer took Kochin to a hallway beyond, lined with a series of closed visitation boxes. His was the one at the far end of the hall.

"Here you are," he said, giving Kochin his privacy and closing the door behind him.

There was no one on the opposite side of the window until the door in the back opened. In stepped Santo, flanked by two guards and hands cuffed. Imprisonment had not treated him kindly; his back, once bent with the gentle lean of an older gentleman, seemed bowed under the weight of his numbered days. The prison had given him a walking stick, and he sported a limp on the side Trin had shot him—still healing, Kochin thought. His white hair, once so trim and respectable, had overgrown; he hardly looked recognizable as Santo Ki Shon.

The only things that hadn't changed were his eyes, holding a familiar dark cunning as he took a seat across from Kochin. Despite the reinforced glass between them, Kochin's shoulders tensed. He'd told himself he held all the power here, yet when he looked at Santo, he was sixteen again, new to the city and already approached by a research director. That pearly shine revealed itself to be the gleam of fangs soon enough.

"Ven Kochin," Santo greeted. "I see the days have been treating you just as kindly as they have me."

In the glare of the lights above, Kochin could see half his face mirrored on the glass divider, the bags beneath his eyes and his unstyled hair. "I didn't come to be belittled by you again, Santo."

"Then what did you come for? To mock me? To curse my name? To gloat?" Santo leaned back in his seat with unbecoming weariness. "Have your fun; I don't care. I already lost everything when that bloodcarver took my son from me."

He'd sympathized with Santo's loss before; this time, he couldn't find it in himself to care at all. Giving Santo no soapbox to whine upon, he said, "I've come for answers."

At that, interest shifted in the doctor's eyes. He leaned back in his chair, looking thin and small between his two guards. "Ah, so you need my help," he goaded.

Kochin continued anyway. "Where did those Daltan texts come from?"

"I figured you would pay me a visit sooner or later, but I didn't think it'd be over Daltan texts, of all things."

"Just answer the question."

"Why are you interested?"

"It's none of your concern."

Santo leaned back in his chair. "Let me guess. You want a story about my *evil*. You want to use my smeared reputation to elevate yourself—when we both know who should really be in this cell."

Kochin's eyes flicked to Santo's guards, but neither showed a reaction. "I've no interest in having my name spoken in the same sentence as yours," he said. "All I'm interested in is how you thought a bloodcarver might possibly bring back your son."

Realization lit in Santo's eyes and his apathy turned into predaceous curiosity. "Oh, I see what this is about."

"Where are they from, Santo?" Kochin reiterated.

"This is about her, isn't it? Because you two *both* entered that operating room, but only you walked out—so, who was it, then, who truly killed her?"

Kochin set his jaw with anger.

Santo continued, undeterred by the death in Kochin's stare. "I see you for what you are, Kochin. A *hypocrite*."

"I'm not sure what you mean," Kochin replied coolly.

"Don't act so brave just because there is glass between us," Santo spat. "When it was my loss on the line, those texts were evil, subversive, unholy. But now—now that *Ven Kochin* has something he wants, suddenly those texts are permitted, aren't they? Now that *Ven Kochin* has lost someone, suddenly he can find it in himself, with his half-formed gift, to heal? Isn't that just so convenient?"

Kochin's eyes narrowed with malice. He glanced at Santo's two guards, wondering if they were trying to make sense of Santo's nonsense. Still, Kochin didn't fear Santo's words anymore, not when he was a disgraced doctor and Kochin looked as Theuman as any other.

"You're growing old, Santo."

Santo met Kochin's livid stare with one of his own. "You're growing audacious. That was her doing, wasn't it? Now, you think you can do anything, maybe even bring back the dead. We know you never could, Kochin. I, for one, am glad she's gone. Potential wasted, but another bloodcarver rid from this—"

Kochin stood abruptly, the scrape of his chair against stained concrete loud enough to halt Santo's words. He had to leave soon; any longer, and nothing would be able to stop him from breaking through the glass and revealing himself as a bloodcarver.

He took a breath to calm his pounding temples and said, "If you aren't going to tell me anything, then I've wasted my time here."

He moved to exit the cubicle, but Santo leaped to his feet. "Where do you *think* I got them from?" Santo said, and Kochin sensed his desperation—anything to keep his physician's aide at his beck and call. But Kochin was no longer the boy who had been beaten and weathered by Santo's abuse. Now, he was bleeding from a greater wound than Santo's brambles.

Slowly, Kochin turned back toward the glass.

"You act as if I've been withholding information to torture you. Despite all you've done to me, I don't hate you. When I first met you, I even thought you were so much like me."

"You were wrong."

"Was I?" Santo said in a tone Kochin didn't enjoy—not because it was cold or derisive. Simply because it was earnest. "So, if I tell you where I found those texts, you won't pursue them? And if I told you it was possible, you wouldn't give *anything* just for the chance?"

Something unpleasant tugged at Kochin's cheek. Santo must've read his answer plainly on his face, because he only barked out a laugh.

"I'll tell you, then. Where else would those texts have originated other than the Daltan base on Yarong itself? So, go on, Kochin. Try to find them for yourself. I'm excited to see where it lands you."

"What a change of heart," was all Kochin said before he headed for the exit. He'd almost hoped for an easier answer, even if it was a perverted one. But to learn that those texts came from an island under Daltan rule, governed by isolationist policy . . . that was almost worse than if those Daltan experiments had taken root somewhere in Theumas.

Santo laughed, and Kochin halted with one foot out the door. "It's not the kindness you believe it is. I've learned this world is not kind to those who try taking more than their due—and you should know best, shouldn't you? Asking for more than you could ever give?"

Enough of this. Kochin turned his cheek. "This is the last you'll see of me, Santo. Enjoy solitary confinement."

As he left, Santo rose into a fury. He slammed his fists against the glass, screamed bloodcarver accusations—anything to keep Kochin for one moment longer. Kochin didn't dignify him, closing the door before Santo could try any other cheap bids for his attention. The officer escorted Kochin back the way they came.

"Is he still talking about bloodcarvers, that Santo?" the officer asked, and Kochin made a noise of acknowledgment. "He's been prattling about them to anyone who will listen."

"It seems he's truly lost his mind," Kochin said.

With a murmur of agreement, the officer deposited Kochin back into the waiting room, where he collected his items from the lockers. Though Kochin had never thought himself one for vengeance, there was sweetness to this, seeing Santo so powerless without his reputation that he could throw around such loaded accusations and not be believed. As Kochin left the penitentiary, a weight lifted from his shoulders—this was the last he'd ever see Santo, and it was he who walked away with his reputation intact.

The disgraced doctor had been useful for one thing: The answers Kochin sought were on Yarong, in the naval base where Daltanny had performed their twisted research. As ironic as it was, because of how Daltanny burned and cut through so many heartsooths, perhaps the greatest documentations on the limits of the gift remained there, behind concrete walls on an island locked by a warmongering country. The only question was how Kochin would get there.

But Santo had been wrong about something, too. They were nothing alike. Santo had let his quest consume him beyond reason. Even when his son was nothing more than dead skin pulled over bones, even when there was no more chance, he'd still persisted. *That's* why the world had punished him.

But that's where Kochin differed. He had bloodcarving, where Santo had only those texts. He had time, where Santo had only a corpse. And Kochin would succeed where Santo had failed.

There was nothing that could stop him.

In the morning, Kochin took himself down the street to the public telephone booths. With his bag of coins and his purposeful strut, he must've looked like a recent graduate on a desperate job hunt. It was around this time of spring, when the university terms were coming to an end, that the workforce saw new blood.

His task was nothing so simple.

With a half-chem coin, he paid for his first call: Mr. Aom, whose industry manufactured underwater seafaring. He considered simply purchasing a vessel himself, but such a voyage would require a crew, and who else would sail to Yarong with him? Who else would have reason?

The line hummed to life and a moment later, a noise clicked

on the other side. "Aom Rang Yatsuu. Who's this?" It was a gruff response, and Kochin wondered if he'd called Mr. Aom's personal line at an inopportune time. For a moment, a bout of social anxiety returned to him, an artifact from the life he'd lived before Theumas. Even his short stint in Chengton had been enough to draw it back.

He cleared his throat. "It's Ven Kochin," he said, his voice adopting a charismatic silkiness. "Poor time to call?"

"Kochin!" In a moment, all hostility left Mr. Aom's voice. "Not at all. I just hadn't expected you. Last I heard, you'd left the city."

"You can take the boy out of Central, but you can't take Central out of the boy," Kochin responded smoothly. "The country couldn't keep me."

Mr. Aom returned a heavy bout of laughter. "I could've told you that and saved you the trip." A silence precipitated and Kochin knew what Mr. Aom was thinking, what he was too afraid to ask.

Kochin offered it freely. "As you know, my previous employer, Dr. Santo, is no longer on good terms with the law. So, I'm looking for new horizons."

"Ah, Santo Ki Shon. A tragedy of man and a travesty of medicine," said Mr. Aom. Kochin anticipated his next question: "I've seen the news, but I suppose you would know best—was it all true?"

"Which part? That he'd been compelled to murder, or that he'd been interested in Daltan vivisections?" At the moment, Santo's entire reputation was scandal, not only his crime but also his interests. Once the reporters had gotten wind of that, his name had been dragged through the mud.

"Both, I suppose."

"Unfortunately, it's every bit as true as the reporters have said. It's one of those things that you look back on in hindsight and wonder how you missed the warning signs," Kochin lied, building up intrigue in the anticipation of a trade: his gossip for passage to Yarong.

"Like what?"

"He always did have a penchant for hiring Yarongese."

"I always thought Santo was so brave for that. Deny their vacation and they might carve you for it, right?" He said it as a joke between two Theumans, with the belief that bloodcarving didn't exist anymore, so it was nothing but a jibe. Kochin had heard variations of this joke throughout this society; it no longer came to surprise him. Now, it only reminded him of how little he truly belonged.

Kochin mirrored his close-lipped laugh humorlessly. "Exactly. I was actually calling about something related. Ever since I heard about Mr. Congmi and Dr. Santo, guilt has been eating me up. It's a lot to unpack, a man who I'd once admired turning out to be a felon." Kochin put on his best act of a tortured physician's aide. In a way, he didn't have to act much.

"It's not your fault, Kochin. You couldn't have known."

"It's why I've been trying to escape the city. I was wondering if you had any charter trips on your vessels. Somewhere out of the city, somewhere I can use my talents philanthropically." Kochin released a breath. "Somewhere like . . . Yarong."

A silence fell over the line until Mr. Aom clucked his tongue. "You'd want to go to Yarong? Is this to atone for Santo's wrongdoings?"

Kochin's eyes flashed to the street; he'd thought he'd seen Nhika turning the corner, but it was just a different girl in the crowd. "Something like that."

"Kochin, I commend your selflessness—really, we should all be giving more to the Yarongese during this time. And I've got cruises to Simbal, or the Daijonas, or Chilmea. But you know I can't get you into Yarong. Not with the travel restrictions."

Kochin wasn't sure what answer he'd been expecting, but he didn't let his disappointment show. "That's completely understandable, Mr. Aom."

"If you're intent on taking your mind off Santo, perhaps a change of employment? My office doesn't have any openings, but I could refer you somewhere, if you'd like it."

The conversation had turned to pity; travel to Yarong through Mr. Aom was a futile endeavor. "I greatly appreciate the offer, but I'll have to decline. I'm sorry to take your time, but I hope you're in good spirits and this terrible news about Dr. Santo hasn't put you off."

"Nothing of the sort! It's just a reminder that even the best of us aren't above folly."

Folly. A choice word for murder and malpractice.

"Well put, Mr. Aom," Kochin said. Then, as much as he fought it, the instinct to maintain good relations compelled him to say, "When next I'm looking for employment, I'll be sure to give you another call. I'll let you return to work now—any longer and I'd feel inclined to compensate you for your valuable time."

Mr. Aom rounded out a laugh. "All right. Talk to you soon, Kochin."

The line clicked.

With a huff of defeat, Kochin crossed Mr. Aom's name out in his notebook, then slotted another half-chem coin into the telephone.

It went this way for the next couple hours, with Kochin placing calls that only ended with etched-out names. Ms. Giom, who manufactured powered aircrafts a few years back, hadn't developed a solo-craft that could survive the trip across the water and back. Mr. Ngut, whose hydrogen-powered dirigibles rivaled the Congmis', couldn't manage a crew that dared fly to Yarong. Even Dr. Peva, known philanthropist, who had aided many conflict zones before, refused to set foot in Yarong for fear of drawing Daltan's attention. He called the city's wealthiest, its engineers and researchers and savants, who'd put metal in the sky and seas, whose medicine rivaled the heartsoothing of yore, whose inventions had elevated Theumas from a forgettable city-state to a technological empire.

And yet, none of them would take him to Yarong. None of them had reason to.

With his purse of chem dwindling alongside his hope, Kochin hung the receiver back onto its cradle, taking a moment to lean against the glass of the telephone booth. What must people have thought of him, slumped over this telephone for hours on end?

He thumbed open the notebook, the names dwindling. Kochin had run out of viable connections half a dozen calls ago. Now, these were just numbers of those he knew, those who would truly have no reason to go to Yarong.

As his finger grazed the final name, he sighed and drew another half-chem coin from his purse.

Nem Boch Kenyi.

Or, as he was now known, Commissioner Nem. The election had been finalized weeks ago, when Kochin had no reason to follow politics, but the results had been easy to foresee—especially when Mr. Nem promised safety and defense against Daltanny, while Mr. Ngut was just a shadow of the late Mr. Congmi.

There was no reason for Kochin to call him, but he found his fingers dialing the number of their own volition. The line ran, and Kochin let out a breath to steel himself when audio clicked on the other side.

"You've reached the office of Commissioner Nem," said a young voice. "How can I help you?"

"This is Ven Kochin, Dr. Santo's former aide," Kochin said. "I was looking to speak with the commissioner, but I can call another time if he's busy." He almost hoped Commissioner Nem was, because he wasn't sure what he was calling for, anyway.

"Hold one moment," said the assistant, and the line fell silent.

When next someone spoke, it was Commissioner Nem. "Good morning, Kochin. I wasn't expecting you."

"I was just calling to offer my congratulations," Kochin said, easing himself into conversation. Before Nem became a commissioner, his industry lay in armaments: antiaircraft artillery, treaded combat machines, mortars. The kinds of inventions retired during periods of peace, and certainly not anything that could get him to Yarong.

"Thank you, Kochin. It has certainly been an adjustment. As I am preparing to move to a new office, hire new staff, I have some positions open—if you were interested. After all, your previous employer . . ."

"Yes, a shame, what happened to him," Kochin said curtly. Again, he was being offered positions, which he would've once leaped at as a university student. But he had just untied himself from Central; he wasn't yet prepared to bind himself again. "Unfortunately, I've decided to take a break from employment, do some self-reflecting."

"I wish I'd done the same at your age," Commissioner Nem said with a huff. "Was there any other reason for your call?"

Kochin hesitated. With each call, Yarong felt more and more impenetrable—this island that his mother and so many like her had tried to escape, and all he wanted was to return. But, if not even a commissioner could get him there, then perhaps it was a lost cause. "No," he said at last. "Just wanted to congratulate you and wish you a prosperous commission. Bye now, Commissioner, and I won't forget your offer."

Kochin was about to hang up when Commissioner Nem's voice stalled the phone at his ear. "Kochin, one more thing, before you go."

"Yes?"

"If you have family out of the city, I suggest you spend time with them while you can."

"While I can?"

Commissioner Nem cleared his throat. "Don't make a habit of sharing what I'm about to tell you—I don't want to cause undue hysteria—but . . . war is coming. Simbal is on its last legs. If it falls, Theumas will become Daltanny's next target; I guarantee it. A boy like you is at the ripe age for a draft. If there's nothing keeping you in Central Theumas anymore, I would suggest you spend the next couple months with those you love."

For a second, Kochin didn't respond, the receiver limp against his ear. At last, he found the words to say, "I'll keep that in mind, Commissioner Nem. Thank you."

"Farewell then, Kochin."

"You too, Commissioner."

The line went silent on the other side.

War. Kochin spent a moment in the ensuing silence, hanging his head with the receiver still in his palm. War was the topic on every mind, the storm front on the horizon. Some called it a tragedy, others an inevitability.

Kochin, however . . . he wondered if he could call it an opportunity. A question pricked at him—*What if?* What if Theumas declared war against Daltanny? What if they rolled up onto Yarong beaches with submarines turned warships and dirigibles turned bombers?

What if Kochin reached Yarong on the tides of war?

"Don't be stupid," Nhika said, appearing on the other side of the glass, her back to the booth. "You heard the commissioner. If war breaks out, you're at the ripe age to be conscripted."

"What are they going to do, send me to Yarong? Oh, the horror."

"That's only if Yarong is their first target. I can think of a hundred other places they might deploy you." She tilted her head. "Besides, wasn't it a bullet that nearly killed you the last time?"

She was right. He hung up the receiver, squeezing the bone ring around his finger. War was not the opportunity he was looking for—too many unknowns. He'd have to get deployed to Yarong rather than the Theuman-Daltan border. They'd have to win the naval base. He'd have to find the research. And, after all that, he'd have to find a way to escape deployment and return to Chengton.

Yet, the idea wouldn't leave him: What if, what if . . .

What if.

⇒⇒ EIGHT ⇐⇐
NOW

NHIKA'S TRAIN WAS COMING UP ON CENTRAL.

The Monkey Borough came first, the westernmost reach of the metropolis. This city never belonged to her, yet she couldn't help but feel relief at its familiarity all the same.

That was, until she noticed the emptiness.

The Monkey Borough was a hub of commerce, and she should've seen autocarriages parked along the streets—commuters with their bikes and umbrellas and scarves. But, when their train tracks passed through the heart of the borough, she found empty restaurants with their outdoor seating closed off—even though it was lunchtime. Where there should've been crowds, there were empty streets. Where parks should've been full, their fountains ran dry.

And when her train finally rolled up to the Grand Terminus, in the heart of the Sheep Borough, there was only a lone smoker to greet her on the platform.

Nhika stepped off the train. Though she preferred the trolleys over the train, she'd been in the Grand Terminus many times before, mostly to solicit things—okay, *always* to solicit things—but this wasn't the train station she recognized. Automatons that sold papers of collected trash were out of operation or absent, the few she saw ill maintained. Many of them were missing core components, their bronze shells or iron innards, almost like they'd been harvested. The station was also a happening tourist destination, but when she walked through its main concourse, where the floor had been tiled with a map of the city, the only passersby came from trying to catch their train. There was no line at the ticket booths and those vendors who sold street foods, sandwiches, or paper-wrapped bouquets had boarded up their stalls.

This city was unrecognizable, like she'd stepped into an alternate version of Theumas. It set her on edge, gave her a dozen new questions, but Nhika pressed on.

At least the trolleys still worked. She grabbed one toward the Theumas Medical Center. It was fitting: the last place she remembered being in Central, and now the first place she'd return to.

As they drove, familiar streets returned to her in unfamiliar ways. When they passed the Sheep Borough's famous market hall, she found the gates closed and the windows boarded. People commuted through with purpose, not simply to loiter and haggle down market prices. All that construction that Theumas was famous for—a city that never stopped growing taller, and bigger, and faster—had halted, too. Color itself seemed to have drained from the streets, gone without outdoor vegetable displays or shining automatons or the flashy parasols of pedestrians.

Nhika realized she *did* recognize this atmosphere: mourning. It was the same gloom that hung over the Congmi manor during Mr. Congmi's funeral, the emptiness of that house and the silence of its inhabitants.

She only wondered what could make an entire city mourn.

The trolley stopped in front of the Theumas Medical Center and her speculations dashed as she hopped off.

How strange it was, revisiting a building that had tried to kill her. The architects had likely designed it to look academic and regal, judging by the many carved details in the facade and the twin statues over the entrance, one woman holding an open book and the other holding a lion-headed staff. To Nhika, it looked like a very large and expensive mausoleum. So many had died within these walls. She'd almost been one of them. With a breath to steady herself, she pushed her way inside.

This was one place in Theumas that felt the same as before. Just as busy, with nurses carting patients around in wheelchairs and families loitering anxiously for news. A constant voice coming from the electronic loudspeakers called for physicians or lost patients to return to their wards—if anything, the medical center seemed *busier* than she'd ever seen it before.

Mimi said Trin had been in surgery, so Nhika would start with that—the post-surgical ward. Along the way, she passed by Santo's old office—and despite everything that place had done to her, she had the urge to visit, as if she could poke her head in and find Kochin behind the desk, Trin in the waiting room chair. Antagonistic physician's aide, stoic billionaire's minder—and not just two bloodstains in an office hallway.

Almost like an automaton with a set command roll, she lumbered through these hallways, preprogrammed feet taking her forward. She followed signs toward post-surgery. The walls grew familiar, and it became clear where those signs led—Santo's old research ward. Within awaited the casketlike contraption that had trapped her, the operating room that had nearly killed her and Kochin. Each step closer made her skin burn hotter and redder, like every nerve was tearing itself apart trying to keep away.

By the time she reached those telltale double doors, her body was split in half. Nhika had always listened to her body, and right now it wanted to be anywhere but here. But her mind kept her feet planted solid—told her jittery legs that this ward hadn't killed her before and it wouldn't kill her now. The signage above the door no longer called it the Santo Research Initiative. Rather, it had been repurposed.

She was just reaching to push open the door when someone else stepped out. At first, she hadn't recognized him when he dressed so plainly, and when his hair wasn't gelled back, but they both stopped and stared at each other.

"*Nhika?*" Andao asked.

"What are you doing here?" they said in unison.

He balked, long enough for her to add, "Mimi told me Trin was in the hospital. You know what I am, right? You know I would heal him if you asked."

"I know. *We* know. But the magic comes at a cost, doesn't it? And you can't bring someone back from near-death without sacrifice, can you?"

"Near-death?" Nhika's throat closed. "Is Trin near death?"

Andao shook his head. "He's fine. The surgeons did their job. We should head home."

"But I just got here."

"Please, I don't have the energy to argue this right now."

"But, Andao—"

A blare came from outside the window before he could respond. She thought it was an autocarriage horn at first, but it didn't cease—only crescendoed. It continued wailing, growing louder and rolling in pitch. It took her a moment to recognize it as an alarm, signaling some emergency she didn't recognize; Theumas was hit by the occasional tsunami or earthquake, but she was far too inland to hear tsunami sirens, and earthquakes announced themselves.

Andao reacted before she did. He grabbed the arm of a passing nurse, pulled her close. Nhika was just barely able to make out the words he whispered into her ear: "The patient in bay six—don't let any harm come to him. Understand me?"

Then he slipped a wad of chem into the nurse's palm and grabbed Nhika by the elbow. Despite her protests, he guided her down the hall, and it clicked what Andao had done. He'd *bribed* a nurse.

Around them, doctors mobilized and nurses disappeared into their wards. Voices came alive over the loudspeakers, instructing workers to get to their stations and visitors to seek shelter.

"Wait a min—"

"Nhika, come with me," Andao said, and all her questions and stubbornness dissolved under his stern voice. She staggered forward, his arm looped in hers.

"Where?" she asked. He pulled her along until they reached a pulsing line of people, all headed toward the lowest levels of the hospital.

"Safety," Andao responded tersely. "Hospital basement."

Nhika had never seen him so tense, not even underneath Nem's heat. "Wh-what about Trin?"

A muscle flickered in Andao's cheek, and his eyes darkened. "He'll be fine," he said, like he was convincing himself.

Something had changed about him. No, *everything* had changed about him—and this city, and her body, and the Congmi household. Nhika almost didn't recognize Andao for how steely his eyes appeared, and for how he'd . . . he'd bribed the nurse. Andao, straight and narrow, using his money as power when Nhika had always thought he'd been the exception rather than the rule.

Andao pulled her deeper into the bowels of the hospital. They descended stairs and passed through double doors, until Nhika was sure this was a part of the medical center she wasn't meant to see—not the mortuary cabinets, nor the exposed plumbing system, nor that graveyard of broken gurneys. Red lights painted their way to the sound of the swooping alarm. No matter how far they went underground, she couldn't block out the noise, and Nhika felt the sudden need to curl into a ball on the floor. The only thing keeping her moving while the crowds eddied around her was Andao's firm grip on her arm.

"What are the sirens for, Andao?" she asked, giving resistance—just to slow down a moment, understand what was going on around them. Andao continued at an uncaring pace.

"It's just a drill," he said. "A false alarm."

"But what is it *for*?" she pressed. He didn't answer, both of them jostled right and left by the rushing crowd. At some point, his hand slipped from her biceps to her wrist, and his grip turned painful. "Andao, please—*Andao*, you're hurting me."

Only then did he stop and look at her. Remorse broke through his expression, that cold spell lifting and clarity returning to his eyes. Still hounded by the alarms, the people around them, they stared at each other until he said, "It's a drill for the air raids."

"Air raids?" She'd heard of those, of course—they happened in Simbal, their northern neighbor. But never in Theumas, because to get raided, one needed . . . "Andao, are we going to war?"

The corner of his lip turned down. His eyes explored her with pity. "Nhika, we . . ." A nervous swallow, but he held her gaze. "We're already at war."

War.

Nhika had never experienced war before. Some might argue she was a child of it, but that didn't mean she'd lived it. Not the way her grandmother had, bidding goodbye to her village, who'd collected enough money to fund her trip to Theumas, knowing she would never see any of them again. Not the way her parents had, growing up in Theumas during a time where every Yarongese was a liver eater.

Theumas, for as long as she'd lived, had never experienced war, either. It terrified her, that the leaders she'd trust to engineer a perfectly efficient city might not know how to handle the irrationality of the human condition.

They were sitting in long lines in the subterranean tunnels beneath the hospital now. These tunnels were once meant to cart away the newly dead out of the public view, and now they served to protect the hardly living from Daltan air raids. There were too many people down here; her lungs could taste the change in the air, waning oxygen. She was swimming with water up to her nose, waiting for someone to fish her out.

Something ruffled beside her. With a sigh, Andao doffed his jacket and draped it over her shoulders. "It's all right," he said. "It's just a precaution—no fighter has reached the city before. Usually, our antiaircraft takes care of them over the Gaikhen Mountains."

She hugged her legs to her chest and buried her chin in her knees. "Why didn't you tell me when I awoke?"

Andao swallowed. "We . . . we were going to. We wanted to ease you into it. I suppose that's not much of an excuse, is it?"

"If I'd known, I wouldn't have run from the villa. Mimi must be fuming."

Andao laughed weakly. "She'll recover." He leaned back, a sigh passing through his lips. "In truth, this war crept up on us almost as quickly as it did you. Our father died, we discovered our closest family friend was responsible, and you . . . you . . ." He caught her eye, faltered, swallowed his words. "It felt like we were bleeding away the ones we loved. Then war broke out, and Trin was conscripted. And I don't think I knew true fear before then. It's why I . . ."

The rest of his sentence was lost to a long exhale. Instinctually, she touched her sternum before remembering she'd given away her bone ring. His words were familiar ones, but she'd already bled away everyone she'd loved a long time ago.

"It's why you did what you did with the nurse," she said, more a statement than a question.

He looked sheepish. "To tell the truth, Nhika, I've done a great many things my father wouldn't be proud of. It's easy to justify it with war, for the safety of the people, the city—but no, it's selfish. I'm selfish. Told myself I was righteous for turning down Commissioner Nem's chem, but as soon as the man I loved was drafted, I backtracked on all my staunch values and used the entirety of my father's empire to protect him. It's as the commissioner said—I'm a hypocrite."

"If I had anyone left to love, I'd do the same."

He gave her a wan look. "I know you would. It's why we didn't want to tell you about the war, about Trin. You'd just come here, try to heal him. Nhika, I swear—if I'd known what it cost for you to heal, I never would've . . . I shouldn't have let you . . ." He shook his head, like the words had dried up on his tongue.

Nhika shrugged. "They're just calories. That's all. But I know my limits."

His gaze bored into her again—somewhat sad, somewhat conflicted. His lips parted like he wanted to tell her something, but nothing came.

"What is it?" she asked.

His gaze returned to the floor. "It's not *just* calories, is it?"

"What do you mean?"

"That night, in this very building, you . . . You don't remember what you did?"

"I bested Santo and I healed Kochin," she said.

He shook his head adamantly. "No, it was more than that."

"What, Andao?" This was the truth, she realized—the answer behind all the little lies that clung like dust mites in the unreachable parts of the Congmi villa. "Tell me."

"The truth will make you question everything. Like it's made us question everything," he said. "If I could unlearn it, I would. So, I'm giving you the chance to just . . . accept that you're safe, and okay."

"You're scaring me."

"I'm sorry." His brows knit like this pained him. "Do you still want to hear it?"

It was her final chance to back out and accept this life the Congmis had crafted for her—a life she'd *always* wanted. A life like Trin's, adopted by Theumas's wealthiest family, feeling no consequences of the war her city-state had entered. But that meant her mask would never come off, and Kochin had warned her so often about masks.

"I want to know," Nhika decided. She had a terrible feeling she knew what it was about—that little inconsistency that had been eating at her since she'd awoken. The laws of heartsoothing, the balance of calories that didn't quite add up. They couldn't *both* walk off that table. Something had happened after she'd gone under.

Andao cast a glance around, as though wary someone might be listening in. When he found no one, he said, "I wasn't at the medical center that night when it happened. But I was there when they returned. And it was with . . . with your corpse."

"But I'm not dead," Nhika said. "I didn't die."

Andao stared at her, eyes growing remorseful. It struck her, as surely as Santo's bullet—those eyes had seen her corpse. They might've even seen her funeral. There it was, the answer to the inconsistency: She and Kochin both couldn't walk off that table, and they hadn't. She'd died. She'd *died*, just as she planned, having passed her bone ring on to the next heartsooth.

Nhika sank against the cold wall of the tunnel. Each breath came out jagged—like she might forget how to breathe if her lungs realized they ran on stolen air, or her heart might give out if it remembered the last time it'd stopped. Her shoulder burned where Santo had shot her.

So, this was the truth, that *dreadful* truth the Congmis tried to save her from. It uprooted her thoughts like buildings, gouged out everything she knew. The war seemed trifling now—because what was death anymore? Nothing but a blink. If there was an afterlife, it had forsaken her, and she'd awoken months later without a hint of rot, and she was still *Nhika*, and . . . and . . .

And the only way she could have returned was through heartsoothing. But heartsoothing had a single rule, and it was the equivalence of calories. So, what did it mean that she'd been brought back from complete death? Who . . . who had given her life?

That was an answer Nhika didn't want to know.

"I understand it's a lot," Andao said, placing a fortifying hand on her shoulder. "I wish . . . I wish there were a more palatable explanation for all this."

So did she. The thought of herself as a corpse made her sick.

Since her heartsoothing had manifested, there had never been a moment where her body hadn't completely belonged to her. In death, it had belonged to everyone *but* her.

"I still have so many questions," Nhika managed.

"Like how you're back?"

She nodded.

"Quite honestly, we don't know. After the night at the medical center, we mourned you. It was the first debt our family could never repay. I . . . I didn't know someone like you could just *die*," Andao said. "But the world moved on. Commissioner Nem won his election and delivered every promise he made during his campaign. War began. Trin was drafted, deployed to Yarong. And, well . . . Next thing we know, we get a call telling us he's back on this side of the water with an injured leg and a sleeping Yarongese girl. That was only days ago."

"Kochin. He must've . . . It must've been him."

"Maybe so. We handed you off to him after the ceremonial burial. He said there were Yarongese customs you'd want. But none of us know for sure. The only one who knows is . . ."

"Trin," Nhika finished. And he was in the hospital, still recovering from surgery. "What do we do now, Andao?"

"What I have been doing," Andao said, his tone forlorn. "We wait. As painful as it is, we wait."

NINE
NOW

IT SEEMED LIKE A LIFETIME BEFORE THE SIRENS finally stopped. As Andao said, it was a false alarm, but everyone crawled out of those tunnels like the risen dead seeing sun for the first time. Andao's warpath was set back toward Trin's side, and Nhika followed him.

It was so strange, seeing how everyone resumed their habits as if it were nothing more than a storm warning. As if they weren't at *war*. But Nhika supposed a place like the medical center couldn't stop, couldn't slow. It could kill heartsooths, condemn doctors, and still chug on as though nothing had changed.

Soon, she was standing before those fateful doors again. Earlier, she'd thought these doors had merely injured her. Now, they were the ones that killed her, and she was staring at the site of her own death.

Andao gave her a sympathetic look. "I'm sorry, Nhika. I hate that he's here, too—but once the war started, the hospital needed more space, and Dr. Santo's research ward had just been emptied. If you need time, we—"

"No. Let's go." She could no longer avoid her own tombstone in this hospital.

When Andao pushed open the doors, Nhika found a completely repurposed hospital ward. It was almost a relief; this hardly looked like the ward that had killed her. Wartime had spat out a veneer over the entire place: the laden stretchers lining the walls, the curtained bays that nurses disappeared into, the surgical tools carted off for sterilization. This hospital ward repurposed, Kochin missing, Trin hospitalized as if she weren't a heartsooth . . . Nhika didn't feel like she'd died. She felt like she'd stepped into a different Theumas altogether, like the events of the past few months had simply been rearranged to write her out of the story. There was no part of this city she recognized anymore, not even the part that had killed her.

At last, they stopped before a postoperative suite, something more than the curtained bays other patients received. Andao stopped before it, straightening his coat like Trin might be awake to notice—or perhaps just to buy time before he had to open the door. But, with a breath, he steeled himself and turned the handle.

Inside, Trin lay soundlessly on the bed, a blanket pulled up to his chest, and his leg, dressed in bandages, elevated by a pulley system from the ceiling. Bandages wrapped his forehead, others his biceps, and a wet towel had been draped over his eyes.

Andao exhaled a long, slow breath, and Nhika couldn't tell if it was disappointment or relief. "He just came out of surgery the other day. Doctors say he'll be here until his leg fully heals."

"I can heal him, if you'd like."

"But you'll—"

"It's fine," she said. "It won't hurt me. I know my limits." And she did. When she'd given her life for Kochin, she'd known exactly what she was giving.

Nhika pulled a chair over to the bedside. Up close, she counted limbs—all four of them, thank the Mother—and snaked her hand under the blanket until she found flushed, sweat-mottled skin.

"Watch the door, would you?" she asked Andao before pouring her influence into Trin's skin.

Nhika felt the anesthetics and pain medications first, like a haze that made her chest bubble with the same warmth as alcohol. Then she felt the pull of stitches, itchy and rough. The wound hit through a moment later in his leg—something tight, red, throbbing. There were a dozen other injuries, bruised ribs and inflamed abrasions and cracked nails, but the bulk of it—the reason he'd come to this hospital—had been his leg. A surgeon had gotten to it first, a long incision along the side of the leg, one that cut through skin and fascia but spared muscle. It was strange, wading through something that was surgically healed, because her influence told her it was an injury where her mind assured her it wasn't. Most worrisome of all, they hadn't stitched up the leg fully, leaving the wound exposed with nothing but a wet dressing around it.

Her first instinct was to close it up, finish their work for them. A moment of further exploration revealed why they had left the wound open: The nerves and vessels of the leg were pinched and choked, and the surgeons had cut open the leg to allow them to breathe. A little crude, and not what she would've done, but Nhika supposed that was all they *could* do.

She would help out the doctors. Moving stores up from her liver, she quelled inflamed nerves and pulled excess fluid back toward Trin's heart. As she did, she realized she hadn't been the first one here. There was the metallic aftertaste of a surgeon's scalpel, the muggy haze of a drug cocktail, but beneath it she felt a strange aura in the anatomy—like an afterimage, only there if she wasn't paying attention to it. When she walked her influence down the vessels of his leg, it almost felt like there was someone just behind her.

Nhika didn't heal the wound to completion, not wanting the surgeons to find a miracle in their hospital bay the next morning. But she helped the injury along, knowing Trin could keep the leg, and the Congmi family could be full again.

When she pulled her hand away, she found Andao staring intently at her.

"How is he?" he asked, his voice strained.

"He'll be fine," Nhika said. "The surgeons will just have to close him up."

Andao's shoulders loosened. "Thank you, Nhika. I'll be sure to reimburse you once we get back to the—"

"No payment," Nhika said, dismissing him with a wave. "I just want him to get better."

Someone rapped at the door. Nhika snapped her hand back, fixing the blankets, but when the door opened, it was only Mimi.

And she looked like she wanted to yell at *someone*, but she just hadn't decided who yet. Then her eyes locked with Nhika, and she said, "Heaven and *earth*, Nhika. Have you any idea how worried I was? You can't just run away without leaving a note. I thought you were . . . that we let you . . ."

Andao touched her arm, mollifying her. "It's all right, Mimi. She's okay. Everyone's okay."

That eased something in Mimi, but the childish irritability was still plain in her tight expression. It only lessened when she noticed Trin on the bed. "Did you . . . ?"

"I did my best."

"I'm sorry. We should've told you about him. In truth, Nhika, there's a lot more we—"

"It's all right. I know." Nhika ran a tongue across her teeth. "Andao told me everything. Everything other than what happened on the other side of the water."

Mimi's eyes fell to Trin. She inched forward until her arm rested on his. "We don't know, either. See, we never buried your body. Mr. Ven requested it. So, last we knew, you were with him. Until you weren't. You and Trin only showed up a few days ago, and we've been trying to put the pieces together, too."

Nhika quieted. It sickened her, just a little, knowing her corpse had been places she didn't recall—that it might've even been to Yarong. It had traded hands, traveled countries, knew all the answers Nhika sought, yet it hadn't been *her*. For her, death had lapsed like a dream, and she'd awoken into a nightmare.

And that pressing question still remained: Where was Kochin? He was of drafting age; it wasn't so outrageous to assume he'd been drafted. But in war, there were a great many things that could kill a heartsooth. Nhika would know, wouldn't she?

"You want to know where Mr. Ven is," Mimi guessed, reading her plainly.

Nhika nodded wordlessly.

"I want to believe he left you in our care," she responded. "So, that's what we've been doing. Caring for you."

How strange; she had always been the one caring for this family. She'd healed their loved ones and found their murderers. So, she didn't quite know what it meant to be cared for by them. It sounded a lot like trust—just as she'd once asked them to trust her. Now, they asked the same.

"Thank you," she said, long overdue. "I'll let you have your time with Trin now."

Nhika stepped outside, giving them their space. Through the crack in the curtain, she watched Andao step up to the bedside, take Trin's hand in his own, and lace their fingers. He brought the hand to his lips, kept it there—like a prayer. Like a promise. It was a familiar scene. Nhika knew well how it felt to be at someone's bedside, ready to give anything just to heal them.

What terrible irony, that she had the gift to cure all wounds and they had the money to buy any favor, yet they could still both know loss. Nhika stepped into the hallway. A nurse passed, and she had the wherewithal to call her.

"Excuse me," she said, stopping the nurse midstride. "This patient, Dep Trin . . . The surgeon meant to leave the incision site open, right?"

It took the nurse a moment to catch up. "Ah, yes, it's standard with a fasciotomy."

"Fasciotomy?"

"It's for compartment syndrome—swelling or bleeding in the leg without a break in the skin, like when a bone breaks and nicks the artery."

"But his bone wasn't broken—I mean, as far as I could tell."

The nurse tipped her head back. "Yes, I remember—the surgeon mentioned it was strange, a blood vessel breaking with no sign of trauma at all to the leg. As though it just burst of its own volition from the inside out. I swear, we get something new every day with this war." The nurse shrugged and continued down the hall as though the thought was completely innocuous.

And maybe to a Theuman nurse, it was. But when Nhika had immersed herself in Trin's bone, there had been the shadow of another in every bundle of muscle, behind every layer of tissue. She knew Kochin had met Trin on the island; it was the only way she'd come into Trin's possession. And she knew Kochin's fingers had traced the vessels of Trin's leg long before hers had.

Now, Nhika asked a dreadful question: Were Kochin's fingers the ones to rip them open?

⇶ TEN ⇷
FIVE MONTHS AGO

KOCHIN AWOKE TO A CLAMOR IN THE STREETS. He blinked, rubbed sleep out of his eyes, and dragged himself out of bed. Unemployment had been destroying his habits—and his savings. Sweeping hair out of his eyes, he crossed to the shophouse window and cracked the shutters. Below, a sluggish crowd had gathered, though Kochin couldn't tell what for—until he saw the papers in their hands. Something lurched in his throat and he remembered Commissioner Nem's words: *War is coming*.

Throwing on a dress shirt and slacks, he stumbled out of the shophouse and found himself in the thick of the crowd. He pushed through, trying to find a newspaper automaton and catching snippets of conversation along the way:

"This'll be war, I tell you."
"Theuman lives for the Yarongese? Disgraceful."
"Finally, the Commission will make a real decision."
"You voted him in. If this means war, that's on you."

War. Commissioner Nem had mentioned it. All of Theumas had been teasing it for months and months and months—and maybe that's why it felt so impossible now, despite Commissioner Nem's election.

Kochin cleared the crowd and reached the newspaper automaton, slotted a chem coin, and wrestled an issue from its arms. There, on the front page, was the headline.

SIMBAL CAPITULATES TO DALTAN RULE—WAR COMES TO THEUMAS

It was cloudless the day of the Commission's address, set on the capitol steps. This year's summer was a sadist, and the crowd outside the capitol was a sea of parasols and hats. Kochin was in the far back of the square, such that the five commissioners were just dots at the top of the stairs. Commissioner Nem's figure was the easiest to discern—broad shoulders, wide stance, a man who held presence among the thin and tall frames of the others.

It was Commissioner Nem who finally stepped up to the podium to speak—a good choice, Kochin figured. He was recently elected, still popular, Theumas's latest figurehead of change. Loudspeakers wired throughout the square carried his voice even to where Kochin stood.

"Good morning, my fellow Theumans," he began. "I understand what most of you have come to learn today, so I won't tax your patience any further. Our closest neighbor, Simbal, has fallen. Daltan's land grab has surrounded Theumas on all sides. Last week, on the sixth day of the Sixth Month, we commissioners five and our Parliament came to the decision to declare war against the growing crisis of Daltanny."

Shock rippled through the onlookers, but this was inevitable, wasn't it? Kochin had already known their decision from a phone call with Commissioner Nem. Still, it staggered him all the same. Daltanny had all but declared war on Theumas by claiming the last of its neighbors, but Commissioner Nem's statement made it real. It created an official enemy out of Daltanny. It meant deployment to foreign lands, the first time the Theuman military had seen battle in decades.

After the square quieted, Commissioner Nem continued. "I understand that war may feel like a foreign and regressive arena. For so long, we've been comfortable to stay within our twelve boroughs. It is not our intent to go to war for war's sake. Rather, it is our intent to fight against a corrupting power who has, since its inception, gone uncontested. And it's not about what we have to gain by fighting; rather, it is about what we have to *lose* if we don't act now. The tragic fates of Yarong and Simbal serve as cautionary tales against the folly of hesitation."

They were grand words, but Kochin wondered if personal interest hid behind them. It was no secret where the commissioner had earned his wealth.

Commissioner Nem went on: "Daltanny defies all the values we hold dear. Where we build, they destroy. Where we cultivate, they conquer. Where we innovate, they injure. This is a tyrant that has stifled the freedoms of many nations before. This is an empire that claims to be our neighbor, yet has prepared weapons against us on the island of Yarong. And they are a deepening darkness that will continue to spread without the presence of light. They intend to wave the Daltan flag over the entire landmass. Let's not make it easy for them.

"It is only because we, as Theumans, have so much to be proud of that we have so much to lose. We take pride in our commitment to innovation. We take pride in all that we've fostered and advanced. As our next chapter, let us take pride in our contribution toward the greater fight for peace and freedom."

Those final words speared Kochin through the chest—their familiarity, spoken to him by a girl on her deathbed. *Peace, freedom, and . . .*

And the word she hadn't managed to get out. Kochin exhaled a shaky breath, turning away from the rest of the address. He'd gleaned all he'd wanted to know, anyway—had found the answer to the only question that mattered to him.

Theumas was at war, and Yarong was finally within reach.

"Wouldn't that be funny? I give you my life in some grand gesture—only for you to squander it on a battlefield a few months later?"

Nhika was haunting him again, trailing behind him as he buttoned up his vest and donned his suit jacket.

"That won't happen," Kochin murmured. Yet, it was exactly the kind of sadistic ploy the Mother would conjure, punishment for him taking the spot of a real heartsooth. But what other choice did he have?

"Emaciated scholar like you?" Nhika said. "You're not exactly a soldier. I give you three weeks, max."

"You're so very inspiring."

"I could go on."

"It won't be necessary."

"What I'm trying to say is that it's a stupid decision, in case that wasn't clear."

"It certainly wasn't subtext." Nhika was referring to his decision to enlist. For the past couple weeks, he'd waited for the draft—but his selection window had come and gone, and he never received the call to service in the mail. In any other situation, he would've been relieved to escape the draft, but this war . . . it was a charter to Yarong. It would be *so* easy to enlist, just a short walk down to the registration offices, and he'd claim a ticket.

"Oh, one other thing," Nhika continued. "No guarantee you'd even be sent to Yarong."

"Fifty-fifty chance," Kochin said. On the commissioner's orders, there were only two stations where he might be deployed: the Theuman-Daltan border in the Gaikhen Mountains, or Yarong. "I've gambled on worse odds."

She raised a leery brow. "Then you're a terrible gambler."

Kochin dismissed her with a wave—because that wasn't the real Nhika. That was some facsimile he'd conjured, his doubt given voice. The *real* Nhika might've even egged him on; wasn't that how she'd convinced him to betray Santo? He'd hauled himself to safety by her noose.

Before he could leave, she beat him to the door, one arm across the exit as though that could stop him. "Kochin, this is bigger than your quest. This is *war*."

"And I've got my gift."

"Heartsoothing can't heal everything. I'll remind you how Yarong fell to Daltanny in the first place."

She was right. He snaked a hand up his chest—right shoulder, where Santo had shot him. Admittedly, most things on the battlefield could kill a heartsooth: land mines, mortars, bullets. Out there, under gunfire, he'd die just as quickly as any other Theuman, especially without a bird in his palm.

"Well then," he said, his smile grim, "I suppose I'll see you one way or the other."

When he stepped through the door, Nhika was gone—and with her, the last trailing doubt in his mind.

Kochin took himself to the nearest registration office in the Pig Borough. On his way, he witnessed a Theumas he'd never seen before—one shaped by fear, anger, confusion. A few shophouses down, a storekeeper swept the broken glass of a shattered window into a bin, muttering something about looters and the end of times. Not five steps more and there was a storefront vandalized by whitewash paint, bold letters that said DEATH TO DALTANNY. Just below it, in red: NOT MY WAR.

The former sentiment must've been the prevalent one in Theumas—otherwise, Commissioner Nem never would've been voted in. Or, perhaps, no one had expected him to act so quickly, or everyone saw him as the milder of two poisons. Still, Kochin had never lived in a Theumas so at odds with itself.

His mother had told him about a Theumas like that, though— the one she'd immigrated to. She knew war better than most

Theumans did, a disease brought to Yarong by Daltan soldiers. She was just a child then, but she still remembered the bombs, the gunfire, the gases. Bullets that tore through skulls faster than a heartsooth could mend them and masked soldiers wrapped in gloves and uniforms, no inch of their skin showing despite the beating humidity of the island. Never mind that heartsooths were few in every village; everyone was treated as a possible heartsooth, gunned down from afar if they could not be captured.

His mother had escaped by boat, adrift on an endless sea until Theuman fishing vessels chanced by them on neutral waters. There, lifted onto the deck by a net meant to trawl mackerel, she had been given new life.

She'd said the city she'd entered couldn't agree with itself—were they the ones offering Yarongese immigrants salvation, or were they the ones who fashioned gloves against heartsooths and adopted that same Daltan insult, *bloodcarver*? Were they the ones exemplifying virtues of peace and progress, or were they the ones turning a blind eye as Yarong pleaded to its mainland neighbors for aid? Sometimes, Kochin still wasn't sure.

A short trolley ride later, and he'd reached the registration offices. There, he was met by a troubling line—no, not a line, upon further inspection. A protest, signs held high that read: PEACE IS PROGRESS and NOT OUR LIVES FOR LIVER EATERS.

Kochin let out a sigh, unimpressed—another mixed bag of sentiments. Theumans never could quite figure out if they were open-minded or if they still clung to outdated ideals.

Ignoring the protesters, he found the true line to the registration office snaking around the block and joined it behind a couple of women nearing their thirties. They shared quiet chatter, just audible beneath the chant of protestors.

"We really thought we could age out of the draft, didn't we?" one of them said with a sigh.

"You almost did," joked her neighbor.

"Just how old do you think I am?" Her indignation was only met by laughter.

"Honestly, I don't see why we can't send automatons instead. We've got automatons that clean for us, automatons that play music, automatons that sell papers. Surely, it's not that hard to make an automaton that can go to war for us."

"Maybe Congmi Industries will. Goodness knows Congmi Quan Andao isn't getting drafted. Perhaps he can help us out with all that time on his hands."

They shared a hearty chuckle at that, and the line advanced forward.

Congmi. That was a name he hadn't heard in a while—not since Nhika's death. Mimi and Andao would be exempt, for sure, one on premises of age and the other for industry. Trin might have to scrounge up a different excuse. One night, a long time ago, he had promised them he would never set foot in Central again. But that was before Nhika had died. Honor was not a concept that a grief-stricken heart remembered. And if they were ever truly her friends, they would understand why he had returned.

At last, the line crawled in through the propped-open doors

of the office, and he reached the recruiter, who only looked up at him in expectation.

"Draft registration card?" he drawled.

Kochin slid his card across the desk and the recruiter flipped through some papers before giving Kochin a beleaguered look. "Your number wasn't called."

Kochin cleared his throat. "Actually, I'm here to volunteer for service."

The recruiter blinked lazily, as though the statement was taking a moment to root. When it did, he lifted his eyebrows in surprise. "For what station?"

Kochin hadn't prepared for this question, but the answer came easily. "Combat medic, sir."

With a grunt, the recruiter stamped his registration card and sent him off to the adjacent station for a physical. The rest went routinely—his physique checked, his vision tested, his height measured.

Then, at last, they shuttled him to a room in the back with a group of other volunteers, right hands raised as they recited the Theuman enlistment oath:

"I, Ven Kochin, pledge to hold highest the safety of my city-state and its denizens. I swear to obey the orders of my Commission and superior officers. And I vow to fight in defense of Theumas for all its people, against all its enemies. This, I place before all else."

Even as he repeated it, he knew it was a lie. He owed nothing to this city—the one that had trapped him, the one that had killed her. When he swept up to Yarongese shores on tides of blood, it would not be Theumas he fought for.

But the oath was the last thing he needed to be sworn in. The recruitment officer pinned a badge to his lapel—I VOLUNTEERED!—and slapped some papers into his hands, promising instructions for training camp by mail soon.

Just like that, Kochin was a soldier.

⇛ ELEVEN ⇚
FOUR MONTHS AGO

THE TRAINING CAMP WAS A FIELD OF BEIGE TENTS set up beside training yards and shooting ranges: Kochin's home for the next six weeks. War had come quickly to a city-state without a substantial military; boot camp packed in the hundreds of medics-in-training like cigarettes waiting for a light, four recruits to a tent. Even after he'd unpacked his sparse trunk, he made no effort to fraternize with his tentmates. As medics, they'd be split off between squadrons, some stationed in the Gaikhen Mountains and some deployed to Yarong.

Nhika had been wrong about one thing: He would not be a scholar on the battlefield. The training made sure of that, six hours a day in basic military training and ten hours learning tactical medicine—how to splint a fracture, clot a gunshot wound, tourniquet a limb.

The first week was the hardest: physical conditioning that burned through his body, rope courses that tested his agility, drills performed in the open heat during the height of summer. His tentmates called it sadism—Kochin called it a test of resolve, and any time he felt his heart might burst, he remembered who he owed the organ to. Every grain of muscle was a debt unpaid; each breath drawn was a breath stolen.

Once he survived the conditioning, he was given his first weapon: a semiautomatic pistol.

Kochin had used one of these before—nearly the same exact make. He'd used it to veer Mr. Congmi's horses over the bend. He'd pointed it at a girl in his shophouse.

Sometimes, Kochin wondered what might've happened if he had pulled the trigger. A bullet through the roof, just to scare her off. Or, if he'd wanted to truly keep her away, maybe a bullet where it didn't matter—through the foot, the hand—because he knew she could heal it. Then she could hate him, and Dep Trin might've even come through that door to arrest him, but at least she'd be *alive*.

Instead, here Kochin was, shooting bottles from a dozen yards away and imagining a mirror at the end of the range—because his own sternum was the only suitable target for a bullet. Maybe the recruits to his left and right were imagining Daltan soldiers, but he found that a little abstract. Daltanny had destroyed his mother's culture, her people, his heritage—but the hole in his heart *right now* was not their doing. There was only one person responsible for Nhika's death, so Kochin was shooting bottles and trying to find himself in the shattered glass.

In the few moments he had to himself—the half-hour meals, the minutes before sleep overtook him—his thoughts were on Nhika. What she was back then. How she was now. The dwindling hourglass, each grain of sand a day he had left until she became unsalvageable like Santo's son. Kochin wasn't quite sure where the divide was—his mission and Santo's futile goal.

He only knew he was running out of time before she was just another stripe of bone on her ring.

"Tomorrow, it'll have been two months."

"What?" Kochin turned on his bunk to find Nhika sitting at his feet.

"Since you left Chengton. You never did tell your family you enlisted, did you?"

"I'll be back before they realize I'm gone."

"Or they'll receive your bloodied ID tags atop a folded Theuman flag." She shrugged, as though the prospect of his death was not such a terrible thing.

But to Kochin, there was no option in which he didn't make it home—because Vinsen was waiting for him with Nhika's casket, and he had an outstanding debt to a girl who'd lent him her heart. "What, no faith in me?"

"A realistic amount of faith in you, I'd say."

"I'm not going to die."

"I thought that once, too."

Kochin raked a hand through his hair. "*Fine*, I'll write a letter if it would please you."

Her smile was smug. "Yes, it would."

And when he turned around again, trying to catch some sleep, she was gone.

Boot camp came and went with the aftertaste of gunpowder and heatstroke. At the end of it, they were lined up in rows and marched by their training officer, who pinned a new badge to their uniform lapel and gave them their first rank: private.

Then came the moment that determined it all: their

deployment. It didn't hit him until the list came out how definitive this was—because if he wasn't sent to Yarong, he would just burn months of time somewhere far from Nhika. He'd have to break his own bones for a medical exemption, go home, find some other way to Yarong. He would have to start over from the beginning.

Kochin hadn't realized it, but his hands were shaking.

Their training officer began. "Under order of the Commission, Theumas will commit two hundred units to the Gaikhen Mountains and a hundred fifty units to Yarong, all of which will require medics. We will begin with those of you deployed to the Gaikhen Mountains, which is as follows: Adau Rin; Ahao Sanna . . ."

A breath nocked itself in his throat as the officer went down the list of names. He was doing the math in his head, that fifteen percent greater likelihood of being deployed to the Gaikhen Mountains, estimating the number of privates in this camp and calculating their division—until he realized the list was merely alphabetical, the divide arbitrary.

And his name, Ven Kochin, was nearer to the end.

His breath released, shoulders fell. That shaking in his muscles still remained, but it was more anticipation than anxiety—waiting for the officer to say his name, send him to Yarong, make it *real*. He'd spent these last couple months working for nothing else.

"And now, to those deployed to the island," the officer went on, and Kochin's name still hadn't been called. "Liy Munna, Long Yin Laory . . ."

Each name, a step closer. Each name, a bullet loaded into the chamber. Each name, the pull of the trigger. Kochin was just waiting for a shot to land.

And then: ". . . Van Nhoa, Vang Ro Miya, and Vei Luuka. If your name hasn't been called, you're on reserve. Transports will be arriving tomorrow to take you to your respective stations. Dismissed, and congratulations."

Kochin's chest was pounding. He waited for something more—because that couldn't have been it. His name hadn't been called. He was meant to go to Yarong. This couldn't be *it*.

Around him, the privates left for their tents and luggage. Kochin stayed rooted, trying to make sense of how he could be so close yet so, so far.

Finally, his feet found the volition to move, and he jogged up to the training officer. "Sir, a moment?"

The officer's eyes flicked to his name tag. "Private Ven."

"You didn't call my name."

The officer checked his list. "That's right—you're first at the top of the reserve list. Lucked out—go home, enjoy the extra time, and wait until we call you."

But Kochin couldn't wait. If he wasn't in the first wave of deployment, there wasn't any guarantee he'd be deployed to Yarong. The island might've even changed hands by then. "What about Yarong? Can't they use another medic?"

"The units are filled. Don't worry; if Theumas needs you, we'll call you." The officer turned, beckoned away by his superior, and Kochin was left standing alone in the yard, wondering if this was an obstacle, or if it was providence.

He hadn't been drafted; he'd enlisted.

He hadn't been deployed; he could return home.

Yet . . . there was something on that island, something the Mother was trying to keep from him. If She were kind, he might've assumed it was his own demise She kept him from. But the Mother had never been kind to anyone who defiled Her art.

Kochin glanced back over the tents. Tomorrow morning, everyone would be off to their stations. Tomorrow morning, Kochin would be sent home, unless . . .

His mind whirred like an automaton. A hundred fifty medics going to Yarong. His name at the top of the list. Just one private who needed to be cut. A hundred disqualifying medical conditions.

And . . . and a hundred ways a bloodcarver could cause them.

Kochin had to make a decision by tonight. Come morning it would be too late, and he'd be shipped home while another went to Yarong in his place. He'd spent the past couple hours sleepless on his bunk, considering the injury until he'd finally narrowed it down to one: rhabdomyolysis. Muscle cells, torn apart after a period of overexertion like boot camp. The onset was delayed, so no one would wonder how it sprang up overnight. It would require hospitalization, which opened a spot for him on Yarong.

And . . . with prompt enough treatment, its symptoms were largely reversible. Kochin had seen it done at the Theumas

Medical Center before. Hell, it might've even been a service, a few weeks of pain in exchange for exemption from the war and the terrors that awaited on the other side of the water. It was a perfect crime.

But . . . he'd have to use heartsoothing. These hands had had no qualms injuring before, but it had never been with his gift. Kochin told himself there was no difference, whether it was a gun he used or his influence. For some reason, his heart wouldn't believe it.

Yet, it had been his heart that misguided him before. The moment Nhika had shown up at the funeral, the moment Santo had given her that business card, Kochin had known he'd needed to push her out. It was his heart that'd convinced him to let her in—his heart that had stuttered when she was near, his heart that had searched for her in every crowded room, his heart that *dared* to imagine her in his future.

It had been his heart that killed her.

Kochin would not let his heart misguide him again. His rationale told him plainly: It had to be tonight. In the morning, he'd be sent home. There was no guarantee Theuman soldiers would be deployed to Yarong again.

And it would be so *easy*. Easier than any of his previous crimes, easier than framing Santo, easier than coming home to Nhika's casket and admitting he'd failed.

As if summoned by his mere thought of her, Nhika appeared at his bedside. "It's a bit extreme, don't you think, rhabdomyo-whatever-you-called-it?"

He didn't respond for fear of waking up his tent, but who was she to judge? He'd seen the Butcher with a bruise in the shape of her handprint, and she'd nearly stopped Kochin's heart herself—how was this any different?

"Well, for one, that Butcher had plans to sell me. And I recall there being a gun involved in our little tussle," Nhika countered. "Your poor victim's only crime would be sharing a tent with a bloodcarver."

At that, Kochin sucked in a breath. Nhika had never called him that—*would never* have called him that. It was her faith in his heartsoothing that had been so intoxicating; under that lovesick stupor, he'd felt so invincible. That's how he knew this . . . this *ghost* wasn't really her. It was only his doubt given voice, and he'd come way too far to let doubt stop him now.

Nhika watched him, and her expression dropped like she'd noticed the shift in his intent. "Mother, you're going to do it, aren't you?"

Kochin couldn't meet her gaze. He pulled off her bone ring, hid it beneath his pillow—and she was snuffed. Even if she wasn't real, he hated the thought of her realizing she'd died for a bloodcarver rather than a heartsooth.

But it had to be done. She could hate him for it when she awoke—he was already accustomed to her enmity. It was her absence he couldn't stand.

And she was right. He was a bloodcarver.

Even though he'd burned that fox mask months ago, he could feel its familiar grooves over his skin as he lifted himself from bed. The world darkened as though he were seeing it out of two small eyes, and his breath echoed in his ears.

Without realizing when he'd moved, Kochin was standing over his tentmate, hand outstretched. Private Rho was curled up in slumber, looking almost like a child—innocence before the storm, dark hair falling over his eyes. He was on the younger side, and Kochin could almost convince himself this was a mercy, giving the soldier back his childhood. Almost.

When he pressed his fingers against Private Rho's skin, the body came into color like a sunrise.

This was nothing new to Kochin, soothing a body without permission. He'd seen patients during surgery, the drug-thick sleep that nothing could penetrate, not even his heavy-handed influence. He'd seen them after, too, when it really mattered— making sure Santo's transplant organs stuck. As he soothed the soldier in sleep, he almost expected to feel the line of an incision curve around his abdomen, the cold taste of scalpel against muscle. But, right now, with no Santo, no surgery, no hospital around him, there was no excuse to soothe. The act felt like violence.

His mission returned to him: rhabdomyolysis. His influence moved toward the leg, and he saw it plainly past the soldier's blanket. It walked fingers through the layers of the skin, the fat, the fascia . . . and found itself at the muscle.

As though he'd sunk his fingers into the tissue itself, he felt a pull against his nail beds—like if he just yanked his hand, something in the leg might tear apart. But he hated the thought of such destruction—like tearing flowers off their stems when someone had taken so long to grow them. No, if he were to do this, he'd pluck those petals off one at a time, feel their softness between his fingers, repentance for an act he was in the middle of committing.

"If you do this, there's no going back," Nhika said, but she was wrong.

He'd passed that point already, months ago: standing before her grave, promising a feat of necromancy. So, no matter how much the Mother asked of him, he couldn't back out now.

Kochin rolled the muscle between his hands like a stalk of rice, the beds of his fingers walking down the grain. There was a moment of reverence, as well as a moment of regret, before his influence sank its teeth.

Cells swelled and burst. He started with just a few—their destruction would bring more. Death spread through the soldier's leg: acid chewing muscle, a spark bringing fire, a rot that wouldn't come until the next morning.

After years spent using his heartsoothing to heal, it struck him how easy it was to destroy.

Kochin staggered back, his exhale tasting like smoke. He wasn't sure what was a greater violation: the fact that he'd destroyed the soldier's leg or that he'd used the soldier's own energy to do it. Something hammered in his chest, his brain— he was so sure it was his conscience, revolting against his own act of violence. He tried stifling it, drawing back under his sheets and letting the darkness take him, but it persisted.

Are you happy now? No, not yet.

No going back. I know.

And then Nhika's voice: *I can't believe I died for a bloodcarver.*

A bloodcarver.

A bloodcarver.

A bloodcarver.

When Kochin awoke, Private Rho was gone. He jolted up in bed, remembering the events of last night—in the clarity of the morning, he almost hoped that was a nightmare, because he couldn't have . . . he didn't . . . how could he . . .

The door flap lifted, and another tentmate entered. Kochin straightened. "Did you see where Private Rho went?" he asked, tilting his head in the direction of his victim's empty cot.

The tentmate's eyes went wide. "He went to the infirmary this morning—overworked himself. Heard he might get shipped back home."

Kochin swallowed, stared at his hands. He still couldn't tell if this was a victory or a defeat. Everything had gone to plan, yet he felt like he'd just branded himself with a scar only he could see. And every time he looked at his palms, it would be there, that charred skin and bubbling blister, a word written so plainly. To everyone else, he was just Theuman. Private Ven. Physician's aide. Yet he couldn't soothe away those deeper scars.

Murderer. Liar. Bloodcarver.

Kochin dragged himself out of bed and donned his uniform. When he reached the infirmary, a portable wooden building, he found his victim already being carried out in a stretcher. The pain looked immense—Private Rho languished on the stretcher, clutching his leg and biting the lapel of his uniform.

For a moment, Kochin wondered if catching Private Rho right now was providence, a second chance. Maybe there *was* going back, and if he healed the soldier right now he might have it all: He'd take Private Rho's place to Yarong, but the boy would return home uninjured. Maybe he could pretend this had been his plan all along, not to disable anyone but simply to put on a show. *Maybe* the Mother was kind.

"Private Ven," snapped a voice behind him.

Kochin turned, then saluted when he realized it was his commanding officer who addressed him. "Sir."

"Private Rho's been discharged on account of injury. I know I said you lucked out, but I fear I spoke too soon. You'll have to take his place."

"What station?" Kochin asked, even though he already knew. He just needed to hear someone say it to make it real.

"Yarong. Pack your things—the shuttle comes for you soon."

Kochin bowed his understanding, and his officer dismissed him. His victim returned to the forefront of his attention, but when he turned, Private Rho was gone.

Perhaps he'd been naive. Repentance had never been his wont. Running, hiding, hurting people—*that* was always his habit. After he'd killed Mr. Congmi, he hadn't repented; he'd only tightened the fox mask. He'd run, hidden, pushed Nhika away.

There was only one crime that he *had* to repent for, and that was killing a heartsooth.

Kochin returned to his tent and packed. The shuttle came for all deployed soldiers later that morning, giving him no time to dwell on boot camp—for which he was glad, because he feared he might only have regrets if he was given time to think.

Kochin and all the other medics deployed to Yarong were taken to a cantonment near the coast, where they awaited the congregation of the troops. He was given a trauma bag, a uniform to distinguish him as a medic, and two ID tags dangling on a ball chain.

It didn't strike him until he saw his name stamped in nickel that there was some chance he might die. That's what the tags meant, after all, one to take home and the other to leave on his dead body, a small bid for remembrance in a war zone that would sooner forget him. But if he didn't make it home, there would be no one to remember Suonyasan Nhika as she truly was.

Perhaps it was *he* who would not be remembered, and all this world would know him for was a dead girl and a dog tag.

On the quiet night before deployment to Yarong, camped in a coastal town in Eastern Theumas, Kochin slipped Nhika's bone ring onto the chain beside his ID tags. He was afraid of losing it if he kept it on his finger—and it was the one thing she'd entrusted to him. That, and her heartsoothing.

He recalled her warning, how he might return home as an ID tag and a folded Theuman flag. It was then he wrote to his family:

Ba, Ma, Vinsen, Bentri:

I have enlisted in the war as a medic. Don't worry about me; I won't forget what I've learned from Ma. But, I hope that the fright of war has not yet reached quiet Chengton. Bentri, I wish you best of luck with your studies, but don't forget to cherish what you have. Ba, Ma, I apologize if this news comes as a shock, but it's something I must do. And, to Vinsen, please take care of everything and everyone while I'm gone. You've always been so good at it. It's a debt I can never repay.

Kochin paused, considering folding up the note and sending it before he could make any more false assurances. But, before he could stop himself, he added:

I promise I'll be home soon.

When morning came, Kochin was off to Yarong.

⇉ TWELVE ⇇
NOW

IT DIDN'T QUITE HIT NHIKA HOW MANY MONTHS she'd missed until the rain came in—autumnal chills, when it should've been the middle of summer. Looking out her window now, she found the dirt road out of this manor muddied from the downpour. There came a sense that she was waiting for someone to arrive—Kochin, Trin, anyone. Or perhaps, she was waiting for a moment to leave.

A knock on her door drew her attention from the window to her doorframe, where Mimi stood with a long gown in her arms. The girl herself was still dressed in mud-spattered trousers, having just come back from some field test with Andao.

After she entered, Mimi hung the gown on the door of Nhika's wardrobe, its red skirt waterfalling down into deep purples and the thighs slit to reveal matching purple pants beneath. Gold flecked the hem like splattered paint—or spilled blood—and the outfit came with glittering golden gloves. Though they were meant to tie the outfit together, their solid shine made them stand out. It looked beautiful. It looked wrong.

"I had it tailored," Mimi said. "I wanted you to have something to wear for Commissioner Nem's party."

Nhika was looking forward to Nem's party—but not for her

usual reasons. The Congmis didn't know what had happened to Kochin, but someone *did*. She had to believe a man of his stature couldn't simply disappear.

And . . . a naive part of her hoped to find him at the party, dressed in a vest suit with bare hands and a bold smile—*I've been looking for you, Ms. Suon*. If she could find him unharmed, she might even forgive him for disappearing on her.

"Where is the party?" Nhika asked. After the air raid drill, she feared returning to Central.

"Nem has a home nearby, in Western."

Western Theumas was as far from Daltanny as anyone could get, so she couldn't blame those with the wealth to relocate. But she imagined her old life in the Dog Borough—imagined watching those warships leave the harbor every morning. She was eighteen—old enough to be placed on one of those ships, even. Being able to escape the war was a luxury Nhika had never expected to possess.

With a sympathetic look, Mimi took a seat beside her. "I know it's a lot. The world you left is not the same world you're returning to, is it?"

"That's one way to put it."

"Well, when my father died and Hendon was injured, you helped us heal. I don't know if it's against your heartsooth sensibilities, relinquishing yourself to the care of another, but I'd like to return the favor."

More than ever before, Mimi looked so genuine and earnest, and Nhika realized she was finally seeing the girl beyond her grief and anger. And there was something precious about her intent—healing Nhika, when Nhika had always managed fine on her own. "You've done enough."

"No," Mimi said. In a quieter voice, she added, "Andao has me on Trin's old duties now, and every time I balance the ledger, I know there's an invisible debt there, one we owe you. I wish we could pay it back with chem—at least that's something we know how to do."

"I'll take chem," Nhika joked. "Now that I think about it, I never did get paid for healing Hendon, did I?"

Mimi laughed. It sounded like music. "I suppose not. We can make good on that debt, too."

Nhika looked Mimi over. She was still the delicate smile, lotus petals on untouched water. Still the bashful doe eyes, the cherub cheeks, pinned hair. But, as with everything, she'd been changed—touched by the selfsame melancholy that had transformed the household and Theumas itself. After sitting through that air raid drill, Nhika was beginning to understand it. It was a different kind of grief than losing a loved one—it was the kind that mourned a life they'd never know again.

"Food, shelter, dinner parties with commissioners," Nhika said. "It's a good start."

The playfulness returned to Mimi's expression. "I'm glad you're coming to Commissioner Nem's party with me—so I won't have to be the only one pretending she's someone she isn't."

"And who are you pretending to be?"

"The Congmi heiress."

"You *are*."

"Then it's working." Mimi sighed again, looking tired beyond her years. "Funerals and parties—at some point, they start feeling the same."

"Don't get me *too* excited."

"I'm only joking. Mostly." Mimi clapped her hands against her lap as she stood, something to dispel the sentimentality. "Besides, it's a dinner party. At the very least, I know you can enjoy the dinner part."

Ah, well, Nhika couldn't argue with that.

Nhika learned the hard way of Mimi's latest venture: learning to drive. In the night, Mimi sped them toward Nem's party in one of Mr. Congmi's old autocarriages, the pale tree trunks of the forested roads blurring by like upright skeletons. At times, Nhika was sure that all four wheels left the ground, but she made no comment—that was for Andao and Hendon to do, both clutching their chairs with white knuckles.

Thankfully, the trip was just a town over. When they reached Nem's property, Mimi finally slowed to join a line of autocarriages at the gate, which rounded the courtyard of Nem's gorgeous countryside villa. Though it was already sundown, the mansion glowed gold with lights—gas lamps at the door and electric spotlights showering the stone facade in honey gold against the darkening blue of the sky. The villa was larger than the Congmis', with a towering central body and expansive wings on either side, cradling the courtyard and gardens in their berth.

The architecture was everything she might expect from a commissioner: the perfect symmetry, the many balconies and pinnacled roofs, the sweeping staircase and pillared entryway. Nhika figured she should've been accustomed to buildings like these by now. Perhaps she'd have to reacclimate to wealth; dying had reset her progress.

When they reached the front of the line, Mimi passed the ignition key to the valet. A butler swooped in to escort her and Andao toward the villa.

The guests strutted up to the mansion like peacocks, each taking a moment to flaunt their dresses or suits at the top of the stairs. Though Mimi had given Nhika a beautiful gown, it didn't quite compare to some others: dragging capes bejeweled like a puddle of the night sky; gloves scaled with delicate plates of metal to mimic dragon skin; or fabric that shimmered with the iridescence of hummingbird throats. Lights flashed, and Nhika took a moment to recognize the cameras of photographers, who'd found time to come out to Western Theumas to capture poorly lit photographs of Theumas's wealthiest.

Mimi was right. Funerals and parties did look the same with this company.

As she neared the top of the stairs, Nhika felt oddly shy. Mimi, walking before her, linked arms with her brother as they both turned toward the photographers. She wore a youthful gown, white melting into threads of gold as it unfurled like the tail of a betta at the hem. Andao wore gold trim to match her. A couple reporters asked about Trin, upcoming marriage plans, but Andao turned away without answer.

Noticing Nhika's discomfort, Hendon shielded her from the vulturelike photographers as much as his thin frame could; they entered Nem's open doors without stopping for pictures.

Inside, a sizable attendance had already gathered in the entryway. Champagne overflowed from glasses and gown trails swept the ground, while buoyant conversation and tipsy laughter created a general air of revelry. Nhika found herself scanning the crowds for a face, coiffed hair and antagonizing smile, but of course Kochin wouldn't be here. It would be strange, attending such an event without his opposition. And she'd dreaded it so much before.

At some point, Andao was called away, and so was Mimi, with Hendon following her—leaving Nhika alone before a crowd of people she barely recognized, who hardly paid her a second glance. It had been *so fun* to pretend she was a part of this company when she'd first joined, but then she'd learned that a mask could be as simple as a pleasant conversation and a business card. The bullet wound in her shoulder, hidden behind beautiful silk, was a reminder that the prettiest snakes had the most venomous fangs.

The only thing that kept her here was opportunity—not the same kind she'd sought before, the desire to wheedle her way into this society like a wood louse beneath mahogany floorboards. But, certainly, among all these people, at least one person would know what happened to Santo's aide.

The first person to catch her eye was Nem. Or, *Commissioner* Nem. His station far outweighed even her fake identity now, but Nhika strode boldly toward him—until she saw the pistol holstered at his waist, a jarring accessory to an otherwise sharp outfit.

Her muscles froze, breath catching. Nhika wasn't sure when she'd become afraid of guns—certainly not when Kochin had pointed one at her. It wasn't the pain that scared her. It was what the weapon *meant*. A chunk of metal and gunpowder that could kill a heartsooth—proof that she could die and *had* died. All her bravado from earlier disappeared, and she turned her sights on someone else: Mr. Ngut, head of Ngut Inventions, trying to enjoy an open bar in peace. Discarding etiquette, she hitched up her dress and strutted toward him, though she could tell he was attempting to avoid her eye.

"Mr. Ngut," she said, bowing, and he gingerly lowered his drink to bow his head. "It's been a while."

"I'm sorry, you'll have to remind me your name."

Her cheek twitched with a smile. "Suon Ko Nhika."

"Ah, Ms. Suon, of course," he said. "Pleasant party, isn't it? So kind of Commissioner Nem to find time in his schedule to host."

There was resentment there, and she remembered they'd both been leading candidates. Seemed Mr. Ngut hadn't been taking the loss well. "Yes, so kind—anyway, I wanted to ask you a question."

Mr. Ngut downed his drink. "I'm sorry, Ms. Suon, but I'm afraid I don't have any positions avail—"

"When's the last time you heard from Ven Kochin?"

At that, Mr. Ngut froze. "Now, that's a name I haven't heard in a while."

"What do you mean?"

"Last we talked was months ago. He gave me a call."

"What about?"

Mr. Ngut pinched his chin, as though trying to remember. "He was asking about one of my long-distance dirigibles. Wondering if I could muster a crew to take him to Yarong, if I remember correctly—of course, that was impossible, so—"

"Why?" Nhika interrupted, and Mr. Ngut gave her a piqued look. "Why was he going to Yarong?"

"Guilt, would be my guess—what with his old employer's penchant, to, ah . . ." He eyed her over, as though remembering the Yarongese could exist off the island, and cleared his throat. "I should probably get going. Would hate to leave the wife to fend for herself."

Mr. Ngut left his empty glass and fled, and Nhika let him; he didn't have the answers she was searching for. But it was a hint: Kochin had gone to Yarong, despite the island being under Daltan rule. She wanted to believe it was about soul-searching—that, after she'd died, he'd been inspired to learn more of their culture.

Somehow, she knew the answer wasn't so pretty.

"Let me go!"

Nhika turned, following the cry—because it had sounded familiar. It sounded almost like the way her grandmother would say it, the way Kochin's mother might say it. It sounded Yarongese.

There, at the entrance, a Yarongese girl was being detained by Nem's security detail. Skin the color of honey, high cheekbones, dark brows—she was tall and elegantly sculpted, but her clothing betrayed her. Despite the shawl she wore, Nhika still spied the plain yellow gown beneath, a shoddy mimicry of the true golds worn by others.

By Nhika herself.

"I'm expected," she protested indignantly, but the guards didn't loosen their gloved holds.

"I'm not seeing a Lana on the guest list," one was saying.

"It's *Lanalay*," the girl corrected in a condescending tone. She spoke her full trisyllabic Yarongese name like a beautiful melody. It compelled Nhika closer, though other guests shied from the scuffle. The commotion attracted eyes, and her thoughts were on the gun at Nem's waist, wondering how he would take to a trespasser, especially one that looked Yarongese.

"Well, Lanalay, you haven't been invited," the guard insisted. "You can either go peacefully, or I can call local authorities to make you cooperate."

Nhika cleared her throat. Eyes turned toward her, and before she understood what she was doing, she said, "Excuse me, officers."

"Ms. Suon." The guard bowed deep, though his apprehension didn't lift.

"She's a friend of mine and the Congmis'," Nhika said. "If her name's not on the guest list, it's simply because no one could spell it."

Lanalay gave her a wary look. Nhika had been hoping for something more appreciative.

"Is that so?" the guard asked.

"Yes. Let me call Congmi Quan Andao over and he can

confirm it," she bluffed, pretending to scan the room. Luckily, he was nowhere in sight—but even if he was, she imagined she could bully him into playing along.

The guard waved his hand. "It's our mistake, Ms. Suon," he said, then turned to Lanalay. "And apologies, Miss . . ."

"Numathai," Lanalay responded, brushing off her gloves as though he'd sullied them with his touch. Yet, they were of the cheap cotton variety, the kind worn for weather rather than fashion.

"Our apologies, Miss Numathai. Please, enjoy the party." The guard waved them in, and Lanalay strode into the foyer at Nhika's side.

"You have my thanks, Ms. Suon," Lanalay said once they were out of range, but her tone was more practical than grateful. She started to leave, but Nhika grabbed her arm.

"Hold on a moment," Nhika said. She eyed Lanalay up and down. Gaudy clothing, the kind of stuff Nhika used to think was fancy growing up in the Dog Borough—bold colors but cheap material; all the right pieces, but none of them matching. "You weren't actually invited, were you?"

"As you said—if they forgot my name on the guest list, it's because they could not spell it."

"Numathai Lanalay," Nhika remembered. "Is that even your real name?"

"Suon," Lanalay returned, looking Nhika up and down. "Is that even yours?"

This was no way to repay a favor, but Nhika let the contentiousness slide. More than anything, she was intrigued—why a girl with a Yarongese accent wanted to sneak into a commissioner's party, and how she thought she could do it dressed like that.

Mother help her, she was starting to sound like Kochin.

"What are you doing here?" she asked.

"I am here for the food. The drink. The company," Lanalay said, but it was a plain lie. "May I leave now?"

"Seeing as I've basically sponsored you in, I just need to make sure you're not—I don't know—planning to assassinate anyone."

Lanalay looked unaffected by the accusation. "I am not," she said, the sentence coming out prideful. "Who are you, anyway?"

"Suon Ko Nhika. I'm here with the Congmis," Nhika replied. She was used to condescension, but usually it came from people above her station. If Lanalay had snuck into high society—well, then they were in the same exact position. "If you have ill intention with this crowd, I can call those guards right back over. Now that I think about it, maybe I mistook you for someone else."

Lanalay's eyes narrowed, like she wanted to call Nhika's bluff, but she said, "Very well. If you must know, I was not invited. Your commissioner has no business with a translator from Yarong, but I have no plans on stirring trouble here."

Yarong. Nhika's suspicions were confirmed; Lanalay was from the island itself. But they must've been around the same age, so for her to have left Yarong meant Daltan had lowered its isolationist policies. Either that, or—

"Ms. Suon!" boomed a voice to her left. Nhika turned just as Nem approached, his arms outspread and a glass of champagne between his fingers. Though he still looked kempt, the gelled hair and a suit already decorated with wartime medals, the redness in his cheeks suggested early stages of inebriation.

"Commissioner," Nhika greeted, bowing low. She looked toward Lanalay, trying to coax the same formalities out of the stowaway, only to find her missing.

Before Nhika could question it, Nem said, "How are you enjoying the party?"

"Just fine, Commissioner." Her eyes scanned the crowd. How much could a girl in yellow blend in?

"And how has your recovery been?"

Nhika gave the commissioner a wary look. "Fine. Why do you ask?"

"The Congmis are my dearest business partners. Any friend of theirs is a friend of mine."

Nhika remembered Andao mentioning the partnership. Nem was a brute, she decided, celebrating the alliance when it clearly brought Andao so much shame. "Would you consider yourself their friend?"

"Something better—their ally. We all have the same goals, do we not?"

"I think that depends on what you fight for, Commissioner." She studied him, the deep trenches of his laugh lines—though he hardly ever laughed—and the hard-set, unyielding eyes. She was looking for a mask. Surely, a man who made his fortune selling armaments fought for different reasons than a man simply defending his lover.

"Peace and freedom," Nem responded. Nhika felt something

tight wrap around her chest, but those words sounded different coming from a commissioner's lips than Kochin's. Here, they sounded like lofty, weaponizable ideals. When Kochin said them, they just sounded like quiet ambitions, the same prayers one might send to the Mother.

When she didn't respond, he said, "What do you fight for, Ms. Suon?"

Nhika's eyes scanned the room for Andao or Mimi, someone who might save her from this conversation. Perhaps he was making small talk, but Nhika was growing wary of those who sought out her company. Nothing ever happened in this society without motive.

But there was no rescuing her, so she responded, "Myself."

Nem snorted. "Your honesty is refreshing."

She was born of war. It had driven her family to Theumas. It had razed her culture and her roots. It had forced her grandmother to teach her heartsoothing off stolen textbooks. It was the reason she could only remember past matriarchs by their bones in her ring—and now, not even that.

"It's just that war has never been kind to my family," she said—and realized her guise had slipped, just a little. "I'm not very fond of it."

"The war you're thinking of is war as the Daltans knew it—spreading an empire like a disease, wanting to control the land and seas. I'm not fond of that war, either," Nem said, and there was verity in his tone. "But when war is brought to you, there are only two options: survive or surrender. It's the surviving that I'm fond of."

"Do you believe we can survive it, Commissioner?" she asked, feeling a little concerned herself. Before that night in the Theumas Medical Center, she'd felt . . . invincible. She'd survived house fires and Butchers and illness. She'd been shot and scraped and bruised.

But then, she'd learned her gift was not bottomless, and this technocratic city did not have enough metal to build walls over its mountains and skies. Nhika had died made of marble, and she'd awoken flesh and blood.

"Yes," he said, his familiar confidence returning. "I can guarantee it."

"That's bold," Nhika blurted before she remembered who she was talking to. "I mean, how can anyone guarantee the tides of war?"

"I have a weapon," Nem responded, a grin peeling back his lips. "A weapon unlike anything anyone's ever seen before."

"What is it?"

"You'll learn—when the white flags wave over the Gaikhen Mountains, when our soldiers come back safe. You'll know." With that cryptic language, he gave her a deep bow. "As much as it's been a pleasure speaking to you, Ms. Suon, I have others to entertain."

He started to leave when Nhika remembered her quest. "Commissioner, one moment."

Nem paused, turned. It was a daunting thing, being the sole object of his attention.

"There's someone I'm looking for, Santo's old aide," she said. "Do you remember Ven Kochin?"

"Ven Kochin," Nem repeated, like he was surprised to hear the name. "Yes. I remember him."

"Do you know where he went?"

His eyes wandered somewhere past her, like he was trying to conjure the details. "Camp Majora. Northernmost tip of Yarong. He was stationed there as a combat medic," he said, as though reading off a document.

"And where is he now?"

Something rueful came over Nem's expression, but she couldn't read it before his stoniness returned. "I wish I could tell you, Ms. Suon. There are many who served overseas or in our mountains. I regret that I can't know all their fates."

He left Nhika with her feet welded to the ground. So, he'd been drafted, just like Trin. They'd met each other on the island—she'd theorized just as much. And . . . and somehow, her body had traded hands, though Nhika wasn't sure how.

She caught a spot of yellow out of the corner of her eye, drawing her back to the present: Lanalay, coming down the stairs. There was nothing upstairs that should've interested a partygoer, and the girl slipped through the crowds and turned the corner.

Nhika followed.

Lanalay snuck through a closed door. Throwing a glance over her shoulder, Nhika did the same. She crept through just in time to find Lanalay disappearing into a study. The door remained ajar, and the light moved with shadows as Lanalay explored the room.

That was Lanalay's first mistake, trying to hide from a girl with an unhealthy amount of curiosity. Her second was doing something so damned curious—Nhika couldn't help herself.

She snuck forward. Shadows moved. This house no longer belonged to an entrepreneur; it belonged to a commissioner. That meant there could be political secrets within these walls— so how treasonous would it be, Nhika wondered, if she'd let in a spy. Could the Congmis protect her then?

Nhika prepared for a confrontation, but when she opened the door, all she found was an empty room with an open window and a draft.

THIRTEEN
NOW

NEVER IN HER LIFE HAD NHIKA JUST SAT AND waited.

Her fingers itched to do something—press snake oils, soothe, anything other than hide behind these silk gloves. Yet, all she could do was wait: for Trin to wake up, for Kochin to come home. Waiting for answers, when she'd always preferred prying them out.

The house looked different now that Nhika had learned it was a refuge from war—not so menacing, just . . . lonely. A little barren. Too big to be a bunker, but too empty to be a home.

At the very least, Mimi kept her busy. This time, it was to reveal the last of the Congmi secrets: their locked carriage house.

"Knowing you, it's only a matter of time before you pick this lock," Mimi was saying as they walked the path toward the carriage house. "So, I figured I should show you now before you hurt yourself."

Mimi had been right. Nhika had planned an expiration date for that lock, and it'd been fast approaching.

"Hurt myself?" Nhika asked.

Mimi gave her a saturnine look. "It's wartime. Our storehouses are a lot more dangerous these days."

Nhika sucked in a breath and followed.

Mimi took her to the carriage house doors and unlatched the lock at the bottom. With all her weight, she cranked a lever and a pulley tightened, lifting the door. Inch by inch, the door revealed a dark storehouse, until Mimi ducked inside and switched on the light. The dim bulbs painted the machines in oily color.

They were automatons unlike any Nhika had ever seen before, built in the bipedal semblance of a human but not imitative of one. No, these were treaded metal suits standing twice her height, somewhere between armor and vehicle. At their sides hung segmented arms with claws and grappling hooks and . . . ammunition belts, which traced back to turrets on either arm.

These were war machines, all of them. This warehouse was lined with rows and rows of war machines. They were in resting positions now, their torso segments bowed, but she could see how intimidating they would've been if they had been standing upright, an untouchable soldier operating the machine from behind a gridded glass window, manipulating arms that housed turrets and spewed flames. Nhika walked up to one of them, taking a stepladder to peer within the cockpit, where she found a dashboard of controls. It looked so simple, like driving an autocarriage. GUARDIAN read the emblazoned letters across its arm. Yet, these machines looked built to kill.

"Striking, aren't they?" Mimi asked, though her words didn't match her somber tone. "My brother's ingenuity knows no bounds."

"Nem mentioned a secret weapon—one he thinks will end

the war. Is this what he meant?" Nhika asked, placing her palm against the cool glass of the cockpit.

"*Commissioner* Nem," Mimi chastised, sounding so much like Trin. "And no, the Guardians are no secret. We've already deployed a few earlier models on Yarong. It was terribly hard, designing treads that gripped sand, but Andao was adamant they be sent to Yarong."

Of course. That's where Trin had been stationed—and the name, *Guardian*, was self-evident. Perhaps these machines were made to save lives and defend Theuman soldiers. All Nhika could think about was how, with these cold metal suits, Andao had unknowingly created the perfect weapon against a heartsooth.

"Now that Trin is back from war, will Andao maintain his partnership with Nem?" Nhika asked.

Mimi looked like she wanted to reprimand the disrespect again, but she only said, "Yes. It's becoming clear that Theumas needs every advantage it can get against a country with two—now *three*—occupied territories."

"Yet, Nem sounded so certain we could win," Nhika said, mostly to herself.

Mimi moved to the workbench, where she unfurled a blueprint of the Guardian. "If there's anything I've learned since the start of this war, it's that there's no such thing as certainty. This is new for everyone. It feels like building an autocarriage while it's in motion."

Nhika didn't like that answer. She needed certainty, and she wanted to believe Nem—because she'd awoken, having lost six months and a heartsooth, to a city at war. So, she needed something that might lessen the terror of it all, like adding sugar to snake oils. Otherwise, she might start to think about all those injuries her heartsoothing could never heal because she'd escaped the draft. She might imagine air raids over the Congmi villa—a fire claiming this family just as it had claimed hers. And she might wonder about a heartsooth, alone somewhere on an island she couldn't reach.

This war . . . it was so much bigger than she was. Nhika had only two hands.

"It's a duty," Mimi said, and for a second, Nhika thought Mimi had read her mind. "This immense power. Six months ago, all our machines did was sell paper, or serve tea, or play strings. Now, they might turn the tides of war. I don't think Theumas would remember us kindly if we turned our backs on that possibility. Well, if Theumas falls, then I doubt they'd remember us at all."

"Do you want to be remembered?"

"Yes," Mimi answered haughtily. "Before the war, I thought that was a guarantee. At this moment I'm not so sure."

Nhika wanted to be remembered, too, but not by all posterity. Just by a heartsooth—it's what she died for. Now, she'd been given a second life, and she had to wonder if it was wasted here, with her hands behind silk. Surely, with her many gifts, there was something more to be done.

She blinked out of her stupor just in time to catch a rag, which Mimi had tossed at her. "What's this?"

"A job—help me polish all these models, won't you?"

"Excuse me? You're making me work?"

Mimi gave her an unsympathetic look. "If I must work, Nhika, so must you."

"That's how I know the world has turned upside down," Nhika muttered, starting on the first machine. "Congmi Mai Minlan is doing manual labor."

Together, they polished. These automatons had been stored for quite some time, so their shiny finishes had already begun to tarnish in the dust and dampness. Mimi was a mean employer, making Nhika polish until she could see herself in the metal.

"If these things are going to war anyway, why are we cleaning them?" Nhika grumbled.

"Commissioner Nem has requested a few models to showcase at his upcoming exhibition," Mimi said. "It's going to be an entire event—all these sponsors and politicians congregating in an airship for the weekend. We have to bring our absolute best."

"Am I invited?" Nhika asked. She'd always wanted to ride on an airship.

Mimi blew out a strand of hair from her face. "Trust me. You don't want to go. Two days of smiling, talking, selling. Lying to people that our machines can save this city." She shook her head. "I'd much rather stay home with Hendon."

"Then stay home."

Mimi let out a light laugh. "It's an upside-down world, isn't it? Congmi Mai Minlan no longer gets what she wants."

They were just finishing up when someone knocked on the side of the building, drawing their attention. It was Hendon, hands clasped behind his back. "Someone has arrived for you."

"I'll be right there," Mimi said, pulling on her gloves.

"I should've specified—she's here for Nhika."

Nhika exchanged a wary look with Mimi. "Er, who?"

"She said her name was Numathai Lanalay. I've invited her to the parlor."

"You know her?" Mimi asked.

"Only by name." But Nhika couldn't pretend she wasn't dying to know more.

Hendon led the way. Nhika hadn't expected to ever see Lanalay again—had assumed she'd made away with the commissioner's secrets. But when Hendon dropped her off at the parlor, there Lanalay was, walking a finger down the spines of Mr. Congmi's books.

Her outfit was, in a word, bold. She'd foregone the Theuman customs of long sleeves and long pants, opting instead for a simple dress with short sleeves and a slit at the thigh that revealed the skin of her legs. A winter shawl wrapped her shoulders, but it was too small to cover all her skin. Nhika couldn't help but notice all the social blunders where she might never have before. At least Lanalay knew to wear gloves in Theumas, but they ended at the wrist when they should've traveled the arm.

She had cuts along her arm—scars, some still red. Nhika's heart fell, knowing that if Lanalay were a heartsooth, all those wounds would be healed. Her arms, too, had muscle, and it set her apart. She didn't look like a socialite. She looked like a soldier.

"Are these books yours?" Lanalay asked.

"They belong to the late Mr. Congmi."

"Well then, he had a fondness for Yarongese stories," Lanalay said. She tipped back one of the books to expose the cover. "This is a translation of the tale of Talahun. One of our most famous."

"I'm not familiar with it."

"It's about the tragic lover Talahun who looked upon a noblewoman and fell in love. When she asks for proof, he has nothing to offer her—except a severed finger. And each time she doubted his loyalty thereafter, he'd give her another finger, then a hand, then an ear—until he'd cut himself up into little pieces for her."

Nhika clucked her tongue. "And here I thought romance was dead."

Lanalay didn't laugh. Nhika found herself missing Kochin—even if he antagonized her, it was still *entertaining*. Instead, Lanalay gestured to the chairs, an invitation to sit, but Nhika still wasn't sure why she'd been asked to meet. From anyone else, Nem or Ngut or Santo, it would've put her on edge. Right now, she was only curious.

They sat across from each other. "I thought you'd made it pretty clear you didn't want to talk to me anymore," Nhika said.

"I need another favor," Lanalay said, but it sounded more like a demand.

"Oh? The one I gave you at Nem's party wasn't enough?"

Lanalay shifted her jaw, like she finally saw Nhika as a person, rather than a tool. "Right, I suppose I owe you a thank-you."

"And an apology." Nhika threw a glance toward the door, just to make sure they were alone. "What were you doing sneaking around the commissioner's home?"

Lanalay's expression darkened. For a moment, Nhika almost feared Lanalay might actually be an undercover agent, and she'd made a blatant accusation—political subtlety had never been her strength. But Lanalay said, "It's not what you think."

"Tell me what it is, and I'll decide."

"I . . . can't."

"Then we have no business, Ms. Numathai."

Lanalay pressed her lips thin. "You know important people. You even know one of the commissioners. Commissioner Nem has an upcoming exhibition in the sky, and I *need* to be there."

That stalled Nhika. This exhibition—the same one Mimi had mentioned—was starting to sound important. But Nhika saw no reason for a translator from Yarong to be there. "I've been warned it's a dreadful affair."

"Let me be the judge of that."

"What's it to you?"

"It's everything to me."

"I've seen the shining lights, Ms. Numathai. Trust me, they're not worth it." Nhika's story was a cautionary tale: called by the gold, killed by the cave-in.

Lanalay leaned forward, hands bunched in her lap. For the first time, she looked desperate, not so cold, nor contemptuous. "Your commissioner has something that belongs to me," she blurted, and only after did she check if someone else might've been eavesdropping. When she found no one, she added, "I need it back."

This seemed earnest. "What is it?"

"The last memory of my grandmother on this earth," Lanalay responded. By instinct, Nhika's hand went to her sternum, but her bone ring wasn't there. There were other Yarongese customs of remembrance, but she didn't know of any that might interest a commissioner.

"Why would Nem have it?"

Lanalay drew closer. "I don't know. My guess is that he believes it will win him this war."

Nem's secret weapon—he'd been so confident. "Well, can it?"

For a long time, Lanalay kept Nhika's gaze. Then she said, "If it could've won wars, then Yarong never would've fallen to Daltanny in the first place."

"That's what you were looking for in his villa, wasn't it?" Nhika figured.

"Yes. But it wasn't there. I realized it must be in that airship, waiting for the exhibition. So, I need to be there. You can help me."

"I don't remember making promises," Nhika said quickly. "I'm not even invited."

"But you know the Congmi family," Lanalay pressed. "You could whisper into the ear of the commissioner himself. Some of us would die for that honor."

And Nhika *had* died for the honor. In Lanalay's words, she saw a shadow of the past: herself, months ago, watching a certain physician's aide traipse among stars and wondering how he could take the night sky for granted.

But Lanalay wanted something from Commissioner Nem. She might've even wanted something he considered a weapon. To get Lanalay on that airship would be nothing short of criminal espionage—and worse, it would put Lanalay within Nem's crosshairs. The girl didn't even know how to match gloves with her dress. Nhika could not steer her toward a commissioner who bullied and drank and had pressed Andao beneath his thumb.

Just like that, she was Kochin at the wake, watching a Yarongese girl from across the room accept a business card from a diabolical doctor. She was Kochin over the phone, wishing that girl on the line wasn't so damned persistent about climbing into her own grave.

And she was Kochin with heartsooth books in his hands, wondering if it would be such a terrible thing to help her in her quest.

Nhika knew how that tale went. She had a bullet wound in her shoulder to remind her of the ending.

"I'm sorry," Nhika said. "I . . . I can't get you on the airship."

Disbelief drew Lanalay's brow. A muscle twitched in her jaw. "You're the only familiar face I've seen since coming to this city-state. I thought . . . I thought you might understand."

That one struck deep. Nhika felt the guilt in her sternum, right where her bone ring might hang. "I *do*, but—"

"You're Yarongese, aren't you?"

Nhika swallowed. "I'm Yarongese-Theuman."

"Do you know what a heartsooth is?"

She wasn't sure how to answer in a way that might satisfy Lanalay. Suddenly, she didn't even know what it meant to be a heartsooth—because she soothed only in the way her grandmother had taught her, in the way that survived in Theumas. That was nothing like the heartsoothing on Yarong. "I've heard of it."

"You may be more familiar with the Daltan term, *bloodcarver*. It's the gift of healing passed through my culture—*our* culture. My grandmother was a heartsooth. When the Daltans came, they destroyed the gift and anyone who might pass it on. They invented a new word for it, *bloodcarving*—that's the name Theumas uses, too, isn't it? They pillaged graves because they believed our corpses might give them the same gift they despised about us. They've tainted the very memory of heartsoothing." Each word drove the blade deeper into Nhika's chest, and Lanalay's glare walled her in. "It's your history, too. Don't you care to preserve it?"

She did—and that's why she couldn't walk Lanalay to her death. Keeping the legacy of heartsoothing alive simply meant surviving, and Nhika had failed that once already. Now, the only other heartsooth she knew was somewhere on Yarong, and she didn't even know if he was *alive*. So this time, she had to be the one leveling the gun on the girl in the shophouse, telling her to leave everything well enough alone.

"Nothing on that airship is worth making an enemy out of Theumas's most powerful man," Nhika said—her final answer. It haunted her just to say it.

Disappointment drew across Lanalay's expression, and the coldness returned. "I see," she said. "I thought we might see eye to eye. It seems I was mistaken."

She stood, paused a moment—like she was giving Nhika a chance to change her mind. But Nhika remained silent, tight lipped as she stared at the floor, and Lanalay left the room. Nhika let her.

Mother, she didn't know how Kochin had done it—seeing someone so much like himself yet purposefully driving her away.

Then again, he'd never been able to pull the trigger.

⇛ ༒ ⇚

Nhika was still thinking about Lanalay that night—all the things she should've asked, should've done. She wondered if Lanalay herself was a heartsooth. She wondered what that meant on Yarong. But in the end, it was for the best she never asked. That was where Kochin had failed—he hadn't been able to keep away.

Piece by piece, she changed out of her outfit and into a nightdress. She wasn't sure when she'd started wearing the aristocratic getup every day, the high collars and the pleated pants and the . . . gloves. But she doffed them, and they came off like ink spilling down her arms.

As Nhika went to unclasp her dress, her elbow bumped the full-length mirror. It swiveled, catching the glint of moonlight off something behind her bed. Nhika stalled with her hands behind her back, still reaching for the zipper, and squinted at the reflection—a metal chain and something silver at the end of it, indiscernible within the shadow of her bed.

Urged by curiosity, she crouched down near the head of her bed, arm clawing behind her frame for the catch of metal. She found it, her fingers closing around something firm and familiar: her *ring*. There was something else there, both of them caught on the woodwork of her bed frame. She gave a firmer yank; something gave, and Nhika drew out her ring on her palm.

Some long-rooted anxiety released from her chest as she saw her bone ring, the familiar matte of its onyx and the jagged crack through its bone segments. It must've been caught on the trelliswork of her bed frame all this time. If she'd known it had been with her, she might've looked for it, but Nhika had expected it to be with . . .

Brows knitting, she turned the necklace over in her palm. She'd always kept it on a cord of woven rope, but now it was on a metal chain, stained with a sediment like rust. Alongside it was something else, something she took a moment to recognize.

It was a pair of those oval-shaped ID tags, the kind collected off dead soldiers. The tarnished engraving on this one spelled out a name:

VEN KOCHIN.

FOURTEEN
TWO MONTHS AGO

ANXIOUS WHISPERS HELD THE WALLS OF THEIR submarine vessel together as much as nuts and bolts did. Kochin and his squadron were in one of many, their numbers lining the walls as they trawled forward. The trip was seven hours long, but Kochin had already lost track of the time.

They traveled by a Congmi vessel. With a shape resembling a prawn, it glided beneath the surface, metal but for the bulbous glass dome at its front from which the captain guided their craft through the abyss.

The others had started the journey joking and chatting. But they fell silent now—perhaps because, this far in, there was nothing left to talk about. Or perhaps it was because there was nothing outside the circular windows but crushing, oppressive darkness. The light had disappeared a long time ago and, with it, hopes of the surface.

Kochin was one of three medics in his squadron of thirty. Theirs would not be the first landing; they would enter into combat, with the sole goal of helping advance the beachhead. Before nightfall, the aim was to claim Langabien, which Theuman operations had code-named Majora after the northern star; it was the northernmost Yarongese labor camp on the island and, hopefully, their first field base.

Beside Kochin, strapped into the hull, was his pack, full of trauma shears, clotting gauze, bandage rolls, saline, abdominal pads. He'd memorized its contents down to the smallest pocket, but all those tools were only just as good as a bird in his palm.

The vessel stuttered as it came to a stop. Privates exchanged wide-eyed stares, knowing that the sand beneath them was now Yarongese soil, and that meant they were in Daltan territory. With the whirring of rotors and stutter of fins, the vessel swiveled so that its rear faced forward; they were preparing to beach.

Nervous murmurs rumbled through the hull, accentuated by some poorly placed jokes, mistimed shows of false courage. A pit of anticipation hung in his narrowed throat, and his dry tongue stuck to the roof of his mouth, but Kochin was not afraid. That only came from having something to lose.

He brought his hand to his chest. Underneath his jacket and undershirt, he felt the prominence of Nhika's bone ring. It was a reminder that he wasn't in this war for the same reason as the rest of Theumas.

Their lieutenant emerged from the cabin, slapping the metal archway to announce his presence. "Attention!" he said. "We're two klicks out from the beach. We'll be entering a firefight—our allies have already started things without us. They've met the resistance of Daltan soldiers in the jungle, so I want the rifle squads to establish cover fire while the rest of us set up mortars at the beachhead. Is that understood?"

The platoon chorused their assent.

Kochin's heart mounted in his chest as the submarine lurched forward. Up there, he would have a different goal than the rest of his crew. Along with the two other medics, he was responsible for keeping everyone else alive—or collecting their ID tags.

Their submarine stuttered to a stop and hollow thuds resounded around the vessel, heralding their disembarkment. Their lieutenant strolled up to the rear, whipping the platoon into preparedness as he did. There was a clamor of buckles and rifles and packs, and then they were all up and facing the great bay door at the back of the submarine. Kochin slung his pack over one shoulder, checked his pistol on his hip, and held his breath.

Water gurgled around them. Machinery clunked in the hull, and the light shifted in the vessel; they'd surfaced. With a jarring lurch, the submarine beached itself on the sands and the bay doors hissed open.

As soon as the beaches revealed themselves, the lieutenant signaled for them to advance. In the dimness of the sub lights and under the speckle of gunfire, they all rushed onto Yarong.

Water infiltrated Kochin's boots as he trudged forward, the humidity of the evening air thickening in his lungs. He kept his eyes forward, head bent, and teeth gritted as their lieutenant carved a path for them toward the first beachhead. In the darkness, the jungle was just a breathing mass of canopy, crackling with the drumroll of bullets like a thundercloud lit by lightning. In front of him was the promise of violence, but behind him was an endless wall of water; there was no way to go but forward.

And yet, Kochin stood frozen with his steel-tipped boots in

the sand. His allies maneuvered around him, kicking up water, but Kochin couldn't move. After all he'd done to get here, enlisting and training and *injuring* that soldier, he could not set foot on Yarong.

In his mother's stories, it was a home, cities set in paradise with their proud, resilient people. In Theuman newspapers, it was just war-torn jungle and beach, nothing more than a tragedy. But right now, Kochin saw neither of those things. He saw the island as though he were soothing it: a body fighting infection, its blood beating hot and heavy just to burn away the virus. He saw Yarong in the shape of a girl, an open wound in her shoulder bleeding into the surf.

And he saw his own gravestone, its epitaph written by the Mother Herself: HIS BLOOD CAME FROM YARONG, AND IT'LL SPILL HERE TOO.

Artillery fire splattered across the beaches, throwing up geysers of sand and tufts of smoke. Kochin's instincts punched back through his skull, and he lunged forward to join the defensive line established by the sharpshooters. His breath was ragged, the air too humid and thick—like his lungs gleaned more water than oxygen from it. Around him, darkness consumed anything that wasn't lit by gunfire until all he saw was the combat, the glow of a rifle barrel and the trails that mortars carved through the sky.

A bullet whizzed past his ear as he reached the beachfront. Kochin fell to the sand, tasting the grit of it in his mouth, just as a cry lanced the air. Blood dirtied the sand before him as his comrade fell, already in hysterics.

Kochin was quick to move, dragging his wounded ally behind

the cover of driftwood. From his bag he emptied an assortment of items, shears and bandages and gauze. Sand infiltrated everything, wet with either salt water or blood, but he worked quickly to strip off the soldier's vest.

The shot had landed in the lateral shoulder. Kochin imagined it shattered the joint, but he didn't voice the fear aloud. Instead, he cut through the shirt to reveal skin, dark with blood.

When he worked under Santo, Kochin had mastered soothing his patients without their awareness. A part of it came from the innocuousness of his Theuman looks, but the other part was the lightness of his touch. Much like sleight of hand, it was about distracting the patient with one sensation while delivering another.

This patient, however—howling in pain and body convulsing in hysterical sobs—needed no distraction. Kochin drew out a wad of hemostatic gauze and pressed it to the soldier's shoulder.

"Hold pressure here," he ordered over the hail of gunfire. The soldier complied, and the flash of a mortar off his ID tag revealed his name: Jint Laom. "Stay still, all right, Laom?"

"Am I going to die?" Laom asked, and his wide eyes betrayed his panic.

For a moment, there was a lull in the gunfire, a gap where Kochin could hear his own thoughts. He almost found it in himself to laugh at Laom's melodrama, because it was only a gunshot wound and this soldier was lucky enough to find himself in the care of a heartsooth.

"You'll survive," he promised, and drew out the bandages. As he worked to wrap the wound, his influence seeped into Laom where his palm rested against biceps. The repetition of gunfire droned to a buzz as his senses drowned, a welcome reprieve from the chaos. For a moment, the battle washed away, and Kochin could imagine he was in one of Santo's examination rooms—just him and this patient and the touch between them. Laom's body came into unnatural visibility, as though illuminated by day. Kochin could see the wound with new clarity, the shattered bone and shorn vessels, even as he concealed it beneath the bandage.

In this state of panic, Laom lacked the lucidity to fight Kochin's influence. As Kochin drew calories from Laom's liver, he knew the soldier would mistake the warmth for adrenaline. He would not feel how his skin sewed itself back together beneath the pain. He would attribute the mitigated bleed to gauze, instead of Kochin's handiwork.

But Kochin would leave the bones as they were; this beach was not the place to piece the jigsaw puzzle of the boy's shoulder back together. He worked quickly otherwise, knotting off the bandage by only muscle memory while his mind was set on soothing. By the time he'd finished, Laom's frantic breaths had subsided to pants.

Laom removed his helmet, the inky mess of his hair plastered to his forehead with a ripe sheen of sweat. Now, seeing him fully, Kochin realized how young he was, just a boy like himself. And here, soothing his first patient, the *momentousness* of the war finally hit him, like pulling his head out of the water. He was a soldier. He was a *soldier*.

And the very same war that had uprooted his mother's life was coming for him, too.

The momentary panic slipped from his mind as the blare of gunfire returned, louder than his soothing. Kochin grabbed Laom's helmet and dropped it back on his head. "Keep your head. It's not over yet," he said, then left to find another injured.

The night lasted indefinitely, a ruthless pocket of time that looped on into infinity, its boundaries demarcated only by the flash of artillery and the wails of the newly injured. Kochin spent it with his belly against the sand, crawling between spattered gunfire to drag fallen soldiers into the cover of the advancing beachhead, which crept its way toward the jungles.

There was no room for thinking between the whistling bullets and hollered orders. Kochin acted only by the guidance of his two hands; his mind was on just what he saw before him, the dark well of blood and pale glare of bone catching his eyes as beacons did. He could smell it, too, the metal tang of blood that arose toward the early hours of morning, frothing with the salt of seafoam and hanging in the smoke-filled air. Over the course of hours, his bag thinned of supplies until he was substituting strips of uniforms for bandages and taking more from livers than he should've. As he stole calories to mend wounds, his thoughts were on Nhika, gifted with the miracle of giving.

The first break came near dawn. Under the orange promise of sunrise, two beachheads connected, and their combined battalion managed to overwhelm the gun tower at their vertex. Sharpshooters clambered up the ramshackle wooden structure in droves, tossing Daltan soldiers from the top and turning the mounted artillery toward the jungle. Those Daltan soldiers found themselves trampled underfoot as Theumans advanced toward their target, Majora.

Kochin watched the Daltan soldiers as he passed. Those who hadn't died sat injured and feeble, stripped of their weapons and left to be collected as prisoners of war after the fight. One part of him wanted to raise a pistol to their temples and deliver them from this fight. The other part begged him to heal them, because some of their injuries needn't spell death and disability if they saw the urgent care of a heartsooth. But he reminded himself that he wasn't on this beach for a moment's whim; he was here with a goal, uncowed by fleeting compassion for an enemy that would sooner shoot him than accept his help.

So, he kept his eyes forward and head low, following the swelling tsunami of Theuman forces as they crept forward through the jungle. Kochin was glad for the growing light; the ground was a thicket of brush and rotten wood, with holes and drop-offs that threatened to swallow any thoughtless step. And swallow they did; when bodies fell, Kochin would have to dive through the foliage to search for them and drag them to cover behind the thick folds of kapok trunks. But, after securing a sheltered grotto of the forest, he and the other medics laid down a bivouac, where he stayed to tend to the wounded while others left to collect them.

This detachment was never something he felt with his patients at the Theumas Medical Center. There, every patient had a name, a history, a family. Every encounter started with a quip, a jest, a story. But here, Kochin found himself categorizing them by wound and priority. Underneath the helmets, with their slick black Theuman hair and muddied skin, they all looked the same to him. So he cut, and bandaged, and soothed, focusing only on what he saw before him lest the terror of the night swallow him whole.

Kochin sensed the arrival of their victory when the battle slowed around morning. The sun had risen in full; the incoming wounded had slowed despite the rising visibility. Kochin managed to take a breath between patients, lifting his gaze from the bodies for a moment to stare in wonderment at that horizon.

Shafts of sunlight broke through gaps between broad tree trunks, melting into the golden sand of the beaches and washing a new warmth into his skin. His gaze followed it to the water, finding the horizon endless and tinged with a morning fog. Now, as gunfire lulled and the jungle saw longer gaps of silence, the tropical birds had returned overhead, inspired to start a cautious melody.

He was here. Two feet firmly on Yarongese soil, having bypassed Daltan mandates and isolationist policies. The tunnel vision that had gotten him here cleared from his mind for a moment, just enough to allow him to appreciate this, how suddenly close Nhika was. If any of his brothers asked, he would've told him he didn't believe in the Mother—but that wasn't entirely true, because how else would he have gotten here if She hadn't had Her hand on his back?

He perked up as a noise grew in the distance. First, he mistook it for a collection of human screams, a mass casualty. But, as it continued, ebbing and swelling, he realized it was cheering.

One of his fellow medics launched past him and up the hill. She crested it, a hand shielding her eyes from the sun as they scanned the jungle. When she looked back toward the bivouac, her face held only jubilation and she yanked her helmet from her head.

"We've done it!" she rasped; perhaps it was the first time she'd used her voice all night, or perhaps she'd lost it yelling to patients over the cacophony of war. "They've taken Majora!"

Now, the medics were erupting into cheers. The wounded, too, where they could. Someone clapped Kochin on the back so hard he stumbled forward and needed a moment to regain his bearings. When he did, his tunnel vision returned with him.

"Let's get the wounded up the hill," he instructed. "They'll have better care inside Langabien's walls." Before the others could question the instruction of a private, he gathered the tarps into makeshift stretchers and looked to the rest of them for help.

They were slow to move, perhaps confused on why he had called Majora by its Yarongese name, Langabien. Or perhaps they were still coming off the dregs of their victory. But Kochin didn't give himself time to celebrate; there would be time for that when Nhika opened her eyes again.

This battle on the beach was only the beginning.

Through the morning, Theuman forces turned Langabien into Majora, one of the many camps they planned to establish before they moved on to the naval base and retook the island.

The labor camp was a compound of dirt and clay in a clearing of tree stumps, fenced in by thick wire and guarded on its five vertices by watchtowers. Stilt houses huddled close to one another on one side, with soldiers gathering underneath their shade as the sun rose in full, while the remainder of the property housed empty yards and lone wooden structures.

They had freed the Yarongese prisoners within, but many stayed. Kochin learned that these were not just laborers; they were rebels, dissenters, members of the Yarongese resistance who had fought for the past nineteen years of Kochin's life while families like his had chosen to flee. Some were young enough, Kochin's age, that they wouldn't have ever seen a free Yarong. They fought anyway—had never stopped fighting, even as Daltanny came in with fire and plague, as villages were razed.

Theumas could've offered its military support a generation ago. Suddenly, Kochin didn't feel so horrible about his city at war.

Some of the Yarongese prisoners returned to their families, but those who stayed picked up Theuman weapons and offered their expertise. While caring for patients at the newly established field hospital, Kochin passed many Yarongese fighters. He wondered if any of them were heartsooths; the art had seen a firmer cull on the island than it had in Theumas. He also wondered if any of these locals could see the Yarongese in him. Even if they could, Kochin's Yarongese half was a breed apart from the Yarongese here. On Theumas, he'd always felt too Yarongese; here, he was nothing but Theuman.

In passing, he heard his lieutenant colonel interacting with a group of Yarongese freedom fighters. One stood at the front of the group: a girl who looked his age, whose features were elegant but roughened, especially with her glower. She was translating from Yarongese into accented Theuman. It surprised him; Yarong had likely been in isolation her entire life, so she could've only learned the language from her family.

"This is our home. We know it better than the Daltans do," she was saying. "Better than you, too—you need us."

The lieutenant colonel's eyes narrowed. "That's not for me to decide."

The girl continued translating: "You are fighting for military advantage. We're fighting for our home. You won't be able to take the naval base without our help."

"The naval base is our next target. We await the arrival of our acting commander in chief. Logistics can be negotiated then."

Acting commander in chief. Kochin ruminated on that—from his classes, he knew that in times of war, the Commission would appoint one of their own to carry out the military decisions of the rest. Considering the current lineup of the Commission, there was only one man learned enough in the art of war to claim that title: Commissioner Nem.

The thought reassured him. He'd always known the commissioner to be brash, prompt, and cunning—if there was anyone who could get Kochin into Yarong's naval base, where he might find the Daltan research, it was him.

It wouldn't be much longer now.

Langabien was the first base to be reclaimed under Theuman control, reerected as Majora, but it wasn't the last. Across the crescent-shaped island, more Theuman forces landed on beaches and stormed labor camps, converting them to field bases: Minora, Lumosa, Exora, Dendura. Upon hearing about the Theuman aid and the chance at rebellion, a few camps freed themselves. Each victory was an inch closer to his goal, but Kochin didn't let himself celebrate with the others. On his end, there was still much to be done. They had to siege the naval base, where Daltanny housed its research on Yarongese heartsooths. More than that, they had to *win*—so Kochin had time to pick through all that research, find something to his liking.

Then, *then* . . . he had to believe there was an answer in all that suffering. It didn't have to be an easy one; he'd pay any price to bring her back.

It was a week before the commander in chief came. Before the sun woke Kochin up, the clamor of privates and crunch of autocarriage tires did. He blinked into lucidity, banishing sleep just before it could drag him back into the pillow, and threw on cargo pants. Half of the privates were already awake, and the others were quick to follow as a commotion outside the stilt house drew their collective attention.

Apprehension came to him by instinct before he peered outside, and his hand flinched at his waist, missing the weight of a pistol. But his fears washed into curiosity as he saw the Theuman utility vehicles bouncing up the knotted path toward the camp. They rounded into the clearing, shedding new privates like a shaking dog shed fleas.

A massive vehicle followed them, swallowing saplings beneath its treads as it made its way over uneven forest ground. Soldiers held open the gates for the tanklike vehicle, which situated itself in the center of the clearing. With a hiss of steam, it opened its wide bay doors.

As Kochin had predicted, out stepped Commissioner Nem, followed by an armed entourage. Cries of admiration followed his appearance, but he waved away the attention, instead gesturing back toward the bay of the vehicle.

Guided by technicians, out rolled one, two, *three* automatons. They were humanoid in shape, but only vaguely: the head a domed cockpit, the torso a breastplate of armor, and the legs treaded like those of a tank. A ladder climbed the back and weapons mounted both shoulders.

"Behold," Commissioner Nem announced. "The Congmi Industries' 'Guardian.'"

Kochin's eyes flared in surprise. He would've assumed the invention to be Commissioner Nem's design, but now he saw the Congmi insignia stamped on the side, a half-circle cog with their name written within. That was a shock, seeing the Congmi symbol in a war zone. Congmi Vun Quan had made no attempts to hide his pacifism. It would seem his son, though he had inherited all the intelligence and savvy, had not inherited his father's ideals.

"Would you look at that?" said a familiar voice at his side, and he startled. When he turned, Nhika was there, so bright in her red robe compared to the sea of drab military uniforms. "Nem must've finally gotten to Andao."

Or the war did, Kochin thought but didn't voice aloud. Briefly, he wondered if there was someone on this side of the water he now cared to protect.

He got his answer as the next utility vehicle rolled into the yard. The reinforcements disembarked, dressed in uniforms and boots that hadn't yet seen combat, and there among them he saw a familiar face that belonged to a different lifetime: Dep Trin.

He seemed the only true soldier in his squadron of boys—tall, broad shouldered, and with the straight-backed posture of someone already accustomed to taking orders. Somehow, he'd gained more muscle since Kochin had last seen him, and he looked better fitted to this career than his last one as an aristocrat's minder. Kochin receded a step into the crowd, not forgetting Trin's ire at him.

The clearing fell quiet again as Commissioner Nem mounted one of the Guardians. He unlatched the cockpit, lowered himself inside, and closed the hatch upon himself. Within, behind reinforced, metal-gridded glass, Kochin could only see the top of his head. He imagined it would take a great number of bullets to pierce the hull; the name Guardian seemed apt.

The Guardian hummed to life under Commissioner Nem's control. Even a brief display was impressive; the body swiveled with a great degree of range and its arms moved as naturally as though they were jointed with elbows and shoulders. It seemed that the Congmis had tired of turning metal to men; now they set their sights on turning men to metal.

"Clear the yard!" yelled a technician, and soldiers and

Yarongese people alike scattered as the Guardian swiveled toward a tree. With astonishing efficiency, it unloaded a round of bullets into the trunk, tearing up shards of bark and wood. The tree began to tilt; a shock rippled through the soldiers as it fell toward a stilt house.

Jets flared to life behind the Guardian's treads, launching Commissioner Nem forward. The Guardian maneuvered with a grace unlike any machine Kochin had ever seen, its treads kicking sand. Before the tree could fully fall, Commissioner Nem had roped it back with steel cables shot from the arms of the Guardian. With a burst of power, he heaved the tree aside.

A chorus of applause drew up from the crowd. Kochin felt his morale soar with them, more confident than ever that they could siege the naval base, that he could penetrate its walls and find the research he sought within.

With a hiss of steam, the cockpit of the Guardian popped open and Commissioner Nem hopped out, bowing after his performance. He didn't need to say anything more; the machine had already spoken for him, its message clear:

The Daltans had best learn how to run.

FIFTEEN
ONE MONTH AGO

THE GENERALS PLANNED TO TAKE THE NAVAL BASE at night. With the base sitting on open beach, its straight-edged walls just brushing the jungle and its campus otherwise exposed, darkness only played to a Theuman advantage. It would be a mobilized attack, consisting of all the labor camps that had fallen and been resurrected under Theuman control, aided by Yarongese freedom fighters. They had the advantage of the dark, local expertise, and the Congmi war armor, yet Kochin still held his breath with aching nervousness. Too much hinged on tonight, all of it out of his control. If they could not siege those brick walls, if he could not find the documents he needed, if Daltanny had never even discovered his answer . . .

Well, then all this would be for nothing.

Kochin clenched his fists to quell the tremor in his hands. They'd divided up the battlefield as a twelve-hour clock with the base at its center, and he'd been assigned to five o'clock—the thick of the jungle, where the hill sloped up to overlook the water. He imagined the island in its prime, back before any foreign touch: the cradle of the earth curving around the bay like a lover curled in bed, the dark water a perfect mirror of the Star Belt, the white-sand beaches unstained by spilled blood.

Now, the geometric, concrete eyesore of the Daltan naval base marred the landscape like a pale scab, starkly separated from the rest of the island by austere walls, cubic compounds, and chained fences. Docks jutted into the water, some lined with battleships but most empty; the majority had been drawn out into naval warfare by the Theuman navy this morning.

Kochin didn't know what conquering the naval base meant to Theumas. There was talk in the air: freedom restored to Yarong, eliminating the closest Daltan threat to Theumas. Despite his mother's roots on this island—*his* roots on the island—Kochin couldn't find the energy to care about those far-off plans. There was only one thing on his mind.

She was with him now in the silence and darkness. Nhika's apparition appeared everywhere and nowhere, her figure lingering at the edge of his vision only to disappear when he turned, replaced by the shadow of a fellow soldier. But he knew she was there, could feel her warmth against the sticky humidity of the jungle night. Perhaps her ghost was hanging on to the outcome of this night as much as he was—because this battle determined everything. Wordlessly, he and the rest of his squadron watched the base, waiting for the signal to advance.

It came as a silent flash in the night: a lone meteor, the blaze of a mortar arcing through the sky with a smoke trail to follow. Half a dozen more launched in its wake, and as they reached their apogee, every soldier around Kochin held their breath.

Sound only returned to the jungle as the mortars landed. The blast was a sharp knife, a clean slice through the whisper of the leaves, and a cloud of debris plumed up from the southernmost naval complex. All at once, the beach exploded to life.

Great lights turned on in the complex, whiter than any electric light Kochin had seen before. It blinded him to look at them, so he kept his gaze low as he followed the forward shuffle of his squadron, picking his way down the hillside. Resembling ants from a crushed mound, little Daltan soldiers scurried around the base, assimilating into some defensive position, as alarms wailed through the jungle. Kochin heard the familiar whir and click of war armor as Guardians mobilized, tearing their way through the foliage.

Now, he was grateful for the weeks he spent in boot camp. With the disadvantage of darkness, this forested slope would've been untraversable if not for the habits formed during that time, the instincts that kept him light on his feet as the ground fell away beneath him and the stamina that kept him going even as his legs burned.

When he reached the base of the hill, the Guardian leading his squad had already breached the fence. The devastation in his wake was animallike, as though an ox had raged through a chain-link fence, dragging the posts with it and bowing metal bars under unnatural strength. Kochin and the other soldiers slipped in behind it, ducking away from the scattered fire of mounted guns.

"Help me!" cried a strangled voice, drowned in panic. Kochin dipped in that direction, separating from his squadron under a spatter of brick dust. Bright beams of light swept near his position, then over the injured soldier. Kochin waited for them to clear before creeping forward, keeping close to the wall as his comrades advanced their front under the cover of a Guardian. By the stroboscopic light of gunfire, the war armor looked like something out of a nightmare, impossibly fast and fearfully strong. Fire sprayed from its limbs and bullets sparked off its plating, drawing fear even into Kochin's throat. The Congmi logo was visible on the breastplate; it may have been the last thing so many soldiers saw before they fell. In Theumas, the Congmi name was synonymous with innovation; to the Daltans, it would mean nothing but violence.

Turning his gaze forward, Kochin reached the injured soldier. PHUA, read her ID tag. She was clutching her shoulder with both hands, a stripe of blood running down her cheek and teeth clenched with grit. She panted heavily, eyes wide with panic though she tried to hide it behind a falsified fortitude.

He dropped to a knee. Slung his pack around. Drew out trauma shears. It was too loud to hear his own breath over the rolling thunder of gunfire, too loud even to hear Phua as her lips moved. She was asking him something, but the words were lost to the clamor.

He made a gesture for her to let him see the wound. Her lips were thin with reluctance as she loosened her fingers, but not so much that he could see the extent of the damage. He soothed her as he sheared away her vest, visualizing the wound even before her blood-damp shirt fell away from it. It was a shot through her ribs, and the metallic taste that rose on his tongue told him the bullet was still lodged somewhere in there. The wound sucked air and he could feel the burble of blood in her lungs, red in his vision. It drew him back in time, to a hospital hallway drenched in moonlight where he drowned in his own blood. There was Nhika bent above him, so close. Tears streaked her cheeks, pupils blown with distress.

He saw the bullet trace a line through the air, spinning on its axis as it embedded itself in Nhika's chest. Time slowed to a crawl as she recoiled, the full spectrum of her shock and pain playing on her face in torturous clarity. Her name snatched the breath from his throat as she fell away, hand gripping his shoulder and eyes glazed with anguish.

"Help me, Kochin," Nhika cried, the words breathless.

Help me. He reached out, but she was too far, and his body had failed under his control. How? How could he help her when his gift could only take from her? When there was no way to return what she had given him? When he was not *enough*? *Help me.*

"Help me!" Hands snatched at his coat lapels, yanking him forward. Kochin blinked back to the battlefield. Phua had grabbed him close, her bloodied grip tight around his jacket and her eyes bugged with panic. "Please."

Kochin let out a shuddering breath, heartbeat ramming its way out of his rib cage. The vision was slow to clear until he saw the glare of moonlight off Dr. Santo's gun was just the blare of the base's lampposts, and the smell of blood was not from him, but from Phua. His hands shook violently when they never had before, and the gunfire was suddenly overwhelming. He wanted to be anywhere but here; he yearned for the warmth of his houseboat, for the comfort of Nhika's palms against his.

Instead, he clamped his fingers down over congealing blood.

"You're going to be all right," he assured her, and whether or not she believed him, some of the tension seeped out of her body.

Now redrawn into reality, Kochin worked fast, digging up gauze and bandages from his bag and stopping the bleeding. It was at least a clean entry, easy to cover with a chest seal. He leaned in close to say, "Can you walk?"

She tried with great effort, but he stopped her when he saw the pain spike in her expression. Kochin expanded the field stretcher hooked to his bag and helped her roll on before draping a blanket over her. Even in the heat of the tropical summer, he worried that shock could set in quickly. He gave her something for the pain before dragging her out under the threat of crossfire. In his luck, his squadron had pushed toward the middle of the naval base, all fronts of combat converging toward the center, the vanguard fronted by those Guardians. Still, Kochin was vigilant for the dark brown uniform of a Daltan soldier, reassured by the weight of the gun at his hip. All he saw was the blue-and-black livery of Theuman infantry as he dragged his patient around the curve of the hill, where the medics had set up triage under the protection of sharpshooters.

His companions rushed to help his patient when he arrived. Kochin set down the handles of the drag stretcher, only now noticing how his palms burned with fatigue. His muscles shook, shoulders aflame, and his heartsoothing felt the sourness of acid in his legs. He'd turned to help his patient when a rumble shook the earth, the sound of a collapsing building and an upward draft of concrete dust to follow. Kochin whipped his attention back to the naval base, eyes widening with horror as he saw a mountain of rubble where one of the towers once stood.

No . . . no, no, no! The word caught in his throat; he was too afraid to say it aloud, too afraid to be anything but a Theuman combat medic, ready and loyal. But the Theuman mortars and armored soldiers were collapsing buildings. The very thing he'd come here for may well be lost under a mound of rubble. If the Theuman forces planned on leveling the naval base in their siege, he needed to find any Daltan research within first.

"I'm returning for another!" he called to his medic-in-arms, then sprinted back toward the base.

Gunfire welcomed him as he reentered the envelope of battle. Kochin threw himself behind a wall as a mounted gun rounded its aim toward him, shielding his head in his arms when its bullets buried themselves into the dirt beside him. Somewhere from the far end of the base, he heard a blast that lit the sky for a chilling moment. Seconds later, he felt the wave of heat pass over him, choking his breath and drying his eyes. Braving the open, Kochin edged toward the corner and threw a glance toward the expanse of the base. If he had to guess, the research ward would've been in the central compound, rather than the peripheral hangars. He'd have to infiltrate the heart of the base, somehow.

Serendipity brought his answer. A mortar rained from the sky like a shooting star, whistling as it fell. It crashed through the ceiling of the compound, its blast carving a yawning hole in the side.

Sensing a lull in the gunfire, Kochin ran. His trajectory took him into the open. Broad-beam lights swept across his path and bullets shrieked past him as he sprinted. His legs pushed harder than they ever had before. Every nerve in his body tensed in anticipation of pain, a bullet to end him or a blast to cripple him.

Someone called for a medic. He registered their voice automatically above the cacophony, and for just a moment, his steps faltered. Their voice was ripe with desperation and muted under hailing artillery. Would anyone else hear them? Would anyone else know?

For a moment he stood frozen in the open, stunned into inaction. But then another mortar glanced off the base, collapsing a portion of its corner, and Kochin started forward again. He drowned out the cries for a medic with the heaviness of his own breathing; there was no time for anything else. In the moment, all he knew how to do was run.

A band of Daltan soldiers found him just before he reached the cover of the building. They called something out in Daltan and his eyes widened as they turned rifles toward him. Kochin leaned forward in a full sprint as gunfire unleashed in his direction, then he lunged for the cover of the wall. Pain traced a length across the back of his neck as he did, a bullet grazing skin.

Kochin hit the far wall of the building hard. He'd made it to cover but allowed himself no time to rest before sprinting through the darkened hallways of the naval base. His hand reached up toward the new wound, finding a steady bleed down his neck. If the bullet had been any lower, he would've been left with a spine too shattered for even heartsoothing to fix.

As he continued on, turning wherever he saw fit, the sounds of the Daltanny soldiers' pursuit dimmed to a silence and the walls of the compound muffled the terror outside. At last, when an empty hallway full of dead lights stretched before him, Kochin allowed himself a moment to breathe.

He was here. After all this time, he'd made it.

This part of the compound had been emptied. Linoleum floors and stark walls made up the interior of the naval base, and there was little here to suggest he was still on Yarong. This was the Daltanny he'd read about in textbooks, the austere concrete architecture carving a place for itself on this part of the beach. All the signage was in Daltan, but the language shared a root with Theuman, and he guessed at the meaning of phrases as he hobbled forward, hand on his pistol. The building shook with the ferocity of an earthquake at indeterminable intervals, the rumbling brought on by the Theuman onslaught.

"Hurry. This building is due to collapse," came a voice, and Nhika's image sidled up from behind him.

"Nhika," he exhaled, so relieved to see her even if only a ghost. For a blissful second, he could almost forget where he was.

"There are lights down the hall," she warned, halting them both. He glanced up at the signage on the wall, determining that the hallway led nowhere good, and turned inward at the first junction he came to. Nhika followed, and he was briefly saddened at how his clearest memories of her were in places they weren't meant to be.

"There!" she said, pointing to a sign above them. "'Rechesh'— research. That sounds promising."

He nodded. It was a part of a longer phrase, with an arrow leading down the stairs. He banked left and hastened down a floor, following signage until he came to an underground part of the base molded out of concrete and lined with cables. The electric lamps overhead still worked down here, though they swayed and flickered with each rumble traveling the earth. Dust trickled from holes in the ceiling, and he hesitated to enter these undergrounds, lest the building collapse and trap him under twelve feet of stone.

But Nhika had continued forward, and he followed her as she strode past the main foyer, where offshoot hallways extended in each direction. From somewhere down the hall, footsteps turned the corner and the shadow of a Daltan group splayed across the wall. Kochin ducked behind a corner just as they turned into his hall.

He tensed. Fire worked through his muscles, down his arm—until he was flexing his fingers in anticipation to soothe.

No, to *carve*.

But it never came to pass. Someone burst out of a bisecting hallway, crashing into the first of the soldiers. Bullets spattered, bulbs burst, and Kochin retreated back into cover. When next he glanced into the hallway, he found a girl standing over the bodies, a pistol in her hands.

It was the translator from earlier, but that role was ill fitting. With her shirt torn, a bandanna wrapping a wound in her arm, and cuts lacing her skin, she was a soldier.

She stepped past the downed soldiers and turned left down the hall. Once she'd gone, Kochin came out of hiding.

"Seems like you're not the only one who abandoned your station," Nhika said.

It did nothing to lighten his guilt, having forsaken those voices outside who had called for a medic.

Kochin moved past the Daltan soldiers—dead. Their eyes were like glass, and in death, their expressions looked like those of an automaton awaiting a command roll. Despite himself, he had sympathy for them—he had to believe the dead deserved some remorse, no matter their crimes. It might've been the only way he'd ever find forgiveness.

Once he found the research ward, he began his exploration. Some of these rooms were cells, others large spaces with empty beds, and he recognized a couple as operating rooms, now decommissioned. With rising disappointment, he wondered if he had wandered into the wrong part of the base or, worse, if any remaining records had all been archived off-island. Room after room, abandoned and desolate, stained with oxidized blood and salt water. His chest squeezed tight with swelling defeat before he swallowed it back down, because he refused to accept this end. He had not made himself a bloodcarver over concrete dust and the whispered memories of tortured Yarongese.

. . . Had he?

"Kochin," Nhika's voice came, delicate and small. He glanced up at her, and maybe the sadness showed through his eyes, because she gave him a wan smile. "It's okay."

"I know. I haven't given up."

"That's not what I meant."

He swallowed. "What did you mean?"

"Are you really doing this for *me*?"

"I..." A dozen responses came to him—that he was doing this for their future, one with her in it; that she'd sacrificed herself so that he could walk home, so he would pay it back in kind—but none of those excuses felt apt. "What else would I be doing it for?"

"I don't know. Guilt. Grief. Loneliness?"

The suggestion burned in his throat. Kochin sucked in a breath through his teeth, collecting the words. There was grief and loneliness sown into his love. Memories of her tormented him because he lived while she did not. He had replayed those encounters over and over, pinpointing every error that had led to her deathbed. First it was the heartsoothing books, the lure that had enticed her into his world, the first thread to tether them together. Then it was the pistol aimed at her head; he should not have asked her to come with him. He should've scared her away with the threat of the bullet, convinced her to flee to the Dog Borough and wipe her hands clean of the Congmis. Finally, it was the truth. He had shown her all of his cracks—she was a heartsooth; he should've known she would try to heal them. But he had asked her to give when he knew he could not reciprocate.

The guilt was the worst of all. It had taken him time and all his mother's reassurances to come to terms with the incompleteness of his gift. He was so sure it came from his Theuman half; his mother had told him the rest would come in time. And it had only taken one night in the Theumas Medical Center to remind him that, whatever his excuses, it hadn't been enough. Not to save himself and not to save Nhika.

Sometimes, he wondered—could he have stopped her from healing him? Could he have given back all that he had taken from her?

"It doesn't matter why I do it. It only matters that I bring you back," he said, stepping past the ghost of her. No one else would do it; no one else had the power to.

A few rooms remained. The Daltans had gone. Kochin was alone down in this research ward, with only Nhika's memory to keep him company. So, he got to work, rifling through room after room, hope dwindling as he did but the determination unshakable. If not in this building, then the next. If not on Yarong, then in Daltanny. If not there, then—Mother damn it all, he'd figure it out himself if he had to.

It was with the final room, one whose counters were assorted with a variety of rusted instruments and whose chairs had been strewn with some level of disarray, that he found it. A metal cabinet nestled into the corner with file drawers he only hoped weren't empty. Kochin fell to the floor beside them, his legs giving out from either excitement or relief, and tried the handle. Locked, of course, but at this point, no lock could deter him.

Kochin yanked on the handle, feeling the give of the lock. Anchoring himself, he pulled harder, until metal popped and the cabinet pulled free, its drawer sliding open. And there were files, papers, folders—the cabinet opened into a trove of answers. Kochin pulled them out feverishly, skimming their contents. All in Daltan, but he looked for anything that might help, photos and scrawled notes. Anything in Yarongese, he kept; anything about vivisection, he threw aside. The answer he searched for was not in a heartsooth's anatomy, but in their technique.

The room shook violently, metal rattling atop countertops and within the cabinet. Kochin glanced upward, hearing the moan of the ceiling and watching as cracks webbed out from the corners.

"Kochin, get out of there," Nhika called from the entrance of the room.

"One moment," he pressed, furiously shuffling through papers. He drew them out at random now, whatever caught his eye, anything with potential. The papers cut his fingers in his haste; the crack expanded overhead. Then he found it, a paper headlined: BLUDCARVER REINCARNE OS CADAVE? For a moment, his mind returned to Dr. Santo's study, to papers that asked the same question.

"Kochin!" Her cry came as a shrill warning, and he glanced up just before the ceiling loosed. Kochin scrambled backward, papers in hand, barely escaping the weight of the caving stone. He stuffed the papers underneath his jacket, racing the expanding crack as it tore its way through the ceiling.

Rubble crushed close on his heels as he ran, each billow of dust stealing the breath from his lungs just as much as his fatigue did. The way he'd come from had collapsed, so he rounded the corner, toward where the Daltan soldiers had headed earlier. With each bound, the collapsing building threatened to swallow him in its closing maw. He shed his pack as he sprinted, no longer a soldier but just a boy outrunning a viper's throat. But at last he saw deliverance, the stairway at the end of the hall. Closer and closer he drew, light dawning in his vision, until—

A blast erupted at his side, sweeping him off his feet. Everything fell to blackness before he even hit the ground.

SIXTEEN
NOW

HER RING, KOCHIN'S ID TAG. HER REVIVAL, HIS death.

Nhika brushed a thumb over his embossed name, trying to make sense of it. She'd never seen one of these ID tags in person before, but she knew what it meant. It was the same thing as her bone ring, a bid for remembrance, passed on after . . . after . . .

After death.

Something happened on that island. She wanted to believe it was a miracle. She wanted to believe Kochin had found some way to bring her back at no cost but the Mother's benevolence.

More likely, because heartsoothing was a science—had *always* been a science—it had been a balanced equation. Calories, nutrients, and macromolecules inputted toward a product. Her life . . . at the cost of his.

No. *No.* She would not accept it. Someone had an answer for this, whether it was Trin or Andao or Mimi. Nhika left her room for Mimi's, just down the hall, and rapped her knuckles against the door.

Mimi had already changed into night linens when she answered. With a yawn, she rubbed sleepiness from her eyes. "Something the matter, Nhika?"

Nhika didn't know how to answer. Her throat wouldn't open to words. Instead, she merely held up the ID tags by their chain. Brow creasing, Mimi cupped the swinging tags in her palm and leaned close, squinting in the dim gaslight to read.

When the name registered, she dropped the tags. Her eyes met Nhika's, and every question Nhika had for Mimi was answered at once.

Mimi hadn't been hiding Kochin's whereabouts out of spite. Mimi hadn't known about these tags. This entire household had no more secrets to hide—but Nhika wished it *had*, because then they might supply some other answer than *this*, and it would be a matter of sleuthing it out as she always had. But if this was truly all Mimi knew, then the simple truth was that Trin had come home with Nhika, and Kochin hadn't, and these ID tags meant he was . . . he was . . .

"Nhika, I'm . . . I'm so sorry," Mimi said, and there was genuine remorse in her brow. She crept forward, reached up, and pulled Nhika into a hug.

It was soft. It was firm. Nhika knew Mimi wasn't mourning the man who'd killed her father, but her sympathy made it real—because Mimi, of everyone in this household, could never have let her vendetta go, not until her father's murderer was dead and buried.

And here she was, holding Nhika in her arms without a single word of ill.

The Vens deserved to know.

Earlier, Nhika hadn't wanted to return to Kochin's family without him. Now, she dreaded seeing them more than anything, but they deserved to know.

The last time she'd come to Chengton, she'd come by river. Nhika hadn't realized how close it was to the Congmi countryside manor; they were both in Western Theumas. This time, Mimi drove her.

Mimi stopped the autocarriage when roads became untraversable, meant only for horse carriage. "Are you all right, Nhika?"

It had been a silent drive. "I'll be fine."

Nhika wondered if she should've been wearing black. She had her fair share of funerals. Nhika wasn't sure if this was meant to be one of them—she'd simply wanted to tell his family that he . . . that Kochin . . .

She wanted to show them the ID tags. They could draw their own conclusions from it.

Bidding Mimi goodbye, Nhika followed the dirt path toward Chengton's main road. This was familiar, the road that stretched toward the river on one end and rice terraces on the other. Ramshackle houses squatted every so often on either side, placed there with little order, their walls colored by dust and foliage.

Nhika scanned the hillside, searching for the glowing white house at the top. She found the fishing flags first, hanging tall. It felt a little strange, returning to Kochin's home without him beside her—she'd always imagined they'd come back together. But that was a lifetime ago.

She started toward the hill. The familiar route returned

to her, the hike that crossed its way up the hillside and the view that overlooked crystalline water. The lingering heat of the autumnal sun made her appreciate the shade of the tree canopy.

Nhika crested the hill to find that recognizable white house, paint peeling and garden bursting with flora. This moment was a memory pulled from the recesses of her mind—there was the line in the dirt that Kochin refused to cross, followed by the excited barks of a dog behind the door. She took a moment to steel herself—every time she'd come here, it was to be some bearer of cryptic news. When she'd pressed down the rising stone in her throat, Nhika knocked on the door, expecting Auntie Ye to answer.

Instead, it was a young man. For a moment, Nhika almost thought it was Kochin—but no, he was older, his Yarongese features more prominent in his tanned skin, thick lips, and wide nose. She saw Auntie Ye's softness in him and he was handsome like Kochin, but in a rugged rather than polished way: a brother, then, though Nhika failed to conjure a name.

"Nhika?" he asked breathlessly, surprising her—because how could he know her name?

The man stared at her. Nhika stared back, cupping the ID tags in her palm until they bit. Her lips parted, but the words wouldn't come—and he was still *staring* at her, like he was seeing a risen ghost, like . . .

"You knew," she said, the words forming by themselves. "He told you about me, didn't he?"

Still stunned, the man nodded. After a quick glance behind

his shoulder, he closed the door and took her by the elbow. "Not here. Come with me. We need to talk."

The man was still rubbing Kochin's ID tags between his fingers.

He'd introduced himself as Vinsen, Kochin's elder brother, and had taken her to a secluded riverbank shaded by palms—a secret fishing hole, somewhere they wouldn't be disturbed. All Nhika had managed to do was give him the ID tags, and it was as if she'd broken an automaton. He hadn't moved since.

This place, returning to Chengton... Kochin was written everywhere. She remembered sitting on a bank like this one, his palm against hers, teaching him to soothe. She remembered looking out over the water and fearing he'd left her and accepted a future under Santo's wrath. She remembered seeing him truly, for the first time, under all his masks. A place like this, blue-green water lapping against hyacinths and the tranquil stillness of the river, was far too idyllic to be haunted by memories of him.

At last, Vinsen let out an exhale that cut the air. "Please, don't tell my mother. Let me deal with this. She... she's not ready to hear."

Nhika nodded. It was a cruel twist; she'd died to let Kochin return to his family. He had barely gotten any time with them at all before war pulled him away. "Vinsen, I don't understand. What happened to him?"

"I was going to ask you the same thing." Vinsen's gaze tore off the ID tags, landed on her. "Who were you to him?"

Nhika wasn't sure how to answer. She was the girl who pulled off the mask. She was the girl who'd kissed him on the operating table. She was the girl who'd died in his arms.

And, apparently, she was the girl he'd defied all laws of nature and heartsoothing to bring back.

"We met in Central," she began. "He was being blackmailed by a man who exploited his heartsoothing, someone who had eyes on me next. Kochin tried to save me, in his own way, but I like to think I saved him better."

She tried to laugh at her own joke, but it came out weak and humorless. After all, what good had her sacrifice been?

"That's what he told me—that you saved him from the city. That you gave up your life so he could come home." Vinsen sucked in a slow breath. "I should thank you, by the way. He did come home, for a little. That was because of you."

"Why didn't he stay?"

"Well, he left because of you, too." Vinsen gave her a shadowed look, and Nhika pressed her lips together.

"Right," she said. "I . . . I guess I don't understand what happened."

"I was about to say the same. He left you in my care. There was this casket, some machine designed to keep your body in stasis."

She knew the one—was all too familiar with it. The thought of being trapped in Santo's device again hatched spiders beneath her skin, but how had Kochin succeeded where Santo had failed?

"The next time we heard from him was months later," Vinsen

continued. "He sent a letter home. Said he'd enlisted in the war."

"Enlisted?" Nhika asked. All this time, she had assumed he was drafted. But, if she placed herself in his shoes, she might've sought answers to heartsoothing's oldest taboo on Yarong, too.

"Yes. I definitely cursed him out when I received that letter. It trapped me at home with a worried mother and a dead body—no offense. Now, I wish I could've just shaken some sense into him." Vinsen tipped his head back, his gaze skyward. "Last I heard from him was only a few weeks ago, and then . . . *this*."

"You heard from him a few weeks ago?"

"When he first left you here, he told me that if he ever found the answer, he'd send for your casket. And, three weeks ago, he did."

"From Yarong?"

Vinsen nodded. "He had an ally on the island—I didn't ask who. I only spoke with a messenger."

An ally? It was the first Nhika had heard of it. Her initial thought was Trin, the only person on that island who might've known of her death. It was wishful, hoping they were allies. Hoping Kochin hadn't been the one to put Trin in the hospital.

"You just handed my body over?" Nhika asked, unsure whether she was allowed to feel insulted.

"To be honest, by then I was just . . . just glad to be rid of the responsibility. He always, *always* did that—hid from his messes, I mean. Like he didn't want to see them, but could never let them go, either. It's just—" Vinsen stopped, as though realizing

→ 191

he was speaking ill of a dead man. "Mother, I could punch him. He's going to make Ma cry again."

For how cold his words were, Nhika saw tears in his eyes, though he blinked them away. "Everything he did was for family," she said. "Family was the very thing his employer had used against him."

Vinsen went quiet. His eyes were on the water, fingers tight around the ID tags. "Is that so? And you got him out of that?"

"I've no family of my own. Figured I had nothing to lose."

"You lost your life."

"Ah, well, guess I figured wrong."

Vinsen let out a sharp scoff, his smile wry. "I'm beginning to see why he loved you."

His words were soft, and Nhika felt something pang distantly in her chest, an organ long dormant. *Loved.* But the Mother had never fated Nhika for lasting loves, had She?

⇛ SEVENTEEN ⇚
ONE MONTH AGO

KOCHIN STOOD ON THE PLATFORM OF A TRAIN station he didn't recognize. In one direction, Western Theumas. In the other, the Grand Terminus of Central. And above him, the sky was a blinding white. His memories came back to him slowly—the naval base, the research, and the . . . blast.

So, this was Heaven? He'd always figured he'd go to Hell.

A woman stepped up beside him. Kochin afforded her a sidelong glance—Yarongese, judging by the roundness of her features and flatness of her profile. Tall, hair past her shoulders, dark eye bags, and a glowing cigar between her fingers. Her lips parted and a puff of smoke wafted onto the platform. The two of them stood side by side in impenetrable silence, staring at the empty tracks and waiting for something, anything, to come by.

"Ask your questions," the woman said at last. "I know you have them."

He gave her another look, trying to place her, but her face was not one he recognized, and he remembered all the Yarongese people he'd encountered in Theumas. "Do I know you?"

"Yes. Whether you believe in me is entirely different."

It struck him, then, exactly who this was. And She was right—Kochin had never quite decided whether he believed in the

Mother. To see Her now . . . was this confirmation of the divine, or a delusion from his proximity to death? It must've been the latter, because the Mother was described as a drop of the sun, infinite love and forgiveness. Not a tired woman on a Theuman train platform, smoking away Her hallowed health. But perhaps She *would* be this cold to him, someone who planned on defiling Her gift.

"Go on, ask," She said again, sounding annoyed. "The question on your mind."

"Why weren't you there?" he said, something cracking his voice. "She needed you all her life. I needed you for three long years. And that night in the Theumas Medical Center . . . where were *you*?"

Slowly, aggravatingly, the Mother took another long draw of the cigar. Then, again, She exhaled smoke—She had no answer for him. "I'm here now."

"It's too late."

"It's all I can offer."

"Then how do I bring her back?" If anyone knew, certainly it was Her.

"And why should I tell you that?"

"Because you took her from me."

At that, the Mother barked out a laugh. "I didn't take. She gave."

Kochin opened his mouth, wanting to protest, when the whistle of a train drowned out his thoughts. Before he'd processed it, the train sped up to the platform, headed toward Western Theumas. It came to a rough stop before them.

"This one's yours," She said, tilting her chin forward as the doors slid open.

"I can't die yet."

"I never said you would."

Kochin took a step closer before pausing. Only now did it strike him how . . . how *tired* he was. He had not stopped to breathe these last five months, and all his body wanted was rest. Maybe, if he just stopped a moment, this train would close its doors and pull away without him. Maybe if he simply sat down on this platform and closed his eyes, he could take the easy path toward Nhika.

But he remembered he wasn't headed toward the same afterlife. The only way he'd see her again came from the papers he'd stashed against his chest. There was no easy way out.

Kochin swallowed the rest of his reservations and stepped onto the train. Before the doors closed, he turned to ask the Mother one final question.

"You gave me only half a gift and punished me for it. Why?" That was Her reputation, wasn't it? With the Trickster Fox—cleaving off his tails just because he couldn't fully share in Her gift. Like he had any other choice.

The Mother's smile was derisive. "I never give half gifts, Ven Kochin."

Before he could speak, the train doors slid closed.

Kochin opened his eyes to darkness. Slowly, meagerly, the fuzzy gray of his vision made shapes out of his surroundings, great mounds of rubble, sparking wires, frayed rebar. There was a grainy mix of blood and dust in his mouth, like swallowing bitter sand.

For a long time, Kochin lay still, working through the Mother's visit. She was right—he wasn't dead—but he doubted he had the energy to even lift his head. Silence reigned, backed by a distant rumble as the rest of the building collapsed around him. As he breathed, each movement of his ribs lancing pain through his chest, he felt the stiffness of the papers beneath his jacket.

So, he hadn't lost those. A pained sigh of relief tapered through chapped lips.

In his grogginess, his influence explored his body. His pain receptors burst through him, most caustic in his chest. He checked his systems in turn—a bleed across his back to match the one in his neck, hematomas across his body, a flailing rib. And then, despite all those injuries that bled and screamed, he found the most grievous of them, one he could not feel but that hailed his soothing as flares did: an unstable fracture through a lumbar vertebra, encroaching on his spinal cord. Any wrong movement and it could paralyze him.

As soon as he felt it, he stilled again. The next breath that came from his lips was one of defeat.

This was the end, wasn't it? He was beginning to realize the extent of the Mother's cruelty, that She would keep him alive but immobile. That a single wrong move could paralyze him, just when he'd finally found his answers. Kochin squeezed his eyes shut, lowering his temple to the floor. He'd come so far—his two feet firmly on Yarong, the naval base sieged, the very papers he searched for against his chest, and yet . . . he would die here, bested by a millimeters-long crack through the wrong bone.

Any other heartsooth could fix this, just a twinge of sugar and a mote of calcium to seal the cracks. Now, more than ever, Kochin saw that he wasn't a heartsooth, not really, because heartsooths could give and his body, down to his very bones, had grown so selfish that it veered toward self-detrimental. Nhika had told him he was a heartsooth, had given him the gift with her very last breath, but she'd been wrong. He wasn't enough—not enough to belong in Theumas, not enough to belong in Yarong. Not even meant to save the girl who had made him feel like anything more than a bloodcarver. All he could do was lie here, too afraid to move and cursing how close he'd been.

"*No*," came a voice. Blinking blood from his eyes, Kochin craned his neck to look up, expecting the Mother's derision. Instead, it was Nhika. "You're not giving up here, Kochin. Heal yourself."

"I can't," Kochin managed, not daring to even shake his head. "I'm not like . . . you. I'm not a heartsooth. Despite what you thought, I never was."

"Then what did I die for? I gave you my gift, Kochin. Do something with it."

"I . . ." His excuses died on his tongue; she was right. She'd taught him her art form, the School of Sixfold. With her dying breath, she'd rewritten what his heartsoothing meant. Kochin felt her ring against his chest and squeezed his eyes shut, remembering how it was to soothe as she did. How it felt to walk through the body as though it belonged to him, to follow the blood flow along lines of influence and ride the axis of his central nervous system. In that moment, the crushing weight of darkness fell away—he was within himself, drawn first to the pain in his chest. There, he felt the grind of the broken ribs in his teeth, tasted the blood on his tongue. It was a visceral sensation, even more so than the pain, and if he reached out he felt that he could align the bone and fuse it back together.

But a flail chest was only a distracting injury. The worst one lay at the small of his back, and he took the spinal cord to get there—a jolt of electricity and he'd arrived, the fracture catching his influence like a fishhook.

Soothing this way, as Nhika had, the injury felt so accessible. Like it was begging to be healed without Kochin even having to seek it out. Like he was one with the fracture, at once the jagged bone ends and the severed capillaries and the shorn muscle fibers. It should've been easy to heal, reallocating a crumb of calcium, a pinch of collagen. But stimulating the processes to break down bone required energy; building up bone was the same—energy that he had only ever sourced from an external organism.

Despite that, it came freely in his blood. He could taste it on his tongue now, the sweetness of sugar, the abundance of calories to be spent. Nhika had fueled her gift from the liver, yet when he extended his fingers to his own, he found only a miserly organ, which ceded not a single calorie.

That was his Theuman part; he was almost certain of it. His Yarongese side gifted him heartsoothing, which was dynamic and magical, but Theuman anatomy was inert by nature, following only the innate instruction of its biochemistry. It resisted his influence, a constant battle, and while it yielded in many places, it remained staunch where it mattered: its capacity to give.

This time, he begged. *Please, take something, anything.* Anything but this dormancy, as if his body didn't even belong to him. This defiance, stronger than the will of his influence. No matter how much he willed it, nothing gave way, and he came to the bitter conclusion that if it didn't comply here, when his life was at stake, it never would. It almost felt incorrect to call it heartsoothing; now, when he needed it most, it was soothing nothing at all.

"I can't do it," Kochin said with an exhale, defeated. When he looked back up at Nhika, ready to admit failure, he found her hand extended through the suspended dust. Her bare fingers were splayed forward with the open invitation of soothing.

With every muscle and nerve combating him, Kochin strained his arm forward, his fingers shaking from the effort. Holding his breath, he curled his fingers over hers.

And she squeezed them back. His eyes flared with a surprise, breath so sharp that it hurt, as Nhika held his hand in hers. Now, she glowed, and he felt she must be real this time, not a ghost or a fragmented memory but something so corporeal as to hold him.

"Nhika, I—" The words caught in his throat, and they stayed

there as the glow dimmed. As the dust settled. As Kochin saw whose hand he really held, not Nhika's but a soldier's.

He snatched his hand away, the motion sparking pain like firecrackers through his core. The soldier only laughed, the sound like wheezing barks through an open mouth.

Slouched forward with his arm still outstretched, the soldier wore the red-brown military coat of Daltanny. He was an older man, somewhere in his midfifties, with enough decoration on his pocket to denote a high status even though Kochin couldn't discern Daltan ranks. A kinked length of rebar jutted from his abdomen, pinning him to the concrete, but his sedated look made Kochin wonder if he felt any pain. The realization dawned on him slowly: that this was not Nhika, that Nhika had never been here, that she was still waiting for him.

"Theuman, Daltan," the soldier began in a thick accent. "We are the same in death."

Kochin glanced beyond the soldier, up the stairs. He saw a sliver of moonlight paint the far wall; it grew brighter, as though breaking through clouds, illuminating more of the soldier as it did.

"I don't want to die alone," the soldier continued, and proffered his hand again. Kochin eyed it testily but didn't speak. "Please. Don't let me die alone."

When Kochin still didn't take his hand, the soldier's eyes crinkled with something near acceptance and he tipped his head back against the concrete that had pinned him, murmuring something in Daltan. A prayer to the Daltan maker, perhaps? Kochin watched him, wondering how it was that they had led such different lives but had come to meet the same fate. Their deaths here were not honorable—a medic who had abandoned his post, a soldier who had hidden from the chaos until the chaos had found him. Their deaths here would entomb them in rubble, and Kochin doubted anyone would find their tags for a long, long time. Perhaps the soldier was right: Their allegiances had departed in a death like this. The only things that remained were guilt, grief, and loneliness.

"I'm a bloodcarver," Kochin said. That was the only term a Daltan might recognize—they'd coined it, after all—and the admission came easily because there was no consequence to it here. "Do you still want to die beside me?"

"A bloodcarver," the soldier repeated, mimicking Kochin's Theuman pronunciation. He gave a sharp laugh, which burbled with the blood in his lungs, and added, "I did not know they remained."

Kochin guarded himself against hostility, but instead, the soldier offered his hand again. "You can put a man to sleep, yes?"

"Yes."

"Then please, let me sleep. I want to think of my family when I die. Not pain."

Kochin slowed his breathing, so surprised by the soldier's request. Maybe this was one of the rare Daltan soldiers not yet indoctrinated by prejudice, or maybe prejudice had left him in the desperation of death. In any case, he was asking Kochin for heartsoothing, knowing not that Kochin was only half a heartsooth.

Kochin took the soldier's hand, diaphoretic but cold.

"Let me think of her smile first," the soldier requested. Kochin, too weak for words, grunted his understanding.

The soldier closed his eyes, his breath leaving him in a slow, long stream. Something played behind his lids and warm relief tugged at his lips before he tightened his fingers in Kochin's hand, a tacit request.

Kochin quelled the overactivity of his brain into a quiet, slumbering rhythm. Let him have his dreams, if only once more. Let them be of family, of a partner at home and children at the table. Let it be painless. His fingers were still curled around the soldier's when the breaths stopped, the pulse deadened to a standstill, and the last static impulse of the cortex tapered out into silence.

For ten long breaths, Kochin let the man have peace in death. After that, he carved.

It felt an act of depravity, stealing from someone he'd promised to relieve. But the soldier had come to accept death; Kochin had not. It was not his time yet, not when he'd finally found the answers he'd gone to war for.

He took only what he needed, leaching calcium to heal the crack in his spine and mend his leg, his ribs. Not to their former strength, but enough to get him out of this collapsed base. Anything more would be debauchery. The vehement warnings that had signaled themselves across his anatomy petered out at his soothing, the discomfort lifting with the pain. At last, Kochin felt confident enough to drag himself off the floor, feeling the weight ease from his chest as he did. The pain of bruises, scratches, and scars still remained. It reminded him that he was still human, not yet the bloodcarver of myths.

He pulled himself beside the soldier's body, clasping his palms and dipping his head in thanks. "Mother keep you," he said, taking the soldier's ID tag from beneath his lapel. Then he lifted himself to his feet, staggered toward the waning swath of moonlight, and climbed his way out of the collapsed naval base.

When he reached the surface, he gulped his first breath of fresh air, though it was colored with the sulfurous scent of gunpowder. By now, the shooting had stopped as the Daltan generals emerged in surrender.

He found a newly dead body. Opened her fingers. Pressed the soldier's ID tag in her palm. With the Daltan papers still flat against his chest, safe underneath his coat, Kochin thanked the buried soldier one more time before heading back to his station.

EIGHTEEN
NOW

NHIKA HADN'T WANTED TO FACE KOCHIN'S ENTIRE family, but there were no more trains back to the Congmi manor at that hour and Vinsen insisted she stay the night. She no longer had the strength to argue.

For that long walk back to the Ven household, she practiced her entrance. Most of all, she was afraid to face Kochin's mother. Vinsen had asked her to keep the ID tags a secret, but she worried one sad look from Auntie Ye would compel all of Nhika's truths to spill out.

When they reached the house, Vinsen opened the door and gestured her in—and there, all but Kochin, was the Ven family.

There was a boy studying at the table and Kochin's father rearranging flowers and Auntie Ye at the stove, preparing dinner. She turned and, at the sight of Nhika, froze.

"Nhika," she said. Broth dripped from her wooden spoon. Then her expression melted into something deeply hopeful. "*Nhika*. If you're here, does that mean Kochin . . . ?"

Nhika glanced at Vinsen, looking for an out. She couldn't speak. She didn't even know what to say.

"Kochin's not home," Vinsen said, a hand at Nhika's back as though to brace her. "Nhika's going to stay the night. I'm taking her up to Kochin's room."

The youngest brother looked like he wanted to meet her, but Vinsen quickly swiveled her away from the family and took her upstairs, for which she was grateful. That relief left when Vinsen stopped her before Kochin's bedroom.

It was him in many ways, yet not Kochin at all. It felt like the part of him he'd hidden in the houseboat, a shelf lined with Yarongese fairy tales and glass jars of dried-out clippings. But it was still boyish—the wooden sailboats he kept on top of his dresser, the garish blue of his bedsheets. It was Kochin before the refinement of Central; it was him before the masks. The blanket looked handsewn, rather than automaton-woven. *Everything* in this house had that unpolished, rough-hewn feel, like it had all been touched and loved and lived in. It made Nhika more comfortable than she ever had been in any of the Congmis' houses.

"Sorry about all the dust," Vinsen said. "No one really went in here after he left."

"It's fine."

"And I'm sorry about the family in advance. I'll tell them you're not in the mood to talk."

"And . . . you? Are you all right?"

A muscle moved in his jaw. He drew the ID tags from his pocket and stared at them like they might yield a new answer. "I've given it some thought, and I don't think he's dead."

Her heart wrung. Nhika hadn't realized, but she'd *needed* someone to say that. She hadn't known Vinsen long, but he didn't seem like the idealistic type, so if he believed Kochin was alive, maybe he was.

"I don't think I believe it, either," she confided.

"He was always too smart to die," Vinsen added. "He was too smart for his own good. I've never seen him fail to achieve something he wanted, and he *promised* the family he'd come home, so . . . so I just need to pray that wasn't a lie."

Vinsen looked at her, a bit unsure and a bit optimistic—like he was asking her to hope with him. "I'll bring him back," she blurted before she could stop herself. "If he's out there, I'll find him."

He gave her a charmed look, like he didn't quite believe her. "Where did my brother find someone like you?" Before she could answer him, Vinsen reached for her hand, opened her fingers, and placed the necklace in her palm. "These belong to you, I think. That's your bone ring, right?"

Nhika made an affirmative noise. As she'd worn it before, she clasped the necklace around her neck, feeling the cold bite of metal through her shirt. "Didn't expect to see this again." Yarongese bone rings passed on in death, but she had to believe this one had returned to her because she *hadn't* died, and not because Kochin had.

"I suppose he never got a chance to thank you in person, so I'll do it on his behalf. Thank you, Nhika, and good night." With a sad smile, he placed a hand on her head and ruffled her hair like she was his kid sister. "You're always welcome here, if you wish."

Vinsen retreated from the hallway. In the quiet, Nhika clutched the ID tags in her palm, a single question on her mind.

What had happened on that island?

In the morning, she opened her door to find the younger of Kochin's brothers standing outside, as though he'd been waiting for her to wake up. He was scrawny, with the curliest head of hair she'd ever seen and freckles to match her own.

At the sight of her, he straightened and cocked his head. "So, who are you?" he asked. "Vinsen's friend?"

"Kochin's, actually."

"Kochin?" His eyes widened. "I've never met a friend of Kochin's before. How did you meet?"

"We, ah, ran into each other on the streets," she said. Not a lie. She would omit their verbal spars, her suspicions of murder, and the fact that she'd stabbed him.

"Did you work at the hospital, too?"

"Not exactly."

"Are you *rich*?"

Nhika barked out a laugh. "Mother, no," she said, then realized she must've looked that way—coming from the Congmi household, wearing unblemished silk.

"Are you a heartsooth, too?"

Nhika's chest warmed at how easily that word passed between his lips, like it was nothing sacred nor taboo. It just *was*. "Yeah. I suppose that's how we met."

Bentri gave her a melancholy look. "Is he okay?"

That almost brought tears to her eyes, but Nhika fought them down—because she'd promised Vinsen she wouldn't tell them.

Because Kochin *wasn't* dead. So, all she said was, "I'll do my best to make sure he is."

After that, Bentri was called downstairs to help with breakfast and Nhika prepared herself to leave. There was a sense of listlessness—she wasn't sure what to do now. She wasn't sure what her heartsoothing could do anymore after having healed Trin and failed Kochin. All this power, her gift and her connections, and Nhika could do nothing.

There was someone at the door downstairs. She could hear them knocking, and a moment later, Vinsen opened it. As Nhika descended the stairs, she realized she recognized the voice: "Is she here? I need to talk to her, please."

When she turned the corner, she found herself staring at Mimi, who looked so out of place in Chengton that Nhika had to blink to make sure she was real.

"Nhika," Mimi said, shoulders falling with relief. There were tears in her eyes, and Nhika assumed the worst until she said, "Trin's awake. He came home from the hospital this morning."

The autocarriage couldn't go any faster—even with Mimi as its driver. Nhika didn't care how many corners they drifted around, nor how many times their wheels left the road. She just cared to see Trin again.

Only a small part of it was for the answers. The other part was to see *him*, to have that little bit of normalcy restored to an upturned world, because Nhika didn't recognize a Congmi manor where he wasn't the shadow to her every footstep.

At last, they reached the familiar gravel driveway of the Congmi villa. Nhika could hardly contain herself as Mimi parked the autocarriage and unlocked the door to the house.

The first thing Nhika noticed when they stepped inside was laughter. It came from somewhere distant, loud enough to snake through the halls. She recognized it as Andao's.

When she looked over, Mimi was beaming, and despite all that was happening—Kochin's ID tags against her chest, the war that raged on the other side of the water—everything seemed right again.

They followed the laughter. Andao's voice was joined by another: deep, masculine, hoarse. Dep Trin. It took them to a parlor, and when Mimi opened the door, there everyone was: Andao, Trin, Hendon. The Congmi family whole once again.

Trin sat on a settee, his leg extended while Andao was fitting a handmade brace. It was such an intimate act—Andao lacing straps through their buckles with utmost care while teasing the state of Trin's buzz cut, Trin squeezing Andao's arm every time a strap was too tight—that Nhika almost felt as though she were intruding.

Until Trin looked up. Saw her and Mimi. And smiled.

"It's been a while, Ms. Suon," he said, and something about the steady, deep assurance of his voice made her chest crack open.

"You have no idea, Dep Trin," she returned.

Laboriously, he tried to stand. The joints of his brace whirred to his aid, and Andao draped Trin's arm over his shoulder to help him up. In five automaton-aided steps, Trin was standing before her. In one more, he'd gathered Nhika into a close, crushing embrace.

"I was told you healed me," he said, putting some of his weight onto her.

Nhika shrugged. "We can give the surgeons credit. Mother knows they have egos to maintain."

Trin pulled away, looking her up and down. "So, you're still *you*." His expression was full of awe. "I can't believe he actually did it."

Her heart stuttered. "You mean Kochin?"

At that, Trin took a step back, leather stretching in the brace. When she saw his eyes again, they were rueful, and her smile dropped.

"I'm sorry, Nhika. I have something to confess," Trin said. Nhika sucked in a breath, realizing she wasn't ready to hear anything Trin had to say. "I need to tell you what happened to Kochin."

NINETEEN
THREE WEEKS AGO

THE MEDICS SPENT THE NEXT MORNING PICKING through casualties. Kochin saw the trail of the arriving injured snaking up the hill toward Majora, where he tended to the wounded. Though Theuman forces had hoisted their flag above the rubble of the naval base, it was still inhospitable for a field base, too many dead and not enough buried. So, the army doctors had congregated in Majora, and because of the nature of his injuries, Kochin was at the field hospital rather than pulling the injured out of the dust, though his Daltan papers enticed him to abandon post again.

He'd stashed them underneath his mattress. They'd been crumpled and abused and stained with his blood but were still legible if he could swipe a Daltan dictionary. He itched to read them, and in his impatience, his anxiety allowed the worst possible scenario to run rampant in his imagination—that they would yield nothing, that it had been all for naught. But the hope brewing in his chest was intoxicating, sure like nothing had ever been sure before. He recognized it from a lifetime ago, the same hope that Nhika dragged into his life when she promised peace, freedom, love. He was almost hesitant to embrace it again. But he let himself appreciate it, just a little, feeling unscrupulous for his boyish excitement while he cataloged names off the ID tags of the deceased.

"I need hands! He's bleeding again," called the army doctor. She stooped over a newly arrived patient and Kochin narrowed his eyes to see the injury. Before she could ask again, Kochin was at her side, staring at a leg cut down to the bone that spurted arterial blood. The soldier cried out in agony, and with a start, Kochin recognized the voice: Dep Trin.

He was mottled in sweat, pupils dilated and every muscle tensed against the pain. A medic was quick to set up an IV line, but that would only help the pain, not the bleeding.

Kochin reached the bedside and clamped his hands over Trin's wound. In the chaos, no one had noticed that they weren't gloved, and when he soothed Trin, he found a femur fracture that had sliced the artery. His eyes met Trin's, but there was little recognition there, just fevered distress and a slipping consciousness. Once the stupor of soothing cleared from Kochin's head, a slew of thoughts took its place. He owed Trin and the Congmis; they'd shown him mercy when he had not deserved it. More so than that, Nhika cared for him, so Kochin could not bring her back into a world where he'd let Trin die. Without heartsooth intervention or a miracle in the surgical ward, Trin would bleed out on this bed, hours after the fighting had stopped. It was a life for a life, then—Kochin had once stolen someone from the Congmis, so it was only right that he returned one.

Sweeping his eyes across Trin's anatomy, exposed by heartsoothing, Kochin soothed again. As the doctor and her medics clamped dressings over the wound, sopping up blood, Kochin pushed his influence inward. Trin's body pulsed underneath his surveillance, alight with pain. Kochin could feel the nerves sparking, the muscles tense in their fascia. It was a body in calamity, unsure of how to mitigate the blood loss and trying every strategy it could conjure: a quickened heart, skin blanched of its blood, rapid breaths that barely moved air.

Morphine entered Trin's bloodstream, eliciting a wave of nausea in Kochin. He reeled, fighting the urge to gag at the flood of bitterness on his tongue, before reorienting himself. But as it suffused through the blood, Trin relented in his convulsing, leg straightening just long enough for Kochin to source the site of injury again. He inched his influence toward where the femur shaft had snapped jaggedly in two, its needle-sharp point nicking the femoral artery. Kochin could not heal the bone like this, but the vessel was the true problem, and that was a quick fix. Fighting the mugginess of the morphine in Trin's blood, Kochin reached up to his liver and stole just enough calories to mend. He dragged those back down, using them to scaffold tissue and seal the vessel. It was an imperfect, rushed fix that left a raised mound on the vessel, like a child had slapped putty over a hose leak. But it worked, and the spurting quelled.

Someone shouldered him away, and his hands disconnected from Trin's leg. The change was sudden and jarring, and Kochin blinked up to find an older medic giving him a reproachful look. "Either help or step aside," she muttered, sizing a traction splint.

Step aside it was. Kochin lingered in the background, holding his hands, slick with blood, away from his uniform. Now that the bleeding had abated, the medics were quick to realign the bone and splint the leg. No one seemed to have noticed his work, how his hands were ungloved—

Until Kochin turned, finding the Yarongese translator staring at him from across the tent. Her eyes had locked onto his hands, dipped in red.

Kochin's throat tightened, feeling as though he'd been caught in a crime scene: hands bloody, victim still fresh at his feet. They'd both caught each other where they weren't meant to be: her in the basement of the naval base, him with his bare hands bloody. He only wondered if she could see past his Theuman looks, find something more.

A noise from Trin drew him back to the moment. A splint had been tightened over his leg, taking pain off the bone, and Trin formed his first coherent word: "Andao," he said, the name formed around a sob. "Andao . . ."

Followed by the translator's stare, Kochin escaped to wash his hands. When he scrubbed the last of Trin's blood out of palm lines and fingernails, he was no longer a heartsooth, simply a Theuman.

There was too much work that day for Kochin to steal time away for his papers. When the sun set, he volunteered for the first half of the night shift, a ploy to have the field hospital to himself. Sunset was late here at this time of year, but as the night fought off the last remnants of sun, the rows of cots took on a quiet serenity, especially as Kochin lit the gas lamps. Within the week, ships would come to take some of these injured back to Theumas, to a true hospital, but Kochin worried that Trin's femur fracture could open the artery again, or else impair him if left untreated.

He passed through the rows like a specter, assessing IVs and watching rising chests for breath, until at last he came to Trin's bed. Even in sleep, a pained grimace marred his expression, the lines at the corners of his nose sharp and brow furrowed in perturbation. Sweat, perhaps from fever or perhaps from pain, prickled at his trim hairline and Kochin checked the scrawled patient record by his bedside for some administration of antimicromials, finding a miserly dose by IV—not enough, if sepsis were to set in.

"If you were here, you'd heal him, wouldn't you?" Kochin said beneath his breath, summoning Nhika to the bedside.

"Yes," she said. "As much as we were at odds, I'd heal him. And then I'd lord it over him for all eternity."

He let out a humored scoff. "If I'm to heal him, I have no excuse not to heal everyone in here to the best of my ability." Heartsoothing was never an art meant to be wielded selfishly, to be hoarded and distributed with partiality and preference. There were tenets to it that he'd so often foregone.

Her ghost simply waved a dismissive hand. "You're only one man, and there are only so many chickens to be used."

She was right, of course. Validated by that self-incepted reasoning, Kochin left the field hospital to find the Yarongese animal pens. Paying mind to the noise, he hopped the fence and opened a roost box, finding the hens asleep in rows. He stole a chick, so small and sweet that he was loath to use it in heartsoothing. It squirmed a moment and its mother roused to peck annoyedly at his hand, but he closed the roost box and enclosed the chick in his palm.

It was never easy to use animals in heartsoothing. When his mother had first taught him, when they'd learned he could not expend his own calories to fuel the art, she had placed a mouse in his palms and asked him to heal the scrapes in his knees. He'd sat for hours with the docile little creature cupped in his hands, crying not from his scrapes but from reluctance, at its big black eyes and inquisitive snout. When his mother returned, upon seeing the mouse still cradled in his hands, she'd sat down beside him to explain the cycle of life. How life sustained life, how it was no different from farming to eat, how calories were either wasted in death or spent in life. So he'd learn to rationalize it that way, calories spent now or later, and slipped the chick into his pocket. He'd served Santo this way, a bird in his pocket while he soothed patients.

Kochin ducked back into the folds of the field hospital, finding Trin still asleep on his cot. Here he looked like a slumbering bear, all muscle and tension, with an expression that made Kochin hesitant to wake him for fear of an instinctive right hook. Nonetheless, he stooped beside the bed and shook Trin by the shoulder.

Nothing. Must've been some morphine. Kochin shook again, more fiercely this time, until Trin sputtered awake, eyes wide as though coming from a nightmare. Before he could make a noise, Kochin raised a finger to his lips.

"Mr. Ven," Trin said, as though he were addressing a ghost. He glanced around, measuring his surroundings—did he think himself dead, having joined Kochin in Hell?

"It's just Kochin here." Kochin rose from his crouch. "Or Private Ven."

Trin's eyes were slow to clear from the languor of morphine, and he blinked quizzically at Kochin, his question plainly readable.

"What are you—"

"I'm going to heal you," Kochin interrupted, making space for himself at the end of Trin's bed. "Is that okay?"

Trin's shoulders rose in apprehension. Beneath the blanket, his splinted leg shifted and he winced, jaw gritted. Without answering, he looked at Kochin, narrowed eyes piercing a hole in Kochin's forehead with his scrutiny. Still absorbed in doubt, he said slowly, "You were there when they found me, weren't you?"

Kochin nodded.

"Did you soothe me then?" His eyes held suspicion.

"Yes. You would've died if I hadn't," Kochin explained. "And if you wait until you reach Theuman hospitals before realigning your leg, you may lose function of it. If it's mistreated, you may even lose your life."

"You'd use your heartsoothing to heal?" he asked, his words holding accusation. Did Trin know that Kochin hadn't killed the late Mr. Congmi with heartsoothing? That it had always been meant to heal?

Kochin raised his hands away from the bedside to placate

Trin. "I don't have to. But I want you to walk away from this war as much as you do."

The scrutiny didn't lift. "Why?"

"Because . . ." Kochin felt the answer was self-evident, but apparently Trin didn't. "Because you're injured. And I can help you."

"I'm not in the business of owing you any favors."

"On the contrary, I owe you one."

"Save your energy, Mr. Ven, and I'll save myself for true doctors."

"A true doctor and operating suite won't be available until you reach Theumas, many hours or days from now. By then, any number of things may happen: Your fracture could reopen the artery, your wound could get infected, or your bone may set in misalignment, crippling the leg forever. With all due respect, Private Dep, isn't there someone waiting for you at home?"

Trin quieted, his lips thin. Kochin knew he was thinking about Andao, the man who had launched war machines to Yarong just to keep his lover safe. Maybe, if the war hadn't started, the two of them would've been thinking of marriage and a future together. He and Trin were similar in that respect, weren't they, fighting not for a city but a someone? The only difference was that Trin's someone was promised, safe behind walled mansions. The least Trin could do was survive long enough to see him again, whatever it took.

Trin's eyes ran down the length of his leg. At last, he asked, his voice raspy with fatigue, "I would heal faster if you soothed me?"

Kochin nodded. "And it'll take away the pain."

Expression set with acceptance, Trin grunted. "Then I have no choice. I won't die here."

"I'm glad you could see reason," Kochin said, then lifted the blanket off his leg. The splint kept traction against the bone, pulling it into near alignment. Kochin eyed Trin as he hovered a hand above skin, a final request for permission.

"Just . . . just the leg," Trin said, hesitant. "Touch nothing else."

With an understanding nod, Kochin began his work.

The bone wasn't completely aligned, the ends slipping against each other—the source of the pain, no doubt. "This will hurt a bit," Kochin warned before pulling on the ankle. Trin sucked in a shaky breath, fingers bunching the sheets, as the two halves of bone pulled apart.

Kochin dipped his influence into the anatomy and the field hospital fell away to blackness. He could see Trin still, his form turned into artwork rather than flesh and blood, the cleaved diaphysis not bone but glasswork and light. With nothing to distract him, Kochin found it easy to align the bone; as they slipped together, he felt a tightness ease from his chest, as though his own heart had socketed back into place.

Holding tension, he dipped his hand into his pocket, where it wrapped around the slumbering chick. Ensuring painlessness, he seeped energy from the chick—calcium, too—until its body grew cold in his palm and its shivering heartbeat stilled. He channeled those calories through himself, past the juncture of skin, pushing them toward the femur. Kochin blinked and matter returned to the anatomy— the matrices of bone, the rivers of marrow. Using calcium and collagen as mortar, he took to fixing the bone, building upon what existed like a potter mending cracked ceramic with wet clay. With his attention to detail, the crack was seamless, the diaphysis smooth, but he left the marrow, muscle, and frayed nerves to mend themselves. The last step was to seal the skin back up, alleviating the greatest source of pain.

Hands shaking, Kochin drew himself away with an exhale. The humidity of the night air returned to him, settling on his palms before he wiped them on his trousers. When he met Trin's eyes, they were dark with consternation, not gratefulness. Even as Kochin stood to retrieve more IV anti-micromials, he was silent. It wasn't until Kochin pushed the drugs into the needle port that Trin blinked out of his trance and spoke. "What are you giving me?"

"Fermicillin," Kochin said. "In case of sepsis."

Trin drew in his leg, still in its splint; Kochin would keep that there for appearances, so no one would question the overnight miracle. Words unspoken passed through Trin's expression, until at last he decided, "I know why you're really helping me."

Kochin paused, needle still in hand. "Do you?"

"Because you know it's what she would've wanted."

Kochin's instinct was to deny it, but the look on Trin's face was not presumptuous, but sympathetic.

"I'm sorry," Trin continued when Kochin didn't reply. "It must've been hard to lose her like that."

Trin had been there when Kochin walked off the operating table, chest still scarred, carrying Nhika's limp form in his arms. He and Mimi had witnessed Kochin's grief firsthand, how he'd collapsed to his knees and cried Nhika's name, anguished and loud enough to shake the walls of the medical center. But, eyes wide and expressions stunned, they could not share his agony because they still had a home to return to at the end of the night. All Kochin had was a newly empty houseboat and a family a city away, who could never love him for his sins as Nhika did.

For an ephemeral moment, Kochin wanted to tell Trin how close he was to bringing her back, not because he wanted Trin to know but because he'd carried on alone for so long on this journey that a familiar face, no matter how hostile, came with relief. Perhaps Trin could understand how the anger at an unjust death could morph into such manic resolve—hadn't they hired Nhika to find Mr. Congmi's murderer? But this was a secret meant to die with Kochin.

"It's all right," he said, because there was nothing else to say between them. Not after what Kochin had done to that family. "You're right. It's what she would've wanted."

"She soothed me once, too."

At that, Kochin met Trin's eye. "I didn't know that." Though, he shouldn't have been surprised—Nhika's art existed to heal.

"She used me as a template to heal Hendon."

"I see." Kochin set the needle aside for sanitation, watching Trin out of the corner of his eye and wondering at the reasoning behind Trin's reminiscing.

The soldier's next words came with grace: "Your soothing felt the same. It . . . it felt just like hers."

Something cracked in Kochin's chest. Despite himself, despite Trin's audience, tears burned behind his eyes and he cast his gaze aside to hide them. The words were few, but their insinuation enormous—that he wasn't alone in bearing Nhika's memory if Trin remembered her heartsoothing, too, that there existed some truth to her ghost, that he still carried her legacy faithfully in her absence. That maybe, if he could touch as she had touched, then there was still some heartsooth left in him, after all.

"Don't put weight on the leg," Kochin advised, drawing a curtain of impassivity over his expression. "It'll still require time to fully heal. If you need me, I'll be making rounds."

Before Trin could see the grief drowning his heart, Kochin turned away, exiting the field hospital. He left for the edge of Majora, buried the chick in dirt, and wept.

After settling emergencies among the injured, Kochin had the rest of his night shift to finally translate the papers he'd taken from the naval base. He opened the bloodstained papers in his lap; in his hand he held a Daltan dictionary borrowed from his commanders' tent. Murmuring to himself, Kochin began translating the documents.

Daltanny had explored a great many things about the heartsooths of yore. The vivisections were the most inhumane experiments, but others came close: torture to tease out heartsooths, those who could numb themselves; asphyxiation by gas, to see if a heartsooth might be able to survive without oxygen; caustic drugs to see what might inhibit or stimulate the gift. Kochin found himself on the fence between hope and dread—hoping

Daltanny had found his answers but dreading how they'd come about it. His gut told him they must've explored reincarnation; Daltanny was known for its infinite armies, spreading like a disease, so he trusted them to take any opportunity to create the undying soldier. But how close had they gotten?

He burned through his papers until he reached his most promising one, the one he'd risked death to grab, headlined, BLUDCARVER REINCARNE OS CADAVE?

Translated: *Bloodcarver reincarnating a corpse?*

This was promising. He flipped through the pages, finding a photograph of a dog. Kochin narrowed his eyes in question, trying to skim the passage for some kind of result. His attention passed by words greedily, translating what he knew and ignoring what he didn't. There was something about a dog, and he caught the word for "healthy." But, when he reached the end, a bold red stamp greeted him: STUDEN TERMINAEN.

"Study terminated?" he scoffed aloud, incredulous. Something had happened in this paper, something miraculous or something deeply disappointing. But why terminate it?

Kochin flipped back to the beginning, prepared to translate every word for an answer. Despite the hour, he felt no tiredness as the text came together, word by word.

This study was from eighteen years ago: an observation of a Yarongese matriarch, a fifty-two-year-old heartsooth taken from her family—a husband, a daughter, and two newborn grandchildren—and placed into internment. The strongest heartsooth of her village, their magistra and doctor, she was compelled to perform acts of her miracle for fear of violence and death. They eased her into it, healing other prisoners. Healing herself. The experiments escalated. Killing animals. Inflicting pain. Practices that conflicted so viscerally with any school of heartsoothing that it must've anguished her to do it. But, under the eyes of the Mother, she defiled her own art. Kochin found himself filled with repugnance, and suddenly this war seemed not premature, but overdue. What could have been if Theumas had cast aside its neutrality twenty years ago? When Yarong beseeched those mainland empires of metal and mortar to help them, their pleas befalling stubborn ears?

He translated on, a question in the back of his mind: Why had the study terminated?

Kochin reached the page with attached dog photos. Now, he saw that word, *reincarne*, and worked feverishly, writing through a hand cramp. *1/12/998—Subject 148 growing restless, exhibits signs of aggression . . . Refuses solid food . . . Dog cadaver provided 24 hours postmortem, no obvious signs of trauma or decay . . .*

His eyes snapped forward in rising fervor. *Reincarne . . . reincarne . . . reincarne . . .*

They dragged back as he continued translating. Here it was, everything he'd been waiting for, searching for, fighting for. *Reincarne.* They'd given her a dog, asked her to bring it back. And . . . She'd refused on the basis of impossibility. She became incoherent, uncooperative. The researchers found incentive: her grandson. Told her to find an answer soon, as she'd need it when they placed a bullet in his head. That made her work.

Through his zeal, Kochin felt the heat of the matriarch's pain, even as transcribed through the pragmatic Daltan text.

He could imagine her wails, the anger and the helplessness. And he understood, more than he'd ever understood anything, the desperation.

She worked tirelessly on the corpse. The text noted all her failed methods: an electric pulse to the brain fizzled into silence; an artificial beat in the heart stilled without stimulation; air in the lungs did nothing to renew the body. As Kochin had done, she'd emulated life atop the body, but it was not the same. It was imperfect. What neither the Daltan soldiers nor the matriarch understood was why, but Kochin had come to understand—life did not enter a corpse spontaneously, holding the same whim with which Death stole. Life was a miracle, a beautiful eclipse of magic and biology, one that couldn't possibly be re-created in a lab or under Daltan intimidation.

They thought the matriarch, who had once brought someone back from the brink of death, was lying to bide time. They gave her a final warning. She asked them to bring her a dog, a live dog.

Kochin's pencil lead snapped. He cursed, grabbing a pocketknife and sharpening it hastily before continuing, his mind forgetting all tiredness in favor of mania.

She held both dogs at once, one dead and the other alive. Before their eyes, she soothed them. Before their eyes, the frisky dog wilted and tired, lapsing into death. In its place, the cadaveric dog, now ten days passed, wagged its tail.

Kochin stopped, breathless. The labeled photos showed the dog, once a corpse and now reanimated. After reading the passage, he saw now how gaunt the dog looked. Gaunt but alive—eating, breathing, panting. His hands were stiff with fatigue, the pencil dimpling his writing callus.

But the study had been terminated. Why, when she had done it? She'd discovered how to bring back the dead. Now, how did she accomplish it?

Over time, the dog grew heartier as she soothed it back to health. Its coat shone; its legs carried strength. But it had been a trained dog before its death; now it forgot simple commands: sit, stay, bark. It wandered, lost and confused. It would lie down for hours at a time without moving. The matriarch contested that it was not her soothing, but the dog's state of decay when they'd given it to her. Kochin had prepared for that—it's why he'd kept Nhika in such stasis.

But how had she done it? Surely, the Daltanny had documented that. As the text drew nearer to its end, Kochin's heart rose in his throat in anticipation of disappointment.

They asked her to replicate her work. She performed it with success on a variety of animals, pigs and hens and cats. They asked her to revive a soldier. They gave her a macaque as fodder. She refused.

Impossible, she said.

Kochin's throat closed as he translated on, each word coming with new dread. The matriarch gave her explanation, this part seemingly translated from Yarongese—an equivalent life was needed, a perfect template. Because she did not create life; she merely transferred it. Soothing them both, she overlaid them, one a template and the other a ready patient. She acted simply as a bridge, funneling energy where it already desired to go.

And not even a heartsooth could turn a monkey into a man; that energy needed to first sift through the cycle of life.

Impatient and skeptical, the researchers presented her the corpse of her grandson. She'd gone into a fit of grief, but no matter how many macaques they provided her, she could not bring him back. At last, they threatened to kill the last of her line: her granddaughter, just born.

Knowing they might make good on their threat, she reached into her own chest and squeezed her heart to a stop.

The final page of the study had been stamped in bold: STUDEN TERMINAEN. Terminated, because the subject herself had died.

Kochin set down the pencil. He hoped to find a second meaning to these words, something he didn't understand with his elementary Daltan. As he scoured the text a second time, he came to the same, harrowing conclusion. An equivalent life was needed. Finding his throat newly dry, Kochin swallowed. Whatever this meant for Daltanny, it meant the same for him.

If he wanted to bring Nhika back, another needed to die. And it would be his heartsoothing that killed them.

Hands shaking, either from the revelation or the ache of writing, he set the papers down on a desk. Kochin almost hoped that when next he picked them up, the words would've rearranged themselves into a more acceptable solution. He'd done horrible things in his life—killing an innocent man for Santo, rupturing the muscles of that soldier's leg—but killing another with heartsoothing to bring Nhika back was personal. Intimate.

Despicable.

But . . . was there any other option?

The reality was just settling in when a pained shout from the far end of the tent called his attention. Grabbing the handle of the medic cart, he wheeled himself over to a wounded soldier, who was experiencing night terrors in her feverish state. Kochin administered brief care, too occupied to do anything but the minimum: another dose of anti-micromials and a change of sweat-soaked towels. His thoughts were elsewhere, consumed by the enormity of his decision.

Just as he'd finished documenting the anti-micromials, the rustle of clothing outside called his attention. He lifted his lantern, finding the shadow of a girl outside—that translator again, for how tall and willowy her silhouette. A breath hitched in his throat and he slipped out of the tent in pursuit, wondering if she'd been lurking long enough to see him with Trin.

When he reached the side of the tent, he found nothing but an empty clearing. Kochin panned the lantern around, but he was truly alone. It wouldn't have surprised him if he was losing his mind.

With a sigh, Kochin took himself back inside, wrapping up the last bit of patient care and wheeling his cart back toward his desk. There, he found his Daltan dictionary still open, as he'd left it. He squinted in the darkness—beside the pencil and the dictionary, the desk was otherwise empty.

His research papers were gone.

With flaring panic, Kochin searched the desk, the floor, wondering if he'd misplaced the papers in the dark. It occurred to him a moment later—that *translator*, the damned girl who had been far too curious about his bare hands. He didn't have need of those papers anymore, having already gleaned their hateful truth; he only worried someone might realize why he had them.

Another medic came in the middle of the night to relieve him. Kochin accepted only because it would be suspicious otherwise, but as he left the field hospital, his heart was a small black pit, knowing that he had left a deadly secret exposed.

TWENTY
THREE WEEKS AGO

KOCHIN DREAMED OF NHIKA AMONG HIS FAMILY. She would've gotten along with every one of them, connecting with his mother over their shared gift and regaling Bentri with tales of her time in the city. She had Vinsen's same quiet judgment and shared his father's deep compassion, hidden beneath layers of stoicism. From the very moment he'd met her at the wake, when she'd returned his insults rather than quailing from them, he knew she would belong.

The dregs of bittersweet happiness were quick to dissolve as Kochin blinked awake, finding himself on his military cot with no memory of falling asleep. The dream left an acrid taste on his tongue. How horribly cruel the Mother was, letting him love someone he was destined to lose. How sadistic She was, giving him a way to bring her back that would cost the life of another. It was, however, fitting: Kochin's gift was so good at taking. This was the only answer that would've worked—he himself was not enough to heal Nhika, so of course he would have to use another.

Last night's revelation came with its own withdrawal: lethargy, discouragement, indecisiveness. He wondered if he'd overlooked something, a caveat to the matriarch's absolutes, but the papers were gone.

And a small part of him, a belligerent voice he tried to quiet, told him he'd already killed before, so what was one more? Why hesitate now, when it was to save Nhika?

Kochin knew the answer but didn't want to put words to it. It wasn't about what he was willing to do; it was about whether Nhika could live with that truth. She'd died to give him back his art, unhallowed by Santo's exploitation. Would she hate him if he defiled his heartsoothing to bring her back?

The voice, ever persistent, insisted: Nothing mattered, her hatred or his heartsoothing, if she was gone.

Around him, other soldiers were dressing. Today, while Kochin tended the wounded, they would be preparing for another attack. Their next goal, now that they had taken the naval base, was to aid the locals in overthrowing the Daltan occupation of the capital. Freedom fighters prepared their numbers, and there were talks in private tents about how long Theumas would stay. It was a multistep venture, one that would take many more months. Kochin had forgotten this war he'd joined extended so far past his goal.

That morning, while Kochin worked, his mind was elsewhere. Half of him was looking for the translator while the other half contemplated a terrible decision. He was slow to react to calls for more narcotics, sluggish in his triage, clumsy with a needle. For a moment, as he remembered the soldiers in the emergency ward—soldiers with uncontrollable bleeds, in the chokehold of sepsis, or hemorrhaging in the brain—he wondered if it would be so bad to take a life like this. It was the cycle of life, calories spent now or wasted in death.

He blinked the thought from his mind, sparing a moment to

be appalled at himself, at how easily the notion came to him. When had he grown so accustomed to this, taking lives? When had those plots come with cold calculation, rather than the reprehension of a conscience?

A collection of shouting drew him from his stupor. When he looked up from his work, he found a commotion across the yard: a Daltan prisoner, free of his binds and sprinting toward the fence. A Theuman private leaped up to intercept him—but the prisoner tackled the young soldier, wrestled him in the dirt, and snatched his pistol.

Now armed, the Daltan prisoner flew to his feet. He brandished the pistol at the private on the ground and someone cried out in panic.

A gunshot rang out through Camp Majora. Around Kochin, the field nurses gasped.

But it was the Daltan prisoner who collapsed to his knees, a bullet in his chest. Kochin was breathless until his eyes panned to Commissioner Nem, standing on the other side of the camp with a rifle raised. The barrel was still smoking.

The camp swelled with applause and relief as the private pulled himself out from underneath the dead man. Commissioner Nem, lauded and fierce, turned to the line of remaining Daltan prisoners, who were all being marched toward detainment. "Let that be a lesson," he said, and Kochin heard the message loud and clear.

No one crossed the commissioner or his city.

At noon, Kochin searched for the translator. She was elusive, never where he expected—not by the tents the Yarongese freedom fighters shared, nor in the spots the girls huddled in for lunch—and he didn't know her name to ask for her. He was just exploring the medic tents when steps approached from behind.

When he turned, he found Trin coming up to him on a wooden crutch, out of bed far too early for the state of his leg, soothed or otherwise. Kochin bristled on instinct—despite his injury, Trin's broad shoulders and stern brow offered him a menacing quality.

"Private Dep," Kochin greeted. They were nearly the same height, but Trin was bigger and older. Kochin's shoulders tensed underneath the uniform as Trin stepped closer, until they were within arm's reach, stares contesting each other. Somehow, Kochin knew Trin hadn't come to thank him.

Trin only jerked his chin down the path out of Majora. "Mr. Ven, take a walk with me."

Pushing past him with an onerous, lopsided gait, Trin started down the path. Kochin remained on guard, wondering if he should've prepared himself for a disagreement. Long ago, he'd promised the Congmis he would stay out of their lives, and he'd done his best to uphold it.

Nevertheless, he followed.

Trin took them down the winding path out of Majora, the same path they'd ascended after storming the beach. While Kochin kept a wary distance between them, he didn't doubt he could overtake Trin in this ambling, impaired state. Still, Trin walked the path in silence, his pace unfearful of the bloodcarver behind him.

"I read those papers," Trin began once they'd left the vicinity of Majora. Realization struck Kochin like lightning then—he'd been wrong. It'd been Trin to notice him translating those papers, to take interest. It'd been Trin to swipe them.

Had he put together what Kochin had planned, why Kochin was on Yarongese soil? He must've, and yet he walked with his back exposed, the skin of his neck bare. Kochin wondered if it was a gesture of peace or a sign of foolishness.

When Kochin remained silent, Trin glanced over his shoulder, his eyes demanding an explanation. But Kochin had nothing to say that Trin hadn't already guessed. They continued down until dirt mixed with sand, but Trin stopped them at the edge of the forest. They both looked out to sea, using it as an excuse to avoid eye contact.

"You're trying to bring her back, aren't you?" Trin asked. He turned to Kochin, gaining false height from his daunting expression. There was a subtle pity there, too, as though Kochin were nothing more than a misguided lover, blinded by grief. As though there was no merit to his plan.

"You had no right to read those papers," Kochin said in lieu of an answer, nose crinkling with indignation.

"Answer the question."

Kochin tried not to flinch at the sharpness of his words. "Yes. I am."

"Kochin," Trin began, and his words drew dangerously close to sympathy. In the moment he seemed years older, having lived and lost more than Kochin could understand. But Kochin wanted neither sympathy nor pity from him, only complacency and a blind eye turned. "I understand you loved her."

Loved her, past tense.

Trin continued, "And I know she cared deeply for you, too. I'd never learned how to read her, but that much was clear. That night, she made a decision. It was her choice."

Throat still narrowed by ire, Kochin said, "What are you trying to say?"

"Is this really what she'd want?"

Anger soured Kochin's throat and he spun on his toes, hands curled at his sides. "You didn't even know her full name. What would you understand of what she wanted?" he hissed, the rage so palpable he could feel it in his heartbeat.

Trin flinched with regret, leaning further on his crutch. "She sacrificed herself for you—"

Kochin lunged forward, hooking his ankle around Trin's poor leg. His hand extended for Trin's neck as he pulled back, toppling Trin and ramming him up against a tree trunk in the same halting motion. The shudder of Trin's body against bark was enough to shake seed pods from the canopy. Fury pulsed in the vessels of Kochin's hand and he extended his influence into Trin's throat. "You think I don't know that?"

His arm trembled as he held Trin against the tree. There was room for Trin to escape him—knock him back with the crutch or knee him—but he didn't, either from weakness or the fear that, with the contact of their skin, it was already too late. Instead, he swallowed, the prominence of his throat bobbing against Kochin's palm. A sliver of air escaped his lips in the shape of a sentence: "I always thought you were a murderer."

Kochin tightened his grip, not a heartsooth act but a human one, until Trin's breath turned into a wheeze.

"But," Trin managed, "I see now that you're not."

Those words stilled Kochin's hands and he narrowed his eyes, the vehemency of his stare drawing more out of Trin.

"Nhika loved you. I didn't understand it. I wanted to be upset at her for it," Trin elaborated, sentences coming in breathless bursts. "But you healed me. You healed Hendon. You may have committed an atrocious act, but it doesn't need to condemn you."

But it already had. If only Trin knew how Kochin had come to be deployed, how Kochin had healed him not out of servitude but guilt, then he would not be so quick to absolve. "You won't change my mind," Kochin responded.

"I won't let you do it."

Gritting his teeth, Kochin raised his hold on Trin's neck, until he'd lifted Trin to the balls of his feet with unbidden strength. He saw nothing now but the anger—at Trin's gall, broaching threats while in a bloodcarver's grip and presuming he knew Kochin so well. "How would you stop me?" he challenged, and his words carried the threat of death. Trin sucked in a sharp breath and Kochin watched the fear unspool in his eyes, like he was looking at the man who had killed Mr. Congmi, rather than the one who had healed his leg. Here, Kochin held all the power; he could steal the last rush of electricity from Trin's chest with a single thought.

So, why didn't he?

There, now you'll have it all. That was Nhika's voice, a fragmented memory surfacing into crystal focus: them both on the operating table, him holding her form, so impossibly light, against the cradle of his chest. Her head resting in the crook of his elbow, the glow already dimming from her dark eyes. Peace, freedom, and . . .

Love. She hadn't been able to say it, but he heard the word on her breath. *Kochin, I love you.*

This anger now, was it love? That was her gift—peace, freedom, and love—but Nhika had left him no instruction on how to use it. In her absence, the gift had morphed into something else: grief, guilt, and loneliness.

His fingers loosened around Trin's neck before he pulled away altogether, leaving the red portent of a bruise on Trin's skin. Trin sagged against the tree, coughing for breath and eyeing Kochin with unmistakable fear.

"She still had a life to live," Kochin said shakily.

"Kochin—"

"What else am I supposed to do!" He resented the vulnerability that had escaped into the tremble of his voice. "How could I live with myself, knowing I could bring her back but choosing not to? If this were about Andao, or even Mimi, wouldn't you do the same?"

From the way Trin's eyes softened, Kochin could tell some part of his appeal had gotten through. But Andao and Mimi were safe behind luxurious walls in Theumas; it was never a reality Trin had to fear, so he could never understand. His answer came out cold, hardened by dogged righteousness. "I won't let you take another life, Kochin. This isn't how you live with loss."

Kochin turned away sharply, leaving Trin breathless against

the kapok, and ascended the trail toward Majora. He paused, looking back only to say, "She's not lost yet."

What a familiar position: deciding whether to carve, a decision he had to make *tonight*—before Trin had time to stop him. Around him, bunkmates snored and murmured in their slumber, but Kochin couldn't sleep.

He could bring her back if he wanted to. Leaving his station would not be difficult—all he had to do was switch out his ID tag with a corpse, mark himself as deceased, and pay a Yarongese charter boat for passage back to Theumas. The island was still seeing battle; a medic casualty would not raise too many alarms, and only Trin might suspect his absence. As for finding an equivalent life . . . not even that would be difficult. Chengton had a small hospital, not nearly as secure as the Theumas Medical Center, where he could find someone near the end of their life. Kochin resented how simple it was.

But the alternative was staying here, with Nhika miles across the water, knowing he had the answer to saving her yet doing nothing with it. He could keep working as an army medic, fighting for the same thing as his peers when he enlisted in this war for something wholly apart.

How could he live with that?

For a moment, Kochin thought—why not? Why not bring her back? He could not face her after, but he would die with the secret of how she returned. She would never need to know it was another life that brought her back. It would not have to haunt her conscience as it did his. But that meant he'd have to leave her because those eyes could compel any secret from him, as they had before.

Knowing he wouldn't find sleep that night, Kochin left his cot and ducked out of his squadron's tent, dipping into the calming darkness of a Yarongese evening. In Theumas, it was hard to see the stars; the city never truly slept. Here, on the island, he saw the entirety of the Star Belt, which lit his path as the last of the sun winked from the horizon.

His feet took him toward the field hospital of their own volition, the voice in his head telling him that if he were to do this, he had to be certain, it had to be tonight. He shuffled around the courtyard, clinging close to shadows to avoid the undue attention of sentries, until he reached the field hospital. A glance through the windowed canvas revealed a medic inside, burning a gas lamp through the night, but they were too captured by tending the wounded to notice Kochin slip around the back.

Toward the bodies.

Behind the field hospital, covered by tarps, lay a line of fallen soldiers waiting to be taken home for a proper burial. The Yarongese heat and humidity hadn't been kind, accelerating the process of decay to the point that the stench alone burned his nostrils and nipped at his eyes. He almost feared lifting the tarp from the bodies and unveiling what lay beneath, whether they be soldiers or merely the echoes of them.

It was a mix of both that greeted him when he threw back the canvas. Flies swarmed, their meal disturbed, and Kochin waved them away from his hand. One corpse called to him in particular—a man his size and build, but whose body was so burned that he could not be distinguishable from any other Theuman. Half of his face was raw, scalp hardly still on the bone, and his uniform had been melted into his skin.

This one would do. Kochin threw a glance back into the field hospital, assuring that he was unnoticed by the medic within. Here was every part of his plan come together so cleanly: the register that documented ID numbers of the deceased, the corpse that could pass as his own, and his ID tag, dangling around his neck.

Yet, for a moment, all he could do was stare at the corpse at his feet. He saw his own face in its gnarled one, his lips formed out of its grimace and his eyes in its sunken pits. The image was jarring enough to stagger him, and when he blinked, the corpse was just a corpse again.

Something stirred inside his chest, a conscience come out of slumber, followed by disgust, because he'd had to see himself in a corpse to make it human. This act, erasing the memory of this soldier to claim this body as his own, was a crime in and of itself. There was no heartsooth tenet against this, nothing but Kochin's own sense of moral rebuke—that all he wanted to do was to heal Nhika, but the Mother kept asking him to take. More and more—taking from the Daltan soldier beneath the rubble, stealing this corpse's dignity in death, and ending a life as the final ultimatum in bringing Nhika back.

It was almost as though She was testing him, trying to see how far he was willing to go.

As far as it took, he'd told himself. Kochin drew out his ID tag from beneath his shirt and cupped it in his palm. The metal was still warm from the heat of his chest, the finish a little tarnished by blood from his ordeal in the naval base. There, beside the ID tag, hung Nhika's ring.

"What would you do?" Kochin asked, wishing bone could talk. He needed guidance—if not from Nhika, then perhaps from the heartsooths of her past. With a sinking feeling, he realized if these bones could talk, they would have no words for him but admonition.

A presence shifted at his side. When he turned, she was there, the image of her. This time, she brought no comfort, not when he'd accepted she was just a delusion and couldn't offer the answers he sought.

"Just say the word and I'll do it, Nhika. I've gone to war for you. I'll kill for you, too, if that's what you want," he said. "But only if that's truly what you want."

Her gaze was distant, as though she were looking past him. "All your life, you've been told what to do with your heartsoothing. When I died, I told you the gift was yours again. So, it's not up to me what you do with it—that's only for you to decide." These were words borrowed from her deathbed. "What does heartsoothing mean to you, Kochin?"

What did heartsoothing mean to him? It meant that he was never quite enough. It was just enough to set him apart in Theumas, but not enough to connect him to the Yarongese on the island. It was just enough to rope Nhika in, but not enough to save her.

And yet, heartsoothing was supposed to mean magic and family. It was supposed to mean surviving; the gift had fled Daltanny, had seeded in Theumas against all odds. It was supposed to mean connection, the one thing that had brought him to Nhika, and Nhika to him.

Just . . . not his heartsoothing. His heartsoothing was what had killed her.

But his bloodcarving could bring her back. Kochin stooped by the fallen soldier, prepared to exchange his tag for theirs, when a voice said, "Not here to mourn the dead, are you?"

Kochin froze. When he turned, that translator was looking down at him, arms crossed. She was tall, made of angles, with muscled shoulders and a long braid down her back—and she'd caught him at another crime scene.

When he didn't respond, she said, "You're not fully Theuman."

"What if I am?"

"I saw you soothing."

"I'm not a heartsooth."

"Ah, so you know the Yarongese term for it."

She'd caught him, but Kochin hadn't intended to lie; he *wasn't* a heartsooth. "You've no proof," he said instead.

"You're mistaken. I don't intend to report you."

"You've been watching me. What do you want?"

"My name is Numathai Lanalay. You have something that belongs to me."

Kochin shook his head. "You must be mistaken."

"Eighteen years ago, a Yarongese matriarch was taken from her family. She was forced to perform acts of resurrection. When she couldn't bring back a human, they killed her grandson. Now, only her granddaughter lives to continue the Numathai bloodline," Lanalay said. "Do you still believe I'm mistaken?"

Kochin quieted. It was uncanny—part triumph, part tragedy—to see the girl from the papers standing before him: alive, resilient, having taken down Daltan soldiers in the naval base without hesitation. It meant that research was something more than words on paper. That matriarch was real, and her legacy was close, and the crimes against her were all the more heinous when her granddaughter still bore the scars.

"I'm sorry," Kochin said, as if it meant anything from him. He could not undo what had been done to her grandmother.

"Where are the papers about her?" Lanalay asked.

Kochin stood to face her, eye to eye. "I don't have them anymore."

Her expression soured with annoyance. "But you *did*."

"Yes. I did. But someone took them from me."

His cheek flashed white with pain before he even realized she'd slapped him.

"You had no idea what you had," she said, seething. "Who those papers belonged to. Why does someone *like you* have them, anyway?"

Her words were formed of anger, but he heard the hurt underneath. And he didn't know which part of him she was reviling—the part that looked Theuman, or the part ready to defile the dead.

Kochin shifted his jaw, the pain cooling. "I wish I could return the papers to you."

She regarded him as one did an insect. "Who has them now?"

Kochin paused, hesitant to give Trin's name to a girl on a warpath—one who had killed Daltan soldiers with such ease. But Lanalay's deathly stare bored it out of him. "Private Dep. He's a good man—he'll return them, if only you explain."

"Good man?" Lanalay scoffed. "Very few have come to this island who were good men."

Seemingly done with him, Lanalay turned from the bodies, her path set toward the barracks. Before she could go, Kochin called, "Are you sure you want to see what the Daltans did to her?"

That paused her. Kochin wasn't trying to deter her from those papers. Even if they were the sole reason he'd come to Yarong, he had no more need of them—and Lanalay was right. They didn't belong to him, never had. It was almost a relief that someone could take them off his hands, like wrapping up the last open end of his conspiracy before he set sail back to Theumas.

But he knew if it were his mother or Nhika in those papers, he would never survive reading them.

"I'm sure," she said at last.

"And what do you plan to do with them?"

Lanalay's brown eyes glowed like embers in the lamplight. "I'm going to burn them."

Kochin furrowed his brow. "All this work, just for that?"

Something mournful overcame her, if only for a second. He recognized it: unspent grief. The desperation that came from coming so close to a single-minded goal that she could no longer turn back, no matter what it took from her. He hadn't once questioned his objective, not even when Vinsen and Trin tried to deter him, so he knew nothing he said could change Lanalay's mind now.

In a disarmed tone, she said, "As long as those papers exist, that's how the world will know her. But in their absence, her memory will be the one I carry with me, the way she sought to be remembered. Even if all that remains of my grandmother are the stories, I'd rather that than have her immortalized as an experiment."

She left him then. In her absence, the night dipped into complete silence—like even the wind had ceased through the trees. Kochin stared at the corpse in front of him, wondering if he still had the energy to fake his own death. Now that he'd met Lanalay, the act felt like a violation more than ever, knowing the Numathai bloodline had nearly been culled for that research.

But the night still held room for unspoken sins.

Kochin yanked off his ID tag. When he did, she appeared—*Nhika*, standing just beyond the tent. Her eyes held depths, like she had his answer: to kill or not to kill. Before he could speak, she disappeared behind the tent.

Kochin sucked in a breath and followed.

Disappearing and reappearing, Nhika drew him out of the camp beneath the watchful eyes of sentries. Her path led him toward the beach, and if she intended to coax him out into the water and drown him, he'd let her. It was an answer, after all—that there were easier ways to reach her.

When Kochin reached the surf, she was gone.

He stood alone at the edge of the water, his hand clasping the bone ring. Take a few steps forward, and he could let the tide claim him. But take a few steps back and he could return to the line of the dead and find one with his same face. Where he'd expected an answer, Nhika had disappeared, leaving him somewhere in between with a decision only he could make.

The waves lapped at his hesitation. He'd always had someone to tell him what to do with his gift. Santo told him to perform miracles. The entire city of Theumas told him to hide it. So maybe that's why he looked to Nhika's bone ring for an answer on what to do now—because there had *always* been someone telling him how to soothe.

Nhika was the only one who gave him permission to use it for himself. But she was gone. And if he was honest, he didn't even know how he wanted to use it.

Did he bring Nhika back, even if his heartsoothing took a life to do so?

"It's a beautiful night, isn't it?" Nhika asked, appearing beside him.

"It is."

"If you're looking for an answer, it's not on the horizon."

"I know." Now, more than ever, the loneliness felt heavy. He felt like he might die from it, on an island far from home with the ghost of the girl he loved.

His eyes fell to the bone ring in his palm. That name, Suonyasan, so beautiful when she said it. There was a space on that black band that belonged to Nhika. That had been her final act, pressing the ring into his palm and whispering an unfinished sentence. *Peace, freedom . . .*

Realization pulled out his legs like a riptide. He fell to his knees, kissing the surf, bone ring cupped in his palm.

He'd been waiting for an answer. The ring *was* the answer—had *always* been the answer. It had told him, months ago, what Nhika wanted; he just hadn't been ready to accept it. The ring was an act of remembrance, so she simply wanted to be remembered. Like Lanalay burning those papers, he had accepted the ring like a duty, the burden of her memory. He'd promised her to carry it with penitence to the end of his life, however short or long.

Nhika had died to return his heartsoothing to him. So, it was as Lanalay had said—he had to carry her in the way she sought to be remembered.

He hung his head, his heart drawn somewhere between the island of Yarong and the city of Theumas—because he had his answer. And it felt more like a defeat than a relief.

"Wait for me in another life, Nhika. I'll find you there." He'd have to, because Kochin realized with ever-growing surety that he could not spurn her sacrifice just to bring her back. It would not be just him who would have to live with his decision, but also her, and he couldn't bear the thought of tainting her heartsoothing with his own.

After everything he'd fought for and fallen for, war on Yarong and a naval base conquered, Kochin would not bring Suonyasan Nhika back. He couldn't.

With the tide calling him, Kochin brought the ring to his lips and pressed his decision into the bone. It was an apology and a promise: that he could not bring her back, but he would keep her memory safe.

Something shifted in his chest, like a knot come undone. It reminded him of notions long passed—peace, freedom, love—but this wasn't any of those. This was . . . acceptance.

It fell like ash over his heart. Slowly, laboriously, he stood, taking a moment to just stand and stare at the ocean. How little he felt here, standing at the edge of the water, watching the immortal swell and ebb of the ocean. Theuman scientists had explained this phenomenon in doubtless detail, had mapped the spring and neap tides to the phases of the moon, the gravitational pull of astronomical bodies. Just the same, Yarongese heartsooths had charted the bounds of their ability with tenets and rules.

It made him feel small and audacious, thinking he could conquer death, the world's oldest guarantee. Maybe he'd never been meant to.

With that realization slow to settle, Kochin started up the beach toward the field base. When he reached his barracks, a man slipped out before he had the chance to enter. He balked as the moonlight limned the man's squared features in silver: Dep Trin.

"Mr. Ven," Trin said, sounding bewildered. "I—"

"You were right," Kochin interrupted. He bowed deep, and when he rose, Trin's surprise had deepened. "I'm . . . I'm sorry. I talked to you then in grief, but I'm deciding now in acceptance. Keep the papers—I've no need for them."

Something tugged at Trin's brow. "You're . . . You're not going to . . . ?"

"No. You won't have to worry about me."

Kochin was wondering why Trin looked so flustered when another figure emerged from the tent behind him, dark coat thrown over broad shoulders and inky hair gelled back. It was Commissioner Nem, who placed a firm hand on Trin's shoulder. In his other hand he held bloodstained research papers.

The menacing look the commissioner gave him turned Kochin's blood to ice.

"No, he won't," Commissioner Nem said, his voice so deep that Kochin's very bones rattled. "Ven Kochin, you've been hiding something from me."

Kochin glanced at Trin, finding a new emotion there: remorse. He was too surprised to feel betrayed.

Dep Trin had turned him in.

TWENTY-ONE
THREE WEEKS AGO

KOCHIN'S HOLDING CELL OFFERED A VIEW OF A Yarongese town. It wasn't the capital—that was still occupied by Daltan forces—but a port town on the northern side of the island that housed the resistance. From his window, he had the privilege of a perspective he'd never seen before: life on Yarong. Real life, not the war stories passed around at Theuman banquets, nor even the panic-fraught memories his mother conjured from her time escaping. It reminded him so much of Chengton—the smell of fish carried on smoke, the women pulling up laden clotheslines, and kids squatting over a game of dice in the streets. The biggest difference between this town and Western Theumas was the absence of automatons, though the Yarongese seemed like they were doing well without. That, and of course, the rebel militia walking the streets—the ever-present reminder of wartime.

Across the street was an impressive building, built in the stony, intricate architecture of ancient Yarong—their town house, with carved arches and handsome eaves and gray pillars. Kochin wondered if he'd be taken back to Theumas for his tribunal or if Commissioner Nem would come to a decision here, as commander in chief.

He hadn't spoken to the commissioner or Dep Trin since

they'd left him here, stripped of his rank. Being a heartsooth wasn't a true crime; carving, however consensual, was. So, Dep Trin must've revealed the truth behind his miraculous recovery to get him indicted.

Kochin didn't have the energy to be mad, or shocked, or upset. All that had been sapped in his resignation: that Nhika was not coming back, and in her absence, Trin had found true justice for the Congmi siblings.

Still, escape was on his mind—Nhika had given him another chance at life, so he would not spurn it in a cell. Besides, he'd promised his family he'd come home.

He could see water from his cell if he craned his neck. Of course, there stood the wooden fence of a makeshift prison yard and a tuft of jungle before it, but it was close. Just a matter of escaping. Now, he wished he knew how to pick a lock. Nhika had once promised to teach him, but they'd never made it that far. And his room was barren—just a cot in the corner and a bucket to piss in—so there weren't many options for picks.

He tried everything else instead: shimmying the bars of his window, hoping to loosen a space large enough to crawl through; carving a hole in the wall with a loose nail, blunting the nail quicker than he dug out the concrete; or calling over the guards, hoping to snag a spare key. He only got slurs and insults instead—apparently, the fact that he had hidden his bloodcarving behind Theuman looks was a reprehensible sin.

Days passed. Kochin only knew from the rise and fall of the sun outside his barred window. They brought him food once a day, water thrice. He was running out of ways to escape.

Then, days later, after his hair had matted from the lack of showers, his uniform dirtied from concrete dust, his guard announced that he would be meeting with Commissioner Nem.

Everything was stratagem with Nem. Kochin knew him well enough from his time as Santo's aide. When he graduated with top marks, Commissioner Nem had even tried to recruit him. So, this long wait, the building anticipation and dwindling dignity—that was just a tactic. If the commissioner planned to have Kochin court-martialed, proceedings would already have happened by now. No . . . there must've been something else.

The entourage came to meet him when the sun was highest in the sky. Kochin did his best to recoup his dignity, shaking the dirt off his clothing and sweeping back his oily hair. Still, when Commissioner Nem arrived, rounding the corner to his private hall, the difference between them was mountainous: polished commissioner with a tailored military tunic, already medaled for his tactics in taking the naval base, versus an unkempt bloodcarver, a socialite so far fallen from his original height.

Kochin rose anyway, meeting the commissioner squarely when he stopped before Kochin's bars. Two soldiers flanked him, highly ranked and armed, but he waved them away with a hand. "You're dismissed," Commissioner Nem boomed.

"Commissioner Nem, with all due respect, are you sure?" one of them asked.

He nodded. "I know this boy. There's no danger here."

Boy. Another tactic, and it worked—Kochin felt small, and uncertain.

Hesitantly, the two soldiers eyed each other, but they did not disobey. It was only after they disappeared down the corridor that Commissioner Nem spoke again. "Ven Kochin, I asked them to get you a change of clothes, but it seems like they never did."

His words were surprisingly congenial, but Kochin reminded himself that Commissioner Nem was not an ally—not anymore. No Theuman who had learned of his gift ever was. But, because he was still a commissioner, Kochin addressed him with respect. "It's all right, Commissioner."

"Do you know what should happen to you?"

"No, Commissioner."

"You would be summoned before a tribunal, your crimes assessed. It might lead to only imprisonment, or it might lead to death, but I couldn't say. There's not much precedent for bloodcarver crimes in times of war, but surely you know past bloodcarvers have been trialed harshly. I can't promise anything. An investigative team would be sent to your family, as well—you had to inherit and learn the magic from someone, right?"

Each word felt like a stake driven deeper into Kochin's chest. He swallowed, trying hard not to show his fear.

"But," Commissioner Nem continued, and salvation clung to that word, "I know you, Kochin. You're ambitious. Smart. You're not some mindless, murderous liver eater, are you?"

The commissioner's words were sympathetic, and though Kochin didn't have the wherewithal to respond to the insulting question, he wondered if Commissioner Nem was prepared to let Kochin go on the basis of their relationship alone. In Theumas, the looks Kochin received from his father had granted him innumerable privileges, which he'd long felt separated him from his mother's side of the family; would this be another one of them?

Commissioner Nem didn't seem all too irked when Kochin didn't respond. Instead, he opened a gloved hand to reveal a key, with which he unlocked the cell door. It swung open until there was nothing between them but air; Kochin could've grabbed the skin of his face and killed him if he were truly the bloodcarver of Theuman superstition.

"There are sharpshooters posted all around the perimeter of the base, instructed to shoot anyone who attempts to flee detainment," Commissioner Nem warned, as though sensing Kochin's thoughts. "But you won't hurt me. Not until you hear what I have to say."

"What . . . you have to say?" Kochin repeated numbly.

Commissioner Nem gestured down the hall. "Walk with me."

Perplexed, Kochin followed. They walked as if they were on Theuman streets, two businesspeople venturing for lunch, not a commissioner and a war criminal. Commissioner Nem spoke as they walked. "You know, being a commander in chief comes with a great number of perks. For one, any news that happens on this island runs through me before it reaches the other commissioners back home. It runs through me, or . . . it stops at me."

"I'm not sure what you're saying," Kochin said, but he had an inkling.

"I'm saying that Theumas doesn't ever have to learn about your secret. That can stay between us. You'd prefer it that way, wouldn't you?"

Kochin's instinct was to thank him, to ingratiate himself

with gratitude. He'd done it so much while trying to rise in Theumas's high society, stroking egos and volunteering favors. But Commissioner Nem's words now came edged in cunning—this was another strategy of his. "I would, yes."

"Well, I would also prefer it that way. Trust me, I don't want to handle the paperwork of a court-martial when there are more important matters to deal with. Especially when your only crime was saving Private Dep's life." They turned a corner and descended the stairs, heading deeper into the maw of the detainment facility.

"I'm glad you feel that way, Commissioner," Kochin responded cautiously.

"I also had a chance to review those Daltanny research papers. It looks like you went through quite some lengths to acquire them, if the blood was any indication. Private Dep also informed me what it was you were planning to do. I almost wish you had brought this to me earlier. I understand why you didn't, but I could've helped you."

At that, Kochin narrowed his eyes, giving the commissioner a wary look. Condemn him or acquit him, but Kochin had never expected the commissioner to *help* him.

Finally, the commissioner stopped before a heavy steel door with a bolted circular window. He opened it and gestured for Kochin to peer inside. There could've been any number of things inside—a shooting squad, a tribunal, even another cell. Commissioner Nem's impassive expression revealed nothing.

The only thing Kochin hadn't been prepared to find was Nhika's casket.

His heart dropped as he rushed to her side, eyes searching the casket for deception or illusion. This couldn't be her—here, in Yarong, instead of at his brother's side—but this casket was the very same, and the slumbering expression beneath the glass window truly belonged to Nhika. A million questions seized him: how Commissioner Nem had found out about her, how he had taken her from Vinsen's watch, what purpose this twisted game was meant to achieve. He was so occupied by his thoughts that he didn't catch Commissioner Nem closing the steel door behind him until it was already bolted.

Kochin rushed to the door and slammed his fist against the window, shouting Commissioner Nem's name in fury, but it was locked shut. Only then did he assess the room around him in full. It was larger than his holding cell, all four walls plain concrete. Above him was a catwalk meant for sentries; right now, it was Commissioner Nem emerging on the bridge. Two personal assistants followed beside him.

"Forgive the arrangement. I just had to ensure my safety," Commissioner Nem said. "I had a talk with your old employer."

Kochin glowered. "You would align yourself with Santo?"

"Align myself with him? No. Trust me, I despise that man as much as you do. I simply requested information." Commissioner Nem gestured to the casket in the middle of the room. "I also sent someone for her, told your brother I'm an ally. And I am."

Kochin shook his head, feeling dread well in his throat. "Commissioner Nem, I don't think we want the same thing." He knew of Commissioner Nem's infamous temper; he'd always gone out of his way to avoid it.

"Maybe I should be clearer. I want to help you bring this girl—Suon Ko Nhika, is it?—back to life." His eyes held excitement. "That's what you were trying to do, wasn't it? With this iron casket, these papers?"

Kochin shook his head, prepared for the ensuing wrath. "I can't. I don't know how."

The commissioner shook his head. "What are you talking about? The papers detail it all."

"It costs a life."

Kochin might've expected disappointment or annoyance at the statement, but the look Commissioner Nem gave him was apathy. "And? We have prisoners of war. You have an infinite amount of tries."

Horror dawned on Kochin slowly, that the commissioner could look at those prisoners not as humans, but as fuel; that he could see this art not as sacred, but as a tool. That he fully expected Kochin to feel the same way. "Commissioner, I can't do that. I can't kill someone to bring her back."

Only now did that telltale wrath pull like a curtain across Commissioner Nem's expression. "Can't? Or won't?"

Kochin swallowed. He could lie, falsify the limits of heart-soothing, but Commissioner Nem wouldn't believe that while holding those Daltan papers. "Won't."

The commissioner glanced at his two advisors, exchanging words through looks alone. "I see." He paced a length across the platform, arms still clasped behind his back. "I'm surprised, Kochin. I had always placed you as someone who never backed down."

"What difference does it make to you that I can bring her back?"

Again, Commissioner Nem shook his head, his frustration showing through the angry line of his brow. Kochin had the unwelcome feeling that he was disappointing someone he should've been impressing. "It makes all the difference. Let me put some things in perspective for you. Daltanny proper has a population of twenty million. Add their territories, even without including their new land in Simbal, and you can double that number. So, forty million people—five percent of whom are eligible for the Daltan Army. That's, what, two million people?"

Kochin nodded, a lump stuck in his throat. He knew exactly where Commissioner Nem was headed with these mathematics.

"And how many *total* people live in Theumas, Kochin?"

Kochin's tongue felt slack. "Two million."

"So, their army alone is as large as our entire population. That's why we build our war machines and submarines and planes. But Guardians can be reverse-engineered, and submarines can be detected, and planes can be countered. We can't maintain the upper hand with invention alone. Sometimes, you need a little . . . magic."

He turned a cold gaze at Kochin, and that lump in Kochin's throat plummeted straight to his stomach. "You think that heartsoothing can make you an infinite army?" That was what Daltanny had attempted to do; heartsooths had killed themselves to avoid performing such taboo.

"I think it can, if you help me."

"It's a life for a life—you can't maintain an army without deaths."

"The battlefield is full of deaths. That won't be an issue."

"You're talking about lives as if they're numbers."

Commissioner Nem rounded an incredulous gaze on him. "And you're talking about them as if they haven't killed, slaughtered, *genocided* so many of your very ancestors. You must know what they've done to bloodcarvers like you—these research papers say it all." He slapped the papers against the railing, which gave a hollow ring. "They'll do the same to us. Now, we either use all our advantages—Theuman industry, Yarongese bloodcarving—to best them, or we become just another Daltan territory. I'll give you time to decide which future you want to fight toward."

Commissioner Nem's tirade echoed still around the concrete walls even as he turned to leave, heels clicking against metal as he did. His assistants trailed out after him, and Kochin was left with nothing but Nhika's casket before him.

TWENTY-TWO
TWO WEEKS AGO

IN THE SILENCE OF HIS CONFINEMENT, KOCHIN went to Nhika's casket. Here, she looked undisturbed, peaceful, and . . . real. The ghost of her never compared; this Nhika was flesh and bone, golden-brown skin kept warm by this machine and eyes still wet beneath their lids, almost as if she'd just been crying.

Commissioner Nem had made it even easier to bring her back. There would be no legal repercussion—a commissioner himself would sponsor his crime. He would not have to worry about the acquisition of an equivalent life when one would be handed to him. As Commissioner Nem had said, Kochin would have infinite tries.

Kochin brushed a strand of Nhika's hair out of her eyes, his influence grazing across her anatomy. The revulsion from soothing a corpse hardly came. He could almost convince himself that this body was still alive.

Almost.

His hand went to his chest, where her ring and his ID tag dangled at the end of a metal chain. There, on the beach, he'd made his decision. It wavered now, seeing her here, knowing how easy it would be. Something about her body drew at his influence, luring him in like a plea, but his fingers around her ring were the only reminder he needed.

Nhika would not gain life through Daltan death. Her revival would not be the product of a commissioner's trial, and Kochin would not make this decision out of desperation.

He wasn't sure how much time had passed before Commissioner Nem returned, but it couldn't have been a full day.

"I've given it a lot of thought, and I can see where you're coming from," Commissioner Nem announced before he even settled on the platform. "It's very noble, actually, your refusal to take a life. Enlisting as a medic, too—you're not even a soldier."

Kochin kept quiet, fearing Commissioner Nem's next scheme. Little did he know, it wasn't about taking a life—Kochin had done that before with Mr. Congmi. It was about killing with his gift when Nhika had died so that he would never have to profane his heartsoothing again. He didn't have the words to explain that to the commissioner in a way he'd accept.

"I understand the hesitation," Commissioner Nem continued, but he didn't. "So, I'm going to try to make it as easy for you as possible." He waved to someone beyond the room.

A moment later, the door behind Kochin opened. He didn't have time to make a break for the exit before a man was pushed inside his cell, hands bound and mouth gagged. The door locked again immediately after.

"This man is Rolan Vasse. Does that name sound familiar to you?"

Kochin shook his head.

"Let me elucidate, then. He is the primary investigator heading all current research on Yarongese bloodcarvers. He is the very man responsible for the torture and death of thousands of Yarongese innocents. The very man who headed the terminated study you translated."

Kochin turned toward Rolan with equal parts horror and disgust. The man returned Kochin's stare with terrified, bulbous eyes. His injuries were numerous—swollen bruises all over his balding head, cracked and bleeding fingernails, a jagged gash across his neck from what looked like a suicide attempt. His figure was bowed, tongue mumbling something behind the gag: a plea for mercy, Kochin guessed.

Commissioner Nem was right. There was no one more deserving of death. It should've been Lanalay, here—she was the one who deserved justice, not Kochin. And Kochin knew from those dead soldiers in the research ward that she wouldn't hesitate to kill, as he did now. This man before him—this pitiful, quivering man—would undoubtedly kill him if their roles were reversed. Not only kill, but torture, maim, vivisect. This was a man who deserved no mercy.

"He's being sent to Theumas to be tried for his crimes, but I know for a fact that he will receive a death sentence for his actions. So, I relinquish his life to you, Kochin. You don't have to worry about taking an innocent life—this man is far from innocent, and he is fated for death anyway."

Kochin explored Rolan's frail state. Sweat dripped off Rolan's forehead in fat beads, and though he was gagged, Kochin saw movement behind the rag—a string of pleas or prayers. It would've been so easy: Take that cowardly life, reweave it within Nhika . . .

But then, just as Nhika walked in step with Kochin ever since she'd saved him, so too would this murderer haunt her new life. Her every breath thereafter would be sowed with the memory of someone who had killed so many Yarongese before. He could not have that.

Turning back to face Commissioner Nem, Kochin opened his mouth to respond before a force knocked him from behind. It was Rolan, jumping Kochin with newfound strength. They grappled and before Kochin could react, he felt Rolan's binds around his neck, shaking hands pulling them tight. Through pulsing vision and ringing ears, Kochin heard Commissioner Nem call for intervention.

Survival instincts returned to Kochin in an instant, and he rammed his head back, skull connecting with something firm. He felt the crack of bone and Rolan fell backward, the weight of his body pulling against the bind at Kochin's neck.

Kochin pivoted, catching Rolan by the collar of his shirt. With his other hand, he carved, stealing from Rolan's very blood to quiet the rhythm in his cortex. Before the man even hit the ground, he was in a deep slumber.

Kochin let out a haggard breath, staggering backward and rubbing the raw skin of his neck. Already, he felt the chafed welts rising and fought back a cough. On the platform, Commissioner Nem had stilled, observing the scene with wide eyes.

"He's dead?" Commissioner Nem asked, not with horror but intrigue.

"Asleep." A cough escaped Kochin's throat.

Commissioner Nem's eyes expanded with zealous curiosity. "So, you *are* a bloodcarver. I knew it was true, but it's so different to see it with my own two eyes. Your gift, it's . . . amazing."

Kochin shook his head. "It's not what you want it to be, Commissioner."

"Why not?"

"I'm not going to bring her back. Not even with this man."

Anger flashed across Nem's expression. It was quick to clear. "I don't understand, Kochin. Explain to me how I can make it any easier for you. I'll do it."

Kochin had always feared Nem's wrath, but now he saw a glimpse of reason. Would Nem so easily let him go if he could explain the sanctity of the gift, explain that all his life he'd used it to take—and he couldn't bear to do that anymore?

When he was just sixteen, matriculating into his university years early, he'd had this dream. He was going to change Theumas, he'd told his mother. Change the way they thought about heartsoothing. Change the way they thought about *heartsooths*. Elevate it from superstition to science, just like the botany his father taught him. From the start, his sights were set on medicine—such a perfect corollary to heartsoothing, a ripe breeding ground for change.

He had failed spectacularly. That naivete had lured him into a spider's web, he a willing pupa. Kochin had not succeeded in changing a single mind, but maybe he still had a final chance— with Commissioner Nem now. If he could convince the commissioner to see it not as a weapon of war, but as a piece of culture, defined by the compassion of its artists, then Kochin could walk out of this cell and hang up his heartsoothing for good—it would not bring Nhika back, but it would also never take an innocent life again.

"I'm sorry, Commissioner Nem," Kochin began, his voice ringing true around the walls of his confinement. "As long as the price for her revival is an equivalent life, I can't bring her back. Only half of it is about the life. The other half of it is about my gift."

Commissioner Nem scrunched his brow. "So, what are you saying?"

"I'm saying that my gift was never meant to take a life. I'd only just come to realize that myself."

"Then what, pray tell, does it do?"

"It heals," Kochin said, growing sure. "It survives. It remembers. It's not an easy answer to war—there are no easy answers, Commissioner, or Daltanny would've found them by now. But when this war ends—and it *will* end—my gift will still exist on the other side. It was given to me by everyone who has ever loved me, so I have to make sure it lives on in the right way. Killing a man, even to bring back another . . . That isn't it."

Commissioner Nem's brow lifted, lips parting—like he'd been moved. Like he might understand.

Then his expression collapsed with its usual ire. "Selfish."

"What?"

"People are dying. *Theumans* are dying. You're selfish, Ven Kochin, to keep this gift to yourself on the basis of something as flimsy as morals. You're so full of contradictions—your gift was never meant to take lives, maybe, but it's been used that way in the past. Or maybe you're too young to know the Liver

Eater, a serial killer with your same gift. So, be consistent—are bloodcarvers killers or healers? Are you a soldier or a pacifist? Are you going to play your moral high ground to keep from taking the life of this murderer, while so many innocents die in his place?"

The words struck deep because they struck true. Kochin gritted his teeth against Commissioner Nem's accusations, knowing that he had shone a light on all of Kochin's inconsistencies. From the very beginning, Kochin had been made from inconsistencies: Yarongese, but with all the looks of a Theuman; a heartsooth, but given only half the gift; a murderer, but one who'd torn himself apart with self-hatred for his act. Maybe Commissioner Nem was right; perhaps, killing this man to bring back Nhika was the correct thing to do. Then a sinful man would die and an innocent would walk in his place.

Kochin stepped toward the casket, lifted the hood. He felt Commissioner Nem's cold approval burn into him as he curled his finger around Nhika's stiff hands. For a moment, her body drew him in a way corpses never did. He glimpsed the channels that had given him life, the energy wrung from muscles and the electricity stolen from her heart. For the briefest of seconds, he almost felt he could save her.

But the reality of his predicament returned to him, and Kochin stepped away again. He saw now how cruel he'd been trying to keep her body alive. These wires circulating her blood, that tube feeding her oxygen—this was not life. It was delusion.

"This is my final answer," Kochin said, reaching into the

mechanics of Dr. Santo's casket to draw out the command roll. The machine slowed, then stuttered, and his heart fell in his chest. This was goodbye; Commissioner Nem had given him the chance to bid Nhika rest in person. But he would not bring her back.

"I'm not sure what's greater, my surprise or my disappointment," Commissioner Nem boomed from the top of the platform. "If you will not bring her back, then there is no reason to exempt you from court-martial."

Commissioner Nem bored into Kochin with his downward gaze, the silence giving Kochin one final chance to renege his hesitance and give in. He hadn't saved Nhika; he wouldn't even make it home to his family as he'd promised. Yet, Kochin only contested his stare with silence.

"Very well, then," Nem said. He gestured to an assistant. "Take him to his holding cell. He'll be shipped back to Theumas in the morning."

In the quiet of his cell, Kochin counted down the hours until morning by how the sun dropped in the horizon. Commissioner Nem was right—he was not one to give up. Not when he'd first come to Theumas, anyway. Back then, he'd convinced himself that the heart of the city was the land of promises. He'd graduated from the university early—earning the highest marks in the past decade of its history, so he was promised opportunity. Kochin learned quickly that it was the land of masks: Murderers worked as doctors; megalomaniacs were voted men of the people; and bloodcarvers could almost convince themselves they were heartsooths.

Since then, Kochin had done nothing but give up. He'd resigned himself to Dr. Santo's service, would've still been there if not for Nhika's intervention. He'd hidden away his heartsoothing behind Theuman looks when he'd promised his mother he'd change the world.

And yet . . . this didn't feel like giving up now. This felt like acceptance.

"So, this is it?" Nhika asked, appearing beside him. It'd been a while since she'd shown her face. A part of him was glad for her company, even if only an illusion. The other part feared being haunted by her forever.

"This is it," he repeated.

"So, heartsoothing truly does die with our generation." She stared wistfully out the window, at the waning sun that numbered Kochin's days.

"It's a good time to believe in an afterlife. Then I might find you there." He settled on his cot, feeling the springs in his back. "But for now, I'm going to sleep."

"You're not going to even try to escape?"

"No."

"Not even for your family? Vinsen and Bentri and your parents, who are waiting for you at home?"

"My insubordination would only endanger them further."

"What about your mother? She'll be investigated."

"They have no proof of anything."

"Kochin, I—"

"*Please*, Nhika. I . . . I can't hope anymore. I don't want to—it's . . . it's how I lost you." He deflated in the cot, feeling the sudden weight of his decision bear down on him at once. "I'm tired."

"Who are you talking to?" came a different voice, and Kochin startled straight. When he turned toward the door, he found Dep Trin standing across the bars.

The hairs of his neck prickled in caution. There Trin stood, wearing a guard's uniform despite the crutch slotted underneath his armpit.

"Volunteered for guard duty, did you?" Kochin asked, not honoring Trin's question with an answer. "I thought I told you that you didn't have to worry about me anymore. I'm not going to murder anyone just to bring her back."

Trin looked unimpressed, staring at Kochin with those impassive eyes. When Kochin had killed Mr. Congmi, it was Trin he feared the most—Trin, well trained with the pistol, who looked like he could split wood with his bare hands and would travel to the ends of the earth for the Congmis. Kochin trusted that Trin wouldn't kill him here—that would be a dishonor to Nhika's final request—but that brought little comfort when Trin rested his hand against his gun.

"I heard you'll meet before a tribunal back in Theumas," Trin said.

Kochin nodded. He couldn't read Trin well enough to know if those words came with vindication or apathy. "Yes. I imagine I'll die by firing squad—the only thing they can trust to kill a bloodcarver."

He hadn't meant the words to invoke pity—they only came

with sardonic truth—but Trin furrowed his brow with subtle remorse. "For the crime of healing me?"

"For the crime of carving." Kochin sagged in his corner of the room. "You must find this end fitting for me. I don't blame you—but please, let Nhika rest. Commissioner Nem brought her body out here, but I don't want her to be left in a war zone."

Confusion inflected his expression. "He brought her here? Why?"

"So that I could bring her back."

"But he knows it would cost a life."

"That didn't matter to him."

"And . . . and you refused?"

Kochin stared into his hands, limp on his lap. "It's as you said—I committed an atrocious act, but I'm not going to let it condemn me."

Trin made a noise of consternation in the back of his throat; the creak of a lock followed it. When next Kochin looked up, his cell door had swung open.

"I didn't volunteer for guard duty," Trin said dryly. "I snuck in to release you. There may be things you deserve to die for, Ven Kochin, but saving my life is not one of them."

Despite the invitation, Kochin didn't budge. What was the point? He would either be executed or he would escape now and reap different consequences—his family investigated, him never being able to set foot in Theumas again. So, Kochin only stared, the open door an empty promise.

"Well?" Trin asked, sounding perplexed. "Aren't you going to leave?"

"There's nothing left for me out there."

"With her gone, you may just be the last heartsooth, no?" At that word, Kochin met his eye. "I won't pretend to understand what that means to you, but ... doesn't that give you some obligation?"

Trin's words were clunky, but the thought behind them sincere. He was trying to connect with Kochin through the memory of Nhika; he was trying to convince Kochin to *live*. That was something Kochin never would've anticipated.

"Why are you helping me?" Kochin asked instead. "You're right—I healed you because Nhika would've asked me to. You owe your life to her, not me."

"Then you're in *her* debt for your freedom. Because if you don't even try to escape death, then she never should have died for you." The words were rough, almost castigatory, but they caught Kochin's attention. Trin cast a quick glance down the hallway. "Now, by my count, the guard will rotate through here again in five minutes. I'll be leaving in two—I'll give you until then to decide. Choose to die or choose to live, but if you meet her in your afterlife, let her know I gave you the choice."

Without another word, Trin turned his back toward the cell, his eyes patrolling the hallway. Kochin righted himself in the cot, realizing that Trin's offer came with no hidden fees—he could escape now or face judgment when the sun rose on tomorrow.

But the decision didn't feel like his alone to make: His family would hear of his insubordination either way, but would the commissioners be fair in their investigation? Or would they find some way to indict Kochin's mother, who could not hide her Yarongese looks as Kochin could? Then again, Trin was right—if he escaped death on Santo's operating table only to die now, then Nhika's sacrifice would've been all for nothing. He'd just accepted the burden of her memory; he couldn't well pass it on just yet.

Kochin stood. With laborious steps, he reached the entrance of his cell. "There are gunners stationed around the compound," he said.

Trin looked unconcerned. "I know. I came in through their blind spot."

"When Commissioner Nem finds my cell empty in the morning, he might suspect you."

"As far as he knows, I was shipped back to Theumas yesterday, honorably discharged for my leg."

Still, Kochin hesitated. Trin gave him a questioning look out of the corner of his eye, a brow raised. No more words passed between them, until at last Kochin said, "Okay. How do we get out of here?"

"This way." Trin waved him down the hall.

They took the first left at the end of the hall; not the way Kochin came in, but a path to avoid guards. Trin had grown adept with his crutch in very little time, his strides fluid even though Kochin knew he hadn't fully soothed away pain. Trin must've felt each step deep in his bone, but Kochin never would've guessed.

They crept down familiar hallways—this was the way Commissioner Nem had taken Kochin before to reach the observational holding cell. Just as Trin banked right around a corner, Kochin stuttered to a halt.

"It's a right here," Trin urged, throwing a furtive glance down the hall; they were all clear to escape.

"Commissioner Nem is keeping her downstairs," Kochin said, drawn to the opposite end of the hallway. "Please—I can't leave her here. I don't trust him to give her a proper burial."

For once, Trin's eyes were sympathetic, and he nodded—the most camaraderie the two of them had ever shared. Then it was Kochin leading Trin through the halls, having memorized his earlier route with Commissioner Nem. A left here, a descent down the stairs, a quick peek around the corner to make sure they were alone, and then they were there. The bolted steel door that had once bound Kochin with a terrible decision.

He opened it now with ease. Inside, Rolan was gone, but the casket remained. When he stepped inside, he found it dead silent—not even the whir of the cogs to fill the empty space since Kochin had turned off the machine. Trin followed him, each foot placed with caution and eyes wary.

Kochin drew up to the casket. There she was, untouched since he had abandoned her. He wondered if Commissioner Nem ever planned on returning Nhika to Theumas, or if he was satisfied letting her rot here. The enmity was fleeting as Kochin removed catheters and tubes from her body, disconnecting her from the machine that had given her false life. Only when he had finished, when this casket looked less like a medical machine and more like a simple coffin, did grief spear Kochin through his heart.

She was gone. Dead six months ago. The reality of it was only now reaching him.

Not ashamed to show his anguish before Trin, he bowed over

the side of her coffin, feeling his throat shrivel, his lungs dry, his heart crack. The piece of her that she'd left with him was truly all that would remain. He reached up to stroke her cheek, the bone ring tugging at his chest. Yarongese tradition dictated that he fit the ring with a sliver of her bone, and he could only do that if he had her body. This was what she'd wanted when she'd pressed the ring into his hands on that operating table: to be remembered in a way that mattered.

"I'm sorry," Trin said. The simple words held a depth of sympathy.

"There's nothing to be sorry about," Kochin said. "It was her decision."

Clearing catheters out of the way, Kochin hooked his arms beneath her chest and her legs. The weight of the task was heavy, but Nhika herself was light. He tipped her head toward him, where it rested against the cradle of his shoulder, the skin of her cheek brushing the skin of his collar.

That touch was enough to pull his heartsoothing in.

Without his conscious control, his influence entangled itself with her anatomy. Something dragged him in—perhaps the remnants of herself she'd left with him, yearning for reunion, or perhaps the empty organs calling for relief, their signal not yet dormant. Earlier, he'd seen the channels in her body that had saved him from death: the path oxygen took as it leached from her blood, the rivulets sugar carved out of her liver. Now, he saw channels that could bring her to life—they were instructions inscribed in her very anatomy, written by Nhika herself when she'd died for him.

His influence intertwined intimately with the secret history of her body as Kochin soothed the way Nhika had soothed: one with the body, not apart from it.

It was as though his feet had lifted off the floor, as though the room had flipped and his body had reoriented to align with her own. The breath rushed from his lungs as he fell into her anatomy, her blood entwined with his. Where there should've been revolt and nausea, the consequences of soothing a corpse, there was only euphoria.

Her body was his body, her muscles his muscles, her heart his heart.

And her heartsoothing . . . that was his, too. He felt it here, still remnant, like the last embers of a dying hearth. Whether it was a figment of his imagination or truly there, lingering still in the strands of her muscle, Kochin let it guide him.

Her bones showed him how they could be more than just stone, how marrow and blood could renew them as tissue. Kochin saw how electricity had discharged from her brain; its deep canyons and folded ridges told him how he might return it. And her heart, that fragile empathy organ, expressed its longing to feel and keep a pulse again.

Her heartsoothing, whatever remained of it, supplied every answer on how he might restore life to her dormant anatomy. It had never been about restoring the processes of her body by machine and influence; that had only been the pale reflection of life. It had always been about listening to her heartsoothing—*his* heartsoothing. Just as wounds cried to be tended, Nhika's body cried for new breath.

Give, her heartsoothing instructed. *Give as she did to you.*

All that remained was to give, yet how could he?

He'd always been unable, his Theuman body stagnant and selfish. He couldn't defy its natural instinct to hoard and reap and reserve. Yet, there came a feeling now, like Nhika's hands on his, unfurling his curled fingers when he never knew they'd been clenched. He saw her on that Chengton beach, their fingers laced, her hand against his heart—wise, gentle, beautiful. In life, Nhika had tried to teach him to soothe as she did, giving and taking in equal measure. Kochin didn't understand until now, but her sacrifice had been his final tutor.

He'd always thought that being half Theuman and half Yarongese had been the divide to his art. Thought that it made him wholly nothing. He was wrong—it made him wholly Ven Kochin, wholly Yarongese and Theuman, wholly a heartsooth.

In its entirety, giving and taking, he was a heartsooth, and this would be his first true act of healing.

Kochin released the inhibition of his influence. As soon as he did, his sugars went where they yearned to go, restoring her blood and tissue the same way she'd destroyed them. Electricity siphoned from his chest to spark her own, until he felt their two hearts beat in tandem. Gases regulated themselves in her lungs as he exhaled a sour taste from his own.

Kochin gave and gave and gave. Nhika grew heavier in his arms while he grew weaker in his legs until at last they yielded underneath him, knees slamming the concrete with a jarring gravity.

"Kochin!" Trin exclaimed, glancing at the door with an urgent look. Only then did Kochin rattle free from his soothing, blinking languidly up at Trin. He still clutched Nhika tight in his arms, but as soon as his influence pulled away, he felt the return of her deathly pallor.

"I can bring her back," Kochin breathed, voicing the revelation aloud. *"I can bring her back."*

But it would be a life for a life, if he gave her back all that she'd given him. He could already feel the ache in his muscles, but he marveled at the sensation, the thought of giving his body so completely, so freely. Something he'd never been able to do before. Now that he could, he'd give it all to her—she would walk away from this compound in his place, the way it should've been on that operating table. Maybe the two of them were never meant to exist together, but it was a beautiful eclipse of fate that they had shared any moments at all.

"Bring her back?" Trin repeated. "But . . . with whose life?"

Kochin's heartbeat was drumming. The organ was going to burst. "Mine," he said, and acceptance settled in. "All I ask is that you get her out of here, keep her safe. Promise me that."

"I . . ."

"Promise me."

"I promise."

Only then did Kochin bow his head and soothe. He gave her back the strength in her bones, the fullness of her muscles, the color of her skin. He returned all that she had given, tracing along lines prewritten, her body his favorite poetry and her heartbeat his favorite song.

In these final moments, heartsoothing wasn't a science, nor was it a weapon, nor even the secret to an infinite army.

It was magic. It always had been. And it was his.

He felt a dark curtain falling over his consciousness. What a marvelous feeling, this selflessness, his body yielding where it had once hoarded. His heart squeezed—the empathy organ, finally living up to its name.

Just as he thought his heart might give out, something wrapped over his arm—warm fingers, new skin.

"We're all walking out of here together," came Trin's echoic voice.

"But it'll require—"

"Take it," Trin interrupted. "Only what you need, but take it. I . . . I trust you."

Kochin bowed his head in understanding, and his influence branched. It threaded itself around three bodies: one dying, one mending, and the third full of life. Faithful to Trin's instructions, he took only what he needed. It was Trin's energy that stitched the last of Nhika's vessels, patched the final cracks in her ribs. It was Kochin's breath that sparked the storm of Nhika's brain, electricity returning along the same paths they'd use to dissipate. When everything came together like this, three bodies in space and a heartsooth to connect them, it was *symphony*.

When it was all done, Kochin nearly collapsed from the effort of it. Trin stumbled, too, pulling apart as he swayed over his crutch. They eyed each other in the ensuing silence, both of them too afraid to speak.

Trin braved the first words: "Did you . . . Is she . . . ?"

Kochin opened his mouth to express his uncertainty when he

felt a movement from Nhika. A muscle twitch. In his arms, a trembling heartbeat gathered strength, muscles tightened with timidity, organs remembered their autonomy . . .

Kochin exhaled hope.

And Suonyasan Nhika drew her first breath.

⇒⇒ TWENTY-THREE ⇐⇐
TWO WEEKS AGO

EVERYTHING BURNED—KOCHIN'S LUNGS, HIS LEGS, the tears behind his eyes—but he ignored it all for the small miracle he held in his arms. Even Trin collapsed at his side, discarding the crutch and sweeping back Nhika's hair to place a finger on her pulse.

"Heaven and earth, Kochin," he breathed, his earlier reservation all but gone. "You've done it. How?"

"I . . . I don't know," Kochin admitted, because he truly didn't. He couldn't say how he restored tissue or cardiac impulse or cranial activity. All he knew is that he had *given*, using the same paths of influence that she had already threaded.

Something rumbled overhead; rivulets of dust rained down on their hair. Trin picked himself up from the floor and offered a hand. "We've got to go."

With a nod, Kochin squeezed Nhika close to him, a bid of luck before he lifted himself off the floor. His legs stumbled in their weakness, but the steady drum of Nhika's heartbeat against his chest urged him on, and he trudged forward with renewed vitality.

They were a clumsy trio, Trin with his crutch and Kochin with his sugar-starved legs and Nhika in his arms, breathing softly. But never before had Kochin felt so much hope—Nhika's form in his arms was the very embodiment of it.

"This way," Trin said, guiding them back toward the stairs. He skidded to a stop when they heard a collective of marching footsteps from above. Their party turned down a different corner just as a troop of soldiers stomped through.

Trin took them forward. Kochin followed blindly. At some point, they rerouted, avoiding the marching footsteps of another troop—then, a cramped stairwell later, they were opening a door into the humid Yarongese air.

Darkness soaked the night. The lights of the village didn't fully reach the sky as Theumas's lights did; Kochin could still make out the stars. Familiar constellations lit their path as he and Trin evaded sentry beams to skirt across the prison yard. The fence was lacking—Trin hacked down a post with three hits of his crutch.

At the noise, a beam of light swiveled toward them. They ducked out into the thicket of the Yarongese jungle, but too late. There came shouting, a voice hollering, "There he is!"

Trin and Kochin continued toward the beach. The jungle was unforgiving terrain, but Kochin held Nhika close to his chest and pressed through, no matter the branches that snapped at his cheeks and the ground that dropped out beneath his step. He kept pace with Trin, who was fighting his own battle through the foliage.

At last, they reached the beach—a breath of fresh air. Trin still pressed on; Kochin followed, only hoping there was a plan beyond this. Behind them, distantly, soldiers had mobilized. Lights roamed the dark. The jungle swayed.

"There's a ship waiting for us," Trin said, urging him on. Kochin wondered if he regretted it now, with the weight of consequences nipping at their heels. All to save a heartsooth.

The ship made itself apparent. It was like the one Kochin had come to Yarong on, only smaller—beached at the moment, its bay open like a wide throat.

Kochin quickened his pace, feet slipping against the loose sand of the dune as he slid his way down to the ship. He reached it before Trin and set still-unconscious Nhika down on the bench, brushed back her hair. In the night, she was starlight.

A cry from Trin drew Kochin's attention out of the vessel; the soldier had tumbled down the dune, his crutch snapped in two beneath him. He clutched his leg, wincing.

Kochin hurried out to help him. Already, those lights were approaching, roving the hill above them. Hurrying, Kochin scooped Trin up over a shoulder, dragging him more than walking with him.

"We have to go," he said, voice urgent. "*You* have to go. They're only looking for me."

"I'm not one to see things halfway through," was Trin's stoic response.

Acid rose in Kochin's lungs as they staggered through sand. His arms burned; his shoulders stiffened. But he lurched on until he'd dragged Trin into the ship, trailing sand and surf behind them. Trin collapsed against a bench. Kochin sent a look over his shoulder. Already, soldiers were cresting the hill—they'd spot him and Trin both. There wasn't enough time to start the ship. Not enough time to get away.

A plan formed. Half desperation, half acceptance—that they wouldn't be able to get through this night without casualty. That Commissioner Nem only wanted him, and he didn't need to take Trin and Nhika down with him. That he'd gotten his happy ending already, bringing Nhika back, reclaiming his heartsoothing. And that had to be enough. Even if he wanted to see her open her eyes, even if he yearned to take her home to Chengton, even if he wanted his freedom, his peace, his *love* . . . This had to be enough.

Kochin's hand wrapped around his necklace. A ring; an ID tag. Her life given for his; the favor returned. A bid to be remembered; a reminder of what was gone.

Kochin yanked the necklace from around his neck and wove it around Nhika's curled fingers. Then he stooped at Trin's side. "Bring her to the Congmis and keep her safe, okay? Promise me."

Already, Trin looked diaphoretic, but he nodded through his pain. "Promise. What are you—"

That's all Kochin let him say before leaving his side. He spent a moment at Nhika's, crouched beside her sleeping form, bending his head low over hers. More than anything, he wished she would wake, if only so he could have a final moment with her. And she'd always had an easy answer, a quick solution, hadn't she? He wondered, if she were awake, would she see some future where they lasted? Or could that only be found in another life?

The moment was brief—it had to be, for Commissioner Nem's soldiers were coming over the hill. Still, Kochin took the time to whisper one last farewell.

"Remember me when you wake, Nhika," he said. "Remember me as a heartsooth. Remember me as Ven Kochin. And remember that I . . . that I love you."

I love you. A quiet confession meant for no one but her, him, the sand and the sea and the stars. Kochin hoped she could hear it. His hand brushed her cheek, and he imagined pouring the confession into her skin the way his influence did—just so that when she woke, she knew she was loved.

All he could do was hope. Kochin tore himself from her side, feeling something crush around his heart.

"What are you doing?" Trin asked again.

"Buying you time."

Kochin stepped out onto the beach. Behind him, with a hiss of steam and a whir of gears, the bay doors lifted. He threw a glance over his shoulder just in time to see Nhika disappear from view.

Then it was just him, this beach, his fate over the hill.

Kochin started forward, climbed the dune. When he came up on the top, he threw up his hands. Lights assailed his eyes and rifles clicked; Kochin squinted, hands above his head, just as a broad-shouldered silhouette cut toward the front of the group.

"Mr. Ven, I'm very disappointed in you," Commissioner Nem said. He peered beyond Kochin's shoulder. "And who is your accomplice?"

"I'm turning myself in," Kochin replied staunchly, yielding nothing.

Commissioner Nem scrutinized him. "If I'm not mistaken, that's a Congmi vessel. One manufactured under my purview.

So, there are few who could have acquired one, Private Dep being one of them."

A stone settled in Kochin's stomach. "He wasn't involved. All I did was send him home with Nhika."

"Doesn't seem that way to me," the commissioner said. "Seems like I've caught him aiding and abetting a fugitive."

Behind Kochin, water burbled. The ship was finally pushing itself off the beach, disappearing into the surf. His chest should've felt lighter for it, but Commissioner Nem said, "It's in my right to have the unknown vessel torpedoed out of the water."

"You . . . you *wouldn't*."

"Give me one reason why not."

Kochin swallowed. This was a bluff. Trin's proximity to Andao made him untouchable, yet . . . Andao would never know the truth of what happened on this side of the water. Here, Commissioner Nem could torpedo the ship with no consequence—just as he'd shot the fleeing Daltan prisoner dead. And Kochin couldn't have that, not while Nhika was alive on board that ship.

"I did it," Kochin announced. "I brought her back. Nhika. She's alive."

Commissioner Nem's eyes narrowed with doubt. "How? With whose life?"

"None but my own." Kochin didn't let his hands fall. "If you want proof, she's on that vessel."

"Are you lying to me, Kochin?"

Kochin didn't drop his gaze. "No."

"This is a surprise," Commissioner Nem thought aloud. His

tone turned lauding. "Kochin, do you understand what this means? This is a wonderful thing you've done—you've rewritten the meaning of life and death and . . . *war*. Has it occurred to you the implications?"

Kochin wanted to deny it, to tell Commissioner Nem that he misunderstood this small act—Kochin had not rewritten anything, he'd just healed along lines already inscribed—but he knew that Commissioner Nem was already cemented in his perspective. To him, Kochin had brought back the dead from nothing. To him, Kochin was the answer to an infinite army.

"If you let Trin and Nhika go without consequence, I'll do it for you," Kochin offered. "I brought her back without using a life in exchange. I don't know how, but I did it. If you can guarantee Mr. Dep's and Nhika's safety, I'll go with you willingly. We can figure out how exactly a bloodcarver revives the dead."

Commissioner Nem grinned at the offer with something between pride and greed, as though thrilled that Kochin was finally speaking his language. In the moment, Kochin felt small and meaningless, grasping for any scrap that Commissioner Nem had to offer—just like when he'd first come to Theumas, so prepared to lower himself to any job just to get a place on the ladder.

"I'm glad that you're coming around to reason," Commissioner Nem said. "And I find it very suitable. I can forget that Dep Trin was ever here—after all, he should be back in Theumas by now. And you're right. The only crime you've committed is saving one life and bringing another back from the dead. I don't see why that can't be forgiven on the island."

Kochin didn't relax, knowing a stipulation was coming.

"*However*," Commissioner Nem began, and Kochin steeled himself, "I will find Suon Ko Nhika. I will verify whether you've truly brought her back. If you can't find out how you performed your miracle, then its only evidence resides in her body. We can't just have something that important scampering off to an unknown corner of Theumas."

Kochin gritted his teeth. Was Nem threatening to . . . experiment on her? After he had so decried the experiments of Daltanny? "Don't you dare hurt her," he growled, and the threat in his tone was enough to coax a couple raised rifles.

Commissioner Nem waved them away. "Every businessperson knows an employee needs incentive to work. That's my one condition. Take it, or chance your fates before a tribunal."

Perhaps Kochin was not so adept at this game as he'd thought; Commissioner Nem had seen right through his ploy. Now, the commissioner expected results for a task Kochin could not reproduce, and Nhika's life was on the line if he failed. Chains, so many chains—out of Santo's binds just to fall into another's. Nhika would've had choice words for him, but Kochin saw no other option.

"Okay," he told Commissioner Nem, holding his head high. "I'll take it."

TWENTY-FOUR
NOW

"SO, THAT'S IT?" NHIKA ASKED.

Trin nodded. "That's it. I haven't seen him since."

She soaked it in; Mimi, Andao, and Hendon were doing the same. Trin's recount of Yarong was news to the entire family. Nhika still couldn't wrap her mind around the fact that she'd been to Yarong and back—or, at least, her body had. The rest of the story was just as unfathomable: Trin finding the research papers, turning Kochin in, and . . . and helping Kochin bring her back.

"Thank you," Nhika said, reaching out to squeeze Trin's biceps. "For helping him. For bringing me back."

"It was more him than me," Trin admitted. "I just can't believe that such a thing is possible. You made me think heartsoothing was a science. But what I saw wasn't science. It was a miracle, Nhika."

Maybe it was. After all, she'd used heartsoothing to relinquish her life and he'd used heartsoothing to bring it back. It capped both ends of her cycle in a way that she couldn't explain with biology, nor medicine. "It couldn't have been easy to trust him with your body. Thank you."

"I'm glad I did." Trin flashed a smile. "I like to think a part of me is with you now."

"Then I hope it's the brawn, and not the brains," Nhika teased.

Trin's smile was quick to sour. "I wouldn't have complained if that sense of humor didn't come back with you."

Nhika placed her hand over the necklace: her bone ring, Kochin's ID tags. These were all the answers she'd been hoping for, yet Kochin was still missing.

Noticing her silence, Trin said in a sympathetic tone, "In the end, he made the right choice. He gave himself up to the commissioner for you. For me, too. Despite everything he's done, he's a good man."

But Nhika didn't want a good man. She wanted an *alive* man. "Don't say that like he's gone."

"I'm sorry."

"What's the sentence for treason of that nature?"

His expression was sympathetic. "I think you know."

No. Nhika could not believe that Kochin had been sentenced to death. It was too cruel—he'd come so far, and he'd finally discovered his heartsoothing again. But if the Congmis didn't know where he was, and Trin didn't know where he was, then that just left . . .

"Nem," Nhika said. Her mind raced, trying to finish Trin's story. Kochin had been detained. Nem had taken her body to Yarong. He'd asked Kochin to bring her back.

So why would Commissioner Nem send Kochin to court-martial right after he succeeded? No, Kochin must've been alive, and Nem must've known where, because a man like Nem was too ambitious to look at a gift like heartsoothing and not see it as an opportunity.

Then it struck her. Nhika knew exactly where Kochin was.

"Nem's exhibition," she said—growing surer. The commissioner had spoken about a secret weapon, one that would win the war: *You'll learn*, he'd said, *when the white flags wave over the Gaikhen Mountains, when our soldiers come back safe*. He'd been so confident he could win the war because he'd been banking on an infinite army. "Kochin is there."

"How can you know?" Mimi asked.

Nhika shook her head. "I don't. But I have to believe he's alive. And if he is, that's where he'd be."

"We can get you in," Trin spoke up. "Can't we, Andao?"

Everyone looked surprised, including Nhika, but Andao shifted his jaw. "I suppose we could. Not with an invitation, but I don't think that's ever stopped you before."

Nhika tilted her head. "You would do that for me? Even . . . even if I'm going up to save *him*?"

"Yes." Andao found Trin's hand, and their fingers laced. "Hate it as I might, I'm afraid I owe that man a favor. But I'm not sure how much we could protect you once you're there. Although the commissioner requires our factories, wartime is unprecedented—so what Theumas knows as 'treason' is very open to suggestion. As Mr. Ven surely realized, Commissioner Nem is good at spinning a narrative. He was elected, after all."

"I'll be smart about it," Nhika promised. She learned from her mistakes.

Mimi looked unsure. "And what's your plan? Find Kochin and break out?"

"Is there any subtlety anymore? The commissioner has seen me dead."

"He's a powerful enemy to make."

"Our goals are opposed. It's inevitable."

"I just . . ." Mimi bunched up her dress at the waist. "I just don't want to see you get hurt again. Not for him. Not even for us."

"Well, I've already died once, and it didn't take," Nhika said. "If you can get me a way on and off that airship, I can find Kochin. And, if worse comes to worse—well, then I suppose he'd just have to bring me back again."

→→→ TWENTY-FIVE ←←←

KOCHIN FOCUSED ALL HIS INFLUENCE ON THE still heart of the chick in his palm. He could see it like a blown glass toy, its miniature vasculature almost like a human's—the heart four chambered and the blood pushed through the lungs. But numerous differences prevented Kochin from immersing in it fully enough to heal it. Humans did not have those now-deflated air sacs, nor the strange positioning of the lungs to the heart, nor any of those other foreign organs that swam in the compartment of its body. So, how could he overlay himself when those organs had no corollary to his own?

Soothing the way he did, his mind one step apart, he could tell the chick's mechanism of death. He could tell that its neck had been broken, snapped by the cruel beak of its mother for being a runt. He could tell the exact vertebra that needed to be mended.

But he could not discern how life had left its body—the precise way the electrical conduction had scattered from the brain, or the cadence of its final heartbeat. This runt chicken had not clutched Kochin on his deathbed, whispering declarations of love, so he could not bring it back. Kochin dropped it back onto the table.

When he'd first learned heartsoothing, his mother had taught him with animals before trusting him to heal his own brothers. Maybe that was why his gift had never fully realized itself—he hadn't developed his skill enough with others to know what it was like to give. By the time he'd grown advanced enough to heal Bentri's and Vinsen's scrapes and bruises, all he'd ever done with his gift was take. Now, it would be easier to practice again on a human.

But Kochin was smarter than to tell Commissioner Nem that. Lest he wake up a corpse on his doorstep.

He stood, giving his muscles a moment to stretch after sitting for so long. The stateroom around him was a luxurious one, if not a little sparse. Burnished wood furniture gave him everything he needed—a workspace, a wardrobe, a bed—and the airship even had its own plumbing and hot water. It was not a military vessel but a recreational one, meant to ferry aristocrats above the silver heights of their city to wine and dine in the sky.

It was almost enough to make him forget he was a prisoner. But beyond those wide windows, curtains pulled open and glass curved to match the hull of the airship, were miles and miles of desolate, neutral waters. In every direction around this airship, there was only open ocean, and even if Kochin could escape his locked room there was nowhere to escape *to*, not unless he could operate, all by his lonesome, a one-hundred-foot aircraft meant to be piloted by fifty flight officers. Even then, he would not know which direction led back to Theumas and they would probably run out of gas and fall from the sky before he figured it out.

That was all by Commissioner Nem's design, this gilded prison. Not so overt as the blackmail Santo kept him with, but binding nonetheless. Occasionally, he would see a ship or a plane arriving, either bringing new fuel or ferrying in Commissioner Nem. Kochin had caught sight of the commissioner's plane against blue skies just earlier, so he knew he was due for a visit.

As though the thought of him had conjured him into existence, the twist of a lock sounded from Kochin's door. It opened to reveal Commissioner Nem, flanked by guards, armed not with guns but batons.

"Any luck?" Commissioner Nem asked, as if they were on congenial terms. He took a seat at the table, eyed the dead chicken, and twisted his lip into a frown. "Not even a chick, Kochin?"

"It's not so simple," Kochin said, knowing better than to voice his true thoughts: that this was an impossible task and Commissioner Nem was stubborn to a dangerous level, unfit for the Commission.

"It's a bird. And I've given you weeks—I thought we'd at least be up to monkeys by now."

That was another one of Commissioner Nem's mistakes—working his way up to a human. That's what the Daltans had done, dogs then monkeys then people, and though that worked for medical research, it didn't for heartsoothing. Humans were humans, monkeys were monkeys, and birds were birds. For a heartsooth, expected to know organs by influence and feel rather than name and equivalent function, such reasoning didn't apply.

"It takes some heartsooths lifetimes to perfect their art."

"Well, we're at war. We don't have lifetimes." Commissioner Nem rested a hand on each knee, elbows square. "You wouldn't be trying to stall for time, would you? Considering an escape? Might I remind you how vital this is?"

Kochin clenched his jaw. "Commissioner, I want to save lives as much as you do, but—"

"Clearly not," Commissioner Nem snapped, and Kochin flinched on instinct.

As though noticing his unchecked temper, the commissioner smoothed away his anger with a pinch of his chin. "I don't think I can understand you, Kochin. So, I'm trying to reason with you."

Kochin didn't speak, fearing he'd ignite something again.

The commissioner continued, "Your family is from Yarong, right? I assume they came here during the first Daltan onslaught of the island. In Yarong, I see Theumas. They prided themselves on a gift, as do we. Their people are staunch in their beliefs, as are ours. And war came to them too quickly, as it did for Theumas. I'm hoping that's where the similarities end. You, of all people, should know to learn from the mistakes of your forebears—a weapon in the very palm of their hands, and they didn't use it.

"History will repeat itself. First Yarong, then Simbal, but I will not have Theumas be next. If any part of you considers yourself Theuman, you'll understand what's at stake."

Those words were moving and true, and Kochin saw how Commissioner Nem had secured himself a place in office with such galvanizing ideas, but he was asking for lightning to strike

→ 295

twice on command, and Kochin was only human. "I'll try, Commissioner."

"I know you will. Andao was the same. All that capital wasted in maintaining a legacy. But as soon as Mr. Dep was enlisted, his tune changed." The commissioner lifted himself off the chair, leaving a heavy depression in the cushion. "I have seen her in the flesh."

Kochin's eyes flared wide.

"That's got your attention, hasn't it? Well, she's walking, talking—wholly restored. Revived. I almost didn't believe you before. I believe you now. And I need you to make *everyone* believe it, too."

He had a dozen new questions—was she okay? Safe? *Happy?* But those weren't questions meant for the commissioner. Instead, he said, "Everyone?"

"Tomorrow is a big day. Politicians and sponsors will be here. Show them a miracle."

"So you can be adulated for turning the tides of war?" Kochin asked, emboldened now that he knew Nhika was awake. "Was it not enough to be a commissioner?"

Commissioner Nem's brow lowered. "So we can actually *win* this war," he corrected. "Everyone has lost hope that we can—until I promised them a weapon that can save us. Now, I've *seen* how it works. Tomorrow, you're going to prove to this whole city such a weapon exists."

With a grunt, Commissioner Nem stood to leave. Kochin stopped him at the threshold of the door. "And if I can't?" he asked.

Commissioner Nem paused, pivoted. "Then all the proof of your miracle lies in the body of the girl. If you can't produce evidence of your gift, I'll have to find it elsewhere."

Kochin swallowed the stone in his throat, narrowed eyes contesting Nem's. "Is that a threat, Commissioner?"

"No," Commissioner Nem said, turning again to leave. "It's a deadline."

TWENTY-SIX

"IS IT TOO TIGHT?" MIMI ASKED.

"No," Nhika said—but she wasn't the fondest of small spaces. Last time she was in a chamber like this, she'd thought she was going to get vivisected by Santo. In comparison, being hidden away in one of the Congmi Guardians wasn't so bad—and she was small enough to curl into the main cockpit without messing with the controls.

But, just in case, the siblings had turned off the machine, lest she accidentally send a round of ammunition through their walls.

"Andao, for the next model, might I suggest some extra padding? Seat warmers, perhaps?" she said.

Andao leaned over to inspect her arrangements. "I'll take that into consideration."

"You'll survive," Trin said with a straight face, closing the domed canopy on top of her. With a hiss that sounded a little too close to Santo's casket, it latched.

"Can you still hear me?" he asked, leaning close.

When she nodded, Andao began gesturing to various instruments. "That red lever there opens the hatch—remember, pull then twist. If it gets stuck, that button there should forcefully eject, just lift the cover and hit it. And if you're in a bind, you can engage manual control of the Guardian by—"

"Andao," Nhika interrupted. "I'll be fine."

He sucked in a breath and straightened his coat. "Right. You're not going to war. Just an exhibition."

That was the plan: sneak her on board in one of the Guardians. Mimi familiarized her with the schedule of events; while everyone was at dinner the first night, she'd be free to find Kochin. Then the pilot would take her home—and she and Kochin would have to lay low in some corner of Theumas until Nem forgot about them. But that was nothing she hadn't done before.

"Remember, Nhika, Andao and I will be up there, too," Mimi said. "Goodness knows, you might be a good distraction from the politicking."

If all went to plan, she would be in and out with no one the wiser, then crash back at the Congmi villa to await the siblings' return, but it was comforting knowing she had support on the ship. Maybe that's where she and Kochin had failed the first time: entering the Theumas Medical Center alone.

"Save me some leftovers from the dinner, all right?" she said.

Mimi nodded. "Are you ready?"

"Ready."

Before they loaded her Guardian into the truck, Trin placed his palm against the glass, a parting gesture. She was a little dismayed he would not be coming on account of his leg, but she mirrored the gesture on the other side. It was good luck. It was goodbye.

When she saw them next, she would have Ven Kochin with her.

It was an hour-long, rattling truck drive to Yibai Airdrome, where one of the Congmis' private aircrafts awaited them. Nhika and her fellow Guardians, three in total, were unloaded and reloaded onto a Congmi airship. They lifted off again after a long and laborious strapping process—for which Nhika was grateful as soon as they took to the turbulent skies.

Now, it was just a matter of waiting. Her legs were starting to cramp, but she didn't soothe them. She was going in on a full belly, but Nhika still had a nervous compulsion to save every calorie.

Time passed. Her muscles grew achy, being contorted into the tight position of the Guardian. Nhika fought the urge to pop the dome and stretch her legs.

At long last, she could feel their aircraft descending. There was lurching around the cabin as it lowered, then a jarring rattle when it made contact. As the bay doors opened, letting in a sliver of light, Nhika craned her neck to peek out through the domed cockpit. She caught a glimpse of the Nem's airship: a beautiful hull of glass and copper shaped like a whale lifted out of the water, suspended by a metal balloon and finned with bright red junk sails. On such a cloudless day, it shone like a second sun in the sky—an airship that promised a weekend of extravagance. Nhika wondered if it was also a prison.

This would be like her and Kochin's previous adventures: Break in, find what she needed, escape.

And this time, don't die.

The aircraft around her settled. When the bay doors opened in full, workers boarded and Nhika shrank back down into the legs of the Guardian. After some shuffling, some clinking, there was movement: her Guardian, being unloaded onto Nem's airship.

She adjusted the earpiece to her level. From inside, she could hear conversation.

"Welcome, Mr. and Ms. Congmi," a steward said. "And your inventory?"

"Three Guardians," Andao replied.

"Any incendiaries?"

"Just fuel. Does it matter?"

"The commissioner is limiting any flammable material on the ship."

"Why's that?" Mimi asked.

"To avoid stray sparks. It's nothing to worry about, of course, but we're simply taking precautions. The Guardians are fine—however, due to limitations, we ask that your ship wait for you back at the airdrome."

"In Theumas?" Mimi sniffed indignantly. "No, that won't do."

"I'm sorry, Ms. Congmi. It's on the commissioner's orders."

"And *I'm* sorry, but I simply can't be on this airship without a way out. It's far too stuffy."

"I'm afraid you'll have to take it up with the commissioner."

There was a tense quiet. Nhika leaned into the earpiece. *Keep arguing, Mimi*, she thought. It was one of Mimi's biggest strengths.

But in a mollifying tone, Andao said, "Very well. We'll ask the pilot to return to Theumas."

Nhika's heart fell. Having a plane waiting to take her

home—that was *half the plan*. Each flight craft that left the airship was another door closed.

Then Andao added, "Surely, you're not sending all crafts back."

"If you're concerned about the operations of the ship, don't worry—we have enough small transports for fuel and resupply."

"Kept on the landing platform, I assume?"

"Yes—but that's for us to worry about. Please, Mr. Congmi, enjoy your evening."

Mimi let out an elegant laugh. "You'll have to excuse my brother. It's the engineer in him. He simply must know how everything works."

But Nhika had understood, loud and clear, what Andao was telling her. If she could make it back here, she could find a vessel and still get off this airship with all four limbs. Piloting and flying it, well—that was another issue, but she wouldn't be alone.

As the workers wheeled her away, she stole a glance back toward the Congmi craft. Its bay doors closed, engines started. Then it pulled out onto the runway, and Nhika watched from the bulbous cockpit of the Guardian as her sure way off this floating prison departed back toward Theumas.

It was nearing dinnertime.

Nhika sat at the bottom of the Guardian, now loaded into

the hull of Nem's airship, watching the hand move forward on the pocket watch by a dim light on the console. Even before it reached the hour, a voice echoed to life on the overhead broadcast system.

"Guests aboard the *SS Justice*, the commissioner cordially invites you to make your way toward the deck two dining hall for dinner."

That was her cue. As Andao had instructed, Nhika lifted the canopy of the Guardian and climbed out, every joint popping with relief. She slid down the ladder at its back and dropped herself into an empty hangar. The pocket watch went around her wrist: a constant reminder of how much time she had before guests moved again. And the ornaments in her hair—they came down, too, not hairpins but lockpicks.

Now, to find Kochin.

She'd work her way from the bottom to the top of the ship. Thankfully, a ship schematic was posted near the exit to the loading bay, and Nhika studied it.

This was a Ngut Inventions airship. No wonder it had such weight limitations. Nhika had never ridden any kind of airship before, but by allegiance alone she assumed Congmi airships were superior—and far less flammable. Ngut was a little behind, still using cheap hydrogen to fill his balloons.

Mother, all those days spent with Mimi were rubbing off on her.

According to the ship map, there were three decks to this vessel. The bottommost—that's where she was now, nothing much but engine rooms, cargo holds, and the loading bay.

But there were also some holding cells, where she'd start her search.

She picked her way through the lower deck beneath gurgling pipes and hissing steam. As she passed by portholes, she hazarded a glance down—and immediately regretted it.

They were so high over the water. It was claustrophobic, knowing there was nowhere to go on this ship but down. There, on the horizon, sat a flat line like a mirage, pockmarked with a little shining dot: Theumas. How very far she was from the Dog Borough now.

Nhika found the holding cells, but they were empty. It was almost a relief—that Kochin was not being treated as some kind of wild, biting animal. But that meant she had to go upstairs.

Deck two: That's where the people were. When she came out of the stairs, she was immediately taken by the stark difference between lower deck to guest cabins. For one, there was carpet—newly laid, colors still vibrant. Little glass lights lined the halls, gently swaying with each bout of turbulence. Everything smelled perfumed, looked golden, and exuded wealth—like she could stick her thumb through the wallpaper and pull out pearls. What a shame, that she had to know this luxury as an interloper rather than a guest.

Ahead, lines of private cabins awaited her. For a second, they intimidated her—too many to pick through in the hour, and Kochin could've been behind any of those doors. But she soon realized they were personalized, a tag at the side of each door for the guests. Even Andao and Mimi had a room each. Nhika walked the rows, finding no room belonging to Kochin, until she heard the quiet hum of chatter.

It was the dining hall. The last of the crowd was slipping inside, ushered by guards, and Nhika chanced a quick peek. It was a room at the front of the ship, windows on either side curving into a large canvas of a sky near sunset—all tea lights and chandeliers and the winking sun to give the hall a warm, orange glow. Round tables, dressed with place settings, circled the periphery.

At the front was a stage. It looked like it should've held performers, but right now, Commissioner Nem stood at the microphone, welcoming his guests aboard. Nhika ducked away quick.

One more floor. She ascended.

Up here was the bridge at the front, with a gallery walk that overlooked the dining hall. Below, Nem continued his speech with a joke—she saw laughter from the crowd. Andao and Mimi were down there, too, sitting at a corner table. It reassured her to know they were on this ship. And it scared her that they might reap consequences if she was caught.

She headed back to the stern. Here were the special cabins, like the captain's suite.

Beside it was Nem's room.

Nhika threw a glance over her shoulder. There was no one to see her draw the lockpicks from her sleeve. It was an easy lock; Ngut had not foreseen criminal trespassing when he fashioned these doors. When it clicked undone, Nhika let out a long breath.

Oddly, she felt fear. She didn't know what it meant if he wasn't behind this door—because she wasn't sure where else he could be. Maybe, he might've truly been dead, and this entire endeavor was to distract herself from the unacceptable truth.

And if he *was* here, Nhika wasn't sure how to act. It felt like just a couple weeks since she'd last seen him on her deathbed. In reality, it had been six months. She wasn't sure how to thank a boy who had gone to war for her.

Nhika turned the handle and opened the door.

Empty.

It was a suite befitting a commissioner, all white and gold. The wall opposite her held an enormous window, so Nem could sleep to a view of the ocean like he owned it. But the bed hardly looked slept in. Instead, furs draped over the back of the desk chair, and the desk was the only worn piece of furniture in this entire stateroom.

She stepped up to it. Miscellany littered its surface, papers and baubles and a pen still in ink. If she were a Daltan spy, perhaps she'd see gold in these documents. Instead, she saw a failed quest.

Nhika rocked back on her feet. Defeat tasted like thin air. She was just about to leave when something dark caught her eye—a bloodstain, dried nearly black. It was on a set of papers beneath the others, wrinkled and tarnished.

Nhika shifted papers aside to uncover it. It was in a foreign language—Daltan, she presumed, from its proximity to Theuman. Someone had translated it in pencil, and she recognized the handwriting: It was the same one she remembered from a napkin, scrawling out an address in the Pig Borough.

She was getting closer and closer to Kochin. He'd been here, his hands all over these papers—so they must've been the ones Trin told her about, research to bring someone back from the dead at the cost of another life.

Someone like Nem should not have had papers like these. The commissioner was a military general; he'd weaponize anything. So, to give him one less idea, Nhika folded up the papers and slid them up her sleeve, just against her biceps.

She was turning to leave when something crashed behind her. Glass sprayed; Nhika yelped, throwing her arms around her head as the air sucked out of the room. Across the floor splayed a shadow: tall and lean.

When she turned, she found Lanalay standing in the frame of a broken window, wind tugging at her hair as she tossed the end of a rope out the ship. Papers took flight, but Lanalay snatched them from the air and slammed them back on the table.

Lanalay leaned over the desk. "Ms. Suon."

"Lanalay," Nhika said. But it wasn't the socialite aspirant who stood in front of her. It was a girl made of metal, wearing a maid's uniform she'd torn and tied into something practical, with a round of rope at her hip and a knife at her biceps.

"What are *you* doing here?" Lanalay asked.

"I should ask you the same thing—didn't I tell you to keep away?"

"You didn't help me. So I had to find my own way."

"Nem shouldn't be trusted."

"Clearly I do not trust him—why do you think I am dressed as a steward?" Lanalay narrowed her eyes. "Now, you haven't told me why you're here."

"I'm looking for someone," Nhika said. "A boy. The commissioner is keeping him here—I know it. It's why I told you to stay away from Nem. Nothing good comes out of a man who has undue interest in heartsooths."

"Why would your commissioner keep him here?"

"I think . . . I think Nem wants him to raise the dead."

Something dropped in Lanalay's expression. "By any chance, does your boy go by the name Ven Kochin?"

Nhika blinked. "You know him?"

Lanalay let out a long string of expletives in Yarongese before she said, in a measured tone, "Yes, I've had the misfortune—he's the entire reason I've had to come to your city-state."

"Why? What happened to him?" Something tightened in Nhika's throat, and she added, "Is he alive?"

"Last I saw, yes," Lanalay said, and Nhika felt all her muscles relax—ones she didn't even know had been tensed this entire time.

"*Where?* Where is he now?"

"I'd love to know that, too—because I have a feeling that wherever he is, so are my papers."

"Wait, your papers?"

All at once, it clicked. Nhika had thought Lanalay had been searching for a memento—but no, she'd been searching for the *research papers*, the last memory of her grandmother, however twisted they were. She was just reaching up her sleeve when the door clicked open behind her.

She whirled. Nem stepped into doorway, two of his guards beside him.

With a defeated breath, she raised her arms in surrender. She glanced back at Lanalay to do the same, but the girl had disappeared—ducked beneath the desk, hopefully. Now, only Nhika stood within Lanalay's wake of destruction, and it must've looked like she'd broken in, which—well, she *had*, but she hadn't done it so gracelessly.

"Commissioner," she said, stowing her picks. "My invite got lost in the mail, so I . . . er, let myself in."

"I knew you were wily, but I didn't think you'd be so bold as to attempt a jailbreak."

Despite her situation, her hopes leaped. A breath of relief escaped her. "So he *is* here."

"He is. In fact, I can take you right to Kochin."

It was kindness wrapped in malice. "Can we forego the chains? They get a little trite after the fourth or fifth time."

"Apprehend her."

"*Wait!*" Nhika protested as the guards stepped forward. Her mind was racing. She had allies on this ship, but she couldn't get to them. However, one such ally crouched behind the desk, if Lanalay could be convinced. With her heel, she tapped the desk. "I saw the research papers from Yarong, Commissioner Nem. Curious about bloodcarving, are we?"

"In fact I am."

"So was Santo."

His laugh was dry. "For all the wrong reasons."

"Are there right reasons?"

He gave her a considerate look. "Of course. Everything has wrong and right reasons—war, for one. Wrong, if waged off notions of power and conquest. Right, if waged for peace."

"And why did you bring war to Theumas?"

"The latter, believe it or not. It's why I have need of Kochin."

"Tell me where he is."

"Like I said. I'll take you right to him." With that, he waved his hands, and the guards descended like Butchers. A hand clamped either wrist; another yanked back her hair. She cried out, squirmed, dropped her weight—but they were armed with gloves.

The guards tightened their hold. Nhika twisted and kicked. And for the first time, her gloves came to her aid.

They twisted off in the guard's grip. Her hands flashed free—just a second, before a guard grabbed her by both biceps. But it was enough; she'd hooked fingers against his collar, her knuckles brushing his neck.

And caught skin.

It was like everyone had scraped in a tense breath, like they were all sharing the same thought: bloodcarver, skin, certain death. And Nhika *could* have soothed him. His anatomy burgeoned under her purview, awaiting her command.

But another guard would simply grab her, and she would still not know where Kochin was. Nem must've had theories of her heartsoothing, but nothing had confirmed them so far. The last time she'd been cavalier about revealing her heartsoothing, Santo had shot her through the shoulder.

So, Nhika did nothing. Let them believe she was simply Yarongese. Nem had his secret weapon. She had hers.

The guard's hold moved to her wrists, yanked them back, and she let herself be apprehended. As her captors turned her back to Nem, she didn't miss the scheming lift of his brow. "So," he began, "not all Yarongese are bloodcarvers."

She glared up at him. "And not all commissioners are honorable."

He scoffed, more humored than put off. "You came here to find him, didn't you? I'll help you with that."

Nem stepped forward, then paused—as though still wary of getting too close. But as the guards tightened their grip, he scrutinized her once more and finally closed the distance between them. She worried he might see Lanalay's shadow beneath the desk—it was so obvious to her.

But he was looking at something around her neck. Slowly, as one approached a wild animal, he extended a gloved hand—until his finger hooked the chain of her necklace and drew it out from beneath the collar of her dress.

Nhika let him cup the ID tags in his hands and read the name punched into their metal. The downturn of his lip spoke volumes, though his eyes revealed nothing at all.

At last, he said, "I promise, no harm has come to him."

Nhika hadn't expected the softness. It made her pause.

"We're all looking to end the war, Ms. Suon. It's why I joined it—call me arrogant, or foolish, but don't call me dishonorable.

Kochin has shown me great promise. I believe he is the answer. And I need everyone on this ship to believe it, too." With that, he dropped the ID tags. They caught against her neck with a chime. To his guards, Nem said, "Take Ms. Suon backstage. Get her food. I've business to attend."

Looking solemn, Nem turned down the hall and left.

⇒⇒ TWENTY-SEVEN ⇐⇐

KOCHIN'S ROOM, NO MATTER HOW LUXURIOUS, smelled of death. He wondered if it was his imagination alone—scented paper lined the drawers, and pouches of aromatic tea were nestled in the furniture, yet all he could smell was the aftertaste of his failed heartsoothing attempts. The bodies of chicks and rodents themselves were disposed of before every meal, of course, but they still piled up in his mind, a growing list of evidence that he could not repeat his miracle. That had only come through the alignment of stars, an irrevocable exchange of heartsoothing that had transcended her death.

But he was coming to terms with the fact that he could stall no longer. That council of war Commissioner Nem spoke about had arrived; Kochin watched the guests come in on their ships—airplanes, dropping off and retreating. If he wanted to escape, find Nhika and steal her away from Commissioner Nem's reach, it had to be today.

Following old habits, Kochin's hand went to his chest for the reassurance of Nhika's ring, but found nothing there—nothing but the welt of scar tissue beneath his shirt, just over where his heart would be.

A knock on the door snapped his thoughts apart. Kochin turned to find Commissioner Nem entering—and with an entourage of armed guards. He almost looked disappointed. "So, in the end, you have no results."

"I can't do it," Kochin said.

But Commissioner Nem only shook his head. "I don't believe that. I watched a corpse become a girl."

"And that's all I'll ever have to show for it."

"I know." The commissioner's expression darkened, and Kochin got the dreadful feeling he'd said the wrong thing. "Put on your gloves. It's time to go, Kochin."

Kochin's muscles stiffened. "Where?"

"The stage," Commissioner Nem replied. "The people are waiting to see my weapon."

"You'll have to disappoint them," Kochin said.

"No," Commissioner Nem replied, and there was something dangerous in the word. "I don't think I do."

He didn't explain the cryptic words further, only ushered Kochin out of his room with a guard on either side. Even though it was a brusque command, Kochin followed—because this was the first time he'd been let outside of his cell since he'd gotten here, and there was now a way off this ship since so many guests had arrived. If he hadn't known the Mother hated him, Kochin might've thought She was giving him an opportunity.

But through their entire walk, the guards on either side of him didn't let up their watch, and their gloved hands rested on the knives at their belts. No good opportunity for escape came before Commissioner Nem walked him through a door: the back of a stage, its ceiling vast and lined with show lights. Just beyond the drawn red curtain, he heard the drum of conversation.

Commissioner Nem halted their entourage just before the curtain and turned to Kochin. "On the other side of that curtain sits anyone and everyone who has any say in this war. They don't believe it can be won. I need you to show them otherwise."

Kochin lifted his chin in indignation. "I can't say I know what you mean, Commissioner."

By way of explanation, Commissioner Nem palmed a holstered knife off one of his guards. "Show them what you are. Show them we have a miracle on our side."

He offered the knife forward. Kochin didn't take it—because he was afraid what he might do with it. Injure a commissioner or one of the guards, and he'd escape, but it would be as a fugitive of the highest degree. He would never be able to return to Nhika or his family.

"You should know better than to give me a knife," Kochin warned—and wondered how true the threat was.

Undeterred, Commissioner Nem pressed the knife into Kochin's palm. If Kochin had intended any malice, the thought was fleeting—because the curtains flew open as if cued, and suddenly he was facing an audience of aristocrats, their expectant glares printed into his skin: limelight on, a knife passed between Kochin and the commissioner, a theater of witnesses.

"Ladies and gentleman," Commissioner Nem said, stepping forward. His back was exposed. Kochin knew which ribs to stab through to make it survivable. "I've promised a weapon. This is something more: an extinct species, last of his kind. A *bloodcarver*."

The audience let out a collective gasp. Kochin's decision

wrapped around his neck like a noose, and the knife felt suddenly heavy in his fingers—because he *could*. He could attack the commissioner, fight off these guards, try his hand at escape. Commissioner Nem had introduced him as a bloodcarver; before this audience of dozens, he could truly become one.

As though noticing Kochin's hesitation, Commissioner Nem stepped back, turned—such that Kochin's gaze followed the angle of his body toward the right wing of the stage.

His gaze landed on Nhika, the delusion. A warning, maybe a sign. A part of him died to see her on this stage because if he had brought her back and still saw these wisps of her, perhaps her memory would never stop haunting him. Or perhaps this was his consolation prize: Bring her back, but never see her again except as a phantom.

Their eyes locked. He beseeched a figment of his own imagination for an answer. Yet, she gave him one, an imperceptible shake of her head and a word mouthed: *No*.

"Need I give you more incentive?" Commissioner Nem asked, lifting his hand in a subtle gesture. One of Commissioner Nem's guards stepped out from behind the image of Nhika—

And wrenched her to the ground. Kochin drew in a sharp breath, feeling as though Commissioner Nem had somehow stepped into his mind, invaded his delusion. It felt impossible. It felt revolting. It felt . . .

Real.

Kochin met Nhika's eyes again, a double take. She was giving him this look, somewhere between resolve and ferocity. *Don't be stupid*, those eyes said. *You're not a bloodcarver.*

But only when he saw the chain around her neck, his ID tags and her ring, did it click.

She was real. She was real, real, *real*—and she was being used as blackmail. He whipped his attention back toward the audience, a breath choking his throat, the knife in his palm now a shackle around his wrist.

Suddenly, he wasn't on a stage, facing an auditorium of aristocrats. He was in a cage at the Butchers' Row. All those faces before him were buyers, waiting on a show. The man standing beside him was not a commissioner, but the head Butcher. Kochin had walked so many times through their inventory, waiting for a bloodcarver to show; perhaps it was fitting he ended up on the other side of the bars.

Slowly, Kochin unsheathed the knife. Its blade sang in the spotlights. With torturous effort, he raised his arm, pulled back his sleeve, and brought the blade to his inner wrist. He pressed the edge against skin—any harder and it would draw blood.

One last time, he looked to Nhika—let her judge him, discourage him, give him some way out as she always did.

But she had disappeared. In her place, a crumpled guard. Commissioner Nem had just noticed, too, and he straightened with panic.

Before he could react, all the lights turned off.

Darkness came swiftly and with a panicked rabble from the audience. Kochin brandished the knife now as a weapon, waiting for guards to descend when something firm wrapped his wrist. He might've raised the knife against it—until he felt a distinct pull, influence grazing skin.

Nhika.

Time slowed in the dark. His fingers tightened over warm flesh, felt her familiar touch against his palms. Something inside yearned to soothe her—because his heartsoothing would know if it was *real*. His mind remembered her as an unattainable dream; his heartsoothing remembered her as she was, the way she smiled when she kissed and how her eyes pinched when she laughed. It had known her in both life and death, so it would know her in this dark; it belonged to her, after all.

She yanked him off the stage and he tumbled out of his stupor. They ran, ducking past Commissioner Nem's rancorous commands: "She's a bloodcarver! Find them! Get the lights on!"

When the lights came back on, Kochin and Nhika had already exited the theater through an offstage door. He wanted to slow down, revel in this small miracle: her hand in his, real enough to squeeze. His mind had gone numb, so fixated on the way the light haloed her flyaways, the way a pant passed through her half-parted lips—nothing like a corpse at all.

"Nhika, how are you—"

"Long story. I'll tell you later," she interjected in that practical, stern tone he'd come to expect.

Nhika turned them down a hall. Kochin yanked her back when he noticed the shadow of the commissioner's guards, and pulled her back into the fold of a utility closet. There, surrounded by guest toiletries and spare towels, they waited in silence for the guards to clear.

At last, Nhika let out a breath—and Kochin did the same, grateful for this moment of quiet to truly appreciate her: warm and sharp and so quintessentially Nhika, like she'd never even died. It felt like he was beholding her for the first time again; at the wake, a familiar girl across the room.

"Say *something*. A thank-you would be appreciated," she said, and he remembered his words.

"You're real," was all he could manage.

"What else would I be?" She fixed him with a teasing look. "Tell me—why is it I'm always saving you, Ven—"

Kochin leaned down and kissed his name off her lips. A breath stifled in her throat, a noise that stirred something inside him, and he leaned deeper into the kiss. How many times had he soothed blood back into her lips and imagined this moment? But his imagination had always been so torturous because their last kiss had been one of parting.

Well, now here she was, and Kochin pulled her in as if he might lose her again, kissing her the way he couldn't on the operating table: his hands on her cheeks, her back against the wall, her hands clutching his shirt. His fingers fumbled into her hair; his influence passed between their lips. He'd soothed her body so many times before, but that had been so clinical. This feeling now—it was music plucked from each of his nerve fibers by her practiced fingers. It was a voracious hunger in his chest, like his heart had grown an appetite. It must've been her heartsoothing—it was the only way he could explain the elation.

At last he drew back, hardly satiated, exhaling her scent on his breath. Her chest heaved with a breathless inhale and his eyes skimmed along her clavicle, eating in the miracle that was

Suonyasan Nhika—dead and back again, there to save him both times. He thought—for a moment like this, the simple privilege of seeing her alive, he'd commit every taboo, go to war, break his spine underneath Daltan concrete. He'd do it again a million times over.

He gave her a satisfied smile, skimming a tongue across his teeth—he could still taste her. "You were saying something?"

"Was I?" Nhika asked, giving him a coy look. It made him want to kiss her again. He leaned in, but she said, "I think they've passed."

It took him a moment to realize she was talking about Commissioner Nem's guards outside. Kochin remembered where he was: on a floating prison, rather than with Nhika in the privacy of a houseboat. "Clever thinking back there, with the lights."

"The lights weren't my doing," she admitted. "It must've been Lanalay."

"Lanalay?" He recognized the name—the translator from overseas who'd slapped him. That must've been why she was here, although she'd come at the worst possible time.

"Yes—she mentioned something about knowing you. And then I got caught."

"You *did* have a plan, right?"

"Please. Do you think I came up here without a plan?"

Kochin gave her an unsure look. "I honestly don't know. Did you?"

"I guess that depends on whether you can fly a plane."

"Nhika, when in my nineteen years do you think I had time to learn to fly a plane?"

"Well, can you drive an autocarriage?"

"Yes."

"So we'll be fine."

"Mother, I'm going to die today, aren't I?"

Nhika only grinned. "Well, it's that or face Nem again."

"Plane it is. Lead the way."

Furtively, Nhika tipped open the door. "It's clear. Follow me."

Kochin complied. All these hallways looked identical, but Nhika seemed to know where she was going. For the first time, Kochin could appreciate the luxury of the vessel. This was the kind of life that had allured him to Central when he was sixteen, having his pick of the top schools in the city: glass chandeliers and scented wallpaper. Now? He'd give anything just to get Nhika home safe with him.

They reached a heavy door, one that looked meant for crew rather than passengers. Kochin helped Nhika unlatch it and they opened it to find a guard just outside. In an instant, Kochin's military training returned, and he stepped in front of Nhika, rounding out a solid right hook. It collapsed the man on impact.

Nhika flared her eyes at him, looking impressed, as he stooped to check for a pulse. "Have you always been able to do that?" she asked.

He gave her a humored look. "I went to war for you. Just so happens I learned some things along the way."

When he'd ensured the guard was okay, he and Nhika continued along the outside of the airship, drawing closer to the landing platform. As they neared, they found two more guards stationed around a small transport craft. They hung back, hiding in the shadow of the hull, and gave each other a sidelong glance.

"So, how are we going to do this?" Nhika asked.

Kochin sized up the enemy. "They're not carrying any rifles."

"Must be the hydrogen—the balloon's full of it," Nhika said. "I've heard it's flammable."

"Very," Kochin said. "But the guards closest to the commissioner were armed."

"Those aren't the worst odds."

They shared a look and, with it, a thought: A gun was the only thing on this ship that might kill two heartsooths. Escape was an easier prospect than Kochin had imagined.

"We don't have to hurt them. Just run past, get in the ship, lock the doors. They can't shoot their way in," Kochin told her.

"And you'll fly the plane?"

"Sure."

"That university education must be good for something."

"I suppose we're about to find out." He gave her a resolute look. "Ready?"

"To get off this flying eyesore? Absolutely."

Together, they raced down the stairs and toward the airship. The guards glanced up at their approach, but Kochin shouldered one out of his way with all the momentum of his sprint while Nhika ducked under the grab of the other. They both reached the aircraft at the same time, Kochin jumping into the pilot seat and Nhika at his side. They locked their doors, Nhika having the foresight to lean over her seat and lock the back doors as well, just as the guards came banging on the windows.

Meanwhile, Kochin observed the cockpit controls. He'd driven an autocarriage numerous times, but this had a dozen more dials, levers, switches. Still, he found a general intuition to all the controls. The ignition switch came easiest, painted orange and labeled, and Kochin flicked it on.

The aircraft hummed to life. Above, a fire started in the balloon and the carriage rumbled, finding slight lift. Still grounded, he tried all the controls in quick rotation—the pedals swiveled the rudder and the yoke opened and closed panels on the wings.

"Kochin," Nhika rushed in a deliberate tone. The guards continued their barrage.

"Working on it," he said, trying to remember which switches and buttons had initiated takeoff.

"*Kochin*," Nhika said more urgently when a crack formed on her window.

"*Trying*," he returned, but Nhika didn't give him any more time. She grabbed the lever at the center of the cockpit and yanked it downward.

The aircraft jerked forward. It rattled down the runway as Kochin pulled back at the yoke. There it was—they were achieving lift, the aircraft bouncing higher and higher each time as the balloon grew hotter. Enough lift to clear the railing and last out in the ocean? Kochin couldn't say; he only hoped.

He pulled back as far as he could. The nose of the carriage lifted upward. Nhika reached over and squeezed his arm in sheer terror.

And then they were flying. Kochin gave Nhika a breathless, hopeful look as their aircraft stayed airborne.

In the next moment, Nhika's window shattered, glass cutting her cheeks and the culpable bullet lodging itself deep in the dashboard. He yelled her name just as his controls went slack and the plane careered back down onto the platform.

Just before they hit the ground, Kochin caught a glimpse of Commissioner Nem standing on the promenade above, aiming over the barrel of his rifle.

⇛ TWENTY-EIGHT ⇚

THE IMPACT TOSSED NHIKA FROM THE AIRCRAFT. She rolled through glass, which bit at her arms through her sleeves. Her ankle flared with pain, and distantly she heard someone calling her name.

Nhika blinked the haze out of her eyes. Their aircraft was a crunched piece of scrap metal, crushed against the railing. The crew members were quick to mobilize, pushing it over the edge before it could alight in full fire.

Her eyes flared as she tried and failed to stand. She hadn't seen him get out—*had he gotten out*? One more push and the ship teetered over the edge and fell to the sea, Kochin's name still stuck in her throat as a scream.

Then: arms around her. At first, Nhika resisted, but when she looked up it was Kochin. She nearly cried from relief.

"Can you walk?" he asked. A forehead cut leaked blood down his temple.

Nhika shook her head.

With a nod, he scooped her up into his arms. Now, with her pounding headache ebbing to a quiet throb, Nhika made sense of the scene around her. Nem stood above them from a passenger promenade, aiming a rifle at the two of them below. For a moment, Nhika thought she saw malice in his eyes—the same malice that had driven Dr. Santo to shoot Kochin, then her.

But he set down the rifle and barked an order toward his subordinates, who rushed back into the hull.

"They're coming for us," Nhika rasped.

Kochin tightened his grip around her. "Don't worry. I've got you. We'll get out of here."

But how? Their only way off this airship was quickly sinking to the ocean bed. Nem wasn't so foolish as to let them set foot near the landing platform again. He could stake them out on this airship forever, eating from its stocked kitchens while they hid themselves away; the only way back to land was if they commandeered the entire thing toward Theumas.

With her in his arms, Kochin started back the way they'd come. Before he could even make it up the steps, the door into the vessel opened, releasing half a dozen guards onto the gangway, none of them armed but all of them gloved. Swerving, Kochin ran in the opposite direction.

They quickly reached a dead end, nowhere to go but overboard. Nhika wanted to heal her ankle, but she couldn't focus—not when she heard Kochin's thundering heartbeat through his chest, when the guards were quickly gaining.

"Nhika, are your arms strong enough to hold on to me?" Kochin asked.

"Yes."

"Get on my back and hold on. *Tight.*"

Without needing an explanation, Nhika shifted herself onto his back with his help, arms wrapped around his shoulders and nose brushing the nape of his neck. She was about to ask him where he planned to go when he took a running start toward the edge of the platform.

And leaped.

Her heart lurched in her chest as they went airborne and Nhika buried her face into the scruff of his hair, her eyes closed against the fearful height beneath her. She held on with all her remaining strength, and even then she almost lost her grip when they came to a sudden stop.

Nhika opened her eyes. Kochin had caught a ladder extending from the gangway all the way up the balloon of the airship. It was their last option for escape.

"Are you all right?" he asked, one hand moving to cup her legs around him. "Hold on."

"I wasn't planning on letting go," she said, and he pulled them up the ladder.

In only a few seconds, they were level with Nem, who still stood on the promenade, his arms crossed.

"You've nowhere to run, Kochin," he said, his voice carried on the wind. "You know I'll find you. Both of you."

Nhika felt Kochin's muscles tense beneath her. He didn't deem Nem's threat worthy of a response as they continued upward, tailed distantly by a line of Nem's guard.

Kochin worked like an automaton, pulling them up the ladder. When they reached the balloon, the ladder became bare rungs affixed to the metal hull, and somehow that made it infinitely scarier. Nhika clung close to him, holding on to his warmth as the air around them grew frigid and fierce. She dipped her influence into him, feeling the ache of his muscles and the raggedness of his breath. With closed eyes and a slow exhale, she mired her influence into his body, letting her energy wean away the acidity of his muscles until his influence barred her, as firmly as if he'd caught her wrist with his hand.

"Don't," he said between breaths. "Just heal yourself. I'll be okay."

"But you—"

"*Please.* We might be stuck on this ship for a while. We need to conserve our calories."

Knowing he was right, she withdrew her influence from his muscles and descended it to her own ankle. The cuts all over her arms were grisly, but not a priority—not when she couldn't put weight on her right leg.

After a brief assessment, she determined it was just a sprain—no broken bones, thankfully. The frayed ends of the ligaments throbbed in bruised and inflamed anger even at the lightness of her touch, though it would be a simple fix. Stealing collagen from her skin and threading it into fibers, she sewed together the tears in her ankle with a seamstress's touch. When she was done, Kochin was just pulling them up onto the very top of the airship.

There were no railings up here. Just the end of the ladder and the vast curve of the hull. Nhika did not look forward to the hike.

"I can walk," she said, shifting so he'd let her down. As soon as her feet hit the ground she slipped, catching herself against him. He made a noise of concern but she waved him away, doffing her shoes for better traction against freezing metal.

"Over there," Kochin said, pointing to a hatch farther down the hull. Nhika followed him, her ankle sore and stiff but at least strong enough to place weight upon. They reached the hatch before Nem's men breached the top of the airship. Kochin heaved it open, and they descended the ladder, dropping down onto dark rafters below.

It took a moment for her eyes to adjust to the dimness. When they did, Nhika found herself on a grid of rafters that extended between innumerable inflated sacs, held into place by a weave of ropes. Every sound here rang out hollowly into the abyss, even the sound of her bare feet slapping against the metal.

"Quick," Kochin said, pulling her into the cover of the hull's triangle support. Only moments later, the hatch opened again behind them, letting in a blinding beam of light. As Nem's men slid down the ladder, Kochin pressed closer against her, the both of them squeezing into their slim cover.

Luckily, the men—without any lights—passed by them farther into the hull. They waited a few more long minutes before daring to relax.

Nhika released a tight breath. Now that the adrenaline was burning off, she felt the full extent of her pain return with every new exhale—the cuts on her arm, the bruises along her legs, and even the ankle, hastily healed. Gingerly, she pulled back her sleeve and began picking glass out of her skin, guided more by pain and influence than by sight.

"Are you all right?" Kochin asked, grunting with effort as he moved to sit beside her. However sore she felt, he must've felt leagues worse.

"I'll live," she said, flicking a speck of glass as far as it could go.

"Here. Allow me," he offered, his fingers grazing delicately over her arm. Despite the pain of her cuts, her skin still tingled at his touch. Where she expected him to pull out glass manually, she instead felt his influence soak into her skin.

Nhika pulled back. "We need to save calories for more important things," she reminded him.

His eyes met hers in the darkness. "This is important," he said, and continued soothing. Her skin mended, the healing tissue pushing out minuscule shards of glass, and only when he'd healed her cuts to red welts did she realize that he hadn't taken a single draw of *her* calories at all.

Nhika's brow knit. "Kochin, did you just . . . ?"

He nodded. "Yes. I learned to use my own soothing. It's how I brought you back."

"But how? Who taught you?"

"You did, Nhika," he said, drawing closer. Gently, with a touch that felt more like a caress, he took her other arm. "I always thought it was a physical limitation, because I was only half Yarongese. But I learned how to give away parts of myself using the same paths of influence you used to save me."

His influence drew down to her skin again, kissing each wound in turn. His healing didn't hurt at all, not even as glass pushed its way out of her skin. "You were always a real heartsooth to me, no matter what your gift looked like."

"I know," he said. "But I think I needed to prove it to myself."

She stared at him, breathlessly, her heart squeezing with a tender ache. That's what she'd died for, wasn't it? So that he might be able to reclaim his heartsoothing, not as something abused or subversive, but as what it was always meant to be: a gift. Now he had, and he used it with such intention that she could feel the warmth behind every touch, as though it were the very extension of his love.

"It's . . . magical, isn't it?" That word had never carried good connotations for her—now no other descriptor felt apt for the way he wielded his heartsoothing.

"It is," he replied, lifting a hand to cup her cheek. Without her realizing, he'd sealed the cut under her eye—a waste of calories, she wanted to tell him.

Before she could, he leaned in and kissed her.

She drew up into it, fingers playing at his shirt, urging him closer. Here, in the cover of darkness and metal, with the hopelessness of their inescapable dilemma, she let herself linger on the kiss. He did, too; she could feel his hunger in his breathlessness, the way his hands explored her waist, how he pressed himself closer until she was flush against the wall. Her fingers wrapped themselves in his hair, tousled and un-styled—she preferred it this way.

It was a kiss with nowhere to go, nowhere to be. A kiss that just was, because they were at the end of their line, broken and beaten and both a little frayed. A kiss because Nhika simply wanted to kiss him, and not because she needed to distract him from her death.

She remembered when they were last like this—him on the table, her bowed over him. Back then, their influences had warred; now they were entwined. His hands were everywhere—and so were hers, but she felt little beyond the exhilaration.

At last, they drew apart. She missed his warmth immediately after. As a parting gift, he skimmed a kiss across her jawline, as though to satiate an urge. They lingered close, still half entangled, and she let herself lean into him, his warmth in the frigid hull.

"What was it like, waking up again for the first time? Did you feel . . . pain?" His gaze was imploring, fingers tentative as they brushed a wisp of hair behind her ear.

Nhika thought back. "Not because of anything physical. But when I found your ID tags, I thought you were . . . dead. Next time, choose a less ambiguous keepsake to leave behind."

Kochin snorted. "Well, you *actually* died, so you're not one to speak," he said, and she snuffed the sudden urge to throttle him. "Which, by the way, we never discussed. Don't *ever* do that again."

"Couldn't you just bring me back again?"

"Nhika."

"Very well. It's not as heroic the second time, anyway," she said, relenting. "But how did you do it, exactly? Bring me back?"

"A long story," he said. A sigh tapered through his lips and he leaned back against the hull. They sat shoulder to shoulder, fingers laced and her legs draped over his, as he began.

He told her of the fallout of Dr. Santo's arrest—the lab closed, Santo's son discovered, his Daltan texts exposed. Kochin had stolen one of the iron caskets to keep her body alive as he combed through those same illicit texts for an answer. But there was none.

He told her how he returned home but couldn't stay. How Nem had warned him of war—and how, when he wasn't ever drafted, he'd enlisted. Then, at the end of training camp, when he hadn't been deployed to Yarong . . .

. . . Kochin told her about how he'd assured it.

"I do it all the time," Nhika said. "Butchers, a constable here or there. Animals, when I need the calories."

Kochin shook his head. "It's different because I didn't have to."

"My body would've started sprouting mold by now if you hadn't," she said morbidly. There came the acidic taste of guilt, knowing he'd had to profane his heartsoothing to bring her back. "But when it came down to it, exchange an innocent life for mine, you didn't."

Kochin nodded; his tale continued—Trin, Nem, the research paper. The pieces would have come together so cleanly, if only he had been willing to take a life.

She knew he hadn't—Trin had told her so—but she felt the terror of the decision nonetheless, then relief when he finally revealed how it was she truly came to live: not through the death of another, but through the awakening of his heartsoothing.

There was some concern at the things he'd done to bring her back, but it was fleeting—she could not judge another heartsooth for what he might do in the name of loneliness. And some part of her, equally lonely, relished in how she could mean so much to someone that they would go to such lengths for her. She'd thought the opportunity dead and gone with her family, yet here he was.

"Thank you," she said, the words feeling inadequate. "For bringing me back, but especially for not using another life to do so."

He drew closer. "When you gave me your life, I think you stayed with me, somehow. Maybe it was my imagination, maybe it was the magic of heartsoothing, but I didn't want the same to happen to you. I had made my peace with losing you—the only reason I brought you back was because Trin and I returned for your body."

"You returned for my body?"

"I intended to add your bone to the ring. I knew it's what you would've wanted." He gave her a soft look, and in the moment, she could've kissed him again. "Ring or no ring, I'll always carry a part of you, and now you'll always have a part of me."

She grinned. "Is that a comfort or a threat?"

He returned the smile. "To be fair, you haunted me for months. It's only right I return the favor." His hands took hers, thumb rubbing the soft flesh of her palm with deliberateness. "Whatever happens, you'll always have me. I promise you that, Suonyasan Nhika."

Her heart swelled, then subsequently stuttered when he leaned closer. His scent reminded her of a house on the top of a hill, with a garden in front and a view of the river. "You know," she said, "your brother Bentri misses you."

An ache shifted across his eyes. "You visited my family?"

Nhika nodded. "Met your brothers this time. Had a long, long talk with Vinsen. You're lucky—two brothers who care so much about you. Although, I have it on good authority Vinsen might want to punch you."

A timid laugh escaped him. "It's within his right."

"He saw your ID tags, but he doesn't believe you're gone—and

I'm going to prove him right. I'm going to bring you home." Nhika squeezed his hand with new resolve. "So, how do we get off this airship?"

His expression grew solemn, a curtain of reality drawn over their quiet tryst. "We're two loose bloodcarvers on a ship of some of the most important voices in Theumas. I'm sure the paranoid among them are already evacuating, which means our options for escape vessels are narrowing," he thought aloud. "It's possible we can wait until Commissioner Nem docks the airship back in Theumas, but I imagine he'll telegraph the mainland for an armed welcome party."

"He can do that? Send a message from out here, the middle of nowhere?"

"Yes, through wireless telegraphy. It sends messages through the air, rather than any cable in the ground." His eyes narrowed in question, reading her easily. "What are you thinking?"

"I'm thinking that I might know some people with airships of their own."

⇶ TWENTY-NINE ⇷

KOCHIN HAD BEEN HOPING HE'D NEVER SEE THE Congmi siblings again.

They certainly wouldn't be happy to see him. When last they'd interacted, Kochin had promised to leave this city—and, well, he supposed they were all currently out of Theumas's bounds.

The hardest part would be getting through this airship undetected. He and Nhika exited the balloon by the ceiling hatch, again braving the perils of the doped hull. It was free of guards or commissioners, nothing but a curved drop and the infinite horizon beyond it, something that would've been beautiful if it weren't so perilous.

They came down the opposite side of the airship from where they'd first come up. Kochin went down the ladder first, prepared to catch Nhika if she slipped, but both of them touched down on the gangway without any trouble. After removing their shoes to avoid rattling the metal platforms, they made their way back into the ship.

In some ways, this confined airship worked to their advantage; there were no more guards than however many had originally come up. But when they reached the level of the passenger cabins, they found where all Nem's personnel had gone: patrolling these halls, two by two. They drew back into the cover of a lounge and Kochin sized up the sentries, noticing that they'd tied bandannas around the lower part of their faces.

"Which room is theirs?" he asked.

"It's on the far side of the ship."

"You mean, past every one of the commissioner's guards?"

"Precisely."

He let out a long sigh. "Mother."

"I've come all this way for you, Ven Kochin, and I've yet to hear a thank-you."

He let out a humored breath. "Nhika, I fully intend to spend the rest of my life showing you my thanks."

That elicited a blush—quickly soothed back from her cheeks, though the pink still lingered at the tips of her ears.

They chanced another glance at the guards. The patrol had neared the end of the hall, and when they turned the corner, Kochin ushered Nhika forward. "*Now*, while there's an opening."

They crept forward. More than once, Kochin had to yank Nhika down a hallway when a guard rounded the corner. This reminded him of escaping detainment on Yarong. He'd seen so many prisons in his short life—the cages of the Butchers' Row and the commissioner-endorsed cells of this airship. The prison that was Santo, and the Central Theuman Penitentiary that held the unhinged doctor thereafter. He had to hope, after all this was over, there was a life for him without bars.

By some miracle, they weren't caught before reaching two doors, one for each of the Congmi siblings. Nhika knocked furiously on Mimi's.

They waited. Kochin wasn't sure the siblings were in—not

until Nhika knocked again, more frantically, and the door opened.

Nhika nearly fell inside. Mimi stood in the entrance, Andao sitting on the chaise behind her. And when Mimi saw him, her expression turned rigid.

"Thank goodness, Mimi," Nhika said, stepping inside. Mimi let her. "So, you might've noticed, but we've run into a bit of a snafu. Namely, our way off is at the bottom of the seafloor and Nem is hunting us. I have a plan, though, if you would . . ."

Her voice trailed off when she noticed Kochin was still frozen at the door. She gave him a curious look, like she wanted him to step inside, away from where guards might catch him, but he couldn't. Not with Mimi standing in front of the door like that, fixing him with a hurtful look. Not when he'd promised the Congmis they'd never see him again.

"Mimi," Nhika said in a small voice. "Please."

With a raised chin, Mimi stepped back, allowing him passage. Yet Kochin still couldn't move. That was another one of his prisons, the guilt. But he knew he might never escape from that one.

Then Mimi said, "Come inside, Mr. Ven. Before I have to lie to the commissioner about what his heartsooth prisoner is doing outside my door."

She'd called him a heartsooth—despite everything he'd done. It wasn't a pardon, but it was a white flag waved. He stepped inside.

Mimi locked the door behind him, then gave Nhika a tired look. "Nhika, when I said I wanted to be distracted from the politicking, I didn't mean turning dinner into an entire show."

"Well then, you should've been more clear," Nhika returned. "Besides, this would've been a lot smoother if your aircraft hadn't been sent back to the Yibai Airdrome."

"How were we supposed to know the commissioner would choose a Ngut airship over one of our own?"

"What's done is done," Andao interrupted. "We can't harbor you forever, Nhika. I'm sure Commissioner Nem has deduced exactly how you managed to get on this ship. It isn't safe for you here."

"We're not planning to stay." Nhika glanced at Kochin. "We just need a favor."

"We'll do what we can, if it's within our power," Andao said.

To which Mimi added, "And everything is within our power."

Kochin let out a humored breath. It was . . . endearing, seeing the way the Congmis spoke to Nhika. And strange, having them on his side—even if it wasn't him they were trying to help. In the past, Kochin had never had many allies. Even then, he let Nhika do the talking for him, afraid the Congmis might find every word out of his mouth disagreeable.

"We need a ship," Nhika said. "Can you send a radio message to Trin?"

Andao hummed. "It's *possible*, but it'll be difficult. The radio would be in the bridge, and I'm not sure Commissioner Nem will let us walk idly in, especially not if he suspects us—"

"We can do it," Mimi interrupted, not a waver of doubt in her voice. "Leave it to us. You worry about keeping away from the commissioner, and we'll worry about making sure a ship comes for you."

Her eyes moved, landing on him. Despite the disdain he found there, she added, "Both of you."

"Thank you," Kochin said. "I can't repay you."

"Keep her safe," Mimi said. "That's all I ask."

Overhead, the broadcast system blipped to life. "All passengers and crew, please migrate to the dining hall. All passengers and crew, please migrate to the dining hall."

They all exchanged urgent looks.

"He's locking down the ship," Andao said. "You can't stay here."

"We'll go to the loading bay," Kochin said. "There'll be parachutes there."

"Parachutes?" Nhika asked.

"Well, I sincerely doubt the commissioner will let us lower a gangway."

With a begrudging look, Nhika looked between the Congmi siblings, like there was more she wanted to say to them. But Kochin placed a hand on her shoulder. "We have to go, Nhika."

"Right," she said—but before she could, Mimi drew her into an embrace.

"Good luck," Mimi whispered. "One day, we'll look back at this and laugh."

Nhika put on a weak smile. "Mother, I hope so."

THIRTY

NHIKA'S EARLIER CONFIDENCE WAS WAVERING.

Strangely, this felt like an echo of the past, a night in the Theumas Medical Center. Maybe it was because they were *so close*—and still without casualty. She had a dreadful feeling like something terrible was about to happen.

And there were so many opportunities for it to arise. Mimi and Andao might never get the message to Trin. And he may not come in time. She and Kochin might never make it off this ship. Nhika figured nothing could go as wrong as that night in the Theumas Medical Center when she'd lost her life, but when she thought of everyone on this ship who'd been pulled into her plight—Lanalay, the Congmis, *Kochin* . . .

She could imagine worse things than death.

"We'll be okay," Kochin said, as though reading her mind. He took her hand, guided her through the ship. "I promise. We'll be okay."

Their path took them down an industrial-looking hallway—the bowels of the ship, where pipes gurgled with fluid and bellows churned like a digestive system. She'd come from the loading bay, so she knew exactly how to get back.

At the end of the hallway, she pushed a set of double doors open into the loading bay, a spacious and cylindrical room.

Shipment boxes cluttered the bay, strapped down with netting, and the floor sloped upward at the far end: the wide door through which her Guardian had been loaded.

The Guardians were still there. For a moment, Nhika wondered if they could hop back into one, because inside she'd felt untouchable. But even if those Guardians had gotten her on, they couldn't get her off.

They found the parachute packs lining the walls, strapped above the emergency seating. Kochin tugged one of them down and fit it over her shoulders. In an instructional tone, he gestured to the various parts of the pack as he buckled her in. "Pull this cord to deploy the chute. Yank this strap to tighten the pack. And, if you get caught somewhere, you can cut yourself free with this razor blade. Does it feel okay?"

She hummed agreeably, a little awed by his expertise. She had only ever known him to be a scholar. "And if it doesn't deploy?"

"Then the ocean surface will hit you like an autocarriage," he said. Nhika gave him a withering look.

He was reaching for his own pack when a rumble shook the bay. When they whipped around, her heart went straight to her stomach, because one of the Guardians was coming to life. Its body straightened with a series of hisses and whirs, its joints cracked like a giant coming out of hibernation, and when the cockpit lit up, Nhika saw the face within.

Commissioner Nem.

His low voice buzzed from an audio horn at his shoulder. "Thought you two might consider jumping. But I can't lose two bloodcarvers to the sea."

Nhika sucked in a breath, eyeing the exit. A dozen calculations looped through Nhika's head: how fast a Guardian might go, how many strides to the exit, the meters of space between them and the commissioner.

But Kochin grabbed her hand, yelled at her to run, and that was all the command she needed.

They sprinted toward the door. The Guardian's hand shot out on a cable, whipping around the bay. Boxes split on impact, spraying shards of wood and shredded paper. Nhika leaped over its extended reach, only to be caught on its recoil—the wire slammed against her chest with disorienting force, knocking her away from the door.

Kochin called her name, but the thud of her heartbeat in her temples drowned him out. She clutched a hand over her sternum, checking her ribs in turn: a hairline fracture here, a bruise across her entire chest, but she was still breathing.

Nem's Guardian had turned its full attention toward her—a soldier encased in metal. A man immune to heartsoothing.

Still scraping herself off the floor, she found Kochin making his way toward her. The Guardian was fearfully fast, treads sparking metal as they skirted around the bay.

"Are you okay?" Kochin asked, reaching her side. He didn't give her time to answer as he scooped her up over his arm and dragged her out of the Guardian's path. It tore through behind them, then circled back to block the only exit.

"What do we do?" she asked, feeling panic rise in her throat.

Even Kochin looked uncertain. "I . . . I don't know. I'll draw him away, and you make a sprint for the exit."

"No. Not without you."

The Guardian's audio horn blared to life again. "Kochin, Ms. Suon, I'm giving you one last chance to come freely. If you continue to resist, I'll have no choice but to detain you against your will."

"We're getting off this ship," she growled, and saw Nem glower behind the glass cockpit.

"We shall see," he said, and shot forth another metal claw of his Guardian.

It snapped between them, tossing her and Kochin apart. She dove on her belly just in time to duck under its extended reach. When she regained her footing, the other arm rocketed out.

It caught her around her torso, pinning her arms to her sides. Kochin screamed her name as the arm retracted into its socket, pulling her with it. With a strangled cry, she flew back through the air and came to a jarring stop at the Guardian's side, squeezed by its tight grip.

Kochin came to a stumbling halt, his arms outstretched as if to quell the metal beast of the Guardian, rather than the mortal man within. Nhika squirmed, but the rigid metal claws around her didn't yield. They crushed her parachute pack against her ribs, threatening to squeeze her to bursting.

"Kochin, Ms. Suon, I am at my wit's end trying to compromise with you," Nem said, his voice crackling across the Guardian's audio horn. "Kochin, we had a very agreeable deal, only for you to treat this as a form of imprisonment. And Ms. Suon, I'm not sure what I've done to make an enemy out of you."

"Don't pretend as if you weren't using me as blackmail,"

Nhika grunted. Her arms flexed uselessly at her side, fingers scrabbling at her backpack. She couldn't reach the tab to deploy the chute, but she could just finger the edge of the knife.

"Commissioner Nem, please, set her down," Kochin negotiated. He feigned calm, but she could read his concern in the twitch of his brow, the clench of his jaw. "You're . . . you're right. Let's compromise."

Within the Guardian, Nem shook his head. "No, no, Kochin. I compromised when I found out you were a bloodcarver. I compromised when you refused to bring her back at my request. I even compromised when you tried to escape Yarong with Mr. Dep Trin. Now, I'm done compromising. I'm looking for *results*."

"I . . . can't," Kochin said, his calm facade breaking as his voice cracked. Nhika extended her fingers toward the knife, muscles aching against the metal grip of the Guardian. At last, her longest finger caught the hilt, and she drew it out of its canvas sheath.

"See, I don't quite believe that," Nem continued. "I'm holding the very evidence that you *can*. What I think is that *you don't want to*, but for the life of me, I can't understand why."

Nhika met Kochin's eye as she began sawing at the bottom of her pack, trying to release the chute. With her hands behind her, she didn't know if he could see her escape attempt. She only needed him to stall.

"You didn't give me enough time," Kochin said, seeming to read her quiet request. "How long did you give the Congmis to build you their machines? Months? I only had weeks."

→ 345

"I would've given you more time if you showed me progress. But there was none—birds and mice and rodents, you couldn't bring back a single one."

Nhika continued sawing, opening a gash from one end of the pack's bottom to the other.

"I can't bring back animals. I only brought back *her*," Kochin said. He swallowed his words immediately, eyes flaring—that had been the wrong thing to say.

Nem lifted her on his arm, grip compressing. The knife fell from her fingers as she let out a pained gasp, ribs threatening to snap and shoulder wrenching in her socket. "Her?" Nem repeated. He went quiet behind the hood, a look passing over his eyes—and Nhika could read it plainly. It was the look of an idea—something twisted, something desperate. It was the same look Santo had given her right before he'd gone to vivisect Kochin, but this time . . . she was the one on the operating table.

Mother, he was going to kill her. Then he was going to make Kochin bring her back.

Kochin held up a hand. Nhika snagged a finger against the chute within her sliced pack, trying to pull out the slippery fabric. "Commissioner Nem, I know what you're thinking, but—"

"So, how many times will she have to die for you to perfect the skill?"

Picking up her pace, Nhika drew out the first inch of fabric, muscle straining against the compressive force of the Guardian's arm. It came out slowly, one handful at a time.

There was true fear in Kochin's eyes. "Commissioner, if you

hurt her, I won't be able to bring her back. You'll be *murdering* her."

"I don't understand, Kochin!" Nem bellowed into his mouthpiece. "I don't understand how you can't repeat something you've already done. Physicians perform procedures over and over and over again until they perfect it. Were you not a physician's aide? So, why is it that you hoard your miracle—is it because you feel that Theumas does not deserve it? Are you really so selfish?"

At that word, Kochin's fear morphed into adamancy. "No," he said, the word resounding around the bay. "I'm not selfish. I love Theumas—it's my home. It's who I am. If I could win us this war through heartsoothing alone, I would. But I can't, because . . . Because that's not what heartsoothing is. It's not a science, to be studied. Nor an innovation, to be industrialized. It's . . . It's a magic, Commissioner."

"What is the point of magic, then, if it cannot even save one's home?"

"To survive," Kochin said. "Isn't that why we're all fighting, Commissioner? To survive?"

That was the first time Nem stilled. The Guardian's claws stopped clamping, and Nhika managed to yank out the bulk of the chute. Like a pustule popped, the chute squeezed out of the backpack and fell to the floor. With it, Nhika slipped out of Nem's grasp, no longer filling the space of his hold.

She landed heavily on the floor, shrugging off the backpack and running to Kochin. He took her in his embrace, holding her defensively at his side. His hands checked her wounds in turn, influence pulling at her pain with a caress that numbed it.

Once he'd assured her safety, he turned his attention back to Nem. The Guardian remained still, unmoving. "Commissioner," he said, sounding so much more assured now that she was free, "how can I change your mind?"

Nhika had never seen Nem unsure before. That man was made of harsh words and even harsher lines, brows drawn with zeal and boisterous confidence. Now, he seemed at a loss for words, stumbling over the start of his sentence.

"I . . . ," he began to say.

He didn't finish his sentence before the ceiling burst.

⇛ THIRTY-ONE ⇚

THE EXPLOSION TOSSED KOCHIN BACKWARD. HE rolled across the floor, scrambling up only to shield Nhika's body with his own. Around them, fire rained and there was the bone-rattling screech of metal against metal, but Kochin only kept his head bowed and his arms over Nhika as violent tremors shook the airship.

When he looked up, he found the explosion had taken half the bay, including its doors. A portion of the ceiling had collapsed atop Nem's Guardian, which teetered on the charred edge of the airship. A metal cable had shot from its arm and embedded itself in the torn wall of the airship, the only thing keeping the Guardian from toppling off the edge.

Nhika stirred beneath his arms, blinking hazily. "Kochin . . ."

"The gas must've sparked," Kochin said, pulling her up on her feet. "We need to get to the promenade and wait for the Congmis. This ship won't last much longer."

She nodded firmly and they started for the door. It was only when a pained cry came from behind that Kochin paused, turned.

Commissioner Nem had popped the hood of his Guardian. He squirmed but couldn't free himself from it. Those flames encroached on either side, and maybe if Kochin were the poetic kind, he might've thought this was justice: the commissioner dying inside a machine of his own making.

Yet, Kochin halted, with Nhika caught at the edge of his arm's reach. She glanced back at him with a quizzical look. "What are you doing?"

Kochin wasn't sure. His feet would not allow him to move because when he looked at Nem, he saw not a commissioner, but just . . . a man.

A man holding a city on his shoulders.

A man who'd started an unwinnable war.

A man who would've done anything, *anything*, to protect the one thing he loved: his city.

In the fire, all that status and power between them had been burned away, and the commissioner was nothing more than a man who needed Kochin's help. And Kochin understood deeply how it felt to need help. There had always been someone to save him at the last minute: Nhika, Trin, Lanalay, Vinsen, the Mother Herself. Save him from making a decision he'd regret and save him from becoming a bloodcarver.

Commissioner Nem didn't have that someone. So right now, he needed a heartsooth.

"Kochin," Nhika reminded him, pulling him toward the door.

Still, Kochin didn't move. "I need to get him out."

Her eyes flared. "No. *No.*" She grabbed his hand again and tugged, but he held fast. "Come *on*, we need to go."

"Nhika, he's going to die."

"So might you."

"Please, trust me."

"Don't be a hero, *please*." She took his arm, dragged him with all her weight, but he pulled back.

"I'm not a hero, Nhika. I've never been. But I need to do this." Again, he untangled his fingers from hers, moving his hands instead to cup her face. "This city—it needs us. If ever we want true peace and freedom, we need to show them that we're heartsooths, not bloodcarvers."

She glanced back at the commissioner. Maybe she understood, too—if a commissioner died on a ship with two bloodcarvers, how that might look. But she said, "We can disappear."

Kochin shook his head. He couldn't live in binds anymore, jumping from prison to prison. Leaning close, he kept her gaze. "Nhika, listen to me. Get everyone on the ship to the promenade for the Congmis. If I'm not there by the time they arrive, go without me."

Her fingers curled around his wrists, not to pull him but just to hold him. He could see the reflection of the embers behind him in the dark canvas of her pupils. A thousand arguments passed behind those fierce, stubborn eyes, but her next words were only a question: "Kochin, why?"

"Because I can save him. You taught me how to use my heartsoothing again—this is what I need to do with it." He grazed a thumb across her cheek, his influence pulling gently at her own in a parting gesture. "Do you trust me?"

The frustration in her eyes said no, but Nhika grabbed the collar of his shirt and yanked him into a rushed, messy kiss. When she released him, the anger in her expression was deadly. "Do *not* die, Mother damn it," she warned.

"I promise," he said through a smile. Only then did she release him. Nhika headed toward the collapsing door, Kochin toward Commissioner Nem. As a bid for luck, Kochin threw one last glance over his shoulder as she squeezed her way out of the bay.

And then it was just the commissioner and him.

Kochin approached the edge of the sinking floor, where the Guardian dangled just out of reach, one tread spinning uselessly over open air. Commissioner Nem was doing everything he could to pull himself up, but the Guardian's support cable was quickly fraying.

"Save yourself, Kochin," Commissioner Nem called from the controls. "A gift like yours is too rare to be wasted here."

Ignoring him, Kochin leaned over the edge and extended his hand. "Leave the Guardian, Commissioner. I'll pull you up."

Looking uncertain, Commissioner Nem glanced between Kochin's splayed fingers and the dashboard of the Guardian. At last, he saw reason and reached up to take Kochin's hand. Their grips locked, Kochin's bare hand in Nem's gloved one, and Kochin pulled.

Nem let out an agonal cry as his body lifted from the Guardian; Kochin released him immediately. "My leg," he said. "It's stuck. I . . . I think it's broken."

"Take off your glove. I can heal you," Kochin offered.

Commissioner Nem didn't act. He only looked at his leg, Kochin's hand, and the controls of his war machine. Even as the Guardian lurched, the wall's metal panel giving underneath its weight, even as the inferno grew around them, he didn't move.

"Commissioner, if you don't let me heal you, you'll die."

"Go, Kochin," Nem said. "I just ask that you use that gift to save this war, even if I'm not there to see it."

"It's never going to win you the war, but it can save you." Kochin opened his fingers again, a gesture of earnestness. "Commissioner, you can either die here or we can walk out of here together."

The hand remained an open invitation; Commissioner Nem needed only to accept it. When Kochin had first come to Theumas, it had been to change minds. To establish heartsoothing as something legitimate, something real. Everything along the way had been a setback—Santo's research, Mr. Congmi's murder, Nhika's death. He'd resigned himself to lose his heartsoothing under the teeth of Theuman meritocracy. Now, he saw that change came only with time, but it came—and altering the opinion of just one man, even one as obstinate as Commissioner Nem, was all he needed.

"After all I've done, you would give me mercy?" the commissioner asked at last.

"That's what heartsoothing means, to give," Kochin responded. "I can't turn the war like you want me to, but I can give you a second chance."

At that, Commissioner Nem drew off his glove and took Kochin's hand.

His uncertainty didn't disappear. Maybe his desperation was just stronger. But when their skin met, Kochin soothed him all the same.

He tumbled through Commissioner Nem's anatomy. For a moment, he almost felt he could see more than just the commissioner's body, but his mind and emotions, too. The tight muscles of his shoulders—that was all his corded fear, the great regret of turning his small city-state toward an unconquerable enemy. And the hammering of his heartbeat, that was his distrust now, not knowing what heartsoothing could truly do. Finally, the pounding pressure against the arch of his aorta came with all his anger, his malice, his wrath—that Kochin could bring a girl back from the dead but refuse to do it again when all of Theumas was at stake.

Kochin could read the question still scrawled through his bones, his blood, his brain: *Why?*

As his answer, Kochin healed.

See how we are connected, his influence said as it collected the crushed shards of Commissioner Nem's leg.

See how this cannot be manufactured or monetized, it whispered as it tied up vasculature with all the meticulousness of an artist.

See how it is a beautiful, wonderful, magical thing, it rejoiced as it sealed split skin.

At last, Kochin lifted his influence from the leg, taking Nem's pain with him. *See what heartsoothing means: a connection with family, with others, with oneself. See how it gives, and gives, and gives. See that it is a miracle.*

His heartsoothing receded; the pressure of the flames returned, still just as oppressive. The look in Commissioner Nem's eyes had shifted—not uncertainty, not fear, but awe, and Kochin knew he understood.

"Can you get out of the Guardian now?" Kochin asked.

With a look of intense concentration, Commissioner Nem tried moving his leg. The pain had abated from his expression, and with a heavy grunt of effort, he lifted himself up. Kochin grabbed him and pulled him firmly onto the sundered platform just as the Guardian's cable snapped. Its frayed end whipped perilously over their heads as it trailed the Guardian into the ocean.

"I'm sorry, Kochin. I'm sorry," Commissioner Nem was saying, but Kochin only shook his head—as the fire closed around them, they had higher concerns than apologies. Hooking one of Commissioner Nem's arms over his shoulder, Kochin helped him toward the door.

"Let's go," he said.

THIRTY-TWO

NHIKA FOUGHT BACK TEARS ON HER WAY THROUGH the ship. She had a terrible dread in her chest, a voice that told her this was *just* like before. It was Kochin taking another bullet; it was another metal coffin. But this time, there would be no chance to save him on the operating table. If this ship went down, they all went with it.

The airship felt like it was rattling apart. From inside, it was hard to determine the change in altitude, but the chandeliers swayed—a tinkling marker of their descent. The halls were growing warmer; the air came like fire in her lungs as she tore her way to the promenade. All that hydrogen gas had been suspended in sacs, and she had to wonder how many had already blown—and how many remained.

When she reached the passenger deck, she heard the clamor of a crowd. She stilled, finding the delayed instinct to hide—but too late. The crowd spilled into her hallway, and she placed her guard up, ready to run and kick and bite.

But they only ran past her. Nhika pressed herself against the wall, feeling small, and found they had greater priorities: the smoke rising from the back of their airship, drawing an ominous curve through the sky.

It took her a moment to realize they were running toward the loading bay, undoubtedly where evacuation protocol told them to go.

"Wait!" Nhika called, her voice small against their clamor. "The loading bay is on fire. Get to the promenade!"

None of them even paused. *Idiots*, she wanted to scream. More champagne than sense in their heads—because sure, why not run *toward* the source of the fire? She had half a mind to let them go, get to the promenade for herself, wait for the Congmis, but . . .

But Kochin had asked her to get everyone off the ship.

"I'm going to die today, aren't I?" Nhika muttered under her breath. She was going to die, he was going to die—they were *all* going to die on this flaming ship, but let the Mother witness that she had been a heartsooth to the bitter end. She and Kochin both.

When she escaped the passenger deck and found herself on the gangway, Nhika saw the full extent of the damage. The tail was on fire, blazing through the gray of a settling fog. It was only a matter of time before the rest of the balloon blew. She quickened her pace.

At last she reached the gondola and burst through its door—to meet a collection of pilots, engineers, and guards trying to mitigate the damage. Warning lights flickered across the console, every dial experiencing its own emergency. There had been a tumult of voices—yelling instructions, announcing new calamities—but they all fell silent when she appeared at the door.

Black flashed in her periphery, a force knocked her from the side, and Nhika found herself newly apprehended. She staggered, too shocked to even feel the indignation—until the guard cuffed her to the railing.

She exclaimed out in surprise and made a lunge for the guard, only to be yanked back by her cuff. The guard pulled a gun and panic jumped in her throat—that pesky fear of bullets, rising as bile. She held up a hand, but remembered the palliative gesture was only a threat among this crowd.

The Mother always did love returning Nhika's acts of goodwill with tests of patience, didn't She?

Nhika lowered her hand again. Her words would have to suffice. "I came here to warn you. Everyone is rushing to the loading bay to evacuate, but it's compromised. I need to get everyone to the promenade instead."

Her plea was only met by empty stares and guarded poses until a pilot stepped forward, speaking for the rest. "Where's the commissioner?" she demanded.

"Kochin is saving him."

"His is the highest in the chain of command on this ship. We await his authority."

Nhika scowled, and her expression won her no favors. "You're making the wrong decision. This ship is on fire—your commissioner's doing, by the way. I need you to send a broadcast to tell all personnel and guests to meet at the promenade. There's a Congmi ship coming for me."

"And why would the Congmis send you a ship?" the pilot asked, and Nhika wondered if she could even answer that question.

"Because they care about me," she said, and had to hope it was true.

From the back, an engineer piped up. "Captain, we're losing altitude. What the bloodcarver says is right—the tail is on fire. We can only assume the loading bay is compromised."

The pilot gave Nhika another long, discerning look. Then she strode to the console, leveled the PA mouthpiece to her lips, and said, "All crew, make way to the passenger-level promenade for evacuation. I repeat, all crew to the passenger-level promenade."

When she replaced the mouthpiece, her eyes met Nhika's. "Your ship better be coming."

Yeah, Nhika hoped so, too.

Before she could respond, a rumble rocked the airship. She staggered off her feet, the cuff wrenching her wrist as it caught her, before the airship made a jarring drop. Screams gathered around the cabin, and then everyone was leaving, *fleeing* the gondola.

"Go to the promenade!" Nhika reminded them as they filtered out—engineers first, then pilots, then the guards. The crowd had thinned about halfway before Nhika realized no one had remembered she was still cuffed.

"Wait!" she called, pulling to the end of her chain. "Wait wait wait—come *back*!"

But it was futile; the ship was shaking as though its hinges had come apart, the crowd had disappeared in a frantic panic, and Nhika was left in the gondola, chained to the railing.

"Mother, you have a twisted sense of humor," she cursed beneath her breath. Nhika wrapped the chain around her wrist, yanked—tugged on it with all her weight. Nothing. She kicked the railing, kneed it until her skin burst with bruises. It held, the fasteners welded to the wall.

The room was growing hot. She wondered if it was because the fire was spreading. She hoped it was just her panic—and she *was* growing panicked. Frantically, she explored the room, trying to find a blunt object within range.

Instead, her eyes found the PA mouthpiece, dangling from its cord. It was at the console; she was near the door, but she dragged her cuff to the far end of the railing and reached out a foot. Her toe tapped the mouthpiece. Muttering obscenities beneath her breath, Nhika leaned forward—until her wrist was chafed raw, her fingers crunched—and managed to snag it. She dragged it closer, brought it to her lips, and pressed the button.

For a moment, she said nothing. The task of speaking felt enormous, and she felt small. Her old natures were returning, and she wondered: *Who would even help her?*

But she remembered Mimi and Andao on this ship. She remembered Trin, who was certainly coming with a ship. She remembered that she was no longer alone—and wondered how she could have ever forgotten.

"If anyone is out there, it's Nhika," she said. "I've been chained to a railing in the gondola. I need help. Right about now would be good." And that was it. Sending that message through the ship with no response felt a little bit like prayer, and Nhika had never much believed in the Mother.

Just then, a dark spot passed the window—at first, looking like the airship's own shadow cast against the clouds. Then, just as sea beasts emerged from the abyssal deep, the curve of a hull broke the even surface of gloom, banishing wisps of fog as it arrived. At last, it swiveled, and she saw the beautiful insignia of the Congmi family painted in gold against its black balloon. Her heart leaped with relief—then dropped in equal height when she remembered her predicament.

Trin had come for her, and she wouldn't even be able to meet him.

Nhika found new determination. As she wormed her wrist against her cuffs, the Congmi balloon reoriented itself parallel to Nem's ship. She saw movement, the beginnings of an evacuation plan—and could only hope that Kochin was among them.

Nhika was seconds away from doing something regretful with heartsoothing when the door burst open. She spun, heart lifting with hope and Kochin's name on her tongue.

But it wasn't him. It was Lanalay.

"Nhika," she said, assessing Nhika's cuffed situation. "I thought you were trying to get off the ship. Not trying to bring it all down."

"Nem's fault, not mine."

"Where are the papers?"

Nhika hung her head. "Is that really your priority right now?"

"Have you tried breaking your thumb?"

"I'm trying to make it out of here intact."

"What? You have heartsoothing. A broken thumb is no matter."

"Can you please just find something to break the chain?"

"Right." Lanalay disappeared. Moments later, she returned with a metal statuette in her hands. Nhika splayed her hands apart, exposing a portion of the chain, and Lanalay slammed the statuette down.

"Watch the fingers," Nhika chastised.

"You can heal them," was all Lanalay said before bringing down the bludgeon again.

Once, twice, *thrice* more and the chains finally snapped. Nhika pulled her hands from the railing with a breath of relief. "Thank you. You saved my life."

"Twice," Lanalay added. "Please, Nhika. The papers."

Nhika couldn't argue. She reached up her sleeve and drew them out. When she offered them to Lanalay, the girl paused. For all her earlier stoicism, her hands were shaking.

"They can no longer hurt you in any way that matters," Nhika said softly. "So, take them."

Lanalay had never waited for Nhika's permission on anything before, but she took the papers. And maybe she would've stayed there frozen, staring at the papers in a descending gondola, but Nhika grabbed her by the wrist and pulled her to the exit.

"Quick, Lanalay. We can't stay here."

Together, they left the gondola. The carnage had spread, fire climbing up the hull of the balloon and seeping into the body of the ship. But the Congmi balloon was level with the promenade, and Nhika found a gangway extended between both ships. She squinted, trying to discern people—but it was too far away.

She was nearing the promenade when she saw two silhouettes at the end of the hallway, gray forms in the smoke. Nhika tensed, but when the figures drew closer, she recognized them.

"Nhika!" Mimi said, her brother trailing her. "You're safe. Thank goodness—we were just coming to get you."

"Did you see Kochin?" Nhika asked.

Mimi shook her head. "He's not with you?"

"Not anymore," Nhika said, swallowing the rest of her fears. "Let's just get to the promenade."

Smoke hazed the hallways. Nhika held her breath until they'd ascended the levels to the promenade. There, most of the crowd had already made it to the Congmi vessel. A perilous walkway spanned their two ships; guards helped shaky aristocrats traverse the terrifying length first before the staff.

And there, waiting to accept them on the other side of the gangway, was Trin. Nhika nearly cried in joy at the sight of him.

"Nhika!" he called, giving her a reassured smile. "Do I even want to know what happened?"

"Best not to ask," she called back. Then, to Lanalay and the siblings, she said, "Go on, get across."

Mimi shook her head. "No. You first."

Nhika gave the crowd another scan, only to be disappointed. "I'm still waiting on someone."

She sent Mimi up. Andao next, then Lanalay, her eyes on their footing until Trin was able to haul them up into the safety of the Congmi ship. Slowly, while smoke expanded around them, the crowd thinned on her side of the ramp and grew on Trin's. Aristocrats first, as they were always accustomed to, and finally personnel.

Nhika stayed last, bidding even the guards to go before her. Every other second, she threw a look over her shoulder—toward the billowing smoke, toward the door—waiting for something to happen. Waiting for someone to come through. As the last evacuee escaped up the ramp, leaving Nhika alone on the promenade, Kochin still hadn't arrived.

"Nhika, come on," Trin urged, holding a hand outstretched.

"No, not yet," she called back, shaking her head. There was a hammering in her chest—she wasn't sure if that was her heartbeat or the drumming of the airship engines. "That's not everyone. Not yet."

She couldn't leave. Not until Kochin came. There was no assurance that the Congmis wouldn't fly away once she was on board. Instead, she held tight to the railing, eyes fixed on the door, even as Trin called her name and smoke poured out of broken windows.

"Come on . . . ," she whispered to herself, a prayer stolen by the wind. He'd asked her to trust him. He'd *promised*. "Come on, Kochin."

The promenade was growing unbearably hot. Fire coursed above, racing along the deck. The railing burned the skin of her palms.

"We have to go, Nhika," Trin implored. "We can't risk catching fire here, either."

She met his eyes, brow furrowed with pleading. He extended his fingers; Nhika drew toward the gangway—

—and Kochin kicked open the door with Nem draped over his shoulder, both in a coughing fit from the smoke.

"Kochin!" she shouted. Relief poured out of her in a heavy breath, and she rushed to aid him, taking the commissioner's other side.

"His leg is injured," he said, lips smudged with ash. When his eyes met hers, they softened. "You waited?"

"You fought on Yarong for me. I bought you a few extra minutes. Now, we're even."

"Sounds fair."

"You can express your grievances once we get off this ship."

Together, they helped the commissioner toward the ramp. Trin met them halfway, hauling Nem up as he stepped off the promenade. Then it was only Nhika and Kochin left on the smoking platform.

"You first, I'm right behind you," Kochin said, his hand tender at the small of her back as he pushed her up. Trin coaxed her on the other end and she climbed her way up the ramp, trying not to look at the plunging descent on either side.

"Okay, it's ready for you," she called back to Kochin once she'd reached the top. Her hands stabilized either side of the ramp as he reached for it.

Before he could climb aboard, the rest of the hull blew.

The gangway escaped Kochin's reach when Nem's airship dove toward the ocean. Nhika screamed his name as pockets of fire bloomed across the airship, quickly gaining toward the promenade. Kochin ran for the front of the airship, leaping off the promenade and falling shakily onto the landing platform.

Nhika whipped around to Trin. "Tell them to lower the airship. I can grab him. *Please.*"

With a nod, Trin disappeared into the cockpit. Nhika sprinted her way up to the bow, running parallel with Kochin—him on a sinking ship, her on a racing one. They were both reaching the end of their line, their ships speeding toward the ocean; the nose of her airship dipped, just enough that she was level with him for a few seconds' time.

"Jump, Kochin!" she called, even though she wasn't yet there. Her ship drew close and Kochin was running out of space to flee the fire.

Kochin leaped; Nhika hurdled the railing at the bow. They both reached for the other.

For a heart-stopping moment, it wasn't enough—the space between them too great, their hands too far. Time slowed to an unbearable stillness, and Kochin wasn't falling—he was flying. Nhika wasn't catching him—she was bidding him goodbye.

And then their hands met. Nhika tightened her fingers around him as time lurched back to regular pace; her other hand gripped the railing.

The force of his fall yanked at her shoulder and she felt the railing give. Half of its bolts sprang free before it swiveled loose, and then they were both dangling over empty air. Nhika's fingers slipped against the metal, grip painful and their combined weight threatening to pull them into the ocean.

"Nhika, the railing," Kochin warned with breathless panic, but she already knew. As the railing loosened, her grip on Kochin only tightened, and she felt her arms pull apart from the tension of it all.

"Don't let go, Kochin," she said, even as her muscles screamed for relief.

He shook his head. "I'll take you with me if I don't."

"Don't you *dare*." Tears burned in her eyes; she pretended it was from the pain, rather than this impending act of goodbye. "I didn't come this far to lose you now."

"It was enough for me just to see you again. To know that I succeeded," he said. The panic ebbed from his eyes, replaced by something softer: acceptance.

Was this how he'd felt when she was on her deathbed? The same helplessness, feeling that if she were just a little stronger, their grip just a little tighter, she might be able to pull him up? Knowing he had made up his mind but hoping he would change it? Instead, all she could do was dangle here, limbs pulled apart and heart torn in two.

"I have to bring you home," was all she could say. *"I have to."* She didn't fear the retribution of the Vens; she feared their grief. And she didn't know how, after all this, she could stand being the last heartsooth again.

"It's all right," he said, letting his fingers go slack. They started slipping from her own, and just as she felt her grip might give, he met her eyes: his, full of awe and reverence; hers, brimming with desperation. Beneath him, Nem's ship tore itself apart, its tatters claimed by the ocean. His lips parted and she barely heard his next words over the roar of the fire. "Nhika, I love you."

Her heartbeat staggered. Was this it, then, a mirror of before? Were they always fated for this ending?

No. Not like this. Those words would not be final words again— this time, the declaration would take no fatalities.

"You're going home," she told him. "Don't argue with me, Ven Kochin. You won't win."

Nhika shot electricity down his arm, shocking the flexor muscles of his fingers—not allowing him to let go, no matter how he slacked. She did the same for hers, even as she felt the muscles tire, even as the fibers sheared themselves apart, even as Kochin stared at her in stunned surprise. The pain coursed through her forearm, and she let out a roar, one part agony and two parts Hell-bent determination, knowing that the moment she gave in they would both plummet toward the ocean. Her fingers, slicking with sweat, slipped from the railing, but she only tightened them. Nhika had never been anything if not relentlessly stubborn and unendingly difficult, and she mustered every ounce of her defiance to spit in the face of whatever fate determined to keep them apart.

Ven Kochin would not die today.

He looked at her in hapless awe, but he didn't fight her anymore, fingers clenched around hers as her tears fell along his arm. In his eyes she saw an echo of a memory, saw every ideal that he had worked for these past months, saw peace, freedom, and . . .

Love. He loved her, she loved him, and she wouldn't let go.

She felt her muscles weaken, tear apart, beg for the relief she wouldn't allow. Tendons threatened to snap, bones pulling loose from the joint, but her soothing bolstered them all. Just when she was about to give—not from the shallowness of her will but from the sheer inability of her anatomy—salvation came.

Arms descended from the platform, hands grabbing her by her shoulder, her shirt. They lifted her up, Kochin with her, and dragged them onto the ship. She managed to crawl against the support of the hull before every muscle sagged, her fingers forgetting how to move. When she blinked the dancing light out of her eyes, she found Trin and Mimi stooped beside her.

"Nhika, are you okay?" Mimi asked.

Nhika was covered in soot, hair ashy from the flames, with ghastly bruises growing on either forearm. "Do I look okay, Mimi?"

A smile tugged at Mimi's lip. "It seems like we managed to arrive just in time."

Nhika's sardonicism softened. "Thank you," she said. "For coming back for me. For saving me. For everything."

"Mimi, is she thanking us?" Trin asked dryly.

"We need to get her to a doctor," Mimi teased. "She must have inhaled too many fumes."

"I *mean* it," Nhika grumbled.

At that, Trin gave her a warm smile. "We know. You're family. Rest now."

Nhika nodded, slurring her next words in sleepiness. "Wake me up when we get to Theumas," she said, and slumped off into slumber.

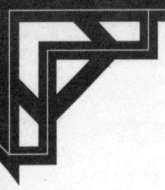

⟶⟫ THIRTY-THREE ⟪⟵

KOCHIN CARRIED A SLEEPING NHIKA INTO THE cabin of the airship, parting bodies as he did. The last time he'd been able to hold her like this, he wasn't all too sure she'd wake up. Now, it was a small miracle that she had, and he relished the way her slumbering breath feathered his clavicle.

Inside, he set her down on a plush bench, where she rolled over and murmured something he couldn't make out. His finger grazed across her arm, thumb brushing the bleed under her skin with the thought to heal it. He decided against that—there would be time when she awoke, but now she needed undisturbed rest. Instead, he undid the cuffs around her wrists and let the skin breathe.

Kochin couldn't take his eyes off her. So much had happened in so little time that he still didn't know if this was real or another delusion, a dream—if he looked away, would he wake up back in that stateroom? Back on Yarong? But the warmth of her skin, the evenness of her breath in slumber, reminded him she was here, and she was real, and through all her tenacity she'd managed to save them both.

Someone entered the cabin behind him—it was Trin, who nodded him toward the deck of the airship with an expectant look. Kochin didn't want to leave Nhika's side, but he obeyed and followed Trin outside.

"Thank you for coming for us," Kochin rushed out, knowing gratitude was long overdue. "And thank you for saving me, of all people."

Trin hummed his quiet welcome. "I'll admit I was hoping I wouldn't see you again."

Kochin met his eye. Trin had helped him far more than he deserved—and if ever Kochin knew how such favors worked, it came at a cost.

Trin continued, "I think, if we had only ever met as privates at Majora, we might've been good friends. As it is, I can't get past what you've taken from us, from Andao and Mimi. All the same . . . I do respect you, so I'll be candid: We're planning to offer Nhika a permanent home with us. An education, a name, a future. Something like what Mr. Congmi did for me. This isn't us trying to take her from you. It's us giving her a choice."

Trin's tone wasn't cold, but its impassivity made his words somehow worse—like being pulled out to sea by a strong surf and knowing he couldn't bargain with the tide.

"Why are you telling me this?"

"So you can prepare for the choice she makes, whatever it might be."

Kochin swallowed a stone in his throat. Once, Nhika had chosen to come home with him. But that was before the decision had killed her. That was before the war, where the Congmis would be able to provide so much more for her than he could. But if she chose them, the family that rightfully despised him, Kochin wasn't sure he'd ever see her again.

"And if she chooses me?" For a moment, Kochin wanted to

be cocky, to tell Trin that of course she'd choose him—had she not died for him?—but he was no longer sure.

"Well then, I should never find her imperiled again. Otherwise, I'd spare no expense to hunt you myself."

Kochin might've feared his threat, but he saw the depth behind it—Trin, in his own way, was preparing to let her go. It only came down to her choice.

With a terse nod to end the conversation, Trin strode away, the mechanism of his leg brace whirring as he did. Kochin was left to his own thoughts, and his eyes drifted to the commissioner, standing at the front of the airship.

In the quiet, Kochin joined him. They both looked ahead, where the ship's bow cut through the sky. The fog had cleared by now, revealing an image that seemed painted in three brushstrokes: the sky, the ocean, and the thin scraggle of land emerging between them. Somewhere, sitting on the edge of the water, was Theumas. Home.

Kochin and Commissioner Nem spent a long moment in silence. It felt strange to share such a calm space with a man he'd considered a threat for so long, but the man standing beside him—shock blanket over his shoulders, hair covered in soot—was not the commander in chief who had imprisoned him. This was a man undergoing revelation, like it was the first time he'd truly seen the sun.

At last, Commissioner Nem cleared his throat. "You asked me how you could prove that your gift could not create my army," he said, voice hoarse from smoke. "I didn't think you could."

"And now?" Kochin asked. "What do you think?"

"I think . . . that you didn't have to save me, but you did. So, I believe if you truly could turn this war, you would. But that's not what your gift is meant for, is it?"

Wordlessly, Kochin shook his head.

Commissioner Nem's eyes traced the horizon. "And what does it mean to you, Kochin?"

Kochin thought on it. For so long, he'd wielded heartsoothing with the Trickster Fox's same shame, feeling like he'd somehow stolen it from the Mother. When working for Santo, his heartsoothing had been abused. In losing Nhika, it had been inadequate.

But, through bringing her back, his heartsoothing was love enduring. It was proof that something inviolable connected him to Nhika, and to his mother, and to anyone else he ever touched—even the commissioner.

"It just means that I'm not alone," he said at last.

"Then, who am I to ask that it be anything more or less than that?" Commissioner Nem let out a low, tired laugh hidden in a sigh. "Perhaps my crime was being Theuman—I considered it a science, reproduceable and dispersible. Now, I see that it doesn't need to produce anything, results or armies or progress. It just needs to . . . exist."

Kochin nodded. "I'm sorry, Commissioner. I know the war is still real. I wish I could help, but—"

Commissioner Nem raised a slow hand. "It's okay. I will keep fighting for Theumas. I'll keep fighting for Yarong, too—because you've reminded me why we're fighting: so that beautiful things can still exist on the other side of conflict. After all, what is this worth, all this fighting and bloodshed, if the very things we fight for are tarnished in the act of war?"

"I'm sorry it couldn't be the weapon you hoped for," Kochin said. "But heartsoothing still lives—barely, but it has a pulse. I need to make sure it continues."

"I understand. And I'll forget all that transpired on Yarong, your gift and your crimes." He gave Kochin a look that held tired humor. "I can't very well lock you up in good conscience now, can I?"

Kochin returned a smile. "I'm glad you could see reason, Commissioner." He swallowed, gathered his thoughts. "What happens next?"

"The fight continues on Yarong. I know now what's at stake on that island—I promise you, I'll do whatever it takes to return it to Yarongese rule. As for you, go home. You've fought for long enough."

Kochin gave him a grateful look. "If you need my talents, you know where to find me."

"And if you ever return to Central, know that it will be waiting for you with open arms."

"Thank you, Commissioner, but I think I'm going to be making up for lost time at home."

Commissioner Nem barked out a laugh. "Well then, know that you'll be missed."

A silence fell between them again, but it was a hopeful one. Together they stood at the bow, watching Theumas sparkle into view as the airship forged its way forward.

The airship touched down on an airdrome in Western Theumas. Passengers flooded down the ramps, exclaiming their relief at solid land. Kochin knelt by Nhika's side, rousing her with a light shake of her shoulder.

"We're here," he whispered as she stirred.

"Am I dead?" she slurred.

"No," he said through a light laugh. "You're in Theumas."

Blinking awake, Nhika gazed groggily around the ship. "We made it?"

"We made it."

Together, they headed for the exit when Mimi's voice stopped them. "Nhika," she called, emerging from the cockpit. Andao and Trin emerged at her side. "We'll be flying back west."

Nhika paused, turned, and Kochin knew what the Congmis would tell her. They would give her a choice.

"If you want," Mimi began softly, "you can come live with us, as you have been. Now that all this is over and Kochin is safe, we can help you start an honest life in Theumas."

Though Nhika didn't speak, she gave Kochin a thoughtful look.

"Or you can go with him," Mimi said. "I understand either way, whatever you choose."

"Kochin, a moment?" Nhika requested, and he acquiesced. Though his heart fell to the pit of his stomach, he exited the ship and gave her space for her decision.

From the airfield, he watched as Nhika spoke with the Congmis.

They exchanged hugs, unbridled familiarity, and Kochin had never seen such a sentimental look on Nhika. When Kochin had first found her at the wake, a ward of the Congmi family, he'd thought it nefarious—he knew they'd bought her from the Butchers' Row. To use her, he'd figured. Now, he saw how good they were for her. Kochin had fought for and spurned his chance to live in Central Theumas, to assimilate to Theuman ideals of progress before all else, but Nhika still had a fresh opportunity. Unlike him, she had a chance to truly thrive there.

Yet, he wanted her to choose *him*. Kochin wasn't sure he could stand to part with her. It took every ounce of will to keep from running up that ramp, falling to his knees, begging her to come with him. Would he regret it if he didn't?

Mother, let her choose him. If She could grant him just this one wish, he'd never ask for anything else.

To quell his nervousness, he paced an anxious path along the airfield. He knew it had to be her choice, but every muscle in his body told him to run to her.

"You got what you wanted, didn't you? I thought you'd be happier," Lanalay said, sidling up to him.

Kochin stopped his pacing, though his lip quirked with an anxious twitch. He eyed her, finding a crinkled stack of papers in her hand. "Seems as though you got what you wanted, too."

"I did."

And yet, she didn't look happy, either. "Did you read it?"

"Yes."

"Ah." He pressed his lips together, feeling remorse for a crime he didn't commit. "What now?"

Lanalay scrounged a lighter from her pocket. She lit it, held the flame to the corner of the papers, and they both watched as the fire licked its way up the sheets until they were nothing more than ashes.

With it, that hateful choice Kochin had once had to make—his last shackle, his near-sin—was gone.

"I'm going home," Lanalay said, smudging the last of the ash beneath her boot. "If you ever see me again, Private Ven, it'll be because Yarong is truly free."

"Well then, I hope to see you again."

With a sly smile, she dipped her head in farewell and rejoined the company outside the airship. Without the distraction of a conversation, all that racking anxiety returned.

He might've succumbed to it, but Nhika appeared at the entrance of the ramp.

"Kochin," she called, and his chest squeezed with nervousness. He tried to discern if that was a "Kochin, goodbye" or a "Kochin, let's go home."

"Yes?" he said, his voice small.

Noticing his agitation, Nhika laughed. "Kochin, can you pay for my train ticket back to Chengton?"

Despite himself, he made an exclamation of relief and opened his arms. She rushed down the ramp and leaped into his embrace, letting him twirl her around—all their sore bones, frayed muscles, singed hair. He held her close, and for the first time, it came with no sense of urgency—for the first time, he knew there would always be another chance to hold her.

Through the window of the cockpit, Kochin saw a stoic Trin,

arms crossed as he watched him. Mimi and Andao joined his side, and Kochin raised a hand—a thank-you, an apology, and a goodbye, all rolled into one. Nhika turned to wave her own farewell and the ramp retracted up the airship as it prepared for another flight.

There, hand in hand and hair buffeted by stirring engines, he and Nhika headed home.

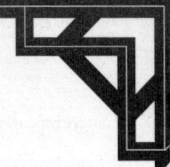

⟫⟫ EPILOGUE ⟪⟪

IT WAS EVENING WHEN THEY FINALLY REACHED Chengton. For the third time, Nhika made her way up the path toward the Ven house. This time, with Kochin at her side, she hoped it would stick. Once, she'd imagined a life here, with a heartsooth family, never thinking it a possibility. Now, she was choosing it.

"How did my brother react to your return?" Kochin was asking as they walked.

"Shocked, more than anything. I don't think he expected you to actually do it," Nhika said. "I . . . still can't believe you achieved such a thing."

"I appreciate your confidence in me."

She laughed. "I just mean that you achieved the impossible."

"Not impossible," he corrected with a shake of his head. "Not if it's for you."

Her cheeks warmed and she tamped them down; he gave her an endearing smile, as though he somehow knew she was blushing despite her attempts to hide it.

They reached the front door. Inside, they heard sounds of a dinner—conversations mumbled through full mouths, the clink of silverware, the scrape of chairs against hardwood. With an incredulous breath, as though he couldn't believe where he now stood, who he now stood with, Kochin raised his hand and knocked.

"I've got it, Ma," came Vinsen's voice. Footsteps, and then the door opened.

For a tense breath, there was only silence. Nhika could see down the hallway to the dining room, where a stunned Ven family stared at her, at their son. Then Vinsen drew Kochin into a tight, fraternal hug. The rest of Vens bolted out of their chairs in their haste to greet them.

They pulled Nhika in—fingers pinching her cheeks, a hand clapping her back, an arm over her shoulder. Auntie Ye clucked her tongue at the bruises on Nhika's forearm, making a promise to heal them later after dinner. Bentri leaped in excitement at Kochin's return, while Vinsen gave Nhika a slow, grateful nod.

I did it, she told him through a look. *I brought him home.*

Very much against Nhika's and Kochin's protests, the Ven family dragged them in, pulled them up chairs, set plates before them. Soup was ladled, rice was scooped, and dishes were moved around the table. Somehow, the best parts of the fish, the fried head and crunchy tail, ended up on her plate.

"How are you home, Kochin?" his father asked.

"Did you really go to war?" Bentri added. "Did you drive any war machines?"

Auntie Ye was still fixated on Nhika's arms, the many welts and bruises. "I'll have to heal these soon, or they'll scar."

Through it all, Vinsen said, "Kochin, Nhika, I'm glad you're both back."

A dinner table had never felt so inviting before. Even the dog tangled himself in Nhika's legs, begging for scraps. Kochin tried to answer all their questions in turn, but they only asked him more. Between words, he snuck looks at Nhika, his smile soft, dark eyes warm. Underneath the table, he reached out and caught her fingers with a squeeze. The two of them were sharing the same thoughts, Nhika knew, the honeyed feeling of being safe after so long.

And the slow-burn realization that they would never have to be alone again.

It was the first time the Ven household had been complete—and, more than that, *full*—in years. They didn't have an extra bedroom for her, but each of the boys, Kochin included, offered her their bedroom in turn. Nhika declined them all. There would be time later for sorting out bedrooms, especially with Bentri headed to Central to study at the university, but for now, Nhika wanted to see their home as it was meant to be.

When the night came, the daytime buzz of cicadas yielding to a cricket lullaby, the household retired to sleep. Bathed and soothed, Nhika was lying on the plush couch downstairs. She wasn't tired, having napped in the airship. Instead, she was antsy—every time she knew peace, it was never for long. But she had hope that this could last forever.

When her fidgetiness forbade sleep, Nhika stood and stepped outside, steeping herself in the coolness of an autumnal night in the country. Here, without the interference of so many artificial lights, she could see so much of the Star Belt twinkling overhead. She wasn't accustomed to a sky that felt like it belonged to her.

"Couldn't sleep?" came a voice behind her, and Nhika realized Kochin had joined her outside.

"I slept on the airship."

He furrowed his brow, looking troubled. "Not thinking about leaving, are you?"

For once . . . "Not at all."

His shoulders eased. "Good, because there's something I wanted to show you. Follow me."

"In my night linens?"

"It'll just be us," he promised—but he draped her with his jacket and she had no choice but to follow.

Kochin guided her down the hillside path, through Chengton's now-quiet main street. Beautiful, she thought, that somewhere in Theumas could be truly quiet at night. She might grow to miss the constant urban burble, but being so close to water, in a family of heartsooths—those were the best parts of her childhood, come to life again.

The walk was a familiar one, so she knew where Kochin was taking her even before he untied the dinghy from the docks and helped her down. Unlike when he'd hidden the houseboat in Central, they didn't need to row far before she saw it, docked beside limestone cliffs. And if she squinted, she could even see the Ven household on the hill, overlooking it. Like there wasn't any reason to hide anymore—and there wasn't.

Kochin tied up the dinghy and helped her on. As he gassed

the engine and turned on the lights, the houseboat returned to her with the warmth of a summer rain: those earthy scents of houseplants and river water, the sun-warmed wood, the gentle sway of the hull. He took her to the veranda, where they could see the Vens' house on one side of the water, the vast Star Belt on the other.

"There," Kochin said, "The houseboat is yours. You know, in case my family is ever too much for you, or you want someplace of your own."

"I . . ." Nhika didn't know what to say. "I can't repay you."

"Since when have you ever cared for settling debts?"

"Since I decided to go home with my creditor."

Kochin huffed out a laugh. "You gave me your life, I give you a boat—let's call it even." Then, in a sober tone, he added, "And you chose me when you could've had the Congmis. I might spend the rest of my life wondering why."

"Isn't it obvious?" she asked, and those words tugged at her lip: peace, freedom, *love*. She didn't say them aloud. "I love your family. You, on the other hand . . ."

Kochin stepped toward her, smile wry, eyes on her lips. When he leaned down for the kiss, his hand on her cheek, she rose up to meet him. It reminded her of their first—just the two of them on the water, a world alone, something blithe and hopeful burning in her chest.

When they parted, he gave her a satisfied look. "That sounds dreadful."

"I can learn to endure it."

Despite her insults, his expression grew soft, and he said, "I never thanked you properly for giving me your life. I owe you in perpetuity. The rest of my life for yours."

Nhika gave him an amused look. When she thought back to the night in the operating suite, she remembered adrenaline, and grief, and . . . love. She'd simply been the last heartsooth for far too long, passing on the mantle. But now she wasn't; neither of them were.

"Did you mean what you said when we were hanging off the railing?"

Kochin gave her a playful look. "When I thought I was going to die and there were no consequences to my words? Hmm, let me think . . ."

"Ven Kochin."

"Yes, yes, I meant every word." He laughed. He curled a finger beneath her chin and lifted her gaze to his. "I love you, Nhika. Even when I thought I only had half a heart, it was yours."

"I love you, too." Her admission paled in comparison to his poetry, but she'd never been one for words. She realized that was the first time either of them had said it back—their declarations had never left any room for reciprocation. "Did you find everything you wanted? Peace, freedom, love?"

"Yes," he said without hesitation. "And are you happy, Nhika?"

"Yes," she echoed, though the word fell short of how she felt. Happiness was ephemeral—she was happy after successfully selling eucalyptus oils as cure-alls, happy to gorge herself on Congmi dinners. But here, with Kochin and his family, Nhika was no longer the last heartsooth. She didn't need to fear being the last of her kind, nor did she worry about being forgotten in death—not when he'd gone to war to bring her back. Here, to exist at all was to be loved.

So yes, Nhika was happy.

But more than that, after all she'd mourned and lost and fought for, Nhika was home.

ACKNOWLEDGMENTS

I have been writing all my life but never imagined I would come this far: publishing the finale of my debut duology. But neither *The Last Bloodcarver* nor *His Mortal Demise* are mine to claim alone. In fact, this duology—from my laptop screen to your hands—has been the product of many people, both those on my publishing team and those who have supported me along the way.

Firstly, none of this would be possible without my editorial team: Emilia Sowersby, Emily Feinberg, and Makena Cioni. Thank you for understanding the heart of this novel and helping me translate that to the page. Of everyone, this story would not be the one I wanted to tell without you.

Thank you to my team at Roaring Brook and Macmillan as a whole. My experience publishing this book could not have gone any more smoothly, and that is in great part due to all of you. To Mia Moran, Emily Stone, Katy Miller, Jackie Dever, Jennifer Healey, thank you for making sure HMD made it to print in its topmost form. I also want to express great appreciation to those responsible for a gorgeous sequel cover: Meg Sayre, Aurora Parlagreco, and Mallory Grigg. Thank you to Charis Loke for bringing Theumas and Yarong to life. To my publicist, Morgan Rath, I don't know how you possibly stay on top of it, but you have my eternal gratitude for guiding me through the people-facing aspect of being a debut author. To my marketing team—Teresa Ferraiolo, Naheid Shahsamand, Samantha Fabbricatore, Carlee Maurier, and Molly Ellis—thank you for getting this book out to as many readers as possible. The same goes to Kristin Dulaney and Jordan Winch: Thank you for helping my words travel the world. Thank you to Celeste Cass for helping this book take shape. My greatest appreciation goes out to Allison Verost and Connie Hsu, and everyone at my imprint for the loveliest publishing journey a debut author could ask for. To Teresa Tran, for your work on both book one and now its sequel, thank you.

This would not be at all possible without my agent and agency, so thank you Ramona Pina and BookEnds Literary. Through BookEnds, my duology has not only found a home, but I have also found a great community within my agent siblings, to whom I owe my sanity.

To my pillars within the writing community, thank you for your ongoing and enduring support. Mia, Selena, Elise, Emma, Trinity: You cheered me on for book one and continue to cheer me on for book two. Tiffany and Sarah Street, I'm blessed to know authors as talented as you two. Sarah MacLean, thank you for being the first to celebrate anything with me.

To friends new and old, thank you for all you do, inside and outside of my writing. Maan, Alvin, Hena, Sarah, Justin, Yoshi, and Lauren: Medical school has been a hoot thanks to all of you. And thank you to all those in my life who have shared my journey with me.

To my closest loved ones, you deserve pages and pages of appreciation, but I'll try to be concise. Charles, thank you for all you've done and sacrificed for me. I appreciate you more than words can ever express. Brendan, you're still my North Star, my Majora (that's a book reference, but please don't read this). Cameron, though I've striven to pave a path for you, you're destined for a greatness beyond me. Caiden, I just know one day you'll do amazing things, and I can't wait to be there to witness it.

To my parents, thank you for your endless support. You've both sacrificed so much for me to pursue both my passions, writing and medicine. I am nothing if not the product of your love, time, and dedication. As such, please know that everything I write is dedicated to you both.

And of course, last but never least, to my readers: Thank you for following this journey with me to the end. You have my boundless appreciation.

VANESSA LE graduated from Brown University with a degree in health and human biology and now resides in the Pacific Northwest. Her writing is an expression of her love for medicine and her Vietnamese heritage. When not writing, she can be found studying medicine, spoiling her two Shiba Inus, or wishing she were writing. She is the author of *The Last Bloodcarver*.

vanessa-le.com
@vanessalewrites